THROUGH THE VEIL

SHILOH WALKER

BERKLEY SENSATION, NEW YORK

THE BERKLEY PUBLISHING GROUP
Published by the Penguin Group
Penguin Group (USA) Inc.
375 Hudson Street, New York, New York 10014, USA

Penguin Group (Canada), 90 Eglinton Avenue East, Suite 700, Toronto, Ontario M4P 2Y3, Canada
(a division of Pearson Penguin Canada Inc.)
Penguin Books Ltd., 80 Strand, London WC2R 0RL, England
Penguin Group Ireland, 25 St. Stephen's Green, Dublin 2, Ireland (a division of Penguin Books Ltd.)
Penguin Group (Australia), 250 Camberwell Road, Camberwell, Victoria 3124, Australia
(a division of Pearson Australia Group Pty. Ltd.)
Penguin Books India Pvt. Ltd., 11 Community Centre, Panchsheel Park, New Delhi—110 017, India
Penguin Group (NZ), 67 Apollo Drive, Rosedale, North Shore 0632, New Zealand
(a division of Pearson New Zealand Ltd.)
Penguin Books (South Africa) (Pty.) Ltd., 24 Sturdee Avenue, Rosebank, Johannesburg 2196,
South Africa

Penguin Books Ltd., Registered Offices: 80 Strand, London WC2R 0RL, England

This is a work of fiction. Names, characters, places, and incidents either are the product of the author's imagination or are used fictitiously, and any resemblance to actual persons, living or dead, business establishments, events, or locales is entirely coincidental. The publisher does not have any control over and does not assume any responsibility for author or third-party websites or their content.

THROUGH THE VEIL

A Berkley Sensation Book / published by arrangement with Shiloh Walker, Inc.

PRINTING HISTORY
Berkley Sensation mass-market edition / June 2008

Copyright © 2008 by Shiloh Walker, Inc.
Excerpt from *Sea Witch* by Virginia Kantra copyright © 2008 by Virginia Kantra.
Cover illustration by Don Sipley.
Interior text design by Laura K. Corless.

ISBN: 978-0-425-22247-8

BERKLEY® SENSATION
Berkley Sensation Books are published by The Berkley Publishing Group,
a division of Penguin Group (USA) Inc.,
375 Hudson Street, New York, New York 10014.
BERKLEY SENSATION and the "B" design are trademarks belonging to Penguin Group (USA) Inc.

PRINTED IN THE UNITED STATES OF AMERICA

10 9 8 7 6 5 4 3

Thanks to my husband, Jerry.
You gave me the idea, darlin'.

GLOSSARY OF TERMS

Anqar
A world overrun by demons and warlords.

Body slave
A female taken from offworld. Since females are taken for the sole purpose of breeding, Warlords and Sirvani search for females of "talented" blood, sometimes taking entire families in the dead of night. Males are put into manual slavery; women are mated to as many as five Warlords.

If a body slave delivers a female child, her Warlord may free her from slavery. Female children are highly prized, and their mothers are well treated, almost pampered, by their Warlord. The Warlord may also decide to formally bond and mate with the slave, elevating her in the Warlord hierarchy.

Commoners
Term applied to the non-gifted race of Anqar. They may own land, but they cannot own slaves. Commoners may marry and mate among themselves, although if a female is born, she may be claimed as a mate to a Warlord. This happens rarely—Warlords only want females that can bear them gifted children, so the female must have some form of talent.

If the female is mated to a commoner, no Warlord would take her as his own. The mating bond is respected among the Warlords. Female children are much more common among commoners, but still very rare.

Daisha

A female child born to a Warlord and a female. Daishan are highly prized, protected, and not allowed to serve in the army, but they may own land, slaves, participate in government, own and run businesses, and serve on advisory councils. Rarely, Daishan will join in the raids on Ishtan—it's considered exotic to observe a raid. However, due to the danger, it only happens rarely. By age twenty-five, a Daisha is required to marry a Warlord or Sirvani, although she may choose her future mate. In times past, Daishan were given away in arranged unions.

For unknown reasons, Warlords rarely produce female offspring.

Dumir

A tough, durable cloth used to make battle gear for Anqarian soldiers.

Gate

A doorway between the worlds. Gates cannot be built. They simply exist and they cannot be moved. Warlords alone have the power to open a gate, allowing travel between the worlds. The ability to open a gate is what separates Sirvani from Warlord. In times past, a gate, once opened, could only be closed by a Warlord. Over time, gates started to close on their own. Opening a gate causes severe natural disruption in both worlds, so Warlords only open gates when they plan to raid Ishtan.

Ikacado demons

More advanced humanoids found in Anqar. They spread to Ishtan when the gates rise, and they travel in packs, preying on the weak, the old or the very young. Fiery creatures, they are immune to most weapons except those that produce sub-zero temperatures.

Ishtan

A realm located between mortal Earth and the demonic realm of Anqar.

Jorniak demons

Primitive humanoids found in Anqar. They feed on human flesh. Physically strong, but with no extraordinary abilities. They travel in hordes and will attack anybody that they can easily overpower. Small groups of people and loners are particularly at risk. Jorniaks are the size of a human male, with long limbs and a short trunk. Their skin is thick and tough, too tough for average-bladed weapons. Lasers are a weapon of choice for killing Jorniaks in Ishtan.

Mating bond

A recognized union between a man and woman of Anqar. Commoners rarely have unity ceremonies. Warlords may never form a mating bond. They will only form a union with a woman that has borne them healthy children. Children are a sign of prowess and good fortune, so many Warlords will simply mate without bonding to have as many children as possible.

Raviners

A more advanced demonic race. Humanoid and bloodthirsty, they often capture humans and torture them to death. They are born empaths and feed off negative energy. They can also force their essence into a human host, destroying the human's mind and turning him into a mindless killer.

Raviners are tall and thin with gray skin and small, pink eyes. They cannot tolerate sunlight.

Sirvani

Sirvani are the offspring of Warlords. If they come into full power, they are then given the title of Warlord. Not all Sirvani will become Warlords, although they are stronger than commoners and may achieve high rank in a Warlord's army.

Sirvani live free and may own land and slaves, run businesses, participate in local political matters or serve Warlords in an advisory capacity. Service in the army is optional, but many choose to serve, as this is the quickest way to secure a female for their own personal use. Although Sirvani cannot open the gates or see through the Veil, they may have smaller mage or psy skills. Sirvani tend to be very loyal to their chosen Warlord.

Talent

Psychic (psy) or mage (magickal) ability. "Talented" blood refers to a family line that is likely to produce many children with talents.

Tersin

A light, concealing material manufactured in Ishtan.

Tiris

A body slave who was formally mated to her Warlord but freed after producing either one female child or a number of healthy, talented male children. In the hierarchy of Anqar, she is in the high echelon. High Lord, Warlord, Daishan, Tiris.

Veil

The barrier between dimensions. Humans with psychic or magickal talents can be trained to see the Veil and beyond.

Warlords

The rulers of Anqar. Their power is bloodborn. Initially, the offspring of a Warlord is known as a Sirvani. If a Sirvani achieves Warlord status, it will be before the age of forty. Rank is obtained through physical and magickal battles—battles are usually to the death. Because of this, powerful Warlords can attain higher rank in a short amount of time.

The High Lord is the most powerful Warlord in Anqar. His rank cannot be obtained through battle. The title is passed to the most powerful Warlord related to the High Lord by blood, and it is only passed with the High Lord's death.

Zandir wyrms

Colossal subterranean snake-like creatures, drawn to heavily populated areas. They spread from Anqar to Ishtan as larvae.

ONE

Her body ached.

It wasn't anything new. Although Lee was only twenty-eight years old, she already felt ancient. Exhausted even upon awakening, with stiff aching joints and bruises that seemed to appear out of nowhere.

Lee slowly flexed her muscles and tried to hold together the fragile wisps of the dream. But as always, it faded away, out of reach, out of mind. *He* faded away.

She didn't know his face. But each night he came to her. Each night, they found each other again. He would look at her with eyes that made her burn and want and wish, and for that brief period of time, she felt whole—complete—and that sensation lingered with her as she drifted from sleep into awareness. But the minute she opened her eyes, all memory of her dreams started to fade. All that remained was an ache in her chest, a knot in her throat and a body that felt as though somebody had tried to beat her to death.

Today, the ache was worse. The memories were fading fast although she tried to hold on to them. Like smoke, though, they faded away even as she grabbed the notepad by her bed and started to scrawl down what little she remembered. She didn't look down while she wrote—instead she clenched her eyes tightly shut and focused on him. Even if she couldn't remember his face, she could remember how he made her feel inside. Focusing on that instead of trying to recall the dream made the words flow more easily.

Blood. Screams. Smoke. The cries of the wounded. Ugly snarls and fetid breath. People clamored for her and they had needs that she couldn't even begin to understand. And him—

Always him. Everything seemed to revolve around him, and everything inside of her yearned for him. As much as Lee dreaded closing her eyes and facing the strange dreams that assaulted her while she slept, she yearned for them as well. Because her dreams led her to him. He would make her laugh, even when the dreams were dark as death. There was a warmth in his presence that filled an empty ache.

But not this past night. There had been distance, anger, and disgust. He'd yelled at her. His fury had been so great that even now she felt chilled by it.

She opened her eyes and stared at the notepad in front of her. She hadn't just written words. She'd sketched out faces of people she'd never met and monsters the likes of which she'd never seen.

She stared at each of the faces she'd drawn, studying its features for something that would trigger her memories again. The notebook was filled with sketches and notes, and none of them meant anything to her. All of them were set against twisted, scarred landscapes.

Some of the figures appeared more than others, like the old woman and the two guys. Even on paper, the woman's smile had a decidedly mischievous bent to it, as though she was laughing and Lee had no idea why. The men were polar opposites, one pale, one dark. One looked like an angel and the other had the devil's smile. Both of them were enough to make a girl's heart skip a beat, but if the man she dreamed of was one of them, she didn't know which one he was.

Furious with herself, Lee hurled the pad of paper across the room and watched as it hit the wall. It slid to the ground, several of the pages bent and crumpled. With a scowl, she climbed out of the bed and stalked to the bathroom.

"He isn't real," she told herself as she turned the hot water on full before turning to tug off her T-shirt. "He isn't real." *He's not,* her mind insisted, even though something inside her heart argued.

Her reflection caught her eye and she stilled, fighting the impulse to turn and look. Damn it, she was going to take all the mirrors down. She couldn't not look, when the mirrors were there.

But every time she saw a bruise, a chill ran through her. It was no different this time. Her eye was black, swollen, raw looking. It had been fine last night. Her mouth trembled as she tried to make sense of what she was looking at.

The doctors had tried to tell her she was doing it to herself. They had even done a sleep study and watched her all night long to determine what caused the bruising.

The study had revealed nothing. And everything.

For when she walked out of the room where they had monitored her body all night, her ankle was swollen, twisted and discolored. It had been fine the night before.

The tape of the study had shown her lying quietly on the narrow bunk, never once rising in the night. She didn't toss. She didn't turn. The only weird thing was a blip in the middle of the tape that lasted no more than a few eye blinks. For that brief span of time, the bed was empty. But she hadn't gotten out of the bed. The probes and lines weren't long enough to allow her to leave it without one of the attendants disconnecting them. They hadn't done it.

Odder still, an attendant had been in the room during the blip. They could see him at the edge of the screen. But he'd never seen her move. She hadn't done any more studies after that. Even though the doctors tried to urge her to agree, it had simply unsettled her too much. So no more

studies. She'd just deal with looking like the loser of a box-
ing match.

Lee leaned forward and probed her eye, touching it gently, wincing at the tender flesh she encountered under her
fingers. The eye itself looked fine, which was a relief. There
had been one morning when she woke up and her pupil
was blown. Her vision had been blurred, and the sicken-
ing pain made her think she had a concussion. By nightfall, though, the pupil had returned to normal and her vision
was fine.

Today, her eyes seemed a little more bloodshot than
usual, and the red looked unnaturally bright against the
nasty mottled blue. Almost festive, the red, white and
blue.

There was another bruise on her knee, like she had
fallen down. The flesh was sensitive, and each step she
took sent pain shooting through her knee. Much as the
knee hurt, it was actually a rather light night. Lee knew
from experience, though, that that wasn't necessarily a
good thing. Light nights seemed to be followed by bad
ones.

Her gut churned as that thought circled through her
head. Bad ones came with concussions, broken bones—
even burns. It had been a while since she'd had a real bad
night, and it was like a little mental clock was ticking away
the time. It wouldn't be much longer before she woke up
one morning hurt so bad that she'd wish for death, just to
get away from the pain.

Even if she did heal fast, pain was still pain and she was
tired of feeling so much of it.

"Morbid, much?" she muttered as she turned away from
her reflection. She climbed into the shower with one goal
in mind. Shower . . . then caffeine. With caffeine, she
could face almost anything.

* * *

Through the Veil, Kalen could see her. Stubborn little
bitch. He could still just faintly smell the sweet scent of her
skin, and his hands still itched to feel that satiny skin un-

der his hands, to feel the silk of her hair brush against his body. The vivid bruise on her face infuriated him, even though her ability to heal rapidly was already lessening the vivid color and the swelling.

The Jorniak demon that had attacked her was dead. Dust in the wind. Not that Kalen had anything to do with it. Lee had taken damn good care of it herself. She was good at that. Always had been. Scowling, he wondered if maybe she was a little too good at it. Good at taking care of herself, good at rationalizing away problems, good at everything.

Clenching his jaw, he turned away from the Veil and prepared himself to face the coming day without her. It was a frightening thought. But it always had been. One never knew what the day might bring. Not in this world.

There had been another demon attack, this time high up in the mountains, striking the small settlement of families living there. They had refused to come down into the valley. Too close to the Roinan Gate. It was as if they thought a few miles would protect them. They had been wrong, terribly wrong, and Kalen had to live with the guilt of not trying harder.

Raviners had killed the few men and taken their time with the women and children. It brought back memories too ugly for him to dwell on, staring at their remains. He couldn't even take a little bit of comfort in knowing that his men had slaughtered the Raviners. If he had taken them down himself, filling their bodies with the dangerous power of the pulsar he carried at his hip, it wouldn't have been any comfort.

They were losing a little more ground every day. The demons were breeding in his world now, and they didn't have to wait for the Roinan Gate to open for more of their numbers. There had been a time when finding a clutch of demons was a rare occurrence and they were killed quickly, if not always easily.

They might have a ghost of a chance if they could shut down the fucking gate. Though the demons were breeding in Kalen's world, they didn't breed easily. Kalen's people could hunt them down and kill them, but every time it seemed the resistance had gotten the advantage, the earth would rumble, signaling another influx of monsters as the gate was forced open.

It was an ugly, thankless job he was doing and one that often seemed pointless. No matter how many demons they killed, more sprung up to replace the dead. No matter how many lives they saved, they'd turn around and find more slaughtered. For every female they managed to save from the raiders, three more were taken.

It was to the point that the men now outnumbered the women four to one. Girl children were taken into the east, away from the gate, but Kalen heard rumors that girls were being kidnapped and sold to the highest bidder. As young as three or four—whoever the winner was, he'd care for the child and then take her to his bed as soon as she was old enough. Some didn't even wait beyond the girl's first menstrual period.

This damn war was turning his people into savages, and Kalen was losing hope. It hadn't been so hard at first—he'd been young and idealistic, convinced that with the loyal, devoted people that formed the resistance, they could face whatever hell Anqar threw at them. Convinced that Lelia would soon join them—truly join them. But instead, he was leading the resistance alone as he had for the past fifteen years.

Facing another day without her—and until she was ready to accept reality, not her idea of what reality was, it wasn't hard to imagine that each new day could be his last.

* * *

Lee stared with focused intent as she wielded the stylus, watching as the image took on life and color. It was a man. His features were familiar to her but that was no surprise. She'd drawn his face easily a hundred times. But he hadn't ever seemed this clear to her. This vivid.

A strong jaw, quicksilver eyes that could glint hot with fury one second and then be as cold as death the next. His long hair blew in the wind, tangling over wide shoulders as he stared out over a land that looked barren and desolate. There was something starkly beautiful about it, though. As if once it had been so lovely, it could bring a tear to the eye. Now it looked like some kind of hell.

He was crouched on a jagged outcropping, wearing a coat that billowed around a lithe, powerful body, tensed and ready . . . She added more color to his hair, a silvery sheen to the dense black. Then she added more definition to the muscles that rippled along his forearms under the rolled-up cuffs of his coat.

Lee worked in a daze. Once she finished with the man, she added to the background, working with the sky, the clouds, drawing in just the barest outline of creatures so monstrous they would have given her nightmares if she was prone to them. In her mind, they already had names. Jorniak demons. Raviners. Sirvani.

Battles raged in her mind as she worked. Hissing calls, furious shouts, the sounds of metal clashing, the hum of a laser weapon slicing through flesh. She could almost smell the scent of burnt flesh.

There were no battles for him now, though. The battles had already been fought. Now he rested. Now he prepared. Now he waited . . . waited for her.

I'm getting tired of waiting, Lee . . . We need you . . .

Then silence fell and she heard him, like he was whispering into her ear, from just over her shoulder. *How much longer will you hide from what you are?*

Lee snorted. "Just because I don't think you are real doesn't mean I am hiding," she muttered as she saved the work. Standing up, she wavered a little, her knees weak and shaky, as though she had just run a mile. Or fought a battle. Pressing a hand to her temple, she laughed shakily. "You're losing your mind, chick."

Actually, you're a little more sane now than usual, Lee. When are you going to stop fighting the truth, pet?

Lee ran her tongue around the inside of her cheek as she started across her studio. "I'm hearing things," she mumbled, shaking her head. "Man, I need a break. A vacation. Drugs. Something."

You need to stop being so blind, Lee.

"Damn it!" she shouted, spinning around. "Would you shut up?" That voice sounded so real . . . Holy shit.

It was him. The man from the picture.

He was standing right there.

In her studio.

With hair that flowed to broad, rock-hard shoulders, eyes the color of pewter, and a coat like Jack the Ripper would have worn. It hung down to the floor and had one of those weird little capelet things. Under the coat, he had a leather harness on his chest and she could see easily five different blades. His eyes glinted like silver and his hair was raven-wing black.

But he was also transparent. Lee pressed one hand to her mouth as black dots started to dance before her eyes. His teeth appeared as he grinned at her, a sensual twist of his lips before he faded away. She managed to whisper, "Oh, hell," before she hit the ground.

Long moments later, Lee groaned and forced her lids to lift. There was a throbbing just behind her brow as she sat up. With her hands on the ground, she stiffened her arms and forced her weight up, swearing as the world spun in dizzying circles around her. "Whoa . . . what in the hell . . . ?"

An image of that man danced before her eyes. "For crying out loud," she muttered, pressing a hand to her forehead. Damn it. "Working too hard."

Yeah. That had to be it. Had to be. She was working too hard, sleeping too little and stressing over it all. That was why he had looked so real to her. There was a life to him that was unlike anything she had ever drawn in her life. Everything, from the texture of his hair, the color of his eyes, to the demons that surrounded him.

She got to her feet, locking her knees when her legs wobbled underneath her. She needed to go to bed. But the dreams would chase her too vividly there. His image would follow her. Haunting her with that dark, quicksilver gaze and that mocking grin that seemed to taunt her every time she closed her eyes.

"I'm losing my mind," she groaned.

Rubbing her eyes, she shut her computer down and left her studio. "That's it. I'm done for the day."

* * *

Kalen watched with a faint smile as she walked away, shaking her head and probing the goose egg that was no doubt forming. She'd seen him. He'd seen the shock in her eyes, felt her gaze connect with his . . . at last. She was already rationalizing it away, but for once, he had managed to breach her conscious mind. He opened his eyes, and the vision of the Veil faded away, replaced once more by the physical world.

Not everybody could see the Veil, or see through it. It took years of training to see beyond what the conscious mind allowed. Kalen had been forced to learn to do it as he ascended through the ranks of their ragtag rebellion. Considering the demons they fought, they needed all the advantages they could get. It wasn't always handy, but the few times he'd looked through the Veil and seen what the Warlords of Anqar had planned for his people, he knew it was worth it. Saving just one life would have been worth it.

Being able to use it to spy on Lee was just a bonus.

Maybe tonight they would speak of something more than the battle against Anqar.

Hours later, Kalen growled to himself, "And perhaps kittens will fly."

Lee stood in front of the front line of the temp base set right at the city limits. Angeles lay before them in ruins. Until Kalen had moved his people here, the only living creatures in the ruined city were the few poor souls that had managed to evade both demon and Sirvani.

She stood quiet and intent, focused on something that he couldn't see or sense, although he wouldn't have been surprised if she was feigning that concentration just so she wouldn't have to look at him. From the time she had appeared out of the forest at sunset, Lee had been ignoring him entirely, like that brief, surreal moment earlier in the

day hadn't happened. If Kalen had thought things would
be different, he was very much mistaken.

It was business as usual for the pale, pretty blonde. The
past few weeks had gone by with an uneasy quiet. It didn't
bode well for them. Other than the encroaching bands of
Raviners and the demon attack in the mountain settlement,
there hadn't been much demonic activity on the radar.
Small skirmishes, but very few outright attacks and absolutely no raids for nearly two months. The gate wasn't
completely inactive—weird little flickers that lasted a few
heartbeats before it fell silent.

Their enemies never went this quiet for long. Lee's presence only added to Kalen's unease. The woman usually
only showed up this regularly when trouble was brewing.
She was silent and tense, her body practically vibrating
from the nerves inside her as she paced the perimeter of
the encampment.

Kalen didn't think it was the devastated landscape that
held her attention.

Much of the city had fallen to ruins, but the inhabitants
of New Angeles were determined not to lose one more
square foot of their land. Anqar had been a blight on Ishtan
for centuries untold. Entire families went missing in the
dead of night. A horde of demons slipped through a gate and
devastated small villages.

But Ishtan had always battled them back. The small
raiding parties that came through were nothing that
Ishtan couldn't handle. But the past two generations had
seen drastic changes, and all of it for the worse. Gates
were blasted open, unleashing a series of natural disas-
ters that devastated the land. Entire armies replaced the
small raiding parties. Demons came through unchecked.

Ishtan was being overrun. Even though their resistance
had battled back the invaders from Anqar, Kalen knew
their luck wouldn't hold forever. When they fell, it was
over.

Not because they were the only hope of an already broken world. Pockets of rebellion were scattered across the
globe. But here in New Angeles, at the base of the Roinan

mountain range, lay the gateway to and from Anqar. There were other, smaller gates but they were erratic and rarely remained open for longer than a few heartbeats. Many hadn't been opened for decades and were easier to protect. The Roinan Gate was huge, big enough for entire armies to pass through, and it remained open for hours, sometimes days, at a time.

There had been two other gates this size once. In Yorkton and in Jivan. A huge earthquake had rocked Jivan, and the shelf of land where that gate had resided crumbled. When the gate flickered next, it had proved devastating to what few people still lived on the big island. As well as to the creatures from Anqar that tried to come through. There was a second earthquake, more powerful than any in recorded history. A huge tsunami had resulted and no one had survived. What remained of the island lay under hundreds of feet of water. Hundreds, thousands, perhaps even millions of humans had died, but it had shut down a dangerous gate.

One hand giveth . . . , Kalen thought bitterly. The earthquake had probably saved most of that continent, at least for the time being.

What happened in Yorkton, nobody knew. York had been the first to fall to the raiders, and nothing of what once was remained. Huge skyscrapers had been decimated by the endless battles. Ragtag rebellions had formed, just like they did with every other gate. The demons came through, destroying enough of the resistance that they would have less chance of fighting. Then the Sirvani came, capturing whatever women they could. Finally the Warlords.

Warlords could tap into the energy of the land with an ability much like Lee's. They fouled it, though. Poisoned it. The land weakened, and eventually the people fought less and less, as though the sickness in the land had spread through them.

The energy fluctuated each time the gate opened. An odd ripple effect. Power erupted from one gate, traveled through the land, triggered something that made the next nearest gate open. And so on and so on, until within a period of days, a hundred gates were open at any given time. Sensitives could feel it in the air when a gatestorm was approaching. There had been a huge storm brewing, centered around Yorkton. Resistance units throughout the world had mobilized, preparing for the coming onslaught.

But it didn't come. Instead there was a power fracture. Almost a hiccup, then an explosion. The resistance there had done something, but what, nobody would ever know. Nothing living survived. Yorkton was little more than a crater in the earth now, a hollowed-out, burned depression that stretched out for miles.

That had been three years ago and still nothing lived there. While it didn't exactly turn the tide, it weakened the remaining gates. The Roinan Gate was the only one strong enough now to trigger the others.

Their intelligence resources in Anqar were limited, but there was a theory that the Warlords somehow forced the flickering in the gates, the surge in power that made a gate open. Once the Warlords had the gate open, Sirvani and demons flooded through while other Sirvani worked with the Warlords to maintain the gate.

"She's tense tonight."

Kalen glanced over at Dais, his mouth quirking in a smile. The older man's face was heavily scarred—a long, ugly jagged mark started at his right temple and ended just above his lower jawbone. It was twisted and puckered, and thanks to days without medical treatment, infection had set in and damn near killed him. That had been forty years ago, a few years before Kalen was born, and he'd grown up seeing the old man's scars. Under the cavinir vest, there were probably twenty other scars. Some older. Some newer. All of them received while fighting the demons back.

Kalen looked over at Lee and studied her. Yes. She was quiet. Her mind was heavy; he could sense it even if he wasn't trying to touch her thoughts. Out of respect, he turned his back to her and focused on his weapons lieutenant. "You left your position to discuss her silence?"

Dais grinned. "No. I left my position to tell you that my

men found two younglings out in the woods. Boys, seventeen or eighteen at the most. Looking for you, Cordain." The older man smirked a little as he used the rare title. Roughly translated, it meant "wise one" or "leader." It was a term that had once been used for governing males in Ishtan, while *corida* was the female equivalent. Over the past century, as their world sank further and further into chaos, many of the traditions had fallen to the wayside. Dais's use of the title now was more humorous than aught else. The man had nearly twice as many years on him as Kalen had, but when the role of leadership had fallen to Kalen over the years, Dais had settled comfortably into his role as Kalen's lieutenant and only rarely made jabs at Kalen's fewer years.

Thinking about the boys, Kalen rolled his eyes. Yeah, he could imagine why a couple of foolish boys were searching for him. Same reason men twice their age searched him out, but at least grown men had a place in Kalen's army. He didn't know what to do with the kids. He knew what they would want him to do, but as desperate as he was, Kalen hadn't taken to putting seventeen-year-olds on the front line.

He prayed that day didn't ever come.

"They have an escort?"

Dais gave Kalen the same look he'd give a dullard. Chances were Dais's men had been watching the kids for days. And protecting them. With a smirk, Kalen said, "Fine, fine. Send them on in. Send them to Eira. She'll know what to do with them." He waved a hand back toward the main camp. If anybody deserved the respectful title of corida, it was Eira. She'd seemed ancient when Kalen was a boy, but she still continued to train those with talent.

As Dais headed off, he beckoned to his men hiding in the trees. They separated themselves from the foliage in a fluid, easy motion, invisible even to Kalen's eyes until they moved.

No. Kids had no place in his army. Kalen knew that, even as he knew that he probably had kids serving under his command. Kids that looked older than they were, had led lives that aged them far too soon. Kalen had been like that, orphaned and forced to fight to stay alive.

He'd been twelve when he killed his first demon, was serving as a courier by thirteen and fighting in battle before fifteen. He would have died on his first battlefield if Dais hadn't found him, lying there with a demon's poison swimming through his bloodstream. If Kalen had been fighting when he was fifteen, then chances were he had other fifteen-year-olds out on his battlefields and he didn't even know it.

It was an unpleasant thought, but there was little he could do about it. He had a war to fight and people to protect and if he started questioning his soldiers about their age and their right to serve on the battlefields, more people would die. So he had to live with the knowledge that he likely had kids serving under him, and it left him sick inside with the image of them out there, fighting and dying.

Unless there was some sort of miracle, it would keep happening. "If we only knew what they did in Yorkton," Kalen muttered as he stared off into the west. The Roinan Gate was quiet tonight. Very few flickers lit the air around it, but he knew that didn't mean much. There were so many demons from Anqar here now, death would come even if the gate never opened again.

Dais's joking use of cordain circled through Kalen's head and he thought bitterly, *Wise one, my ass. What's the term for useless one?*

"You want to see your home turned into another crater?" Lee asked softly, silently appearing at his side and interrupting him before he could travel too far down the path of self-flagellation.

Kalen didn't bat an eyelash. "If it meant shutting down the Roinan Gate permanently? In a heartbeat."

He would try to evacuate the area as best as he could, but if the knowledge to destroy the gate ever fell into his hands, Kalen knew he'd sacrifice himself and every soldier in his unit if it meant destroying it. If the Roinan Gate fell, this world might actually have a chance.

Without that knowledge, Kalen didn't know what he was going to do, and he didn't know what to say to his men when they looked to him for answers. The rebellion followed their leaders, Kalen Brenner and Lee, with a blind, fearless devotion that was almost slavish. None of them knew her last name. They didn't know where she lived. They didn't know where she came from. Nothing more than her first name and that she fought like a woman possessed and that when she was in the battle, the battle was likely to be won.

That was all they knew. They spoke her name in hushed tones, even the ones who had fought beside her from the time she was old enough to fight. Yes, that utter devotion was a bit disturbing. Even more so considering that not one of them had ever seen Lee by the light of day.

Not even Kalen.

She came and left in the dark of night, lingering only a few hours and then disappearing. Sometimes weeks passed between appearances, and then there would be months when she showed her pretty face on a nightly basis. He had known Lee for more than twenty years. She had appeared out of the darkness when she was hardly more than a pretty, cherubic little thing with big, angelic blue eyes and dimpled cheeks, her curling hair pulled into a ponytail high on her little head as she pushed a meat-filled sandwich into his bony hands, whispering, "You're making my belly hurt."

He'd been so hungry. Starving. Locked in the basement of the house where the demons had set up camp, he had been waiting for death. The Raviners that had captured him weren't known for quick deaths. They preferred to torture their victims slowly, feeding off their pain and their screams.

Being caught by a Raviner usually only had one of two outcomes: slow death by torture, or possession. A boy of ten was ripe for them, a good prize—especially one weakened by days of abuse, starvation and fear. They'd killed his mother, right in front of him, and Kalen spent long hours in the dark wishing they'd killed him as well.

But even as a kid, he'd known the Raviners had more in store for him than just a simple death. Raviners had a unique ability of forcing their evil into the soul of weakened victims, making them into mindless zombies intent on one thing—devastation. But Lee had saved him. She'd fed him that night and the next. The third night, she had appeared next to him holding a small, thin disc—the key to the synergistic bonds that kept him immobile. She freed him and disappeared into the shadows of the basement. When he went to look for her, she was gone. Like she had vanished into thin air. He'd waited until sunrise to escape because Raviners, like most of the hell creatures out of Anqar, were weaker during the day. Come sunrise, he'd slipped out of the house and run for his life, sparing just a few thoughts for the girl who had freed him.

It wasn't the last time he would see her, or the last time she would save him. Three years passed, and when he saw her next, he was a courier for a rebel army just outside of Orleans. Even though she had grown up a little, he still recognized her as the child who had freed him from the little hell of his prison outside the fallen city of New Angeles.

"What's your name?" she had asked. Perched atop an aboveground crypt, she had sat swinging her feet, that dimpled smile exactly as he remembered it.

"Kalen Brenner."

Her brow puckered. She frowned a little. "You have really long hair for a boy." She tugged on her short curls and glanced at his hair with a wistful sort of envy. "Your hair is prettier than mine."

He hadn't thought so. Kalen had liked those pale yellow curls. But he didn't say anything. She had just continued to stare at him for a while, then she giggled. He wanted to ask what she was laughing about, and where she was staying, was she safe . . . but somebody had called him. In the few seconds it took him to look behind him and then look back, she had disappeared.

Gone from his life for another five years. Kalen went from serving as a courier to fighting in a rebel army to leading one. The next time he saw her was when she went to pull him out of the way when one of his lieutenants would have slashed his throat from behind. Dais had warned him that men weren't going to like following somebody so young, and the old war dog was right. Lee had saved his life again, and after that, Lee started fighting, not just sliding in and out of his life like a wraith, but fighting. Small things at first. He hadn't wanted her in danger. She was just a kid—she might have just been three years younger but she hadn't grown up fighting to stay alive, not like he had. She'd been too soft. Too pretty—and not just because she was a girl. But for all his instincts to protect her, Lee had a knack for finding dangerous situations and defusing them. Or finding innocent families, trapped and helpless—Kalen had long since lost count of how many people she'd been responsible for saving.

At first, she'd simply appeared and led Kalen and his men, but eventually, she'd started showing up with people in tow. People she'd saved. Now he led yet another band of rebels, but this one was larger, more organized, and they didn't just fight small skirmishes. They fought on the most dangerous front left in their world, with the gates in both Yorkton and Jivan decimated.

They fought to keep the demons from spreading past the Roinan Mountains. Lee, always an enigma, came and went like the wind, appearing out of the night like a shadow, full of whispered secrets and magicks that saved countless lives. Most of their witches were useless when it came to fighting near the gates—it was as if something from the gates froze their power. What they could do was divert the energy flow that fed the gates, but it wasn't easy work and usually required the strength of a good three witches.

Lee, though, was different. A witch, yes, but the gate's energy didn't affect her at all. Even more, she was quick, canny and intuitive. The woman should have been leading this army. If Dais truly wanted to call somebody a leader, then it needed to be Lee. Leader, wise one, corida—for all her young years, the titles suited her. She was a leader and Kalen was simply a soldier. He wanted to be out there fighting, not issuing orders and playing the diplomat with fellow rebel leaders.

Crouched on the twisted rock outcropping, Kalen watched as she issued orders to the rebel soldiers with ease, the sunny banner of her curls gleaming in the false light as she shook her head in response to a question. Tonight's agenda was the same as it had been for the past week: recon and salvage.

This had to stop. There had to be a better way to fight this war than this. Gaining a little ground on one front, only to lose it on another. But Kalen didn't know what the other options were. One of his best warriors was about as insubstantial as a wraith. Until she opened her eyes . . .

The screams painted the night like blood. Hot, vivid washes of it. Kalen jerked to his feet and all around him, people stared.

The screams hadn't come from here. He'd heard them echo through the Veil—a warning, but he had a feeling it was already too late. As he stood, he grabbed the plasma assault rifle from the ground and slung it over his shoulder. His feet passed silently over the uneven ground as he moved closer to the source of the turmoil. Too many screams. He ran for the rebuilt solar-powered glider and powered it up with a silent prayer. It came to life with a muted roar and he breathed out in relief.

"I don't like this."

He shifted his eyes as Lee slid out of the darkness, running along beside him effortlessly. Her hair gleamed like silver in the darkness of the night, her blue eyes colorless. "You heard the screaming."

Her lips flattened. "The very dead heard those screams," she whispered. The glider moved over the ground with blurring speed, and she caught her hair in her fist to keep it from blowing in her eyes.

Miles passed in silence. As they moved closer, other tran-units joined them. As they slowed to a halt, he heard the soft whimper that rose in her throat before she could stop it.

Kalen had to bite back his own furious scream of denial. Clenching his jaw, he drew the rifle from over his shoulder and leveled it at the Jorniak demon that was still feasting in the middle of the death and devastation.

Lee lifted her hand and the pure silver energy that flowed from it was the same as the beam that shot out of the laser pulsing from Kalen's plasma rifle. Like most men, Kalen couldn't control the energy of the land, although he could sense it. It never ceased to amaze him how easily Lee could call that energy to her hands. She carried weapons—all his soldiers did—but she rarely needed them. Lee *was* a weapon.

The Jorniak demon screamed, the hissing quality of his death scream making their skin crawl, while the stench of his blood made their eyes water. Jorniaks never really stank, unless they bled. Once they bled, the smell of them was enough to make a grown man's eyes water and his stomach rebel.

"Did you have to kill him so fast? He could have been useful," Dais muttered from behind Kalen. From the corner of his eye, Kalen saw his lieutenant crouching over one of the fallen.

Lee's bolt had killed him. Kalen's pulsar blast had gone through one of the thing's three lungs, enough to hurt him, enough to keep him from running very far. Dais had taught Kalen well and Kalen liked to ask questions.

But Lee . . . well, her anger sometimes got the better of her. Eh, maybe actually leading the army wasn't the wisest course of action for her. She acted first, asked questions later. She was a dangerous piece of work, true, but she had little use for talking to the demons.

Kalen had learned the value of asking questions.

But he understood why she had destroyed the thing. This small unit had been basically a hospital on wheels. A few soldiers, but most of the dead had been healers, the deirons who used the elusive healing magicks and the medics, untalented but skilled people who relied on science to bring a person back to health. They had been harmless, all of them. Healers had little use for fighting unless they were threatened.

"He killed them all, Kalen."

With harsh, jerking motions, he shoved his plasma rifle into the harness at his back. Fury and grief burned inside him and he wanted to howl out his rage to the night sky. But at the low, rough sound of her voice, he turned to look at her, a fist closing around his heart. There were tears sparkling in her cerulean eyes.

She blinked them away before they could fall, but still the sight of them was like a punch to his already battered system. Lee never cried. "Damn it, how much longer do we have to keep doing this?" she demanded, her voice shaking and hoarse with barely suppressed emotion.

Kalen cupped his hand over her neck, drawing her against him, his body jumping to life as her sleek curves came into contact with his tensed muscles. "Until we win, darlin'. Until we win," he replied. *Or until they kill all of us.* The words hung between them, unsaid, but understood.

It made no sense. The brutality of the demon attacks had increased over the past decade with an intensity that sickened and scared all of them. There had been a time when the Anqarians had policed the demons themselves. It had only made sense—they used Ishtan as their breeding ground, so they wouldn't want it totally decimated.

But lately, it was as though Anqar didn't give a bloody damn. Not that Kalen wanted to go back to simply evading slaving expeditions or fighting to free the females before it was too late, but this sudden reversal made little sense.

"And when will we?" Lee asked. But she didn't seem to expect an answer, and that was just as well. Kalen had no desire to lie to her simply to comfort her, but from where he stood, their future looked grim.

A shudder wracked her body and then she sighed. The soft sound was broken in the middle by a weird little hitching hiccup. He gritted his teeth as he felt the soft push of her breasts against his chest, the smooth plane of her belly cuddling up against his cock.

He could smell her. She smelled so sweet, so warm and alive. The scent of her body took him away from everything—for just the briefest moment, he could imagine himself reaching for Lee, holding her body against his. Feeling the warmth of the sun on his flesh, feeling her silken soft body moving against his own.

A few seconds of peace—the rebellion faded away. The stink of his decaying, dying world, for a moment, was replaced by the warmth of a woman. Then, it was over. Lee stepped away and seemed totally oblivious to the effect she had on him.

She turned to face the destruction and death that lay before them. Kalen watched as she shoved a shaking hand through her hair. Lee always hated being stared at. She slid him a nervous look and then jerked her gaze away. He sighed and turned away, forcing himself to walk into the splattered circle of blood.

Akira was dead. She had been a twenty-one-year-old medic that Kalen had known since she was a kid. A tic throbbed in his jaw as he studied the gore that had been made out of her once pretty face. Her eye was missing, half her cheek, and bone gleamed in the moonlight. Blood shone wetly, her throat a raw, open wound.

He closed his eyes and rested a hand on the smooth, unmarked skin of her brow. "Blessings on your path, little sister," he murmured, the traditional farewell to a dead or dying friend coming harshly.

At least she had died quick. And most likely first.

Akira had been an anomaly, a true healer also blessed with telekinesis. Psychic skills weren't common among those who went into the healing arts. The only talent common among them was the ability to heal using magick. All Akira had ever wanted to do was help people, and because of that, she was dead.

If she hadn't died fast, and first, she could have called for help. Akira's ability to heal had been invaluable, her other abilities even more so—with her around, her unit hadn't needed a designated telepath. The soldiers that moved with the med-unit were some of his best, but none of them had any kind of telekinetic skills. He'd counted on Akira being enough. Now she was dead and he'd have to live with that. With a hand that shook, he reached out and gently closed Akira's one remaining eye.

She was already cold. Damn it, she had just been fine . . . a few hours ago.

Rage boiled inside his heart as he straightened up, turning his head, counting every last body. His voice was a rasping snarl as he demanded, "Are there any survivors?"

Silence fell as his men fanned out and searched for any sign of life. Kalen knelt in blood, gore and other things that he didn't want to think about as he checked the still bodies for a pulse, for breathing—any sign that someone had survived. There was nothing. He found himself standing at the edge of the clearing, staring at the unidentifiable remains of the Jorniak demons.

"Kalen."

He lifted his head and stared at Dais. The old man's lined face was weary and his eyes glittered with rage. "There are none left alive," Dais said, his voice oddly gentle, as though that made the news any easier to hear. But Kalen already knew. Rage pounded inside him as he slowly turned around and stared at the devastation before him.

The entire med-unit was gone, along with every patient that had been in the small roaming clinic. He counted twelve patients. One or two of them seemed familiar, but beyond that, he knew none of them. But the med-unit staff, he'd known all of them. Five friends dead. Blood roared in his ears, while reality seemed to freeze in front of him.

"Leave," Kalen whispered.

"Son?"

Kalen lifted his head and stared at Dais, his eyes burning. A muscle jerked in his jaw as he repeated it, "Leave. All of you. Take the men back to camp."

"But the dead . . ."

Kalen laughed bitterly. "The dead will still be dead in an hour, Dais. Get the hell out of here. Now." Kalen didn't bother to watch them leave; instead he turned his head and stared at Lee. She sat cross-legged by the body of a young child, holding a limp hand between hers. The tears had finally started to fall and her shoulders were wracked with the force of her sobs.

Even in the middle of the massacre, the sound of her grief tore at him like jagged claws. He wanted to go to her. But standing over Akira's body, he couldn't. Rage shook him, ate at him, and the longer he stared at Lee, the hotter his rage burned.

This could all stop.

Lee could help them stop it.

It was within her power. Kalen didn't know how he knew that, but it was true. Magick wasn't uncommon in his world. More than half of the women who served under him had magickal abilities. Many of the men had psychic skills of some sort. Save for the med-units, easily half of his forces had either magickal or telepathic skills. But none of them had the kind of potential that he sensed within Lee.

She moved in the shadows of their world, always at night, fighting the demons while the moon rode in the sky and the demons were at their strongest. She fought them and she won. Somehow, she was their chance out of hell. He knew it in his gut. But none of that would do any of them a damn bit of good until she accepted who she was. If Lee would do that, they just might have a chance. He reached out to her and she ignored him every time. She came and did what she had to, and when it was done, she turned her back on them while Kalen's people continued to die.

His heart pounded in his throat and the bitter taste of anger lay heavy on his tongue as he stared at her. "How long will you hide, Lee?"

She lifted her head, and a breeze blew by, blowing long strands of her silken hair across her face, hiding from him everything but those azure eyes. For long moments, she stared at him, unmoving.

Kalen moved to her, the thick soles of his combat boots thudding dully on the rubble-strewn ground. It was thick with garbage, dirt, tossed medical supplies . . . and things he'd rather not think about, gobbets of nasty wet things he didn't want to see. By the carcass of the senior medical officer, he paused and knelt. He felt a knot swell in his throat as he stared down into the man's wizened old face. "God-speed, Jacob," he whispered. He blew out a tired breath and ran a hand down his face before snagging a blanket from the rubble. Gently, he covered Jacob's body before rising and meeting Lee's gaze over the distance that separated them.

Purpose filled his eyes, his gut, his steps as he moved to her. He curled his hands into loose fists and wondered if he would be able to control his temper this time. Kalen saw the trepidation enter her eyes, watched as her throat moved, the fragile skin shifting, betraying the nerves he suspected she was suddenly feeling.

He could see the pain in her gaze, but it came nowhere near the pain he felt. Lee barely knew these people. She hadn't been there when Akira returned from her medical training and forced her way into Kalen's unit. She hadn't been there when Akira helped deliver Jacob's first grand-daughter. She hadn't been there when Akira sat by Jacob's side as his wife died.

No, Lee came and went. She never risked herself for anything longer than a few hours a night. A few nights a week. Weeks would go by when she wasn't seen at all.

It cost them lives. People depended on her.

She had proved time and again she would only come when she couldn't stay away any longer. Her conscious self didn't even know what was going on. She hid behind the veil of her memory, safe inside her normal world, where demons didn't exist, where everything was safeness, security and light.

Here, in this darker reality, where things existed whether she liked it or not, she could join them, save lives . . . but she refused.

Closing the distance between them, he loomed over her, staring down into a face he knew almost as well as he knew his own. "When are you going to open your eyes, Lee?"

She blinked. He could seen the tension that suddenly tightened her body, stiffening her shoulders, drawing her back ramrod straight, tiny little lines fanning out from her eyes. Her lashes lowered, the spiky little fans hooding her eyes, shielding her gaze from him as she murmured, "What do you mean, Kalen?"

"When you are going to come into the open? Join us? We're dying while we wait for you," he growled, reaching down and closing firm, unyielding hands around her upper arms as he drew her closer to him.

"I've been helping you for twenty years, since I was a kid, Kalen. What more do you want?" she demanded. "I gave you my childhood."

"I want you to join us. Not to just fight when you can't hide from your dreams anymore. What do you do when you're not here? Where do you live? What is your home? I don't even know your full name—do you?" She just stared at him and the irrational anger surged higher in him. "Damn it, what is your name?"

With every harsh question, he watched her flinch. Even here she couldn't answer. Even when she was here in her subconscious dreams, she was too afraid. With a rough, disbelieving laugh, he let her go and turned away, reaching up to rub a hand over his stiff neck.

"You come and go like a shadow in the night, Lee. You're like flashfire, baby," he whispered. "Just as reliable. Just as hot. Just as deadly. You can cause a hell of a lot of damage to the Warlords' armies. You can cut through demons like you're cutting down grass. But too many of our people want to depend on you to always be there. People have launched entire campaigns, thinking that at the critical minute you will come and pull off a miracle. When they are right, it's been amazing. But when they are wrong . . . it's been too devastating for words. I can't let them depend on you anymore. I can't depend on you."

Turning back to face her, he felt a hollow ache settle in his heart. "You belong in my world. I know this—in my gut. You know it, you always have. Otherwise you wouldn't keep coming here. You wouldn't even know we existed."

Kalen plunged his hands through his hair, fisting them, resisting the urge to tear out hunks of hair, anything to relieve the building pain and frustration inside him. They needed to end this. They had to find a way to unite and drive back the monsters through the gate separating Kalen's world from Anqar, a way to stop the Warlords' ever-increasing raids, and they had to do it soon, or it would be too late.

A sudden surge of weariness flooded him and he had to fight to stay on his feet. All the fighting, endless, seemingly useless fighting, inches gained only to loose yards on the next front. Staring into the sky, he studied the flickering lights of the auroras. They had once been much brighter, so beautiful it made the soul hurt just to look at them.

Now he couldn't even see the stars. The auroras grew fainter with each passing season. The skies were clogged with smoke and fumes. The fire-bearing demons were only partially responsible for that. Encampments relied on fire to keep back many of the demon breeds, so there were always fires burning. Some of the demons breathed out a noxious gas, adding to the already polluted air.

Time passed and the skies grew more and more hazy, until the sun became little more than an indistinct bright circle behind the smog.

Kalen couldn't remember the last time he had seen stars.

His world was falling apart. His people were being killed to extinction.

"What are you waiting for, Lee?"

"Kalen—"

Cutting his eyes to her, he whispered silkily, "Don't. Just—don't, Lee." Crossing over to her, he cupped her face in his hand, tightening his hold when she tried to jerk her face away. "You aren't here every day. You haven't been the one to go into a safe haven and find entire families slaughtered, wiped out, from the elders to the babes. You haven't had to comfort friends as they had to watch the women they love slowly go insane because they were raped by the Warlords' men.

"You live there, in your reflection of this world, safe and secure, blind to what happens here. Except for your dreams, where you can't block us out. And then, you come and you go—but you come because you can't resist it anymore. You never come for us, for me."

"Damn it, I've saved your fine ass a number of times," she sneered, jabbing him in the chest with a fingernail. It was bright, bold red, the color of junyai rubies, precious gems once found in the mines of Jivan. "Your life. This army. All of you."

"Yes. Because something disturbed you in your sleep, while you rest safe and sound in your safe little world. Damn it, I know what's going on. You know. A part of you has always known," he whispered passionately. The wind started to kick up and his hair blew around them like a cloak, winding around her slim shoulders as he moved closer, nudging her toes with his.

"Known what?" she demanded, rising onto her toes so that she was snarling into his face.

Her mouth was just a breath away from his . . . just one breath . . . Kalen could almost taste her, taste her fury, her fear, the hunger she tried so hard to hide. He laughed softly, releasing her chin to stroke his fingers over her eyes. "Known what you are. You don't belong in the mundane, powerless realm. You're magick. You're power . . . You're a warrior and you belong here. You see things in your world that other people don't see, but you block it out. You feel things, hear things, sense things . . . You are like a wraith in that world. A mere shadow of your true self. When are you going to come home? Come to us, fight with us?"

"I fight with you all the time," she whispered, her lips trembling, tears welling in her eyes as she stared at him, hands clenched into tight fists at her sides. "You act like I'm in some other world, but I am right here."

"You're still blocking it out. Even after all this time." Kalen shook his head. "Still. Lee . . . you are here. Part of you. Part of you lingers there. But you're nothing but a shadow of yourself in either world. You have to open your eyes and start seeing your reality, instead of the one somebody created for you. Otherwise you'll remain in the shadows."

Lee gritted her teeth, a tiny shriek of frustrated anger slipping from behind them as she spun away and punched her fist into the ruined wall of what had once been a mercantilery. "Damn it, what in the hell are you talking about? You always talk in riddles, you overgrown, self-righteous, hypocritical bastard!"

He said her name softly and waited until she turned around to glare at him before he asked quietly, "Where do you go when you aren't here? Do you know?"

A blank look entered her eyes, one he had seen before. Often he tried to probe her mind—sometimes she deflected him, but sometimes, he knew she honestly didn't know. Her face turned mutinous, a line forming between her eyes, that lush pink mouth puckering into a sullen, sexy little scowl. "What does that have to do with anything?" she demanded. She shoved a hand through her hair, pushing the blond curls out of her eyes.

With a tired sigh, Kalen rubbed his forehead. "You don't even know. Damn it, Lee, doesn't that strike you as pretty fucking weird, that you don't know where you go in between flitting in and out of my life?" he demanded, flinging a hand in her direction before letting it fall limply to his side as she just stared at him, her lids flickering, her eyes glittering like diamonds in the faint light.

"What did you do yesterday?" he asked. *Damn it, prove me wrong . . . prove me wrong!* It would be so much easier if she was just some elusive witch from the mountains. From anywhere—so long as she lived on this world.

But he already knew the truth.

When she remained silent, he felt something inside him die. "You can't," he answered for her. "Because you don't remember."

Something broke open inside him and he lunged for her, drawing his blade from the sheath at his hip, grabbing her forearm. She shrieked and shoved at him, startled. He could feel the fire of her magick as she pressed her hands against his chest. One hand pressed against the dull sheen on his cavinir jacket that he hadn't zipped up. But the other landed on his chest, just a little off center. Above his heart. The heat of her power burned into his skin.

Gripping her left hand, he wrenched her palm away from his chest. He could smell the scorched stink of burned flesh as he pinned her arm down. Stony-eyed, he used the blade to slice a shallow mark into her arm. His heart bled as he heard her soft gasp of pain. "Explain that . . . when you wake in the morning. Explain your bruises away, however you will. But explain a knife cut."

Turning from her, he stormed away. He felt a little sick in his gut for what he had done. He closed his eyes and fought the urge to scream and rail at her. It wouldn't do any good. She hadn't listened to him in all this time.

She wouldn't listen now.

"Leave, Lee. Leave and don't come back. We'll fight this war without you."

And if she kept coming back, he would end up doing something that would destroy them both.

TWO

Lee woke with tears drying on her face and an ache in her heart.

She stretched slowly, searching for any new aches and pains. Nothing felt outwardly painful, which was odd, because she felt like she had run the gauntlet. Usually when she woke feeling like this, she had myriad bruises all over her body.

From her feet up, she stretched, rolling her ankles, tensing then relaxing her calves, her thighs, her buttocks, arching her spine. As she started to stretch her arms over her head, she yelped. A fiery pain exploded in her left forearm.

Slowly, Lee sat up and cradled her arm close to her chest. She didn't want to look at it. She didn't want to see. This pain, whatever it was, felt different. Lee swallowed, the sound of it echoing in her ears. Foreboding filled her, hot and thick, as she slowly lowered her arm and stared at it. Watery sunlight filtered through the curtains, falling on the long, thin slash.

It was three inches long, the dried blood on it forming a scab. It was hair-thin. It would heal quickly and probably wouldn't even leave a scar. He hadn't wanted to scar her. Just scare her, just make some sort of point.

Terror bubbled inside her mind as she stared at the cut and wondered where that thought had come from.

Explain that.

An angry voice flooded her ears, and eyes loomed large in her vision, flooding out everything but their molten silver essence.

We'll fight this war without you . . .

Swallowing, she rubbed her chest. The ache there expanded as his words echoed in her mind over and over. *Explain that.*

Explain it—there was no earthly way to explain it. Well, there was one. She was going crazy. She was going crazy—having bizarre, insane dreams—and she had cut herself. But even as she thought that through, she knew it was wrong. This felt like no dream.

It felt like a memory.

A man's face shimmered into her mind's eye.

The man from that piece she had been working on the other day.

Kalen. His name was Kalen. His face had haunted her dreams for so long.

Kalen, standing over a bloody mess of chaos and destruction, turning to look at her with pain and disappointment in those amazing silver eyes. His hair was a silken black cloak that hung around his shoulders, halfway down his back . . . and he was angry, so angry the air around him all but vibrated with his rage.

You belong in our world . . .

She closed her eyes, pressing her hands to her face. Behind her eyelids, she saw a world that was overwhelmed by war, by chaos, pitted, blackened areas that had once been cities, forests stripped of everything green and pure, a world so ugly and torn. Smoke filled the air and fires always burned. It was a terrifying, ugly image, as close to hell on earth as she could imagine. But like an afterimage . . . another world wavered, just beyond the reach of her sight, something green and lush and rich.

That was the world as it had once been. Before something, or someone, had torn open a hole that led straight to hell. Now it was a feeding and breeding ground for something evil, something vile.

Too real . . . too real . . .

Lee whimpered in her throat, wrapping her arms around her knees and resting her chin there. *You're going out of your mind . . .*

That low, raspy voice, with its odd accent. Like Ireland, but heavier. Almost more ancient sounding. *You belong in my world . . .* It sounded like music to her ears: *Y b'lon in me world. Ye know it . . . ye always have.*

His eyes were pools of molten silver, and just as hot. Damn it, there was no way she could have imagined a creature as fantastical as he was. Or as angry. The rage she sensed inside him was practically tangible. He seemed so real . . . Whimpering, she curled on her side in the bed and whispered, "What's going on with me?"

The entire dream, she remembered all of it. She had closed her eyes to go to sleep last night and had a brief moment of nothingness . . . then she had opened her eyes, seeing a murky display of greenish purple lights just beyond the thick cover of clouds. A strange sense of purpose had filled her, and she had moved through the bizarre landscape of empty rubble-strewn streets, shells of buildings, trees that were twisted and stunted. Walking those roads had felt familiar, and she had seen faces that she had known.

The more she thought about the dream, the more memories she seemed to find, like they had been buried just under the sand and a wind had come, blowing the sand away and exposing the memories. Curling her hands into fists, she clenched her teeth against another onslaught of them. *What is going on?*

***

Lee spent the day wandering the house, thinking she had lost her mind, her hold on reality. If she didn't settle down and focus, she might just lose her job. She had four pieces due by the end of the week, but damned if she could focus on anything.

After dropping the drawing board and the stylus for the third time, she gave up on trying to work. Her equipment was too expensive to keep getting abused like that, and it wasn't like she had accomplished anything today anyway. Not even crap. If she had finished a crappy piece, at least it would have been something she could try to rework tomorrow.

She felt disconnected from everything around her. Even sitting down and trying to watch reruns of *Law & Order* was a waste of time. She couldn't follow the plot to save her life, not today.

His words kept echoing in her ears—*Open your eyes . . .*

Damn it, what in the hell did those dreams mean?

Why didn't they feel like dreams? Dreams felt vague, blurry—or more often than not, she didn't remember them at all. So often she woke up and felt like she had walked through an entire other world, but recalling those dreams was nearly impossible. But this dream? It all felt too real for words.

She could remember the feel of his hands on her arms, the agony and the self-directed fury she saw in his eyes as he sliced that blade down her arm. Lee remembered the quick flash of pain—it hadn't hurt, not at first. The pain came a few seconds later, but the pain wasn't what had her so shaken.

He'd cut her. He'd deliberately hurt her. For some odd reason, she felt betrayed by that.

The cut . . . She lifted her forearm, staring at the cut with wide, troubled eyes. Anytime she had ever gotten hurt in life, it had healed with amazing speed. She hadn't ever taken much notice of it, until another kid from the foster home she'd been living in when she was twelve came home with stitches in her leg from a laceration she'd gotten when she'd been hurt in a bike accident. Lee hadn't seen stitches before.

Technically, she'd heard of them. But weren't they for more serious things? Little cuts like that healed in a couple of days. Well, they always did for her. But Toni had kept those stitches in for more than a week, and the nasty gash on her leg took weeks to heal.

The cut on Lee's arm was still raw. Still open. Like it wasn't healing at all. Lee blew her bangs out of her eyes and dropped her arm, spinning away. "You weren't in some magickal world last night. Some magicked blade didn't cut your arm. You are you, nobody else."

A mantra, she repeated it to herself over and over. But there was another voice, *his* voice, and it was louder, drowning out everything else. *You're nothing but a shadow of yourself . . . a wraith.*

"He talks about me like I'm not real. Like I'm not here," Lee muttered. She hardly realized she was talking to herself. "I am here. I am real." The sound of her raised voice startled her and Lee clapped a hand over her mouth, locking the argument inside.

"Stop it," she mumbled against her hand. "This is just nuts." Crazy. That's what it was. She needed real, professional help. Her hand shook as it fell away from her lips, and she clenched it into a tight fist. A dream had done this to her. Had her shivering and scared, like a child afraid of the dark.

"That's it. This has got to stop." She took a deep breath and left the living room. There was a phone book in her office. The yellow pages had all sorts of professional help. She'd find herself a shrink, get an appointment—today if at all possible. If it took a bunch of pills and hours on a therapy couch, she was going to stop these damn dreams.

You're nothing but a shadow . . . Just outside the door to her office, his voice whispered through her mind again. She froze in her tracks. Then she started to run. Lee ran down the hall, tripping over the runner on the wood floor, skidding on her knees to a stop in front of the bookcase where she kept her photo albums.

"I'm not a fucking shadow. I'm not a wraith. What in

the hell is a wraith anyway? I am real. I'm real," she said, her voice harsh, her breathing erratic. Her hand shook as she opened the heavy cloth-covered board that made up the front of the album. The pictures had been taken last summer, at a barbecue when a friend sold a book to a publisher in New York. Lee preferred to be behind the camera, but this time, she had consented. A few pictures . . .

Her eyes lingered on the very first one. One of her with her arm linked around Moira's neck. Moira's face was clear, her eyes sparkling and bright, all the excitement and joy about her book deal showing in her eyes. But Lee's face . . . it was like the lens had been wet. Foggy, or out of focus. Jason had been taking the pictures that day. Moira's husband was a professional portrait photographer. He didn't know how to take bad pictures.

Turning the page, she looked from one picture to another, and in every one her face was distorted or blurred. The sob started as an ache in her chest, building as she threw down the album and grabbed another one, this one from when she and Moira had gone to Ireland, three years before her friend had met Jason.

All of them. Blurred. Distorted. Out of focus. They hadn't looked like that when she'd put them in this album. She knew they hadn't. "No," she whispered. With her fisted hand pressed to her lips, Lee stared at the picture of her and Moira in front of Dromoland Castle. Moira's face was clear, her smile wide and easy. Her arm was slung around Lee's shoulders. The image was so clear that Lee could see the numbers on Moira's oversized watch.

But Lee? Her image was totally out of focus. Even her clothes looked blurry.

"No," she whispered again.

Her mind whirled, e-mails she remembered coming to mind. Professional portraits she'd had taken to be used with the bio on her website, only to have the photographer e-mail her and tell her they'd need to do the pictures again, the images were blurred. Lee hadn't bothered with it at the time, hadn't wanted to mess with it, and she probably wouldn't have if Moira hadn't kept nagging her about it.

With startling clarity, Lee recalled when she'd finally given in to Moira and agreed to let Jason take some new pictures for her to use on her site. Those pictures had been fine. Perfectly fine. She had loaded them onto her computer right after Jason had taken them. They had been fine. They would still be fine.

Gingerly, she placed the album on the ground and rose, wrapping her arms around her body. She was freezing. She felt so damn cold. Lee stood there in the middle of scattered pictures and albums and rubbed her hands up and down her arms. Chilled to the bone, she turned away from the albums and walked to the office, one slow step after another.

The photos were going to be fine.

They were great pictures and everything was fine, she told herself as she walked into her office and crossed to her workstation. She sat down at her desk and opened the drawer.

Rifling through the scattered notes and paper clips, she looked for the envelope where she had put the disk with the picture files. Her hand was shaking as she put it into the disk drive, watching as the computer screen came to life, the flickering lights of her screensaver disappearing as she touched the key.

The sight of those lights touched another memory in her head.

That clouded sky. The lights behind a shield of dust, fumes and smog . . . Closing her eyes, Lee whispered, "Sweet heaven. I'm going nuts." She had designed the screensaver from those lights, like the northern lights she'd seen when she went to Alaska. They'd amazed her, enthralled her . . . but these lights were different. Muted, almost broken. The lights seemed sad.

"I really have lost my mind," she murmured. Covering the mouse with her hand, she opened the folder where the pictures were stored. She didn't have to click on it any more than once before the sob that had been building in her throat tore free.

"No!" she screamed, standing out of her chair so fast it toppled over. With one vicious sweep of her arm, she knocked the keyboard, the mouse pad and the mouse from the under-the-desk platform, jerking the cords out with vicious pulls of her wrist, screaming as she hurled the keyboard across the room.

It landed with a clatter on the floor as she turned to stare back at the computer. All the thumbnail images stared back at her. And every single one was blurred, distorted, out of focus. She couldn't so much as make out the color of her eyes. *No.*

Open your eyes . . .

Like a wind in the desert, the echo of the voice seemed to scorch her flesh, echoing all around her, echoing inside her head. She pressed her hands against her eyes and demanded, "What in the hell am I supposed to see?"

The world shifted under her feet. Lee gasped for air, throwing out her arms for balance. Noise assaulted her ears, and when she spun around to stare out the window, colors were so vivid, she felt as though she was staring through a kaleidoscope.

Trees seemed to glow, a golden light emanating from within. She could see each individual blade of grass. Hear the sound of a bird call. The ground still seemed to be trembling, but the leaves outside weren't even moving on the trees. Well, that wasn't exactly true. They were trembling, ever so minutely. A fly buzzed by and she whimpered as she realized that the fly was a good forty feet away. She could see it, so incredibly clear, as it landed on one of those minutely trembling leaves on one of the trees that seemed all glowy.

A wild laugh escaped Lee's lips as she fell to her knees in front of the window, propping her arms on the sill, tensing as the wood seemed to pulse and throb under her arms.

Open your eyes . . .

Lee tried to stand up. But the bones of her legs seemed to dissolve and she collapsed to the floor, darkness rushing up to greet her.

***

Lee heard them talking at the table. They were in the other room and they were talking the quiet way adults do when they don't want you to hear, but she heard them anyway.

Her head hurt. It felt all funny, like somebody had smacked her across the back of her head and then packed her aching skull full of cotton. Her tummy felt funny, tight and achy, but she couldn't eat. The food here all tasted so weird. They gave her something to eat called a hot dog. She didn't eat dogs. She played with them.

Where had Mama gone? One second the noises had been getting so loud, loud, loud . . . roaring in her ears, and then something wet on her face and the sky overhead was so blue it hurt her eyes. It was pretty though. The sky at home was darker. A deeper blue. And at night, it was so black that stars sparkled like diamonds, huge and bright in the sky and glowing with the red and purple and blue lights of the 'roras. She barely remembered the 'roras.

It had been a long time since she'd seen them. Now, the skies were cloudy and the air was smelly. The monsters did it. Monsters that turned things into fire with a touch, monsters that smelled so bad they made her tummy hurt, and other monsters, monsters that looked like people until you saw their eyes. She hadn't seen them much. Mama and her hid. Mama really knew how to hide.

But she still remembered.

But now Mama was gone. And this wasn't home. Although the air didn't smell so gross and the sky was a pretty pale blue, it wasn't home.

". . . found her in a field. The hunter was scared to death he had shot her. She gave him a terrible scare." That was the lady with the streaky hair. She had nice eyes, but she looked so tired.

A deep voice spoke up. "I don't understand it. How can

a little girl just appear in that field? The nearest town is seventy-six miles away. And talking to her, you can't get anything out of her. Nothing she tells you makes sense. Talking about fire-things and smelly monsters. Says the sky here isn't right. She talks like she used to see the northern lights, but how in the hell would she go from there to here?"

"Have you investigated anything about a fire? Maybe a chemical fire? Tar or something? It smells something awful when it burns."

Lee rolled away, reaching out and picking up a cracker. That was what Miss Carson had called them. Crackers. Crackers weren't so bad. Salty. Better than the hot dogs. Even if the hot dogs smelled sort of good, she wasn't eating dogs.

They didn't understand her name either. Lelia Rass. That was her name. Lelia Rass. But they kept calling her Leah Ross. Leah was kind of pretty. But Ross didn't sound right. It wasn't her name.

This wasn't her home . . .

* * *

Lee sat up so fast her head was spinning. Whimpering, she pressed her fists to her head.

Damn it, how could she have forgotten that?

Foster kids got bounced around so often it wasn't even funny, and a lot of them tended to block out memories that weren't pleasant. But how could she have blocked out something so important?

She remembered the colors. The colors of the sky—like the colors on her screensaver. The smelly things . . . Jorniak demons. Her head throbbed. Opening her eyes, she stared in front of her, seeing through tunnel vision, like she was staring through a hollowed-out crystal prism. Time slowed to a crawl and she could feel the air pulsing around her.

Open your eyes, Lee.

You live there, in your reflection of this world. Reflection.

She felt a ripple in the air. Then tension. Like a storm was brewing. She could feel it, something powerful, lingering just beyond her reach. Icy cold, she climbed to her feet and stood. She swayed, rocking herself back and forth, and let the power in the air wrap around her. And music—Lee could hear the faint strains of music. Alien music.

The tension in the air became thicker, heavier, until she had a hard time even breathing it in. Heavy and warm, like maple syrup. She took a step and it was like the air had formed a physical presence, clinging to her. It wrapped around her body like an embrace, caressing her body in a way she had never noticed before.

Like a floating feather, she drifted into the bathroom, walking past the partial mirror over the sink. Lee pushed open the door to the walk-in closet, keeping her lashes lowered until she was standing mere inches before the mirror.

When she lifted them, a slight sense of disappointment seemed to fill her, and she felt the tension drain out of her like water.

Nothing but her reflection.

***

Kalen felt it like an electric shock through skin. Her touch. He knew her touch, her presence like he knew the sight of his own hands. All she had to do was be in his world mere moments and he felt it.

But it was daylight.

Lee hadn't stepped foot into his world while the sun shone in years, decades. Cutting his eyes back to the Elder, he tried to follow along as they prayed over the graves of the most recently fallen. It was like the Elder was speaking in some ancient, foreign language though. None of the words made sense. Kalen couldn't concentrate. Couldn't focus.

He felt something touch the Veil. It rippled. As attuned as he was to the Veil's energies, that light touch hit his system with the force of a jolt from a plasma charge.

Something was brewing in the air. Looking around

him, he knew he wasn't the only one who felt it now. Some of his men and women looked like somebody had jabbed them with a hot piece of iron. Startled, jumpy and worried. Understandable—changes in the air usually came just before a gatestorm—like nature was giving them a warning.

Kalen wasn't worried, though. There was no room in his mind for worry, not when it felt like his entire system was singing. This—whatever it was—wasn't a gatestorm. His mind raced, blood rushing through his veins like he had just run the gauntlet. A muscle ticked in his jaw. His gut was tied in knots and his heart pounded with anticipation.

Once the final prayers were said, Kalen knelt over Akira's grave and whispered, "I'm sorry, mycera." Little sister. He could remember holding her hand when she was a child, and wiping away her tears the day their fathers had died. The men had died together and it had forged a bond between them—until now, Kalen had thought it was unbreakable. "Wherever you are, you're happier now. Godspeed."

Before anybody could stop him, he slid through the crowds, eyes narrowed, following that little pulse in his gut. The tension in the air mounted. It had him wound so tight, he felt like he was going to splinter into little bits and pieces if it didn't break soon.

And then it did.

Kalen hit the ground as the earth rocked under him. Distantly, he heard the comm unit at his belt sound off. He ignored it as he climbed to his feet. All was silent. The pressure in the air was gone.

Kalen felt her. Damn it, he actually felt her. By the time he had reached the clearing outside the encampment, his entire body was tense as a bowstring.

Slowing to a halt, he stood there, his eyes scanning the distorted terrain.

* * *

With a disheartened sigh, Lee let her hand fall away from the mirror. "I'm insane. I've lost my mind."

Turning away, Lee tipped her head back, staring up at the ceiling. Under the halter top of her pajamas, a cool wind chilled her skin, bringing with it the scents of things long forgotten. Smoke, soot, something noxious and cloying . . . but below that, something wild, the forest, the air, the earth.

The earth pitched and rolled beneath her feet. Literally. It threw Lee forward, and she threw out her hands to catch herself before her face got up close and personal with the bathroom floor.

Throughout the house, Lee heard crashing. As if in slow motion, she looked up and watched as a framed faerie print went crashing into the floor. Something warm and wet flowed down her arm, and numb, she looked down to see blood flowing from the gash in her arm.

It trickled down . . . down . . . down . . . Dread curled inside her as one fat drop plopped onto the floor. Followed by a second. When the third drop fell, there was a noise, a god-awful noise, like the earth was groaning and screaming. Lee licked her lips and stared, frozen with shock as a crack appeared in the floor, right where the blood had fallen. It raced along the floor toward the mirror, upward. The mirror split in two. The wall behind the mirror cracked. Little fissures ran out from the larger crack and, thankfully, just shy of the ceiling, it stopped.

The floor shuddered and shook. She heard crashing echo through the house, and the lights flickered off and on. A huge glass bowl fell from a shelf that had hung over the toilet and the razor-sharp shards of it stung her feet. Logically, Lee knew she needed to get out of the house before it came down around her. Oddly enough, she didn't want to leave. *Couldn't* leave.

She heard—something. That music, a strange, tribal rhythm that pulsed deep inside—calling to her. Her entire body trembled and tears stung her eyes as she stared at the mirror. There was a huge crack in it, one that ran from top to bottom. The left side of the mirror reflected her broken image back at her. But the right side . . .

"Oh, sweet heaven," she whispered. Running her tongue

over suddenly dry lips, she reached up and touched her fingers to the surface that she knew should be there, but couldn't see.

What she saw was the twisted landscape from some of her work. Dark, brooding, hauntingly beautiful in a disturbing way. Tears stung her eyes, rolled down her face as she pushed her hand against the barrier that had wavered between her world and the other. It resisted. Under her palm, she felt the smooth, slick surface of the mirrored glass.

She looked down at her other hand. The blood wasn't flowing as heavily now, but the blood trail on her arm was still wet and shiny. Her hand was slick with it. Without knowing why, Lee looked back at the mirror and then pressed her bloodied hand to it.

For a second, nothing happened. Then the mirror shimmered. Softened. Changed. Under her hand, it went pliable. It was like pushing her hand through Jell-O, thick, clinging. She hissed out a breath between her teeth and jerked her hand back. The second she did, that weird, tribal music beating through her system swelled to a crescendo. It threatened to deafen her, echoing in her head like drumbeats.

Demanding. Commanding. With horrified fascination, Lee watched as she pushed against the mirrored glass. It gave under her hand again, and this time she stepped forward, holding her breath as the thick barrier molded to her flesh. For a long moment, the world fell out from under her feet and the breath squeezed out of her lungs. Darkness took her vision. She couldn't breathe. She opened her mouth to scream or to gasp for air, and nothing happened. She couldn't move. Couldn't see. Couldn't breathe.

It was the most terrifying feeling of her life.

But more terrifying than that was the bizarre feeling she had done this before.

Just when her lungs couldn't take it anymore, when they were screaming for air and her head was spinning from the lack of oxygen, the cloying barrier parted around her body and she stepped onto solid ground. Solid, uneven ground that bucked and rolled under her feet.

She wobbled and fell forward. She hissed out a harsh breath as something sharp shredded the thin cloth of her pajama bottoms and cut into her knees. Her hands, one clean, one bloodied, pressed into the earth, and just like that, the shaking stopped. Wind tore at her hair, blowing the wispy ends of it into her eyes as she looked around.

Her legs felt unsteady as she stood, and for one humiliating second, she wondered if she was going to pass out. Slowly, her head stopped spinning and the nausea churning in her gut slowly eased. But as she looked around, she wondered if unconsciousness might be a little easier.

It would certainly be a lot less terrifying.

All was barren in front of her. Stunted, malformed trees. Bare ground. She felt like she was looking at it through a camera lens, her mind only letting her take in one small thing at a time.

This land looked familiar . . . very familiar. But she had seen it last with lush green trees, mountains that towered into the sky, their caps covered with pristine white snow. The world had been too beautiful . . . the sky sapphire blue and streaked with auroras at night. "I thought I'd only dreamed this place," Lee whispered, wiping her tears away halfheartedly.

Those dreams she remembered from time to time. But they were just dreams. Dreams of a paradise unlike anything she'd ever known. Some whimsical paradise she'd created out of some need to escape the real world.

"Lee."

His voice, low and rough, sent shivers up her spine. Slowly, she turned, and whatever door had let her step into this world was gone. Standing just behind her was a tall, rangy man, with eyes that gleamed like pools of liquid silver, a square-cut jaw, high, almost harsh cheekbones and a broad forehead. He looked almost brutal. His mouth was unsmiling, the sensual line of his lips unyielding as he stared at her with disbelieving eyes. Kalen . . .

Even before he said anything else, Lee knew how his

voice would sound. Deep, dark and velvety, with a lyrical accent that thickened with emotion. He opened his lips and she shivered at the sound. "You haven't stood in this world while the sun shines in years."

"Oh, hell."

Lee felt her knees wobble under her. The earth started to churn again, except Lee had a bad feeling the earth wasn't really moving at all. Everything grew dark, and just as the world rushed up to meet her, she saw his eyes widen.

* * *

He watched as her eyes rolled back until nothing but the whites showed. Her skin was a pale, ashen gray and he swore, leaping forward. She fell into his arms and he grunted as his body absorbed the impact. Her skin was soft, she smelled sweet and clean, and her body was a lethal combination of curves and muscle.

Kalen gnashed his teeth. It was almost like some dream come to life. He had Lee in his arms—really in his arms—after all this time, and she was half-naked. The soft, thin clothes she wore did absolutely nothing to hide the body underneath. He could see the shadow of her nipples, the cleft between her thighs and every damned inch in between.

He eased them to the ground and shrugged out of his jacket. He balled it up and stuffed it under her head. Not the most comfortable pillow—the cavinir was pliable, moving with his body, conforming to it and protecting it at the same time, but it was still armor. But he wasn't going to let her put her head on the ground, and he sure as hell couldn't rest her head on his thigh. He was too close to jumping her as it was.

He crouched beside her, examining her. He wished he could be detached about it, but that wasn't going to happen. He saw the pallor, most likely brought on by shock and exhaustion, but he also saw the smooth, subtle gleam of her flesh. He watched her chest rise and fall in a regular rhythm, but he also found himself staring at the tight little buds of her nipples, pressing into that pathetic excuse for clothing. She moaned, a soft, husky sound that had him gritting his teeth.

The hungry, needy bastard in him couldn't help but wonder what kind of noises she'd make when he was inside her. Self-preservation had him straightening and moving away. She moaned again, and from the corner of his eye, he watched as her lashes fluttered, then lifted.

Her gaze arrowed in on him, but he still didn't look at her.

"You." She spat it out like she had something nasty on her tongue. Kalen couldn't particularly blame her. Something else he'd seen while he made sure she was unharmed—the long, thin wound on her arm. It was bleeding sluggishly, and he knew from experience it probably burned like crazy. Treu metal did that. It was like something in the metal caused a reaction when it cut into a living being. It was particularly useful against Raviners and Jorniaks. That was why it was a favorite among the resistance.

Lee had given him the blade years ago. He'd used it to mark that soft flesh . . . Grimly, Kalen acknowledged the guilt and then he shoved it deep. He'd done it. He regretted it. But he wouldn't take it back.

He wouldn't avoid her over it either. Slowly, he turned and faced her. She looked—different. But the same. Almost like she was more substantial. Her skin had always been pale—now, in the light of day, he saw that she had a porcelain complexion and there was a light blush of color on her cheeks. Her eyes were a vivid, almost surreal shade of blue. The skies had once been that same shade of blue. Her hair was loose, and it fell more than halfway down her back in a tumbling riot of curls and spirals. It was the palest shade of blond imaginable, shot through with darker streaks.

God in heaven, she was beautiful. There was a life inside her, something that made his skin buzz being this close to her.

"What am I doing here?" she asked. He saw a muscle

jerk in her cheek, and he realized she was clenching her jaw together. It didn't help much. Her soft mouth trembled as she spoke, and he realized belatedly that she was absolutely terrified.

Lee hadn't ever been this scared in her life. The man in front of her was partly responsible. As familiar as he seemed, there was also something alien about him. A look in his eyes that shook her to her very core. A faint smile curled his lips and she figured he was trying to reassure her. "Don't be so afraid, Lee."

She blinked at him. Yeah. Right. Don't be afraid. Afraid didn't even begin to cover what she was feeling. "What in the hell is going on?"

"I don't know," he responded, shaking his head. The long black silk of his hair flowed around his shoulders with his movement, and his face was as unyielding as stone.

"I know your face," she whispered, shaking her head, feeling the knot in her throat rise and threaten to choke her. "Why do I know you?"

As he shrugged, she felt her eyes drawn to the thick pad of muscle that covered his shoulder. He wore dull black clothing that resembled leather, but she suspected it served a more serious purpose than just standard clothing. The sleeveless shirt ended at his waist, a trim narrow waist, and her eyes traveled on down the long muscled length of his legs, also covered with the weird pseudoleather. Licking her lips, she stared back into his eyes.

"I think I've had enough of this," she muttered, more to herself than anything. Shoving to her feet, she looked around and wondered why in the hell she hadn't made that call to the shrink. "Get me back home and I'll make the call. I swear."

"You can't go back so easily now," he murmured, his eyes scanning around them as he moved closer. "The doorway that let you in has closed. I don't understand how you crossed over as it is."

As he started across the uneven ground, she stepped back, but a sharp rock cut into the tender flesh of her instep and she flinched.

"So I'm stuck here?" she demanded, terror seizing her as she thought of never seeing home again.

A tiny smile finally appeared on his granite-hard face. "Well, most people would be. I doubt you are. You'll find a way. But it will take some time," he said. "But while you're here . . . I've a promise to keep."

"A promise?" she whispered.

The smile widened and his eyes gleamed with devilish intent. It should have warned her, but before she could even think of moving away, hard, scarred hands were cupping and lifting her face, as his mouth lowered and took hers. Lee gasped as his tongue pushed hungrily into her mouth, stealing her breath away. With a delicious forcefulness that had her swimming, he took and claimed, threading his hands through her hair as his tongue stroked across hers.

Lee whimpered deep in her throat, rising on her toes and curling her hands into the surprisingly supple material of his shirt. With teeth and tongue, he kissed her, making love to her mouth with a thoroughness that she knew would leave a mark on her for the rest of her life.

An animalistic growl rose on the air as he withdrew to nip on her lip and then kiss a hot, stinging line of kisses down the curve of her throat. Lee grabbed at his hair, the thick, silken locks sliding through her fingers. "This shirt you wear—I can see the shadow of your nipples through it," he rasped as he traced the low scooping neckline of the halter top. The pale lavender top knotted at her neck and low on her spine, and she wore it with a pair of harem-style pants that rode low on her hips. The sheer material of both garments was entirely too transparent to wear anywhere outside of her office, but since she hadn't exactly been planning on going visiting when she put it on, she hadn't thought anything of it. "Why bother wearing it at all? You might as well be naked."

Her cheeks flushed pink. "I . . . ah . . . I sleep in them," she said.

The embarrassed flush only spread as he bent her back over his arm and ran his palm down the center of her torso.

He petted her through the thin material as he mused, "This wasn't something made for sleeping in. It's made to drive a man mad. If you were to lie beside me wearing that, and then expect me to sleep . . ." His voice trailed off and a wicked smile curved his lips. "I do like it, Lee. Quite a lot. Too much."

Kalen stared at her breasts through the pajama top. His eyes were hot, so hot she could almost feel the burn. His dark head lowered, and she cried out as the wet, heated silk of his mouth closed over the distended tip of her nipple, his tongue circling over it delicately before he bit down lightly.

The groan that rumbled out of him vibrated up her skin, and she shivered as he slowly straightened, holding her tight against him. She pressed her fingers against her buzzing lips, still staring up at him.

Kalen's eyes were opaque and unreadable, but hot flags of color rode high on his cheeks and she could see a pulse beating rapidly in his throat as he reached up and flicked at the long silver strand of stars that hung from one of her ears. "I've wanted to do that for years," he whispered.

"You haven't ever?"

A hot smile curled his lips and he shrugged. "How much do you understand about what's going on?"

Scowling, she said flatly, "Nothing." Trying to shrug his arms away, she shoved at his chest, but his arms never loosened. "I don't understand a damn thing."

Kalen laughed, hugging her just a little closer. Since she had her hands pressed flat against his chest, he couldn't draw her upper body too close, but her lower body—she felt the heated length of his cock through the material of their clothes, hard, pulsating against the soft pad of her belly. A rush of blood heated her face as she stared up at him.

"I wanted nothing more than to do just that, every time I saw you. But saving lives is a little more important than discovering if you taste as sweet as you look. And part of me suspected that if you knew how much I wanted you, you'd take off running," he whispered, burying his face in the heavy mass of her hair. "But you can't run away now. Not yet, anyway."

His voice went all raspy and intent, practically vibrating with all the emotion she could feel coming off him. "You can't run."

* * *

She was here.

Kalen wasn't going to question whatever twist of fate, whatever quirk of God had brought her here.

But she was here.

The waistband of his jacket just barely skimmed the taut little curve of her ass. Through the sheer material of the flimsy pants she wore, he could see the outline of her legs, and he wanted to tear the pants away and run his hands over those barely hidden curves.

She called the clothes pajamas. Said she wore them for sleeping, or sometimes to work. He had to wonder what sort of work she did wearing clothes that looked like they had been designed just to drive a man insane.

Damn it, if another man had seen that sweet body he probably would have leveled his plasma rifle at him until the fool had the sense to direct his eyes elsewhere.

Get her into base camp and get her dressed. Into some cavinir before some enterprising Sirvani saw the bright head of hair, all that pretty, pale skin, and decided she'd make a nice prize for his superior. All he'd need was a quick moment to use the poison made from the kifer weed. One little shaft that pierced the skin and Lee would be helpless. The poison never killed, just stunned and weakened, giving them a chance to capture their prey and make the journey through the Veil to Anqar.

The Warlords would wage war to get their hands on Lee. Beautiful and ripe with power—and totally defenseless. He sensed the raw, exposed power inside her and knew he didn't have much time before someone, or something, else sensed it. Right now, she would look very appetizing. Anqarian bastards had a fondness for swiping talented females, and Lee was about as talented as they came.

The chilly air felt good along his heated flesh. He wore a black sleeveless cavinir tunic that left his arms bare after he'd taken his jacket off for Lee. She stumbled, and he moved to her side, sharp ears catching the whimper that escaped her lips before she clamped them shut.

With a scowl, he hunkered down by her feet, lifting the one she had jerked off the ground, probing the little gash with his finger. "Damn it." He scowled, standing up and reaching into the pouch at his utility belt. "You'll heal up quick enough but I imagine it hurts."

Kneeling back at her feet, he directed a curt "Hold on to me" at her before lifting her slender ankle in his hand and applying a psi-skin bandage to it. Standing up, he saw the mutinous look on her face and rolled his eyes. "What?"

Crossing her arms over her chest, she snapped, "I didn't exactly plan on appearing here, slick. I might have packed some hiking clothes if I had."

Running his tongue along the inside of his cheek, he suppressed a smile. "I wasn't scowling at you," he finally said, knowing he'd guessed right when her eyes flickered. "I should have thought of your bare feet."

"Nothing we can do about it, so why does it matter?" she said. He had a desire to lean over and catch that sullen lower lip between his teeth, catch one more sweet taste of her mouth.

Crooking a grin at her, Kalen responded easily, "Now, I never said there was nothing I could do about it, did I?" Slinging his pulse rife over his shoulder, he caught her up in his arms, hooking one hand under her knees, the other bracing her torso, chuckling as she yelped and threw her arms around his neck.

It was nearly a mile back to the base camp. Foot travel had become routine again after so many years of using jetcars and avilifts. Even during the day, the motor and rumble of the machinery disturbed some of the bigger creatures that dwelled below. After a few years of nonstop attacks every time somebody climbed into a jetcar for a trip to the mercantilery, the people of Kalen's world had

learned very well how to live without some of the technology they had once thought so vital to their way of life.

The devastation of Yorkton had seen to that. Even before it had been leveled, the once thriving city had been a
feeding ground for one of the most deadly intruders.

The ever-present rumble of the substation traffic had
made it a prime attraction for the zandir wyrms. Those hell-
beasts had truly devastated Yorkton. After the wyrms had
wiped out the substations, they had gone aboveground in
the dead of the night, seeking out the ever-present nightlife
and the ongoing flow of cars that rumbled even at three in
the morning.

A cool finger stroked down his cheek. "You look pretty
glum, buddy." Cutting his eyes to Lee's face, he finally voiced
the question that had been lurking inside his mind since he
had seen her standing just beyond a shimmery mirage of
light.

"How did you come to be here, Lee?"

Her lashes dropped, covering those pale blue eyes. Finally, she lifted her head and stared at him dead in the eye.
"I really don't know. But I kept hearing your voice. You
wouldn't leave me alone," she said quietly.

A slow smile crept across his lips as he continued to
stride over the ground, his long legs eating up the distance
between the clearing and home. Safety. "You haven't left
me alone for twenty years. High time, I'd say, that I returned the favor," he drawled.

"I was a kid twenty years ago. I didn't start dreaming
about this place until I was a teenager." Her voice was quiet,
her face averted.

"You saved my life the first time when you were seven,
Lee. You brought me food. Then you disappeared. A few
days later, you freed me from where I was being held in
some tiny little hellhole." Eyes grim, he said quietly, "If
you hadn't freed me, and I still don't know how you did it,
but if you hadn't, Raviners would have had a bloody party
with my sorry ass."

THREE

Lee's head was spinning. And it wasn't just from the unbelievable pace he kept up as he carried her across the uneven, rock-strewn terrain. Too much had changed. Too many things that should have been impossible were actually happening—and what was most bizarre, she wasn't even questioning that any of it could be real.

She knew it was.

Knew he was real, even though a man like him seemed to defy every law she had come across when it came to the opposite sex. He was drop-dead gorgeous, a body covered with rock-hard muscle, a warrior, yet it seemed she recalled him asking for her help, time and again. That was almost like men asking for directions . . . wasn't it?

She chewed nervously on her lip, staring as they rounded a bend of half-burned trees. In the distance, she could hear faint sounds, voices floating on the wind, a booming pulsation of sound that echoed in her belly, myriad weird sounds that she couldn't place. "What is that?" Lee finally asked as the booming pulsation rippled through her chest one more time.

"Ion cannon. We managed to get into a fallen military base and we . . . ah—liberated some badly needed supplies. The ion cannon is a bloody powerful weapon, but none of us were exactly sure how to use it. One of the older men was in the army when its predecessor came out, so he's helping us work the kinks out. Before we have to use it."

"Oh," she said faintly. An ion cannon, of course. *I feel like I'm trapped in some weird science fiction movie.* "Why am I so important to this?"

"The ion cannon?" he asked, a smile curving that hard mouth. Her belly quivered as she imagined arching up and pressing her lips to his. His taste still lingered in her mouth and she wanted more. But bad enough she had been making out with a man she didn't exactly know. She wasn't going to kiss him when she suspected they would have company at any minute. "No, pet. We can figure the ion cannon out for ourselves."

Lee scowled at him, her brows drawing low over her eyes before she sniffed and averted her face. "Smart ass," she muttered. "That wasn't what I was talking about. And you know it."

Under the arm she had wrapped around one shoulder and his neck, she felt him shrug. "If I knew why you were so important, don't you think I would have tried to do something about it before now? I'm a soldier, not a seer."

Her cheeks heated as she felt his eyes lingering on her face, the slow sweep of his thumb on the underside of her knee. Through the fragile cloth of her pajama pants, she felt that slow, rough stroke as though he were touching naked flesh. A gasp locked in her throat—images slamming into her mind, that long hard body arching over hers, sweat gleaming along his flesh, muscles bunching and flexing as he pumped his hips against hers, the sight of his eyes, gleaming and hot, as he stared down into her face . . .

"Sweet bleeding saints, would you stop?"

Lee gasped as his arm fell out from under her and she was dropped without ceremony onto her feet. With bemused eyes, she watched as he stomped away, his big hands closing into fists at his side as he paced the path before her, keeping his eyes away from her face.

"Don't bloody do that!" he finally bellowed, spinning around and glaring at her.

"Do what?" she demanded, propping her hands on her hips and glaring at him. "I didn't do anything!"

A sexy little snarl crossed his face and she felt her belly quiver. She was already dazed and hot from that wicked line of thoughts dancing in her mind, and this wasn't helping. He looked entirely too—biteable.

Yes. That was the word. She wanted to walk over there and catch his face in her hands and sink her teeth into that sullen lower lip, maybe into the tendon in his neck . . . then the gleaming perfection of his muscled shoulders . . .

"That!"

Her face flushed. No way. He couldn't possibly . . .

"When you're a strong projector, anybody can pick up. But I'm a fairly talented receiver, which is how I knew you were here, how I always know you're here, and damn it, would you stop?" he snarled. "You've got enough fucking chaos to deal with right now, trying to figure out what is going on, and you haven't even grasped the full extent, but if you don't stop tempting me, I'm going to . . ."

Lee couldn't help it. Lifting one brow at him, she smiled slightly and asked, "Going to what?" And she really couldn't help it, no more than she could stop thinking about him, and her, together . . . Damn, had she really . . . ?

"Not yet," he growled. "But keep this up and we will. Right here in broad daylight. As to what I'm going to do—bloody hell, I'll just give you what it is you are dreaming about."

Lee rolled her eyes. "Male testosterone is obviously on the same high levels here that it is back home," she drawled. "Arrogance sure as hell isn't in short supply either." Balancing on one foot, she lifted her right one, staring at the deep gash and poking at it with a gentle finger. Not as sore. Lowering it back to the ground, she lifted her head. And jumped.

Kalen was standing right in front of her, having crossed the good twenty feet between them in total silence. "It's not arrogance when we both know it's the truth," he murmured, using one finger to tip her face up to his. "Now, is it?"

Her breath was trapped in her lungs as his mouth slanted across hers and his tongue plunged boldly into her mouth. His tongue tangled with hers, rubbed sinuously against it, withdrew, and then started the dance all over again. Under the thin cloth of her halter top, her nipples beaded and swelled. One broad sweep of his hand opened the jacket he had placed on her shoulders and it fell to catch at her elbows, leaving her shoulders bare.

Lee whimpered when he pulled back enough to nip at her lip as his fingers tangled in her hair, tugging her head back, exposing the line of her throat. The sharp sting of his teeth had her pulse racing. The brush of his fingers caressed her nape and she arched into his touch, only to have his hands retreat moments later.

Cool air stung her breasts and she glanced down, watching as the top of her halter fell to hang at her waist. "I like this," he purred, reaching out and circling one finger around the swollen pink tip of her nipple. As she shivered, she felt his eyes on her and she looked up through her lashes, seeing the stark hunger on his lean face.

Lowering his head, he breathed into her ear, "You know one of the most amazing things about being a receiver? I can hear and feel every thought that passes through you, since you don't seem to understand how to guard against such. And when I touch you—I can feel just exactly how much you like it."

Forcing a breath into her tight lungs, she said weakly, "That's not exactly fair, is it?"

Kalen laughed, reaching up and closing his hand over hers. "Well, now, I don't know that it isn't fair. After all, you can imagine how touching you affects me just by . . ."

Her eyes met his as he drew her hand to his erection, closing it over the hard length covered by the thick material of his dark pants. Swallowing, Lee trailed her fingers slowly up his length, feeling the slight pulse even through the layers of clothing. "See?" he whispered as his cock jerked under her touch. "I think this makes us even."

Lee was pretty certain there was something faulty with that reasoning, but the way her brain was functioning, or rather, wasn't functioning, she'd be damned if she could figure out what the problem was. With a slight smile, she dragged her hand back up his length. She'd figure out logistics and thought and everything else later . . . much later . . .

The rumble of the ground distracted her for a minute, but only a brief minute. As she arched up into his touch, Lee slowly massaged his cock, dazed pleasure suffusing her entire mind.

Damn it, his body was so hot. His mouth closed around her nipple, sucking on it with hard, rough pulls of his mouth. Lee fisted one hand in the thick black hair at his nape, holding him tight against her, whimpering as the very earth seemed to shift beneath her.

Kalen arched her back over his arm, one hand going to her waist, to the tie of her harem-style pajama pants, and she let go of his neck, reaching to tug at the knot even as he was trying to tug them down her hips. One second later she was all but naked and he was fumbling to complete the task.

The next second, he was gone, turned away from her, slinging the gun from the harness at his back as he rasped out furiously, "Son of a fucking bitch!"

Lee whimpered, her brain still buzzing and trying to catch up. "Kalen?" she whispered.

He cut her a disbelieving glance and shook his head. "Bloody hell, what have we gotten into? Climb a tree, pet. We've got company coming."

She stared at the trees surrounding her with vague eyes, even as the rumbling beneath the ground intensified. "Sweet heaven," she whispered. "What is that . . ."

But even as she whispered it, part of her knew. "Raviners . . . what in the hell are they doing coming out in the

daylight?" she asked. She felt like there was a curtain within
her mind, dividing her into two separate parts. Every once
in a while, it would part and allow some of the knowledge
the women from this world had to slip through, letting Lee
absorb it.

"You, pet. They felt you." He glared at her, pointing to
the tree. "Climb, damn it. The higher, the better. They don't
like daylight. If you are too high to be worth their while,
too far out of reach, they may just go back to their hole for
a while."

The ground in front of Kalen split apart, and Lee
screamed as black-robed creatures came spilling out. Blue
light pulsed from Kalen's gun, but he was only one man
and there were nearly two dozen of them.

That odd curtain parted again, letting more knowledge
slip through. *Psychic energy . . . magick . . . they love it. It's
a feast to them.*

I sent out a damned invitation, she realized in self-disgust,
backing up to the tree. Lee turned and scrabbled up to the
nearest sturdy branch before glancing back down. "If you
fall, no chocolate for a month." Images of every B-movie
heroine leaped to mind, the cute teenaged coed, scantily
clad as always, falling to her doom just as freedom appeared within her reach.

The tree she had picked was dead, like most of them, but
it towered nearly fifty feet into the sky. Like a squirrel, she
scrambled upward until she was a good twenty-five feet off
the ground, and then she turned and stared down at Kalen
as the circle of dark-robed creatures closed around him.

The Raviners weren't true demons—or rather, they weren't
natural ones. They'd become demons by choice. They were
something that had once been human, or close to it. Living in
the world of Anqar, they had worshipped a dark lord, practic-
ing blood magick, taking his dark power inside themselves
until they were no longer mortal. They needed no food to
live, needed little rest, and they thrived on energy.

Cruel, cunning, full of madness and power, they loved a
psychic or magickal feast, a man or woman with budding
powers that they could feed off of during torture.

Wincing at the information bombarding her brain, Lee muttered, "This is a little too much info to process right now. Can we slow it down a bit?"

The knowledge that had been whispering through her mind fell silent as she watched Kalen stumble when a Raviner lashed out with a hooked staff, slicing at his chest. The black tunic covering his chest resisted the blade but his bare arms didn't and blood flowed. Lee glanced down at the black jacket that covered her arms and flushed. His armor. This was armor. Would have protected that long, powerful body . . .

Rage boiled inside her as she saw the blood welling on his flesh. She descended the tree so rapidly, she barely even remembered the trek down, and the last ten feet she jumped. She landed without even feeling the impact and stood there, staring at the black-robed creatures as images swirled in her mind.

Broken, destroyed bodies, as empty as husks, their eyes staring upward in sightless terror . . . all at the hands of something that wasn't even a demon.

Rage had a feel, a mind, a color all its own, and it brewed hot and powerful in her belly as she stared at them. They never even noticed her as she started to move closer.

Use the power. Harness it . . .

Her body suddenly felt like that of a marionette, and she could watch as her hand lifted, seemingly of its own volition, pointing palm out toward the throng of Raviners. There was a river of power flowing under the earth, calling to her. In turn, she reached for it and it flowed into her. The crackle of power jolted up from her belly, zinging out her arm like a crack of lightning, and she cried out as the blue light exploded from her hand.

The scorching smell of flesh flooded her nose and she watched as a swath of Raviners fell. The saner part of her mind started to babble in terror as the blue light wrapped around the humanoids and fire exploded, burning them away until they exploded like a pile of ash and soot, like a TV vampire.

This is sooooo not happening, she thought helplessly,

even as she jerked to the left and flung out her hand again. Again, and again, and each time, more of the Raviners fell.

Kalen broke free of their circle and fought his way to her side as the throng of creatures tried to regroup. But from their earlier number of several dozen, less than ten now stood. Blood roared in her ears. Her heart pounded frantically as fear gnawed a hole in her gut. But the Raviners all fell back, scrambling away from them. They watched Lee and Kalen from the depths of their hoods, hate radiating from them.

Lee's hand fell to her side as they all rushed to the tear in the earth where they had ripped through only minutes before. As the last one disappeared from sight, her knees buckled and she started to collapse slowly, only to have Kalen's arm come around her, supporting her weight against his body.

"This isn't happening," she muttered, shaking her head. "Not happening."

Lifting her face, she looked up at him, seeing his lips move but hearing nothing as the roaring in her ears increased and a sudden blinding pain exploded just behind her right temple.

***

Kalen stood in the back of the small mobile hospital, brooding. Morne Ramire knelt over Lee, his long-fingered hands absorbing the negative energy from her wounded body, one hand on her forehead, the other resting between her breasts. The deiron's hair fell around his face like a shield, hiding his features from Kalen, and the relaxed posture of his body told Kalen nothing.

Kalen had seen him that calm and serene as he guided a dying child into the arms of the ever after. Lee could be dying, and Kalen would never know just by looking at Morne's face.

When Morne finally spoke, his deep, soft voice was weary, but Kalen heard a nuance in it that gave his heart hope even before he finished processing what the healer had said.

"She overextended, too hard and too fast. Your lady will wake up with a headache the size of a wyrm hole, but she'll be fine," Morne said, rising to his feet with boneless grace, turning to stare at Kalen with probing black eyes. The deiron's face was as exquisite as if he had been formed by heaven's own angels, but those eyes had more knowledge than Kalen would hope an angel would ever know. The shock of those black eyes in his pale face, surrounded by hair a soft, silvery blond—Kalen imagined his rather poetic looks had subjected him to endless tormenting as a child, but whether it had bothered Morne much was anybody's guess.

He was . . . contained. Very, very contained.

He was also the most deadly soldier in their ranks, quite possibly even surpassing the skill of Kalen's legendary father. Dead many years, Astrin Brenner had fought back the demons in their small haven for decades before he was finally cut down.

That a healer, of all people, was the one rising to meet that legend was unheard of.

Kalen hunkered on the ground by Lee's head and ran his fingers through her tangled blond hair. He cupped a hand over her neck and contented himself with the slow, steady rise and fall of her breathing. "She scared the hell out of me. I've seen witches kill themselves by pushing too hard," he murmured.

Behind him, Morne chuckled. "That lady would have to come close to leveling our world before she killed herself— you know magick is physically draining to the bearer, but Lee has more control than this." He frowned and shrugged. "That little bit of magick I sensed earlier shouldn't have even fazed her. Why did it? Lee's been throwing blasts around since she was old enough for you to notice she was female."

Kalen cut Morne a narrow look before looking back at Lee's still face. "Would you believe she's never really been here, my friend?"

The laughter that followed Kalen's slow question wasn't exactly what he was expecting. Rising, Kalen turned and met Morne's eyes with a level stare, lifting one brow and waiting.

"The average warrior wouldn't notice, even your warriors with all their gifts. And that's most of what we have here. But a good healer knows when he is facing a person's shade," Morne responded, shrugging. "Still doesn't explain why she made an amateur's mistake and damn near put herself into a coma." He focused his black eyes on Kalen's face and simply waited.

"She doesn't realize what she's been doing here," Kalen finally said after a lengthy silence had passed. "She came in her dreams, and when she woke, she forgot them."

"And you've known this for . . . ?"

"Always. Or at least it seems that way." Kalen closed his eyes, trying to recall a time that stood out when he knew that Lee wasn't exactly of his world. "I've always known there was something odd about her presence here. Time passed—and I just knew."

A soft sigh left Morne, and Kalen glanced up to see a faint frown on the man's ageless face. "You're dealing with a very powerful weapon, and she hasn't a clue as to how to use a damn thing that is inside of her. This could be interesting."

At the man's mild tone, Kalen scowled. "Interesting? Bloody insane, that's more like it."

"Well, I've been told I am a master of understatement," Morne said drolly. From the utility belt at his waist, he pulled out a small stack of minuscule circular pain patches and handed them to Kalen. "In case I'm out when she wakes." He grabbed a pack from the ground and flipped it open, reaching inside and pulling out a sealed pouch of tea bags. "Chances are, she will not like it, but some insian tea will help. Restore her energy and clear up the headache. Let me know if I'm needed."

Kalen didn't respond. If something came up when she was waking, and Morne was needed, the deiron would already know. On rare occasions, a witch rising out of a slumber like this had trouble—in the form of seizures, or Raviners lurking nearby as they waited for a chance to possess the weakened body. Either one would release a burst of energy that Morne was unlikely to miss.

Kalen moved one of the small cots over by the sturdier, more comfortable patient bed. The patient beds were thick, cushioned jela pads, but the cots were just tough cloth strung over a metal frame. The jela pads were too few and far between a luxury for anybody other than the very sick, the wounded or the very old to use.

There had been a time when the jela pads were standard. Once he'd been able to prepare his food with just a simple thought that activated the thought-sense trigger in the food prep area of his parents' home. It seemed like a different life.

Perhaps it had been. More than twenty years had passed since his father died. He'd just been a kid. And that was when the world seemed to come crashing down around him.

For so long, Astrin and his small defense force had kept many of the demons at bay, away from the small valley in the Roinan Mountains. For a long while, they'd been beneath the notice of the larger demon packs. Astrin and a small army of vigilant, dedicated soldiers had kept the smaller ones back. Sirvani had focused on larger cities and not the small rebel bands that hid in the mountains. Months at a time would go by with not even a single sighting of the enemy.

Astrin's death seemed like it had been the beginning of the end.

More than twenty years later, Kalen still tried to defend the land his father had protected for so long. They held on to their lands, but everywhere were the signs of devastation. The once lush valleys of the Roinan mountain range had been slowly turned into wastelands—either arid stretches of land where nothing would ever grow, or smoldering, stinking marshes where even the very air tasted foul.

Kalen just didn't know how much longer they could keep pulling off miracles. So many other places had fallen.

There were rumors that some countries no longer had any humans living free. Many eastern countries were believed to be completely overrun by demons. Even the fall of the Jivan Gate was little consolation—those lands were already lost.

The lands to the far north were believed to be the only true sanctuary, as many of the demons couldn't tolerate the extreme cold of the polar regions. But the cold was so harsh, many of the mortals in Ishtan couldn't live there either. Damned pity, too, because there were no known gates in the far north.

The Union of Aishen might well be the last nation in his world to fall . . . but if something didn't change, they would fall.

They killed the intruders, the raiding parties of Sirvani, the occasional Warlord and the demon races that poured out of Anqar, but Anqar's numbers were so vast.

Men taken as slaves worked until they collapsed and then they were killed. Women were used as breeding machines, kidnapped from their homes in the dead of night, dragged across the Veil, where the Warlords raped them until they conceived and then repeated the process over and over until the woman's body gave out.

Humans were being pushed to extinction, and their world would soon be nothing more than a memory.

"No," he murmured to himself. He shook his head. They would not even be a memory—in time, there would be not one soul left that remembered Ishtan or the resistance.

Turning his head, he stared at Lee as she slept. She looked innocent, almost frail in her sleep, and he tried to reconcile the woman he saw before him with the woman he had fought beside for so long. She was just a woman—mortal, like him. She ate, she drank, she slept—she hurt. Mortal. More than that, she was a mortal who didn't even understand the power inside her veins. She didn't know who she was or what she could do.

How was it that she could be so very important to this war? Kalen did not know the answer, but it didn't matter, not to him. She wasn't just important. Lee was vital. If they stood any chance at all, it would be because of her.

* * *

Lee woke with a groan. Even that small sound set her head to screaming, and she clamped her lips closed as she felt another moan rising in her throat. Her entire body was abuzz with pain—too much sensation for her to even locate the source of it.

She almost felt hungover, but Lee couldn't remember drinking. She didn't care for liquor much—hated the loss of control that came with tying one on. As a headache pounded inside her skull, she thought back to the past night.

For once, there was something more than a surreal blur of thoughts. She actually remembered much of what had happened. And talk about bizarre.

"Oh, man, what a weird dream," she muttered. Her belly pitched and she swallowed down the bile burning up her throat. She wasn't going to throw up.

Her hands brushed the surface of the mattress, the slick, soft material, and her eyes flew open. Everything spun in dizzying circles, but none of the circles dancing before her eyes were familiar. Slowly, the tan circles slowed and coalesced into one solid form. Wood. A wooden ceiling. Exposed beams, lanterns swinging from those beams by long chains.

Where in the hell was she? Lee tried to remember something before the dream, but none of it made sense. Nothing seemed clear.

Well, that wasn't entirely true. She wasn't in her bed and she wasn't in her own room. That was clear. She also felt worse than usual. Since she usually woke up feeling like she'd been through a battle, that was a bad sign. Her belly pitched and rolled as she slowly flexed her body. The bed under her felt unbelievably good, molding to her form and cradling every last inch of her. If it weren't for the fact that she didn't know where in the hell she was, she might have been tempted to just keep lying there.

She did a quick check on her body, rolling each foot at the ankle, tensing the muscles in her thighs, closing her hands into fists. All sorts of various aches but nothing that really hurt—well, her foot hurt a little, but nothing to account for this pain. Finally, all the aches and pains stopped humming and she could locate the source of the pain.

Son of a bitch! It coalesced behind her eyes, exploding into a mind-searing burst that probably singed her eyeballs. "Oh, hell," she mumbled. Lee carefully lifted a hand and covered her eyes. Her throat was scratchy. She felt like she hadn't had anything to drink in months. Her belly was an aching, empty knot, but even though hunger screamed through her, the thought of eating anything was enough to have her gagging.

With the pain in her head, puking would not be a good idea. Not at all. She heard a sighing sound. Logically, she realized it wasn't that loud. It was the same kind of noise somebody made when they were sleeping—just a heavy little sigh. But it echoed in her ears like a tortured scream. She wanted to clap her hands over her ears, but even the thought of touching her head was enough to have her shuddering in pain.

That sound, though, meant she wasn't alone. Not alone meant that maybe there was somebody who could do something about this pain in her head. And an explanation wouldn't be a bad idea, either.

Slowly, she turned her head. A shock of recognition jolted through her when she saw the hard, chiseled lines of the man whose face had haunted her subconscious and appeared in so much of her work.

Did going insane hurt? Because that was the best explanation she could come up with. She was seeing a guy that only existed in her work and in her dreams. If insanity hurt, that could certainly explain the pain in her head.

Everything about him was exactly as he appeared when she reproduced that hawklike visage on her work pad. The arched, sweeping brows, the black silk of the hair that framed his face, the hard sensual lips, relaxed ever so slightly in sleep. Even the small scar that bisected his chin.

Her eyes moved back to his mouth, and she briefly wondered what he tasted like. And then memories from yesterday slammed into her. The voices in her head. The mirror. The field, so empty and desolate, and him. The feel of his hair in her hands, on her body, the hard, unyielding press of his mouth against hers, and his taste.

Like a digital image, it was crystal clear in her mind, every last memory. Insanity wouldn't be this vivid, would it . . . she wondered.

The thick black fan of his lashes lifted. Even before she found herself staring into the molten silver, she knew his eyes would be that color. "This is really happening," she said, keeping her voice level, trying very hard not to sound like she had the screaming meemies.

Which of course, she did, but she refused to let anybody else know that. Nobody else needed to know that she couldn't make up her mind between screaming or breaking out into nervous laughter. Although the creatures she had seen yesterday didn't exactly inspire laughter. The screams, definitely. Laughter, not in this lifetime.

Both laughter and screaming would only make her head worse—and if it got much worse, Lee suspected her head would split in two.

"Aye," he replied, his voice just as level and so soft it only hurt her ears a little. "It is really happening. How does your head feel?"

"Terrible."

He sat up, tossing his hair out of his face and propping his elbow on his knee, resting his chin in the cradle of his palm as he studied her. "You could have hurt yourself," he finally said.

Touching her fingers to her temple, she muttered, "I think I did."

He laughed. He reached out and stroked a finger down her temple. "That is just a headache. A bad one, I imagine, but it is a headache. I've seen people send themselves into comas because they pushed themselves too far with their magick."

The noise that left her was little more than a squeak. Clearing her throat, she said, "Muh-magick?"

Kalen made a tiny noise that sounded suspiciously like a laugh. "Well, it was not puffy white clouds drifting from your hands yesterday. Yes, pet. Magick."

Lee shook her head. "Magick isn't real." She licked her lips as she said it, and wondered why those words felt so . . . wrong.

"I think you know it is."

Thinking made the pain in her head worse, she decided as she squinted at him. "You are confusing the hell out of me."

He leaned forward and she found her eyes lingering on the bulge of muscle in his arm. Another memory surfaced. His hands on her body. His mouth on hers. She had kissed him, had wrapped herself around his body like she wanted to crawl inside him. And he'd kissed her back with the same hunger. Blood rushed to her cheeks and she dragged her eyes away from his muscles, forcing herself to focus on his eyes. But the dancing light there had her groaning. He knew, exactly, what thoughts were running through her mind.

Gingerly, she rolled onto her belly and buried her head in her arms. Even that was enough to make that bright, throbbing pain double in intensity. She moaned her way through it and as the wave of pain peaked and then ebbed away, she muttered, "Why is this happening to me?"

His fingers, long and warm, came up to stroke down her neck, before he settled into a soothing massage. She could have whimpered as he worked the tense muscles until they felt about as loose as putty. "I have no answer to that. At least, none that I could explain. But you belong here. How you managed to get from our world to the one you call home and then back—I have no explanation." A long moment of silence passed and he sighed. "But you have a great deal of power within you. The creatures from Anqar are attracted to power. Without strong protectors, a great many children with gifts like yours die before they even reach puberty. Die or are taken. So however you ended up in that world, it was a blessing."

"What is Anqar?" she asked. But before he could answer, a flash of pain exploded behind her eyes and she had to stifle her whimper in the odd-feeling mattress beneath her. "Damn it, my head . . ."

"Roll over," he ordered gently.

She resisted, and his hands came up carefully, but forcefully, turned her onto her back. "This will help." His voice sounded odd, tinny, as though he was speaking to her through a tunnel, as he touched his fingers to the middle of her brow. Almost instantly, cool, sweet relief started to ease the pain inside her head. After a few minutes passed and the pain had all but abated, Lee chanced opening one eye and looking up at him.

"Are *you* magick?" Touching her fingers to her brow, she felt something small and smooth against her skin, something disc-shaped. And to her touch, it felt cool.

"It's medicine," Kalen responded with a faint grin. "No magick needed. I should have not even waited until you woke. There is some tea you need to drink. It will settle the nausea in your belly, and help your strength to return faster."

She closed her eyes, sighing blissfully, and murmured, "If it works as well as this, give me a gallon of it."

Moments later, though, as he forced the cup back to her lips, she pressed against his wrist and snapped, "That tastes disgusting." She would have thrown it, except he wouldn't let her. The taste of it coated her tongue, seemed to cling to her throat. Sewer water would have tasted better. It was bitter, pungent, and there was a faint moldy taste to it, like something in it should have been pitched ages ago. He pushed it toward her again and she turned her head. "Get that crap away from me."

Kalen arched a brow and said, "The sooner your energy comes back, the sooner those headaches will stop. That pain patch will not stop them forever."

With a curl of her lip, she said, "I'll just use the patches, thank you."

Turning her head away, she started to lie back down, only to have him fist a hand in her hair and yank her head back. She gagged on the tea while he literally poured it down her throat. Choking on the vile stuff, Lee jerked against his hold. When he finally let go, she spat what remained in her mouth out at him, gasping and rubbing at her stinging eyes. "You jackass!" she shouted in between coughing fits.

"Next time, maybe you'll drink it on your own," he responded levelly.

"Next time, you can kiss my ass," she wheezed out, snatching the cup of water he held out to her. At least, she hoped it was water. Water or cyanide. Right then, she couldn't decide which she'd prefer. It was just water, though, cold and oddly sweet. She downed half of it before shoving the cup back at him and flopping down on the bed.

"I would be rather happy to." A cold cloth wiped over her face, and her eyes flew open as she batted his hand away.

"Happy to what?" She rolled onto her belly and buried her face in the mattress. She would have cut her arm off before she admitted that the churning in her belly had eased.

He slid a hand down her back, and Lee tensed as that hand cupped the curve of her butt. His hair fell down around them when he bent over her, sliding along her bare arms as he murmured, "You suggested that next time I could kiss your ass." Through her thin pajamas, she could feel the heat and strength of his hand on her there. He squeezed lightly, and she had to clamp her mouth shut to keep from sighing a little. "I would be happy to."

He nuzzled her neck, his warm breath drifting over her skin like a caress. An involuntary moan slipped past her lips. She tried to make up for it by tensing her entire body, but she felt limp and loose as putty. Fortunately, she did have a little control over her voice, even if her damn body had developed a mind of its own. "Leave me the hell alone," she snapped, and she was pretty pleased that she managed to sound more like a shrewish bitch than a sex kitten.

Kalen laughed and slid his hand back up her body, his

fingers trailing along the slope of her hip, the slight indentation of her spine, the curve of her breast. He brushed her hair away from her face and pressed a kiss to the corner of her mouth. "I will . . . for now." ·

"I think for the next fifty years would be better," she mumbled. The nausea was completely gone, and the rest of the pain in her head had completely receded. The lack of pain didn't make her mood improve, though. She could still taste that repulsive tea, and her face was still hot with embarrassment and irritation over the little trick he'd pulled, forcing that crap down her throat. Oddly enough, she would have been a little happier if she was still wracked with pain.

He cupped his hand over the back of her neck. "Feeling better?"

Obstinate, she lied. "No. I feel like hell."

His finger tapped her nose and he whispered, "You are entirely too stubborn. Get some more sleep."

Although she was exhausted, sleep was now the last thing on her mind. She wanted to stay awake, just because he had mentioned it. But only moments after he walked out, her lids started to droop.

Before she realized it, she was sleeping, a deep, dreamless sleep.

FOUR

Kalen barked out a series of orders to the small unit before him. Two of the members of that unit stood in the front, their eyes full of pride and purpose. The purpose reassured him, but the pride made him worry. They were so damn young— Kalen cut off that train of thought before it could go any further. Young, yes, but he'd been younger than the twins when he first started fighting. And the sad fact was that they were safer in his unit than they would be if he turned them away. They just would have sought out another resistance to join, if they lived through the journey.

He had heard the soft footsteps behind him, but he didn't turn in Lee's direction as he finished reminding the two younger men before him that this wasn't a game, or a contest about who had the bigger dick.

"Lives are on the line here. We have to hold that line. No foolishness. No playing around. No antics. Just plant the plasma charges and get back here. It's Morne's job to stay there and monitor. Not yours. I don't want any heroics or stupid acts of so-called bravery. I just want—"

"The charges planted and our asses back here before

nightfall," Dagon repeated, rolling his grass-green eyes as his brother pretended to at least look somber.

He didn't like it, Kalen thought as he studied the brothers. Dais stood at his side in silence and Kalen slanted him a glance. The older man just smiled. They were ready. Or at least as ready as any of them could get.

It's not that dangerous a job, he told himself. The biggest danger this time of day was the charges themselves, and the twins were techno-wizards. They could handle a couple of charges. Finally, he blew out a sigh and said, "Go. Get on with it, and be careful."

Dais clapped a hand on his shoulder and murmured, "Don't worry so much, Kalen. They are smart, strong kids. They'll be back, and soon." He grabbed a pack from the floor and slung it over his shoulders. "Now I have a watch to finish. Lelia." He nodded at Lee on his way out the door, but Lee never took her eyes from Kalen.

Behind Lee stood Meghan, a sixteen-year-old courier who had been running messages, supplies and weapons for the past two years. She was itching to get out on the battlefields, begging for Dais to take her on and get her battle ready. So far, Kalen had managed to avoid that, but it was only a matter of time.

"Thanks for showing her here, Meg," he said dismissively before striding back over to his cluttered desk and dropping into the seat.

Meghan had already beat a fast retreat, leaving the door to bang closed behind her. Kalen looked back at Lee and decided she was still too damn pale to suit him, but time wasn't exactly a luxury they could afford. If she was well enough to walk on her own two feet, he wasn't going to waste his breath trying to talk her into resting a little more.

Lee's gaze focused on the backs of the twins as they headed out. "Did I hear you right? Those two kids are going to set off some kind of bomb?"

Kalen blinked at her. The word "bomb" was a little antiquated, but the plasma charges did go boom, and then some. He glanced at the twins and said, "Yes. There's a weak spot on the front line—every night a few more Raviners manage to slip across. So far, we've brought most of them down, but we have to do something to keep more from coming across."

"They look like kids," she said, her voice tight and rusty.

"They turned nineteen last week," Kalen replied. The simmering guilt inside him went from a low-level burn to an all-out fire. It spread through him, festering, and made his mood go in a quick downward spiral. "By rights, yes, they should be out doing whatever young punks that age like to do. But their parents were killed in an attack five years ago. They want some blood."

"So you send them out merrily to let them have it?"

Kalen arched a brow. "No. I send out well-trained soldiers and hope they can remember that they are soldiers now. That they don't need to impress the others or do anything else besides the job. Better to dwell on that than their parents. That will just rub salt in the wound."

"You think that's a good enough reason to send kids out there?"

Kalen tried to remind himself that Lee really didn't grasp what was going on. Not really. Too many of her memories of this world were still hidden. Still, he was pissed off. Did he like sending Dagon and Willim out there? It was a dangerous job. No. But he didn't have too much choice. Most of his men weren't that much older than the twins. "We're fighting a war here, Lee," he said. His eyes narrowed on her face and he took a step toward her. She didn't back away. He lowered his head until they were nose to nose. "Those kids stopped being kids years ago. I'm not going to insult them by telling them they have no right to fight."

He started to pace the tight confines of the war room, turning away from her, the guilt she made him feel. Yes. Dagon and Willim were kids. But war destroyed innocence. They would find a way to fight no matter what he did, and if he made sure they were trained, they had a better chance at surviving.

"We are at war, Lee. Whether you understand that or believe it, it's just a fact. What should I do? Turn them away? And everybody else like them? These men and women are here fighting because they lost somebody. We've all lost something to Anqar, and if we don't stand and fight back, we'll lose even more."

"They are kids, Kalen."

He rose from his desk and turned back to her. Her soft blue eyes were dark and troubled, but he couldn't say anything to help her. She was troubled because she saw him sending a couple of kids off on a war mission. He was troubled because he knew if he didn't, more lives would be lost. "I know this isn't something you can understand. I know you don't remember much, even though you've spent so much time fighting at my side. I feel as though I know every thought that runs through that canny mind of yours. But in war, you make choices. Surely even you can understand that."

The corners of her mouth turned down in a sullen frown. "Doesn't mean I have to like it," she muttered.

Kalen sighed, crossing over to her and cupping his hand around her neck, arching her face up to his. "Does not mean that I have to like it either. But there's been little in my life I've enjoyed over the past twenty years."

Her breath whispered across his mouth as her lashes lifted and she stared into his eyes. Before he could give in to the temptation to taste her again, Kalen moved away. "How is your head?"

He heard the soft sigh in her voice as she replied, "Better. A lot of better. I don't feel like drilling a hole in my temple just to release the pressure."

"Good." His ears heard the light footsteps falling on the ground just outside the shelter and he said quietly, "I hope you feel ready to work."

"Work?"

Just then the door swung open, and the tiny, stooped figure in the doorway said, "Yes. Work. I hear you've forgotten everything I taught you, so now they make me teach you again."

"Corida," Kalen said, smiling despite his dark mood. The top of Eira's head didn't even reach his shoulder, and she looked entirely too frail, but Kalen knew from experience just how *not* frail Eira was.

The old woman ignored him as she moved in, leaning on the cane heavily, her blue eyes still sharp and bright even though she was nearing her first century. "Well. You look the same. Feel the same, just a little . . . hesitant. That power, hmmm, I can taste that power of yours. Sweet as the water from the mountains used to be," she murmured, moving in on them, staring at Lee with those sharp eyes.

"Um, do I know you?" Lee asked, her brows winging up as Eira moved closer.

The old woman laughed, the sound a dry hollow cackle that echoed through the small unit. "You hate my guts—surprised you don't remember that," Eira finally said, wheezing with laughter.

Lee's cheeks flushed a very charming pink. Kalen covered his smirk with his palm as she opened her mouth, then closed it without saying anything. Finally she gave Kalen a dirty look and he returned it with a bland smile. "I really doubt I hated you," she finally hazarded, tucking her hands into the pockets of the jacket Kalen still hadn't taken back.

Eira smiled, lifting one brow. "We will see. Mmm, yes, we will see."

***

"I hate her," Lee stated with utter conviction.

They'd spent three days sleeping out in the mountains, her and that old witch, Eira. And she didn't mean witch as in hocus pocus and spell books. She meant witch as in that woman is evil. Lee had slept on the forest floor with nothing between her and the rocky, uneven ground but a thin blanket, nothing between her and the chill of the night air but another thin blanket and her borrowed clothes.

Every last muscle in her body hurt, and her belly was so empty, she was so hungry, she actually ached with it. Three days. It had only been three days since Kalen had turned her over to Eira's hands, but it felt like a decade. That woman had done her best to kill Lee. She was certain of it.

The first two days, that wicked crone wouldn't let Lee eat. Then she was allowed to eat, but nothing but bark and leaves. Lee wanted a steak. She wanted a steak so bad she could cry. She wanted a bed. She wanted a hot bath, a good book and a glass of wine.

Instead of getting any of that, she was stuck in a gloomy, sunless world where apparently imminent death was commonplace and some ancient, evil bitch was in charge of her. Lee hated anybody being in charge. It was one of the reasons she'd gone the artistic route—she had the illusion, at least, of being in charge of herself.

"Your mind is cluttered."

Eira's voice was like a bee buzzing in her ear, but smacking a bee away would have been easy. Eira wouldn't go away so easily. "Clear your mind, Lelia, and focus on the flame."

Lelia—it was a pretty name. But it wasn't her name. Instead of saying anything, though, she tried to focus on the damn candle burning inches away from her face. If she managed this, maybe the mean little pygmy would shut up.

She stared at the lone flame, watched it flicker, sway and dance. She hadn't ever noticed how sensual fire was. How sinuously it could move. As she stared at it, everything else in her vision seemed to fade away until there was nothing but the flame.

Eira continued to talk, but her voice wasn't quite as intrusive and Lee managed to tune her out a little as she stared at the flame. The yellow and orange were so pretty—she could see the wick, faintly red, burning down to black. Wax melted and dribbled down the side of the candle, fat white tears that rolled down the side and puddled on the stump.

"Focus, Lelia! You aren't just doing an artistic study on fire."

The flame flickered, and the odd, spellbound trance

shattered into a thousand pieces. Lee was once more aware of the hard, cold ground, the rocks digging into her ass, the empty aching hole of her belly, her dry mouth and throat and the painful tension that turned all of her muscles into knots. "Damn it."

She blew out an irritated breath and surged to her feet. Lee felt Eira watching her, and she turned around to glare at the old woman. "I'm hungry. I'm tired."

Eira shook her head, a queer smile on her lips. "You don't understand what tired is, vassa." Eira had been calling her that for the past three days. The first day, Lee had pretty much decided it meant "target," but Eira had told her on the second day it meant "young one" or "one who learns." Basically a student. Lee had a feeling "target" and "student" probably had the same meaning to Eira, though.

"Lelia. Sit back down and focus."

She opened her mouth to say something, but she found herself just snapping her mouth closed. Lee wanted to argue. Hell, forget arguing. She wanted to storm away and lock herself in a room so she didn't have to see this crazy woman again. But every time she said much of anything, she ended up feeling like a kid who'd just gotten caught swiping candy.

That mental image was enough to keep her from sitting down like Eira had ordered. "I can't focus until I get some food."

"You've forgotten all of your control."

Those words circled around and around in Lee's head and she wanted to choke that witch bitch. Desperately. And judging by the way Eira looked at her, Eira knew exactly how Lee felt. "My control is just fine," Lee grumbled. If she hadn't had any control, she would have already killed the crone.

"Bah. You hardly understand the meaning of the word," Eira said. Then she waved a hand. "Go on. Go rest. Go and eat something before you come back in the morning, but do not gorge yourself. We still have much work to do."

Lee didn't wait another second. Turning, she headed back. It was a long, exhausting walk, and for several reasons she had to move slower than she wanted. The first one, she was so damned tired, she felt like she was going to collapse onto the ground. The second? She didn't trust Eira, and she was listening to make sure the old woman wasn't going to sneak up on her again. Eira had sprung trap after trap on her during the past three days. Tests, she called them. Lee knew without asking that she had failed every one.

When she saw the twins standing guard at the gate, she wanted to cry with relief. Almost there. Finally, after what seemed like hours, she arrived at the small, squat cabin that had become her new home. At least temporarily.

She shoved a hand through her hair and winced as she realized how dirty she was. There was no damned way she had the energy for a bath. No way. Her hands trembled as she shoved off the jacket, and the clothes reeked. She was hot, sweaty, and dirty, and her hair was oily and matted.

But Lee was too damned tired to give a damn. She was even too tired to mess with finding something to eat. The empty, aching pit of her belly was just going to have to ache awhile longer.

Tears fell down her cheeks as she stared at her hands. Her nails were broken down to the quick. Although it seemed like a whole different life entirely, just a week ago, she had paid thirty-seven fifty for a manicure. The remnants of a sparkly coral still clung to her nails. Now her cuticles were ragged and her hands already had calluses.

Lee hadn't ever thought she was big in the personal vanity department, but for some reason, looking at her ruined hands made her feel even more depressed. She lifted her eyes and stared at the exposed timbers that made up the small barracks-style house she now seemed to call home. It boasted a bed, a washstand and what looked like a camp-style stove. A toilet behind a privacy wall. A desk. That was it. She'd seen motel rooms with more luxuries than this.

When she had to bathe, there were communal areas for it. Granted, they were impeccably clean and the baths were wonderful, some kind of mineral spring that felt amazing.

She had left behind a home she had designed from the bottom up, to come to this. She wore clothes that didn't belong to her, clothes that didn't fit and stank to high heaven, and her body was filthy, sweaty, and she didn't have the energy to get undressed or clean up or even fill the empty hole in her belly.

Eira had finally told her the three days of fasting were over and she could eat, but lightly, mind you . . . and Lee didn't want to so much as look at food. That steak she had been drooling about just a little while ago now sounded about as unappetizing as the bark and leaves Eira had made her eat.

Lee just wanted to sleep. Her legs felt like they'd been strapped to cinder blocks as she shuffled over to the bed and fell face-first down onto it. She still had tomorrow to go. And the day after. And the day after.

I want to go home . . . , she thought darkly. Back to her nice comfy bed, back to sanity, back to her safe job. So what if she got a little lonely, and she was plagued by dreams that made no sense—haunted by a bastard with silver eyes and a mouth that made her weak just thinking about it . . .

Home . . .

But she didn't know how in the hell to get back there. And even if she did, these people were desperate. Kalen, damn his fine ass, seemed to think she could make some sort of difference.

"Insane," she whispered bleakly. "Whole damned world has gone insane."

Whimpering, she curled into a tight ball and sank into the warm arms of oblivion.

* * *

Kalen watched from the surveillance tower as Lee came dragging back in to the base. He hadn't ever seen a woman look so tired before.

Although he wanted nothing more than to go to her, he had watch duty for another three hours. He had no doubt that by the time he got to his quarters, Lee would be fast asleep and dead to the world. Sympathetic, he watched as she entered the encampment, her shoulders slumped and her gaze downcast. He'd been there before. Eira was a hellish taskmaster.

"Speak of the devil," he muttered. He felt the tingle race down his back long before he really sensed her. Eira was a disturbing woman, very disturbing.

She'd been one of the first people to successfully face off against a Raviner when the things first started invading their world fifty years earlier. Not only had she fought him off and lived to tell about it, she'd killed the thing. More often than not, when Raviners attacked, there was little more than a drained corpse left behind. Sometimes not even that. But Eira hadn't just survived attacks, she'd killed her assailants.

Eira had trained his father. She'd trained him.

Although she no longer fought, she continued to serve by training the witches and guiding the psychics. She'd continue to do it until she no longer could. They had others who could teach, but they were young enough that Kalen couldn't justify taking them out of the field for it. So it fell to Eira.

"She looks like you made her run the gauntlet."

Eira moved into the corner of his eye, just barely in his field of vision. "She is stubborn. Behind the wall in her mind, the knowledge she needs lies in wait. But she won't look. So for now . . . I train her as though she just discovered her magick," the old woman said, lifting a shoulder in a negligent shrug.

"Which means you made her run the gauntlet," Kalen said dryly. "I know how your mind works, corida. You push and you push—eventually she will tire of it, and strike back. You think that through action she'll rediscover the pieces of knowledge that are missing."

She smiled and reached up to pat his cheek. Then she hobbled over to the stool in the corner of the tower. As she sat down, she sighed wearily. "I am tired, Kalen. Do you know how very tired I am?"

"Eira—" Kalen floundered for words. Yes, he could see

how worn out she was. But there wasn't much he could do. He opened his mouth twice, only to shut it without saying anything.

Eira waved a hand at him. "Let it go, boy. I am old. I am tired. We are in the middle of a war, and unless you have some spare messengers sequestered away somewhere, we cannot make contact with the other units. Sending them out just to find a replacement for a tired old woman is taking them away from where they need to be. Our sat-relays are unreliable. Whether we like it or not, we are stuck."

She looked off to the east, and Kalen knew she was thinking about her family. Six months ago, she had finally convinced her granddaughter to take her family farther away from the Roinan Gate. Since the fall of the key gate in Yorkton, it was a little safer in the east. Elina had inherited her grandmother's magick skills—getting her to leave had been nearly impossible. She was a warrior and she wanted to fight. But Elina was also a mother. Her husband had fallen in battle, and Eira had used that to convince her to leave. Elina didn't want her children orphaned.

Kalen wished he could have urged Eira to go with what remained of her family. But he needed her here. "Elina is a strong woman."

"Yes." Eira nodded. "I know. Otherwise, I wouldn't have let her leave my side. But worrying about Elina is not why I am up so late tonight." She draped her cane across her lap and gave Kalen a beatific smile. "It's your woman that has me up so late."

"Lee is not mine." Kalen looked back out into the night.

Eira laughed. "Your words do not match the look in your eyes. Tell me, Kalen, how long have you known Lee isn't from our world?"

"Always." Then he shrugged. "I don't know exactly. Awhile. A long while. I tried to track her once. We'd just freed a family from a small clutch of Raviners. Lee helped me get the family to the encampment. She went back to clear the trail. I went looking for her. She'd been upset— there had been a child who didn't make it. I wanted . . ." His voice trailed off and blood rushed to his cheeks. He wasn't going to tell the old woman that he had gone after her just wanting to wrap his arms around her and hold her. He shrugged it off and looked back at her. "She wasn't there. I found her trail halfway to the house. She'd cleared that much. Then she was gone. I didn't lose her trail, Eira. She just disappeared."

"None of us just disappear, boy." There was a thoughtful look on her face and she looked westward, staring at the flickering lights. "Not even the Warlords with their infernal magick, and saints know they have a vast power supply. What did you feel?"

Kalen shrugged restlessly. Something flickered out in the distance and he lifted the night specs. The lenses digitally enhanced and magnified objects, and through them, he saw easily a hundred times better than he could with his naked eye. Just a boar.

He did a visual sweep with the specs and then lowered them. He thought back to that night, absently rubbing a hand down his face. The light beard growth there was getting thicker. "Nothing."

Eira narrowed her eyes. "There had to have been something. A ripple in the air. A shift in energy. Something tangible. Unless, of course, you did lose her trail."

Without looking back at her, Kalen snorted. "I didn't lose a trail. There was no trail. And I felt nothing."

"Hmmmm. A puzzle." She followed his gaze westward. "We're surrounded by puzzles, aren't we, Kalen? Lee is the newest—and yes, one of the more elaborate puzzles. She has always been such an enigma. Now as much as ever before. She is fighting to accept it, when most people would do the opposite. It's almost unnatural."

"Perhaps it is because so much of her remembers. Every moment that passes brings more and more remembered knowledge," Kalen suggested. He lifted the night specs again, this time studying the far eastern quadrant. The specs let him see nearly three miles away, and through them, he saw nothing. But without them . . . were there odd colors dancing just above the tree line? He had an odd itch low in his gut, and foreboding crowded his mind.

The small skirmishes they had dealt with lately had him on edge. Small skirmishes, no real battles—too quiet all in all. Even the Raviners that kept trying to encroach along the western line had fallen back without much of a fight the past two nights.

"I don't know the why of it. I'm not even sure the why of it matters. Right now, she's dazed. Whatever magick let her enter our world has clouded her mind. And part of her remembers . . . before."

"Before what?" Kalen asked, but he wasn't really paying attention. Other things in the night called to him. He reached out with his mind, trying to find it, but it was too insubstantial just yet.

As though she sensed his unease, Eira looked out to the west. "What do you see?"

Disgusted, Kalen shook his head. "Nothing," he muttered, lowering the night specs and leaning against the waist-high wall that surrounded the surveillance tower. He squinted, staring into the dark, trying to find whatever had him so uneasy. But there was nothing. The night was quiet. "I don't really see anything."

No threat, no sign of the enemy, just those odd colors dancing in the dark that might not mean much of anything. But the knot in his gut said otherwise. He switched to the inner sight that let him look across the Veil, but he could see nothing out of the ordinary. Raviners hovering near the gate, their favorite place to be. Any little flicker let them cross over in twos or threes. Sirvani in their evening rituals. A Warlord with a woman who didn't look like a native of Anqar—

Helpless anger twisted inside him and a snarl formed on his lips. His hands closed into fists and the rage inside him spun itself into a maelstrom. Eira touched his arm, jerking out him out of the trance required to see through the Veil. She stared at him and he saw an answering anger in her faded eyes. "Sometimes I wish I had never taught you how to see through the Veil, Kalen. We cannot save those already lost to us. All we can do is try to keep from losing more."

It was an old argument, one Kalen didn't feel like having again. Weary, he replied, "You know as well as I that if I couldn't see across the Veil, more lives would have been lost. That knowledge saved lives."

"And it's taken over yours."

Kalen shrugged. "If it saves others, then I call it a fair trade." He pushed the worry and fury in his gut down, burying it deep. The emotions were nothing new to him, and late at night, when he was alone and cold in his bed, he'd let them rise to the surface. Not the most warming bedmate, but at least dwelling on them kept him from being as aware of the empty space next to him.

Although he wondered if that would continue with Lee sharing his living space. And that was just another problem he wished he didn't have to deal with—the problem of what in the hell to do with a warrior who didn't realize she was a warrior. "You mentioned something about before?"

Eira's smile was all too knowing. Too unsettling. But she seemed content to let it go for now. "Before she went to the other world. You know she wasn't born there. She belongs here—always has."

He knew that. Part of him had suspected just that for years, but actually hearing somebody else voice it lifted a weight off his shoulders. It was like a reaffirmation of his gut instinct that Lee was the key to their nightmare. Somehow, some way, they could win—so long as Lee was there to help.

"I knew it," he whispered, and he sighed, some of the tension inside of him easing just a bit. "I knew it. But it still puzzles me. How did she leave our world for theirs? She was just a child when I first met her, Eira. Only the Warlords have the power to open a gate."

She shrugged, her eyes thoughtful. With a lined, age-spotted hand, she tugged off her knit cap and ran a hand over thick, snow white hair. "She was sent there, perhaps. I don't understand the how of it, but I cannot imagine she found a way to pierce the Veil on her own at such a young age."

She cocked her head and a faint smile appeared on her lips. "Yes. Perhaps that is the answer. Someone took her across—to hide her. Part of her remembers. That is why she crosses back and forth between the Veil in her dreams; part of her still remembers her true home. And I wouldn't be surprised if she started trying to cross back to the other world in her dreams. Part of her will try to cling to that life. It's human nature," Eira said.

She turned her head and gazed out into the darkness, staring into the west, following Kalen's stare. "Demon fires. Echoes of the unrest in Anqar. Nothing to fear in itself, but we'll have another raid soon."

"Another storm," Kalen said. He had known it in his gut. The uneasy quiet of the past few months was a bad omen, and even though he had known it was just a matter of time, it ate at him. Feeling Eira's compassionate, understanding gaze on him, he spun away from it and started to pace. Fury and desperation—they were emotions he lived with on a regular basis, and emotions he hated. But he couldn't control those emotions any more than he could control the coming raid. It would happen; men and elders would die, and women and children would be dragged across the Veil.

"Pacing will not stop it."

Kalen shot her an evil glare. "What is the point of this, Eira? Was our world created just to provide them with breedable women? Can't they rape their own women and leave ours alone?"

She had no answer. None of them did. For as long as the raids had been happening, those left behind had sought answers and there were none to be found.

"I wish I had a sure and certain answer for you, lad. I do. But I have none," Eira said. Her shoulders seemed to slump just a bit more, as though the burden of the war was too great for her to handle. Then she took a deep breath and slid down from the stool. As her feet hit the ground, she winced a little and rubbed her left hip for a minute. Her first few steps were more awkward than normal, and Kalen could tell by the look in her eyes that every step hurt.

Morne came and visited the old woman twice a week, doing what he could to ease the pain in her aging joints. Kalen suspected the healer needed to visit her a little more often. He forced his mind away from Eira's ailing health and back to Anqar. "Am I a fool to hope we can beat them, Eira? This war has been around for centuries and the raids will not stop so long as the gates exist. I know that. Yet still we fight. I make my people believe there is hope. Am I wrong?"

With an enigmatic smile, Eira replied, "As long as there is life, there is hope, Kalen. Believe in that even if you believe in nothing else."

Hope . . . it seemed such a foreign word. Even now with Lee at his side, hope seemed so out of reach. He turned his head and looked out over the war-torn, twisted landscape. The base camp was sturdy and strong, surrounded by earthen barricades that could be set to flame in seconds. Beyond the fire walls, there were other barricades, made out of rubbish and salvaged metal from the fallen ruins of nearby New Angeles. They were strong and as impenetrable as they could make them—and they were ugly as hell.

The landscape itself had long since started to show the ill effects of a war lasting too long. Most of the standing trees were ancient giants. Saplings couldn't grow in the poorly nourished soil, and the scant sunlight didn't help much.

Food supplies hadn't yet become scarce in their part of the world, thanks to the copious rainfall through the summers, but eventually, even their food supplies would be compromised. Other parts of the world were little more than barren wastelands, either too arid or too swampy to grow crops. As food became more and more scarce, so would the animal population, and fresh meat would be hard to come by.

They no longer had the technology to use synthetic food sources, so as time went by, it would get harder and harder. Theirs might not be a dead world yet, but it was coming.

The Warlords and Sirvani never remained in Ishtan. Once they got their supply of human flesh, they returned to their world and never stopped to think about what would happen if the demons continued to breed unchecked in Ishtan. Ishtan's ecosystem hadn't been created with demonkind in mind.

"We live now, but for how much longer, Eira? We'll withstand this raid, and the next, and the next . . . but what about a few years down the road? We'll start to starve. The snowcaps and rain still provide adequate water, but how much longer until the streams and rivers are as poisoned as the rest of the land?"

She had no answer for him, and dread lay in his belly like a jagged hunk of metal, cutting into him, weighing him down. The darkness that had been pushing at him for weeks felt like it was expanding, exploding. Like it was going to swallow him and everything around him whole.

Voice tight and raspy, he asked Eira, "We truly are running out of time, aren't we?"

"Only the good Lord and his saints know the answer to that, Kalen. Time is of no consequence, though. If it is within our power to end this once and for all, it will happen when it is meant to and not according to some unseen timetable."

She made it sound so simple, Kalen thought darkly. He turned back to look where the odd green lights continued to flicker sporadically in the sky. "Of no consequence," he repeated.

Eira patted his shoulder. "Have heart, Kalen. We still live. While there is life, there is hope." Then she hobbled off, leaving him alone to brood.

Kalen stared off into the bleak darkness. There was one simple, unsaid fact. As long as the gates existed, invaders from Anqar would continue to rain down holy hell on Kalen's world.

There seemed to be only one solution: the Roinan Gate had to fall. It was the last remaining active gate that was strong enough to trigger the smaller gates throughout their world.

If the Roinan Gate fell . . . well, that was a hope that was actually worth believing in. If only they could figure how to make it happen.

* * *

Kalen found Lee sprawled facedown on his bunk, sleeping a deep, exhausted sleep. Her hair lay in a matted tangle around her shoulders and there wasn't a visible inch that wasn't dirty. Occasionally, a gentle, sighing kind of snore escaped her. Kalen lowered himself to the bunk, resting one hip on it as he brushed her hair back from her dirt-smudged face.

"Damn, Eira, what did you do to her?" he murmured.

A light touch on her mind showed him she was sleeping dreamlessly, so exhausted his touch never even stirred her.

He rose and moved down to her feet, grasping one narrow ankle in his hand and loosening the laces that held the oversized shoes on her feet. One of the supply runners had her measurements. He'd hit his sources and try to find her a pair of shoes that fit, but for now, she had to make do with the boots. He tossed them aside and rolled her socks down, wincing as he saw the nasty blisters forming on the back of her heel.

Damn it, what he wouldn't give for them to be able to use the synthit. He could just program in her sizes, and in a matter of moments, the synthit would have her a set of clothes and shoes that fit, not just stuff she had to borrow. But they couldn't use most of their machinery. The vibrations were like a siren's song for the wyrms.

Smaller equipment wasn't too much trouble; solar power was safe, but anything large-scale was downright hazardous. Even if it hadn't been such a danger with the wyrms, they had to conserve their supplies. If he used the synthit for Lee, then when there was a real emergency, what they needed might not be there. He couldn't take away from somebody who would need it more just because he didn't want to see Lee's feet bruised and bloody.

Medical supplies, weapons, food necessities, material for clothes, all the things needed for fighting an endless war . . . did a pair of decent shoes really count when an abundance of boots lay around?

He left the bed and rummaged through the medkit for some antiseptic and skin sealant. After he cleaned the raw patches of skin, he applied the sealant, gently running his hands over her narrow feet, looking for any other mark.

A few more blisters on her toes and along the ankle, but none were as ugly as the ones on her heels. After he cleaned the rest of them up, he put the medical supplies aside and gently rolled her over. He eyed her from head to toe, studying the battered condition of her gear. Mostly just dirt and wear. Eira's granddaughter, Elina, had left behind most of her clothing and the women were of a similar size, so at least Lee's clothes fit.

And she had more than one set of clothes. Thank the saints for that. What she was wearing was filthy. Beyond filthy. Caked with dirt, soaked with sweat. He did a mental tally, thinking through the work rotation for the nonfighters. He was pretty sure one of the women near his bunker was on rotation with the cleaning staff. The fighters all took their turn through the work rotation, but the last thing Lee needed was more work heaped on her. Eira wasn't done with her yet.

Once Eira gave her a chance to breathe, Lee could pick up the rest of the grunt work they all had to do, but until then, he'd pull rank and get her a little help. Decision made, he reached for the seal of her jacket. The edges peeled apart and he cradled her against his chest like a doll as he tugged the jacket off. The sleeveless top she wore molded to her sleek curves like a second skin, the hem of it ending just at her waist, inches above where the waistband of her pants started.

He ran his fingers over the narrow strip of skin and watched as the muscles in her belly rippled. So soft. He remembered how Lee had looked standing in that field, her hair falling in a riot of curls around her shoulders. She had been all big blue eyes, soft curves and golden hair, wearing those slinky, silky garments that outlined each and every curve.

Looking at her had hit him on so many levels. A fist in the heart, actually seeing her and knowing she wasn't going to disappear with the sunrise. An uppercut that left his head reeling as he tried to figure out what this could mean for him, for his world. And then there was the more basic reaction—the one that had his cock standing at attention, bringing to the surface all the urges he had been forced to bury for so long.

Getting her naked, getting her beneath him, all warm and open and waiting for him. Desperate to feel the heat and softness of her sex as he pushed inside. She would be hot and soft. He knew it without even touching her.

Soft—Kalen couldn't remember the last time he'd experienced anything soft in his life. War had a way of hardening things. For a minute, he was jealous. Jealous of Lee and the world she'd left behind. Life would be hard there as well, in some ways. He wasn't fool enough to think that the magick-blind world was without its difficulties. But a man there would have more time to slow down and enjoy a warm, soft woman.

There were women in the resistance. Even among his fighters. But Kalen was in a difficult position. It wasn't a wise idea to fuck a woman if he knew he might be sending her out to die the next day. Or, with the nonfighters, it was just too damned messy. The few lovers he'd had ended up thinking that being in his bed automatically equaled special treatment.

The men Lee knew in her world weren't trying to live in a war zone. They could have sex one night and go about their lives the day after without fearing that they'd find their lover in a bloodbath. In one form or another. Soft didn't belong in Kalen's world. And Lee wouldn't stay soft. He couldn't help the regret that filled him as he thought about that.

Unable to resist, he pressed a hand flat against her belly. She sighed in her sleep and Kalen watched as the smooth, pale flesh undulated under his hand. Silky soft. Soooo soft . . . His lids drooped as he ran his hand from her belly down over her hip, until it rested on the curve of her thigh. There was firm, supple muscle under his hand. Thoughts of the war, thoughts of securing supplies or soldiers—all of them fell away and he found himself lost in a fantasy. A fantasy where he found himself wondering how those long, slender legs would look wrapped around his waist. How her body would feel under his, how her hair would feel wrapped around his hands while he kissed her.

He wanted to feel her mouth again. Wanted to taste her again and again, but just a kiss wasn't going to do it. Kalen groaned and flexed his hand against her belly. He traced a finger around the tight, neat little circle of her navel and then lower, staring at the covered curves below her waist.

She's asleep, he reminded himself. Sound asleep, totally unaware, and he was sitting there, staring at her and practically pawing her. It took a monumental effort to drag his gaze away as he loosened the thick belt that cinched her pants tight. He stripped the baggy material off and kept his eyes locked on the ceiling.

It wasn't that big a help. Even though he stared at the ceiling, his peripheral vision showed him the lacy triangle of the undergarment she wore, the smooth flare of her hips, the shadowed cleft between her thighs. He wanted to push her thighs apart and lie between them. Press his face against her. Taste her there—push her to orgasm and listen to her scream, then do it all over again.

Instead, he just finished stripping her pants away. "Being a bloody gentleman will be the death of me," he grumbled. He tossed the pants into a pile of dirty clothes and then flipped a light, worn blanket over her.

She was still dirty, with smudges on her face and her hair in a tangle on the pillow. And beautiful. So damned beautiful. Lee was just going to have to sleep dirty. There was no way in hell he could do anything else. Better that she sleep dirty than to have him fall on her like a beast in rut as his control snapped. It was dangerously close already.

His cock throbbed in the tight confines of the skin-skimming shorts he wore under his combat pants, and his muscles were tensed and ready. His hands felt too empty, his skin felt too tight, and he was dying for another taste of her. A bigger taste, a deeper one.

No, he wasn't going to do another thing while she lay sleeping like that. Aching and frustrated, he turned away from her. He grabbed his bedroll and threw it on the floor. He could ignore the sleeping woman. He had to.

Dawn would be here all too soon. And you never knew when an attack would come. Rest while you can, eat when you can, always be ready.

It had become a way of life.

He didn't have the luxury of curling up beside a soft, warm woman and holding her close. Didn't have the luxury of cuddling her against him . . . pushing her thighs apart and rocking against the warmth he knew was waiting there.

"You're into self-inflicted torture," he muttered, driving a hand through his hair as he kicked off his boots and shucked his shirt. Dropping down onto the bedroll, he closed his eyes and willed himself to sleep.

Tomorrow wasn't going to be any easier for her.

Or for him.

FIVE

Doddering, stupid, arrogant fool—

There were other words that could be used to describe High Lord Taise. Crazy. Paranoid. Canny. Lucky.

But Raichar Taise had been serving his uncle for the past fifty years, and he had watched the man's descent into madness. Maybe he had sped him down the path a time or two. Planted false evidence to make the High Lord believe his advisors were out to get him. An ambush or two. Paranoid people were so ridiculously easy to manipulate. Char had his own agenda, but right now, it suited him to go along with the old fool's delusions, and add to them, on occasion.

Taking over a world, what had the man been thinking? It had been decades since Taise had upped the aggression against the other world. What had pushed his uncle over, Char didn't know. No longer was he content just to take the females needed for the warriors and Sirvani coming of age—no, he didn't want just enough, he wanted an excess.

Wanted them all. Perhaps Taise's inability to produce a son of his own had been what pushed the old man over into the realm of insanity. And Taise truly was insane.

Char had known it from the very beginning. A lucid man would have seen the effects of the continued raids on Ishtan. Considering that they needed the offworld females to breed, a rational man would have shown more caution. Char knew well enough why the other Warlords had yet to question the High Lord. It simply wasn't done, but then again, none of them had been living with Taise's madness. From their safe distance, Taise's mad decisions may well have seemed to be calculated risks.

Certainly the Sirvani that were bound to the High Lord weren't going to do anything. Bound to the High Lord through blood and oath, their very lives would be at risk should they ever say anything against him. That bond also likely colored how they saw things—they would see things as their ruler saw them, unless they were powerful enough to resist the bond taking them over in such a way.

Taise's insanity they would see as sheer genius, just as Taise saw it. His foolish, arrogant risks would be seen as confident and thorough planning. If this campaign wasn't so bloody stupid, so bloody dangerous, even Char could have ignored much of it.

But it was stupidity. It had gone beyond the realm of arrogance into madness decades ago. And time was running out for them. Char had known it for a while, and it was only a matter of time before others began to see it as well.

Arrogance was a trait common among the Warlords, but their arrogance wouldn't continue to blind them. It was a waiting game and one he was truly tired of. How much longer before the other Warlords realized that Shonar Taise's sly war tactics were actually the machinations of a lunatic?

Char had his own plans, and if he wasn't cautious, the lunatic could ruin them.

If the old man would just die—

Char cut that train of thought off before it could go any further. Taise's psy abilities were all but gone, thanks to age and madness, but he was surrounded by loyal men. And more, men who were like Char, loyal only to themselves, who wouldn't hesitate to use Char's thoughts against him.

"What of the last contingent we sent through the Veil? How much ground have they gained?" Taise would have said something else, but a deep, wracking cough robbed him of his breath.

It was a deep, phlegmy sound, and altogether disgusting. When he looked up at his second in command, Taise had bits of yellow-brown mucus in his grizzled, matted beard. Char hid his revulsion and at the same time found himself somewhat cheered. That cough sounded worse today. It seemed to slowly worsen on a daily basis, and Taise would allow no healer near him. Could be pneumonia. Or the lungrot. Taise had a taste for the disease-causing shaf. Shaf addiction had killed more than its fair share in Anqar.

Perhaps fate would smile on Char and eliminate the old fool before Char had to act.

"Char? Damn you, boy, I asked you a question."

Char hadn't been a boy for many decades. At eighty-five years old, Char was in his prime. The Warlords were a long-lived race. The commoners in Anqar lived to perhaps a hundred, but Warlords usually saw three or four centuries, or more. Taise had been ancient for as long as Char could remember. The High Lord's exact age was unknown. Taise wouldn't give it up, and he had a nasty habit of killing his rivals, or anybody in the vicinity when he was on a tirade. Eventually most of the people who could have made an educated guess were either cold in the ground or had long since left the High Lord's lands. By now, many of them were probably dead. Power was life in Anqar, and the weaker people died earlier in life, either by another person's hand or because their bodies simply wore out on them.

Taise was a powerful bastard, but even his power had limits. Char had watched him carefully over the past few years and he knew the High Lord's strength was dwindling. Of course, his mind, though crazed, still functioned. Char could all but hear his uncle gritting his teeth. He looked at Taise and answered, "We've brought back eighteen small families. Thirty-eight females near or at breeding age."

"Thirty-eight females?" Taise snapped. "We sent a hundred and fifty men. We should have brought back three times that."

"There were—circumstances." Taise hadn't planned on elaborating or explaining how a couple of plasma charges had brought down the side of a mountain, killing sixty-three of his men—and twenty-two families that they had grabbed on their sojourn. But Taise obviously wasn't going to let it go. Just another sign of his madness.

A hundred fifty men was nothing to the High Lord. Even the families meant little. The men and boys would be castrated and put into use at High Keep. Women and girls became body slaves, mated to as many as five warriors. The man that impregnated her could keep her. But they had thousands of body slaves living in High Keep or in the surrounding warrior camps.

In truth, if the raids weren't a way of life for them, they could have stopped the raids a hundred years ago, two hundred. Perhaps even longer. They had enough breedable offworld females, but very few chose to even consider that it was time to slow down, or completely cease the offworld raids.

Thousands and thousands of years ago, Anqar had been an insular world, relying on nothing and nobody. But then, for some reason, fewer and fewer females were born to the Warlord bloodlines. Commoners still bred easily, but their blood diluted and weakened the Warlord blood. Children often didn't survive childhood and too many were born without talent.

Power was life in Anqar—and the Warlords had to pass their power on. Eventually, they realized that if they didn't find a way to get more females, they would die off completely. According to the ancient texts that all Sirvani studied, even in those times long past, there had been those among them who could see through the Veil.

Char imagined it had been pure torture to stare upon Ishtan—the inhabitants would have seemed as primitive to Char's ancestors as Ishtan seemed to him now. But, primitive or not, it would have been a ripe world. Char could remember his first raid and staring into that amazingly green world, so different from the arid climes of Anqar and so ripe with women—women of power. Unlike among the commoners of Anqar and within the Warlord bloodlines, power flowed freely in Ishtan. It didn't mark every soul born in that world; it hit each generation in an equally random way, so that for every untalented child, there was also one born with talent.

Looking through the Veil and seeing that, Char wondered how the idea first came to be, the idea that perhaps they could pierce the Veil and take some of those gifted women for their own. The idea took root, and within a few generations, the Warlords of old had perfected the skills of raising a gate, and crossing the gate for the first time became a rite of passage.

But all things must come to an end. Char had tried bringing the idea up rationally to the Warlords after he'd learned that the women they had taken from offworld would be enough to sustain them indefinitely, provided they exercised thought and caution. They could bring female blood back into the Warlord bloodline, but none wanted to listen.

Time had taught Char that, eventually, they would have no choice. Each passing year, the gates became more unstable. But Char had long since learned to hold his peace. Several of the advisors that served Taise had attempted to tell the High Lord all of this, only to die before they'd uttered more than a few words on the subject.

The High Lord wouldn't listen to reason. But Char didn't need him to—all he needed was for the High Lord to die. As the High Lord's second in command and his closest blood relative, the mantle of High Lord would be passed to Char upon Taise's death and then he would begin anew. The old ways would change.

"Circumstances," Taise spat, drawing Char's attention back to the less than successful raid. "How many dead?"

"Sixty of our men, forty offworlders," Char said, keeping his voice neutral. The loss of his men mattered little to Taise, Char knew. It was the loss of the slaves that had the

High Lord so enraged. His mottled face had gone a bizarre reddish purple, and Char amused himself with images of the Lord having a brainstorm, collapsing to the floor dead. Or better yet, alive, but trapped in the prison of his own body. Char liked to think of that.

By the time he had finished explaining, it wasn't a stretch to think Taise might have that stroke. His breath wheezed in and out of his lungs and spittle foamed around his mouth. His wrinkled face had gone from that mottled purplish red to true purple, as though the High Lord had forgotten how to breathe.

Disgusting old man.

"You lost my body slaves." Taise's hands clenched into fists and he glared at Char with black, angry eyes.

Not like you can get any use out of them, Char mused. Of course, that didn't stop Taise from trying. He killed a body slave on a regular basis, or had her beaten. Useless whores—can't even ride a man right. That was Taise's reasoning. Of course, Taise wasn't much of a man anymore. Char could even feel pity for the girl put in front of that and expected to do anything useful with him. It was a waste. Taise always wanted the pretty, young ones, and more often than not, he killed them when they couldn't arouse him.

"We lost a few, yes, High Lord." Then his tone turned cajoling and he gave Taise a charming smile. "But you should see the young ones we did manage to bring through the Veil."

For a moment, Taise's rheumy eyes brightened, and then his face darkened once more. He tugged at his lip and started mumbling under his breath about the Veil. As delusional as Taise had become, the Veil was one thing he was right to distrust. The High Lord was in direct control of the Veil itself, but each subordinate Warlord had his own territory, a province he controlled. Stronger Warlords sometimes received a gated province.

There'd been a time when nearly all Warlords had a gate of their own, but the number of functioning gates had dwindled. The last generation saw a rapid decline in the gates, ending with the spectacular collapse of their second largest gate along the Surachi Province. Gorin, the Warlord who controlled that territory, as well as his protectorate were gone. Eighteen thousand lives, gone in an instant, and more injuries than their healers could handle. Another four thousand died in the days following as the healers and their workers struggled to keep up with the injured.

Twenty-two thousand gone and nearly double that displaced. The Surachi Province was a wasteland now. No crops grew, no wildlife would live there, and the few who tried to return to their homes either committed suicide, went mad or ran screaming back to the safety of the nearest province. It was as though the gate's destruction had damaged something in the very earth, poisoned it, and it bled out into the land, affecting any that tried to live there.

It was unclear exactly what had happened, and Char suspected they'd never know the full story. What little they knew was scattered, and he wasn't sure how reliable any of the information was. Reports came in slowly, but apparently there was a huge disruption in the Veil right about the time disaster hit the Surachi Province. There was a power surge in the Veil, but most of the gates were down and the only outlet for that power surge was the lone open gate.

The Surachi Gate.

The fall of that gate decimated all of the smaller gates for miles around, and now the Roinan Gate, located in the heart of High Keep, was the only gate strong enough to trigger the smaller gates that still remained.

For the time being, at least. Char knew they were on borrowed time with the Roinan Gate as well. Weaker Warlords had to settle for serving under another, stronger Warlord. On occasion, there were assassinations when a subordinate tried to overthrow his superior. If he was strong enough, he just might succeed. If he did, he had the province—and the gate.

All Warlords had the magick inside them that gave them control over a gate. The power took time to develop, and sometimes it never did. Until it developed, they were Sirvani, formally serving under a Warlord, earning their place in the hierarchy and completing their training.

For some, that would be their life. Not all Sirvani would become Warlords. The power passed through the blood, but with some, it would never fully manifest. While many high-level Sirvani would master the ability to maintain a gate, the ability to control a gate, to raise and lower it at will, was the mark of a Warlord. That power was what set the Warlords apart. The Warlords were the only ones in known history who could open the gates. It was also that power that gave them their physical strength and longevity.

Char didn't know the why and the how of it, why the power manifested in one generation and then skipped the next two. Why twins were born and one would have the ability to raise the gate and another would never be able to do more than look through the Veil. No, he didn't understand it; nor did he care to. All that mattered to him was that he was born into the bloodline and his powers manifested before he finished the rudimentary education all children received.

He was placed into the formal Sirvani training at twelve, and before he turned eighteen, he was placed into Warlord training. He was by far the youngest Warlord, and more important, he was a Warlord born into the royal bloodline.

Power was his due. When the old man finally returned to the earth, Char would rule this land, and the gates. And he'd damned well not make a fool of himself the way Taise had. Paranoid and obsessed with his lost youth, his waning power and the gates. The damned gates.

Char knew he only had a finite amount of time to finish the job he had set for himself all those years ago. Finding what was stolen from him. After he had obtained that objective, then the damned gates could close forever and he wouldn't give a damn. Char would be the next High Lord and he was prepared to lead Anqar into a new age.

It baffled him to think that he was the only one in the royal bloodline to see how shortsighted it was to keep depending on the slave trade to keep his people flourishing.

The offworld slaves could breed well. In recent generations their matches had produced offspring with the same powers common in their native land. More, they steadily produced female offspring, thereby securing future mates for his men.

It would take time to get his men accustomed to the new way of life, to the end of the raids. When making the transformation from Sirvani to Warlord, a Warlord's first successful raid was cause for celebration. Weeklong celebrations where the wine and ale flowed like water and the female slaves were introduced to their new lives.

Yes, changing their old ways would take time. However, it was only a matter of time before it was forced on them by fate. Char wasn't fond of fate's surprises. For years, ever since he realized how unstable Taise had become and the strain the High Lord was putting on the gatemagicks, and the inevitable faltering of that magick, Char had been working on this solution, and he had been working in this direction for decades. He had already been putting his theories into practice in his personal household with much success. The slaves still produced talented female offspring—provided that at least one-half of each mated couple had psy or mage abilities.

Their world wouldn't die when the gates could no longer sustain travel. Let Taise have his delusional dreams of dominating worlds. Char just wanted one. His mark in history would be laying the foundation for their new way of life, a life that didn't rely on offworld raids just to ensure their survival.

The gates—they were the start of all his troubles, and when the last one fell, he would be satisfied.

Almost as if the High Lord could still sense thoughts, he felt Taise's gaze focus on him. "How fare the gates this trip?"

With his hands linked behind his back, Char faced Taise and responded, "Secure. I did not notice any instabilities. I think the key to maintaining them is moderation, High Lord. Endless use, or forcing them to remain open, that seems to cause the fluctuation in the gate's power."

Even though Char delivered the words in a diplomatic, level tone, Taise erupted. "Damn those gates! Moderation—no. It's raiding season. The nights are long and my men are ready to hunt." He jabbed a gnarled finger in Char's direction. "You will find a way to stabilize the Roinan Gate. It's the key. If it is stable, the smaller gates will be as well."

Char inclined his head. Stabilizing them was the last thing that Char would do, even if he knew how. But pacifying the High Lord suited him right now. "Of course, High Lord."

* * *

Waking up was rarely a pleasant experience for Lee. Caught in the grip of dreams that she couldn't remember— but that terrified her nonetheless. Terrified her so that when she lay in bed, she was covered with sweat and had to resist the urge to pull the blankets over her head and hide like a child.

But pulling the blankets over her head wouldn't do a damn thing to ease her fear, and she knew it. Didn't stop her from wanting to try again, but pride wouldn't let her. Even without the dreams lingering in the back of her subconscious, waking up was a bitch.

Today, though, today wasn't just a bitch. It was a colossal she-bitch from hell, and Lee wished she could just close her eyes and escape into unconsciousness. Lying there with her mouth as dry as cotton and an aching hole in the pit of her stomach, she was too nauseated to eat. No, waking wasn't any fun in her experience, and the only thing that made it tolerable was coffee. Oh yeah, today was going to go down in the records as far as bad mornings went. Every last inch of her body ached, her heels were a blistered, screaming mess of pain, her soles were even worse than that, and her head hurt so bad, she figured a visit with a guillotine would be an improvement. All of that she could have handled, so long as she had some coffee.

No. Not some. *Lots* of coffee. Strong and sweet, with just a little milk and a hell of a lot of sugar. Anything could be faced, as long as there was enough coffee. Lee was pretty certain that was part of her problem. This damned place had no coffee. After the second night here, she knew that she wasn't dreaming all of this. Even in her worst nightmares, she wouldn't conjure up some dream world unless it had coffee in it.

So she was either in some bizarre, alternate reality thing—or she was dead and trapped in hell. Lee was pretty sure there wasn't any coffee in hell. Of course, by that reasoning, maybe this really wasn't an alternate reality, where she had to deal with no coffee and a sexy warrior that she didn't know how to handle. Maybe she really was in hell and this world had been conjured up to serve as her punishment, with Kalen as her keeper.

With a pitiful whimper, she rolled over on the bed and pressed her face into the pillow. It was daylight out. She could see the light streaming in around the weird-looking curtains. They looked like they were made of some sort of organic material. They blended in perfectly with the walls and they felt weird to the touch. Rough, at first, like the wood that made up the bunker, and then softer—almost like flesh under her hands. They changed color under the contact as well, going from a weathered gray to a pale ivory nearly the same tone as her skin.

They blocked the sunlight so well, she never would have known it was morning except that the curtain was just a little too short and pale golden slivers of light fell through. They did something to muffle the sound as well, and she could just barely hear voices outside.

The encampment was never quiet. That was one thing she'd learned pretty fast. Right now, she'd have given anything for some silence, some coffee—and someplace to hide from that evil woman.

If the sun was burning in the sky, then Eira would be here soon. Actually, Lee was pretty surprised Eira hadn't shown up already to drag Lee's exhausted ass out of the bed.

"It's safe to get up. Eira won't be bothering you until later today."

At the low, rough sound of Kalen's voice, Lee turned her head just a little, enough so that she could see him if she opened one eye. The sight of that dark angel face was enough to make the morning a little less depressing. Lee would have had to be dead for that face to leave her unaffected, and she figured she hurt too much to be dead.

Kalen was crouched down by the bed, staring at her with a faint smile. The little scar on his chin was very faint, years old. There was another one that bisected his left eyebrow, stopping just short of his eye. A little lower and he probably would have been left without any sight in that eye.

"I didn't know you were here," Lee said softly.

He reached up and brushed her bangs away from her face. His fingers lingered, trailing across her cheekbone. "You have slept more than thirteen hours. There could have been a gatestorm and I don't know that you would have awakened."

Gatestorm—Lee wasn't sure what that was but it sounded ominous. Her brain wasn't ready for ominous, so instead of asking him what it was, she turned her face back into her arms. If she tried, maybe she could go back to sleep. She sure as hell was tired enough.

"Eira has a way of making somebody feel like they've run the gauntlet."

She cracked an eye back open and slid him a dirty look. "She's evil. You know that? Just plain evil." Then she sighed and pushed herself up on the narrow bed. That was when she realized she was mostly naked. She flushed and tucked the sheet around her legs, and when she did, she caught sight of her undershirt. It was stiff and dirty, and unless she was mistaken, it stank to high heaven. Lee probably wasn't in much better shape. That evil woman hadn't let her take a bath. There had been a time when Lee would have been desperate enough to dive into arctic waters to get clean, but Eira wouldn't have it.

Too much of that soft world clings to you, vassa. We need to sweat it out of you.

"People usually survive a gauntlet. I don't think Eira

wants me to survive. She wants to torture me to death, slowly." Lee shivered a little, the cool morning air kissing her flesh.

Kalen's quarters were barren, a barracks-style cabin that boasted little more than the bed and a huge desk. It was a single unit, though. Or at least it had been until she showed up. From the first day, she had crashed on his bed and Kalen made do with a pallet on the floor. She kept waiting for him to cart her off to a double unit where she'd share with some stranger, but it still hadn't happened.

From what she had seen, most of the people here shared. She had an idea why Kalen was by himself, but she felt weird asking. She felt weird not knowing the answer, if she had to be honest. She felt like she *should* know, and was embarrassed that she didn't.

Too many things here felt too familiar—she found herself recognizing people, knowing them by name, even though she hadn't ever met them. Or at least, not while she was awake.

She rubbed her hands over her face and muttered, "It's too early for this. Thinking before coffee ought to be outlawed. Hell. A world without coffee shouldn't have ever been allowed into existence."

"Coffee." Kalen said the word slowly and Lee squinted up at him. The faint light still seemed too bright for her tired eyes.

"Yes. Coffee. I can't wake up without coffee."

He said nothing, but she knew by the look on his face that he didn't know what coffee was. "If I had to wind up in some twilight zone dimension, you could at least have coffee for me."

Kalen reached out and traced a hand down her cheek, then tapped her nose. "We do not have coffee. But . . ."

The tone in his voice gave her hope. When he turned and left, Lee mumbled, "Maybe they have chocolate." It wasn't quite the same, but it had caffeine. It had sugar. It would work. She could make do with chocolate. Hell, she'd make do with hot tea, so long as it wasn't some kind of herbal crap or whatever vile concoction he'd made her drink the other day.

However, she wasn't going to hold her breath. If they didn't have something as simple as coffee, she wasn't going to hope for candy. By the time the door opened a few minutes later, she had forced her stiff body out of bed and gone to stand in front of the minuscule sink. She found her clothes in a pile by the door and decided that Kalen must have stripped them off, because if Lee had done it, the undershirt would have come off as well. She didn't have any other clothes, but she couldn't walk around half-naked either. Even if Kalen had already seen her in the undershirt and panties.

She found one of his shirts draped over a chair, and after hastily stripping off the undershirt, she pulled it on and then immediately wished she'd waited a few minutes. It was clean, warm and it smelled of him. While she stank.

A week in the shower might help, but it wasn't an option. Kalen's small cabin didn't have a real bathroom. There was a toilet behind a little wall that she assumed was supposed to make it a bit more private. There was a sink and running water, so Lee figured she shouldn't complain. These people were living in a manner she'd never imagined, but technically she knew it could be worse. A lot worse. As soon as she could stumble her way outside, she was going to the communal bath. Those mineral springs were seriously excellent. A day at a spa couldn't beat those mineral springs.

She splashed water on her face and glanced at Kalen's reflection in the little mirror. The round piece of glass was barely large enough for their two faces. A blessing in disguise, Lee figured. If she looked at her full-length reflection, she might cry. Lee wasn't overly vain, but her filthy clothes, the ragged lengths of her nails and her tangled hair would have been enough to have even her crying.

Then she caught the scent of something seductive. Something rich. Something she would have happily chopped off an arm to have. Slowly, she turned. Her eyes narrowed when she saw the metal cup in Kalen's hand. It had steam rising off it, dancing in the cool air.

It was the most beautiful thing she'd ever seen. "Is that . . ."

The look on her face was so erotic—she looked like a woman tumbling into orgasm, not a woman staring at a hot cup of kion. One thing they weren't lacking, thank God, since the Kona beans they used to make kion grew naturally in this area. She stared at the cup with the same kind of greed he'd seen in the eyes of a teenaged boy seeing his first naked female. "Kion," he supplied. "Careful. It's—"

She grabbed it from him and a little of it splashed on her hand, but she didn't even notice as she lifted the cup. "Hot," he finished lamely. Her lashes fluttered closed and she made a sexy little moan.

How ridiculous was it to feel jealous? Kalen had dreamed of hearing her make that kind of sound for years, and when she finally did, it was over a bloody cup of kion. She took one sip and then a second one before she looked up at him. The fog of sleep cleared a little and he saw satisfaction in her eyes. "You're my hero," she said.

He laughed. "Over kion."

"Absolutely. You saved my life. If I had to go another day without caffeine . . ."

"You would have lived," Kalen said, his voice dry. "Even if some people around you wished otherwise." He felt just a little bit of guilt, too. The woman had an addiction to caffeine that probably bordered on unhealthy and she'd gone four days without it. Not that Eira would have allowed her to take any into the field while she was being trained. He reached for the bag he'd brought when he first came in. "I also have clean clothes, although I doubt you'll be as thankful for those." He smiled faintly as he studied the tunic she wore. "That looks better on you than it ever did on me."

She flushed and shifted from one foot to the other. "Sorry. Should have asked but I couldn't keep that shirt on any longer. And you obviously don't know me that well if you don't think I'm going to love the clothes as much as the coffee—kion, whatever," she muttered. She glanced toward the mirror and used her free hand to finger comb through some of the tangles in her hair. "Clean clothes are worth their weight in gold. I can't stand to be in the same room with myself. I don't see how you can stand to be that close to me."

It wasn't that easy, but it had nothing to do with what she did or didn't have on, with whether or not she'd taken a bath in the past few days, her tangled hair or anything like that.

His shirt hung on her so long it came down to her knees, and her nipples peaked against the soft cloth. Her eyes were still heavy with sleep. Just standing there was hard because he had to resist moving any closer.

Being this near was both heaven and hell. Heaven— because he only felt complete when she was with him. Hell—because she wasn't ready for what he needed from her. Things he'd always needed from her, but circumstance and fate had kept him from it. Just as circumstance and fate now kept him from her. She was confused and exhausted. Beyond that, there was the war with Anqar. Every day was a battle to survive. Even with the gates relatively quiet, Kalen's forces had their hands full with the demons that had already taken up residence.

Kalen had a bad feeling their time was running out. He didn't understand it, but every day he woke with the urge to hurry riding him. Fortify their position. Get the new recruits trained and combat ready. Stockpile food, weapons and whatever armor they could scavenge. Hurry, hurry, hurry. A clock ticking away the seconds in his mind, always there, and now they had a new problem thrust upon them. Lee. Although he looked at her and saw salvation, there was the problem of getting her ready for this life. Each day it seemed she remembered a little bit more, but would she be ready in time?

If she wasn't, he would lose her.

So definitely thoughts of heaven and hell tormented him whenever he thought of her, whenever he saw her. It was torture, having her there. Actually there. Even though he'd waited for this moment, Kalen hadn't really expected it would ever happen. Now that it had, he was learning the true meaning of frustration.

Kalen had wanted Lee since he'd been old enough to understand what it was to want a woman. She had just been a girl then, and he'd been a boy forced to grow up way too soon. He'd spent too many nights having hot, sweaty dreams centered on her, but when she was at his side in combat, he could focus on the job, on the war. Lee had always had a knack for showing up in times of trouble, and even a hormone-crazed adolescent could put wet dreams to the side when facing down a cadre of demons and Warlords.

They had always been surrounded by people before. There had also been a distance between them, an uncertainty on his part brought on by Lee's very presence. For as long as he could remember, he'd known there was something strange about her. Something strange about how she showed up in time to free him, then disappear. Reappearing on the sidelines when the resistance went to thwart a raid.

That distance was gone now. Lee was here, alone with him, and she wasn't going to disappear the second he turned his back. It would be so easy to reach out to her, to pull her against him and kiss her until neither of them could breathe. So easy to strip away the shirt she wore and lick the salt of her sweat away, then make her sweat all over again as he fucked her blind.

Lee wanted him.

He could see it in her eyes, in the way she held herself around him. He could see it in the way she made sure she never met his eyes for too long. Yes, Lee wanted him, maybe every bit as much as he wanted her. It would be so damned easy. He could find some peace and solace and pleasure, even if it only lasted for a little while. He could stroke away the shadows in her eyes, ease the tension that tightened her body.

And it would solve nothing. Lee was still lost, like a boat cut adrift, and he'd be damned if he'd use that to bring her to him. She needed to find herself first. Needed to get her legs beneath her and understand what she had gotten caught up in.

Her safe, secure world might be lost to her, forever. Selfishly, Kalen hoped it was. He hoped she couldn't ever go back, because even if by some miracle they could send the Warlords screaming into hell, he didn't want her to leave. Ever. If that happened, he wanted her to accept it willingly. To come to him because she had the same need for him that he had for her, not just because she wanted some sex, and some comfort, of the skin-to-skin variety.

But he did have to touch her. Instead of pulling her to him, he went to her, stepping behind her. Kalen rested a hand on the nape of her neck, felt the tension mounted there. He dug his fingers into the tight muscles, and almost immediately, Lee moaned and dropped her head forward. He brought up his other hand, massaging until the tension slowly eased from her neck and shoulders. "I saw you come in last night," he murmured.

"I bet I looked like something the cat dragged in."

His mouth quirked. He didn't quite understand the words, but he grasped the sentiment easily enough. "Today won't be so bad."

"Yeah, but what about tomorrow?"

He smiled at the grouchy, surly tone and wished he could say something that would make her smile. "It will get a little easier, with Eira, at least." The rest of it, though? Her problems were only beginning.

"At least?" Lee asked warily. She wanted to look at him and try to decipher the meaning of those words, but that would involve pulling away from his hands. Those heavenly, wonderfully strong hands—no way in hell was she pulling away. At least not willingly.

When he didn't answer, she just shut her eyes. "What have I gotten myself into?"

Kalen didn't answer her. He did that a lot, and even though it irritated her, on some level she was relieved. He didn't try to offer false comfort or promises. Things were bad around here. When things were bad, people tended to say all sorts of meaningless things, just to make a person feel better. But Lee wasn't much into falsehoods, even those that were well meant.

He slid his hands down her shoulders, massaging her upper arms, then back up. One hand cupped over the back of her neck, lingering there for a minute. Then he stepped away. Lee shivered a little at the loss of his warmth, and then she focused on the mostly full cup she still held in one hand. It wasn't quite like coffee—sweeter, darker—but it had the same kick that espresso would have. She licked her lips and looked up to see him watching her.

For just the briefest second, there was a look in his eyes. A hungry, greedy look that made her heart skip a beat, a look that turned her muscles into putty. Then it was gone.

Good thing, too, because if he looked at her like that for too long, Lee wasn't sure what she'd do. And she had enough problems right now, thank you very much. She sure as hell didn't need to get tied into emotional knots over the dark angel with the silver eyes.

* * *

"Do you see?"

Lee just sat, staring into nothingness. See what? The only thing she could see were the trees in front of her, most of them stunted and dead. She could feel the warning of a vicious headache brewing at her right temple, but she hoped if she ignored it long enough, it would go away.

She couldn't deal with the headache right now.

Not the headache and this.

"This" being *her* again.

How much longer were they going to stick her with this crazy old woman? Eira Cantrell was crazy. There was no other way to put it. For three hours, she had sat on a damn tree stump and listened to the woman's raspy, almost hypnotic voice.

Look . . . it's there . . . . you have seen it before.

Look at what? That was all Lee wanted to know. If the old crone would tell her what Lee was supposed to see, then Lee could look for it.

The Veil . . . look for the Veil.

The Veil. Great. And exactly what was the Veil . . . ?

Lee couldn't focus. She wanted to focus on her irritation with Eira, but she couldn't. She tried to focus on the trees and couldn't. She searched for whatever it was she was supposed to see, but the more Eira spoke, the harder it was to focus on anything, and the longer she sat there . . .

Her eyes grew heavy.

She felt like she was falling asleep. But she wasn't. When her eyes closed once more, she didn't see the darkness of sleep but something shimmery, silvery gray—almost the same shade of silvery gray as Kalen's eyes.

"There . . . you see now . . ." Eira's voice sounded different now. Felt different. Like it was echoing on the inside of Lee's skull, coming from within instead of without.

Lee opened her mouth to speak, but she couldn't. She tried to move and couldn't. She felt frozen, like she was weighted down by something she couldn't see. *What is that?* she wanted to know, but she couldn't seem to form the words to ask.

"The Veil. You're looking at the Veil," Eira said. "The barrier between the worlds. It separates our world from the one you grew up in, and it separates us from the dark realm of Anqar."

Anqar—

The shimmery gray faded, stretched out, until she could see beyond it. It was like looking at something through a transparent piece of gray silk. A desert formed. Hot, arid and dry—she could feel the heat of the air on her face, feel the scorching winds blowing through her hair. She heard voices. She felt chaos. She sensed despair, anger, greed and arrogance.

Each emotion seemed distinct. If she could hold on to this vision long enough, Lee thought maybe, just maybe, she could trace them back to their owners. She wanted to follow the despair. It made her heart hurt. She wanted to help.

But the avarice and greed were stronger. They intruded on her thoughts, demanding her attention. She found herself staring at something alien. Something foreign. Oddly beautiful, terrifying and deadly—a face, but not the face of a human. Too long and thin, stretched out, with dark, hollow pits for eyes, and skin that glowed a burnished orange. Deep inside, she sensed a strange melody, high-pitched, rhythmic and so full of evil, it made her shudder. Her voice shook a little as she said, "There's something here. It's waiting for us."

Eira's voice was soothing, gentle as she murmured, "No. Nothing is here. It's on the other side of the Veil. We're safe. Tell me, what do you see?"

"No. No, we're not. It's there . . ." The face wavered, the music in her head swelled.

"Describe it for me. Tell me what you see." Eira's voice was calm, as though they were discussing the weather.

But Lee couldn't be calm. The thing that seemed to hover in front of her like a mirage had her petrified. Its mouth opened and a horrifying screech filled the air. Lee flinched and instinctively closed her eyes. When she opened them and tried to see the thing again, it was gone.

The shimmery gray veil remained and she could see the alien landscape, but the creature, whatever it had been, was gone. "It's gone, Eira."

"Then tell me what you feel . . ." Something touched Lee's head and she realized Eira was stroking her hair. Oddly, it comforted Lee. It felt strangely familiar.

In this strange, bizarre place, Lee would gladly accept anything that felt familiar. Sometimes, it felt so natural, and she could almost accept what Kalen told her, that she belonged here. Part of her felt as though she did. The world itself was oddly familiar, kind of like a movie she had seen ages ago but forgotten.

They had guns. But the guns looked more like something out of a sci-fi flick set three hundred years in the future. They had field hospitals like those Lee had seen when she had spent a few months in the Middle East, but the technology used here was so far advanced, it left her mind reeling.

Even more baffling than the technology was the magick. Real magick. The kind that shouldn't exist but the kind that she apparently could do. And the Veil—staring at it gave Lee all sorts of conflicting urges. She wanted to pull away. She wanted to reach out—it was insubstantial, like fog, and would probably fall apart if she managed to touch it, but she wanted to try.

"Tell me, Lee . . . what do you feel? What do you see? What do you hear?"

"Just the Veil, Eira," she whispered. The silvery shimmer of the Veil thickened, wrapping around her until it was all she could see. When she breathed it, it was like she took some of that barrier inside her, like breathing in smoke.

She felt terror. Not just her own, but like it was coming from others. "I can't see anything. It's all gone silver again. But—there's fear. I feel it." Her voice started to shake, and it was harder to separate the emotions she felt coming from the outside and what she felt on the inside.

The terror rose inside, choking her. Her vision dwindled down until the pretty shimmer of the Veil was replaced by a pinpoint of darkness. There was a heavy weight sitting on her chest, crushing her, squeezing all of the air out of her lungs, and she couldn't breathe.

She wanted to curl in on herself and hide, but she was frozen. Trapped and helpless, and when it came for her, she wouldn't be able to run. Wouldn't be able to hide. Lee didn't even know what the "it" was, she just knew it was deadly, knew it killed, and she knew it was ravenous.

A whimper slid free and finally she could move, but small, surprisingly strong hands closed over her arms and wouldn't let go. They tightened to the point of pain and then Lee realized Eira was there.

"Pull away from it for now, Lee. Just pull away. The Veil will be there tomorrow. Relax . . . breathe . . ." Eira's voice grew rhythmic once more, soothing, gentle . . . quieter and quieter. The fear faded away and Lee could finally breathe. "You feel their fear, Lee. You have power inside you that comes from the land, and when the people of the land live in terror, it can reflect back on any soul that has a connection with it. But you can't let it control you."

Lee took a deep, shuddering breath. "I couldn't stop it."

"Just breathe. You have to breathe through it, breathe past it. You can't block the fear, but you can keep it from taking control of you." She rubbed her hand over Lee's back in a slow, soothing circle. "You need to center yourself. Focus. Breathe . . ."

The remnants of fear slowly faded away and Lee was left with only the sound of her breathing to keep her company and the soft monotone of Eira's voice. Time stretched out. Lee was caught in that weird place between dreams and waking when everything felt both too real and not real at all. Time moved at a crawl. Darkness gathered around her and still, she drifted. Eira's voice faded away but Lee never noticed.

There was a weird, muffled sound. Lee came hurtling back into awareness with a jolt and jerked on the stump. It was nearing twilight. And the small clearing she sat in was completely empty, except for herself.

Eira was nowhere in sight. A breeze drifted by, bringing with it a sharp, metallic scent. Blood.

Lee licked her lips. "Okay. I'm now officially freaked out." She didn't like knowing what blood smelled like. She didn't like knowing that she knew she should know what blood smelled like, and worse, that she had smelled it before.

Part of her wanted to walk away. Screw walk.

She wanted to run. She was alone in a weird place and the woman who had been with her had disappeared into thin air. Lee was pretty sure that Eira couldn't literally disappear, right? But would she have just left? Or had she been taken?

"Eira?" she said quietly. She didn't want to call out. She didn't want to make too much noise, because then it would hear her.

It. That nameless, faceless evil that she had sensed when she looked through the Veil, but Eira had told her that nothing was there. Eira had been wrong. It was out there in the woods, something devastating and deadly, waiting in the darkness. Her skin felt tight and her heart pounded within her chest, a horrid, breath-stealing fear that whispered to her, *Run—run away and don't stop*. She couldn't run, though. Not until she found Eira.

She kept seeing that stooped little figure in her mind, how Eira had looked out at the base camp, her black eyes softening as she spoke of times long past. There had been a longing, an emptiness in her voice that had brought tears to Lee's eyes, as she told Lee, "It hasn't always been like this here . . . Once it was different."

"Different, how?" Lee had asked. She shouldn't have asked.

"It was better." Eira had laughed bitterly, staring out over the broken landscape.

Lee hadn't thought. That was all there was to it. She should have thought before she spoke. "Better? Holy hell, what wouldn't be better than this?"

Eira had looked at Lee with tears in her eyes. "Aye. Even hell would be better than this, love. And this is the only home I've ever known."

Blocking the memory of that voice in her head, Lee blew out a breath. "Where are you, old woman?" There was no answer. Nothing but the rolling crawl of evil that she sensed in the air. It stung her skin, like a hundred angry hornets. It left her with a nasty taste in her mouth and the urge to just run away. Run far and fast. But Lee didn't know where she'd run to.

Somewhere in that black forest, there were monsters. Like the kind she used to have nightmares about when she was little, except these monsters were real. Staring out into the night, she whispered, "If I live through the night, God, it's going to be a damned miracle."

She pushed up off the stump where she'd been sitting. Her muscles were aching and stiff, but each beat of her heart sent adrenaline pumping through her veins. The tension changed, going from the stiffness of inactivity, to the tight, preparatory state, to fight or run.

Run—she only wished. As much as she wanted to take off and get as far away as she could, it wasn't going to happen. No, the adrenaline buzzing through her system was preparing her to fight.

Her body didn't even feel like her own. Lee didn't usually move this quietly. She wasn't a klutz, but she was pretty certain that when she walked, she made noise. People did make noise, right? Yet her feet moved over the uneven, unfamiliar ground with an easy grace, sidestepping the hundreds of little things that would have given her away—a stray leaf, a skinny branch.

Part of her mind was screaming and raging, demanding she run somewhere and hide. Hide from the monsters. *You've lost your mind, Lee! Run away before you get yourself killed!* The weird thing was—she knew she wasn't going to get killed, not now, not this time.

Lee felt alive. She hadn't ever felt this alive.

Her mind was ticking away, cool and clinical, taking note of everything. She could see each obstacle in her way: a fallen tree limb, some dead, dry leaves that would crunch and crackle underfoot. She automatically took the quietest path to the tree line, not the quickest.

She couldn't even hear herself breathing—she felt it. Damn it, she hadn't ever been so aware of her own breathing. But it was like she could feel the air moving in and out of her lungs. She could feel each beat of her heart. A bird flew overhead, and she imagined she could feel the change in the air currents above her as the falcon's wings pumped up and down.

There was the faintest lessening of the darkness ahead of her. They hadn't set a fire. These particular demons didn't need to. They were fire. Ikacado demons. The fire things from her dreams. More—it was one of them that she had sensed when she looked into the Veil. Eira had said there was nothing, but the old woman had been wrong.

And because Lee didn't know what in the hell she was doing, something bad had happened to Eira. And Lee herself was in a heap of trouble. Lee wasn't sure exactly how she knew that, but the knowledge was there nonetheless. It was like some weird curtain in her mind had parted just enough to let little bits of knowledge filter inside.

Ikacado demons. Lee hated the Ikacado. They weren't walking pillars of fire—they were humanoid, but their skin got fiery hot in battle, hot enough to melt flesh and internal organs. That wasn't their only built-in weapon, either. They were living, breathing vacuums, feeding off the terror and fear of others.

Psychic and magickal energy was a particular treat for them. Random little memory flashes danced through her mind. People killed by the Ikacado—their bodies melted down so that they no longer looked remotely human. Bodies drained of power and left behind like empty husks.

Even though the Ikacado demons were formidable bastards, they acted more like coyotes. They didn't attack outright. They stalked. They hunted. They looked for the weakest link: the old, the sick, the young—the solitary.

If it wasn't for her magick, the old woman probably looked like a damned feast to them: old, weak . . . alone. But Eira *did* have her magick. Typical Ikacado wouldn't have wanted to fight that, not without a hell of a lot more firepower—literally—on their side.

They would have left her alone . . . right?

Unless . . . what if Eira had gotten hurt *before* the Ikacado showed up? What if she'd gotten hurt, or sick . . . Oh, hell. That would have explained it. More of that weird knowledge flickered through her head. Ikacado were scavengers by nature, usually bypassing anything that could put up much of a fight.

Lee drew close, pressing her back to a tree and peering out at the horde of Ikacado with narrowed eyes. The things couldn't see too well unless magick was being lobbed around—Lee bit her lip as she absorbed that piece of information.

All the statistical kind of information filtering into her head wasn't going to do her any good. Because Lee was in no way ready to fight something like that. What she needed was a good, old-fashioned cell phone, or this world's version of it, so she could make a 911 call. Lee had gotten this far. But she didn't know where to go from here and she was likely to end up dead.

A misshapen head turned her way, and she eased back out of sight, pressing against the tree. Closing her eyes, she prayed silently. This is stupid. Stupid stupid stupid.

High-pitched, chittering shrieks rang out. Had they seen her? But before that thought had even really circled through her head, she knew the answer. The words made sense when they shouldn't . . .

I don't want her. She's old. Old power is tough. I want something fresh. Let's go to the human camp. We can find one of the guards.

I'm not going there.

Coward! Humans—bah. Thin-skinned things. They break and tear too easy.

Lee wanted to press her hands to her ears to block out those ugly, alien voices. It was almost easier if she didn't understand. Because now she had to wonder, what else did she know?

You know how to hurt them. This voice spoke to her from inside her own head, sounding oddly like her—yet not.

Everything inside her went still. That curtain wasn't just parting and letting little bits filter through. It was like it had been ripped wide open and she could see herself standing on the other side. Well, at least, it looked like her. Physically.

She wasn't just looking at a reflection, either. She could hear herself arguing. With herself. The urge to laugh wildly and hysterically rose inside her as she met her other self's gaze. The blue eyes were her own, but they were filled with cynical, cool knowledge that made Lee feel vaguely useless.

Fight them. You know how.

No. I don't.

That reflection of herself smiled a little. *Yes, you do. Fire creatures do not like anything that is not what they are. They are fire. Be what they aren't.*

Then the curtain dropped again, cutting off the weird, internal dialogue. Once more, Lee felt like she was alone in her head. Alone and totally, completely confused. A little scared, too, because as much as she'd like to write everything off as a hallucination, as much as she might like to think she was suffering a mental breakdown and that was the root of the strange twists her life had taken, Lee knew she couldn't.

It was all real. Every last bit of it was truly, completely happening. That was what really scared her. Bravado worked wonders, though, even when she used it on herself. Instead of acknowledging that fear and letting it swamp her, she muttered, "Great. Not only am I arguing with myself, I'm doing it in riddles."

Then she edged out and found herself staring with measuring eyes at the Ikacado. *Be what they aren't.*

They were fire. Their skin glowed a dull ruddy orange. They didn't look hot, and from where Lee stood, she didn't feel heat. But she could almost remember battling them. Heat that scorched, melted and burned. She slid her gaze just a little to the left. Up against a tree, she saw a slumped, still form. Eira . . . she wasn't moving. She was alive. Lee didn't know how she knew that, but she did. Hurt, but alive.

Be what they aren't.

Everybody insisted that she had some kind of magick inside, learned and forgotten. None of that made sense to Lee. Nothing made much sense right now. All Lee knew was that Eira was hurt, probably in serious trouble, and Lee was the only one close enough to do anything. Too damn bad Lee felt like she couldn't fight her way out of a wet paper bag, at least not in this world. Back home, she might be confident enough in her abilities to defend herself.

Here? Different story. But that voice inside her head kept whispering, and she knew it wasn't going to shut up anytime soon.

The knowledge is already inside you—stop fighting what you are . . . what we are.

Scrunching her eyes closed, Lee muttered, "Damn it, I've gone and developed another personality on top of my other problems."

Then she opened her eyes. Looked down at her hands.

She could do this.

The Ikacado were talking, gathering together and

murmuring to themselves. *Hungry . . . the camp. Wait until they go scouting, then we could . . .*

Lee narrowed her eyes. *My ass, you will.* Not that these things would likely pose much threat to Kalen or his camp. Not enough of them, and Kalen's people were too well trained, too disciplined to make the kind of fatal mistake the Ikacado were hoping for. But she'd be damned if she'd risk it.

Be what they aren't . . . The voice was seductive, compelling. It kept whispering to her over and over, until Lee was more focused on the voice than on what was happening in front of her. Lulled by that compelling, demanding voice, Lee was only vaguely aware that she had moved. She never realized how pale she had become. How cool her skin was getting. Her feet moved, but she didn't feel connected to the movement in any way. She didn't feel the ground beneath her feet and she didn't feel the wind blowing hot on her face.

All she was aware of was that voice in her head. *Be what they aren't . . .* The high-pitched chitter of their speech hit her ears, but this time it didn't make much sense. It served like a bucket of cold water thrown in her face, though, and she realized just how close she stood to them.

She couldn't hear anything past the roaring in her ears. Some part of her was terrified, but that terror never made it to the surface. Confidence settled over her like a cloak, and Lee faced them down and knew she wasn't afraid. They couldn't beat her.

One rushed for her, touched her like he was going to knock her to the ground. He fell away screaming, as if the touch of her skin hurt him. Another lunged for her. She lifted one hand and it felt like somebody else was controlling her movements—a puppet on a string.

Something white and gleaming launched out from her palm—icy cold. It struck the lone Ikacado in the chest and Lee watched as it fell down, its dull orange skin turned black.

Two more were left on their feet, and both attacked. She

went down under them, the weight of them crushing her into the ground. Clawlike nails tore at her flesh, and fists that felt like lead weights pummeled her. Their touch burned. She wanted to scream.

She sucked in badly needed air and nearly choked as the heat of it blistered her lungs. The temperature of the air had risen with the fury of the Ikacado, and it was burning her, burning her alive. Their hands were hot on her body, and they grew hotter with their fear. It scalded her, and dimly she was aware of the pain, but her mind shoved it away before she could even begin to analyze it.

Lee screamed out in fury, and as she did, something changed. Ice surrounded her, and flesh that had been scorched and hot was suddenly cold. The Ikacado crushing her into the ground screamed out—their rising voices blended in the air, a symphony of anger and pain, and then abruptly, it was cut off, as the rushing in her ears grew to a cacophonic roar. Bright, blinding pain flashed behind her eyes.

Vaguely, she realized she was freezing. Ice cold. And wet—rivulets of something hot and thick flowed over her body. The things were gone. Nothing grabbed at her and the high-pitched, enraged chittering of the demons had gone silent.

But none of that mattered because that pain in her head was expanding, and even if the demons were still there, they wouldn't have a chance to kill her. The pain was going to do it.

Something touched her ankle, and that icy shroud that wrapped around her seemed to grow. It expanded. There was another screaming growl. A wave of darkness washed up and pulled her under.

SIX

Damn it all to hell.

Kalen felt the cold wind dance along his flesh, and for one second, he almost froze from the terror. All morning, he had been cooped up in one of the watchtowers with Laisyn and Dais, debating over whether or not they should send for reinforcements from the east. They needed them, desperately. Laisyn, the only other witch with moderately noticeable power, had agreed.

Laisyn wasn't the powerful witch that Eira was, but she was a wonder with the smaller magicks. Not to mention the fact that she had been born a fighter, not forced into it by lack of choice. Even if they had lived in a peaceful world, Laisyn would have found a way to fight, and win. She understood strategy, she understood that loss of life was inevitable in war, but she never lost her compassion, unlike many wartime leaders.

Her jet black hair was cut close to her skull, and her ice blue eyes had focused as she listened to Dais explain the risk of sending for reinforcements and why he felt they needed to wait and see how things progressed before tak-

ing that risk. Then she had politely dismissed him and repeated her own assessments. "We're running out of time,
Kalen," she'd said, her words an eerie echo of his own gut
feelings.

Dais would have argued the point for hours, but the flicker
from the gate had made Kalen's decision for him. Laisyn
had sensed activity from the gate as well. It wasn't even
midday when they felt the ripple. It was brief, very brief,
but the gate had flickered for a few moments, and he knew
something had come through.

Brief or not, it spelled trouble. The gate hadn't been active long enough to disrupt the energy flow, but it was still
bad news. It wasn't even close to night, and the Warlord
bastards rarely tried to use the gate during the day. For
reasons unknown, the gates' powers were far too erratic
during the day. With the sun still burning its way behind a
thin veil of clouds, they should have had a few more hours
of relative peace.

"I've made my decision, Dais. Laisyn, find a small team
and get them on their way. I want them out of here before
noon." Laisyn acknowledged his orders with a respectful
nod before she left in silence. Dais opened his mouth,
probably to object, but Kalen shook his head. "I don't have
the time or the patience for this."

As if to underscore those words, the power swelling
through the air spiked, and Kalen took off at a run, following the trail of power. As he tracked it, rage and fear
tangled inside him. He knew that power, recognized it as
well as he would his own. Kalen knew the scent and feel
of it. It was Lee. He had no doubt, no question of that. It
was more magick than he'd expected to feel from her for a
while—deadly and controlled, the way her magick should
feel.

He also sensed the oily, slippery darkness of demon
magick. Ikacado demons, he suspected. This was bad, bad
news, and it was just getting worse. The gate opening during the day, a pack of Ikacado—the feel of Lee's magick in
the air and the conspicuous absence of Eira's.

He felt a whisper of power touch his mind. "Whatever it

is, you have to handle it, Morne," he barked as he ran through the woods. He clutched his plasma rifle in one hand and a long, wickedly curved blade in the other. He used the blade to cut through the manderkay vines that hung down from decaying trees and tried to wrap around anything that passed underneath. "I've got a mess on my hands."

A bigger mess than you think. Sirvani, my friend, and moving close.

"Bloody hell." He didn't waste his breath talking out loud anymore. *We need reinforcements in the clearing along the eastern boundaries.* He cut off his mental link with Morne and focused on Lee.

The trail of magick was fading fast. He needed a transport. Fucking transports. Bring in a transport and he ran the risk of the wyrms. So he continued on foot, running through the woods and praying he'd make it in time. He was getting closer—closer, but the power trail was gone. His gut knotted. He didn't sense the Ikacado either.

Magick didn't just stop like that. An abrupt end to a power trail could only mean one of two things—the magick worker was dead or seriously injured. An ugly dark inkling moved through his mind, but he cut the thought off before it could fully form. She was fine. He hadn't waited for her all this time only to lose her so quickly.

God wasn't that cruel.

Almost there—he smelled blood. Lots of it. The acrid, bittersweet stink of demon blood. It was thick and heavy in the air, making it impossible to smell anything else. So much blood—

Far off in the distance, he heard the low, melodic chanting.

Of all the threats he could have to face, the Sirvani were probably the last ones he wanted to deal with right now. Raviners, Ikacado, even the wyrms could be deterred. Granted, the wyrms required plasma charges planted in the trails, but they could be turned back.

The Sirvani? No. They wouldn't turn aside, especially not if they had caught scent of Lee. Young, beautiful and so full of a barely tapped power, she all but shined with it. They would turn back when they had Lee and not before. If they caught sight of her, death was the only thing that would stop them. Killing one Sirvani, or even a few, wasn't the hard part, though.

Their sheer numbers were the problem. Kill one, ten would take his place. Where in the hell had they come from? The gate hadn't been active long enough for the Sirvani to come through. They never traveled with any less than an army, and that took several hours to mobilize. Had they been waiting . . . ? Shit. Or trickling through in twos and threes—the odd flickers from the gate could have been the Sirvani. Coming through in small groups and lying in wait.

The fear was taking hold of his brain, but he battled it into submission. He had a job to do, and panicking wasn't going to help Lee or Eira. Besides, this was Lee. Whether she remembered it or not, she had a gift for getting herself out of trouble. She could handle herself with the Ikacado. Kalen had to believe that.

All he had to do was get to her before the Sirvani did.

*　*　*

Get up.

The voice was back, drumming into her mind, nagging her, pushing her out of the warm cocoon of oblivion and back into the bright, blinding pain of consciousness.

She wanted to go back into the darkness, but that voice in her head wouldn't let her. Finally, Lee opened her eyes, but she wished she hadn't. She was covered with—stuff. Slimy thick goop and things she didn't want to put a name to. She lay shaking on the ground, trembling, drenched, covered with—

Oh, shit. Bits and pieces of ice and other things clung to her hair. Frozen, disgusting little gobbets of flesh, tissue and . . . It hit her like a sledgehammer what she was covered with. Body parts. She was covered with body parts. And the demons . . .

No. No. No . . . Lee huddled into a fetal position and

closed her eyes, trying to block out what had just happened.

It hadn't.

That's all. None of that had happened. She hadn't just killed seven . . . seven things in seconds. She was an artist, for crying out loud. An artist—not a warrior. But she was surrounded by bits and pieces of dead Ikacado demons. She was alive, and they were not. They had bodies that were living, breathing weapons. And Lee had just a soft, human body.

She was alive.

They weren't. Son of a bitch, most of them weren't even in one piece.

Slowly, she hoisted herself into a sitting position, shoving her wet hair back from her face and looking at the mess in front of her. Just to her left, she saw Eira's still form. The old woman hadn't moved.

Her eyes were still closed. Just barely, Lee thought she could make out the faint rise and fall of Eira's chest. Breathing . . . thank God. If they'd killed her— A knot rose in her throat even considering it.

Resolutely, Lee insisted that the tears blurring her vision were because she'd hate to think she'd put her neck on the line all for nothing. But as she got onto wobbly legs and made her way over to the huddled form, she felt a wave of relief sweep through her that left her too weak to stand. Collapsing beside Eira, she wrapped herself around the old woman and muttered a quiet prayer. Without even realizing what she said, Lee murmured, "You're safe now, corida."

Corida—it meant "wise one," and how Lee even knew the word, much less its meaning, she didn't know. She swallowed the knot in her throat and tried to think. She had to get Eira away from here. But how . . . She brushed Eira's wispy white hair back from her face, tapped the old woman's cheek and hoped she'd wake. "Come on, old woman. Wake up and talk to me. Help me out. I just saved our asses, now it's your turn. I'll be awful pissed if I went through that and then we get wasted before we get to safety."

"Lee."

The sound of his voice was just about the sweetest thing she'd ever heard. Lee rolled to her knees and looked at him. She went to stand and realized that things were dripping off her, like water rolling off a raincoat. Bits, bones and blood—vomit boiled its way up her throat and she was going to be sick. She knew it.

She lifted her hands and stared at them. She whimpered as something pulpy dripped off her hands. Hypnotized, Lee watched as it fell to the ground, landing with a wet plop. Hysteria rose inside her. She could feel it, a screaming, whimpering, pathetic sound echoing through her mind.

"Lee."

She blinked and looked up at him. He crossed the clearing and knelt in front of her. He reached out to catch her hands, but Lee jerked away. "No. This—it's all over me."

Kalen didn't even blink. "I've seen worse," he said flatly. He pulled her up and stared down at her. "Hold it together, Lee, okay? Just for a few minutes."

Lee shook her head. "This stuff—it's all over me. It's in my hair. It's all over my hands . . ." Her voice rose, climbing higher and higher. Hysteria had her tight in its grip, and Lee didn't think she could hold anything together, not for another second.

He shook her. Hard. Her hair flew into her eyes, his fingers digging hard into her flesh. "Look at me." His voice was hard and angry, and she blinked in surprise. But she looked at him. His silver eyes had darkened to a thunderous gray, and anger etched lines into his face. But his hands gentled. He reached up, and Lee realized he had something in his hand. It felt soft against her skin as he wiped some of the blood from her face and hands. "You can hold it together, Lee."

"Fuck me." It was a low, amazed murmur, full of shock and maybe a little bit of pleasure. The new voice intruded and Lee flinched.

She followed Kalen's gaze and saw a man enter the clearing. She jerked against Kalen's gentle hold, ready to run and hide. She couldn't handle any more right now. She knew it. Kalen didn't let go though. "All is well, Lee. He's with us."

There was something alien about the new man. He was tall. Ridiculously so. His pale hair was so blond it was nearly white and his skin was pale, pale as snow. But his eyes were a deep, dark black. His gaze skimmed over the clearing, and a faint smile tugged at his lips as he looked toward Lee. "Well done."

A hysterical giggle slipped free but turned into a sob. She pressed a hand to her mouth and managed to stop the flood. Temporarily. She knew it was temporary. She was going to break down soon, but she couldn't do it now. She didn't want to do it here. She wanted to be someplace safe when she finally broke down.

Well done.

For some reason, that just amused the hell out of her.

Well done.

She had body fluids and body pieces all over her.

Well done.

She was bordering on hysteria.

"Shut up, Morne," Kalen muttered.

The tall blond, Morne, Lee assumed, just shrugged. "Eira . . ."

Eira—the weird amusement died and Lee swore. She started toward the old woman, but Kalen's hands wouldn't let her go. She smacked at him and demanded, "Let me go. Damn it. She's hurt."

"Morne can take care of her." Kalen caught her hands and forced her to look at him. "You've done enough, Lee. Let us handle it now."

That sounded awfully good. *You've done enough*—hell, he could say that again. Those creatures were pulpy nasty things now, not much of a threat. "Yeah, enough," Lee mumbled.

Kalen gave her an odd look but then looked back at the other man. Lee blinked. She felt kind of sleepy all of a sudden. Nothing felt real—it was like she was trapped in some hyperalert dream state. Man, another angel face—but he wasn't a dark angel like Kalen. No, he was a fair one.

There was nothing pure or innocent about him. He'd be fun in front of the camera—

Kalen said something, and the sound of his voice distracted her from Angel Face, and she looked at him, squinting a little. Forget the angel boy. Lee wanted Kalen in front of the camera, with his hard face, quicksilver eyes and that black-as-sin hair. Naked. Oh, yeah. She'd take a dark angel over a fallen one any day.

Kalen glanced at her again and there was a weird look in his eyes. Like he was worried or something. Then he looked back toward Eira. He muttered something hard and unintelligible under his breath. "We don't have time to do this here, Morne. The Sirvani—"

"I know." Morne glanced toward Lee and asked, "Will she make it to camp?"

Lee scowled. Angel Face was talking about her. She didn't like being talked about. She frowned at him and said, "I can speak for myself." At least, that was what she planned to say. All she got out was . . . "I." Then her teeth started chattering and she couldn't focus her mind on anything. Not talking. Not walking. Nothing.

Dimly, she heard Kalen's voice. Then she felt his arms come around her and her feet left the ground.

". . . move. They're close."

". . . daylight . . . . no sense . . ."

Their words were a blur, blending together and not making any sense at all.

Who were they? Lee didn't know what they were talking about. She could hear the steady, rapid beat of his heart and feel the warmth of his chest against her cheek. Wind on her face. They were walking. Practically running.

And there was a noise—she could hear it. Almost like singing. Rhythmic. Almost tribal. Faint, but getting louder and louder . . . *What is that?* she tried to ask. But the words couldn't get past her tight throat.

She didn't have to ask, though. That voice was in her head again, whispering, *Sirvani.* The monotonous, tribal beat of drums. Voices that rose and fell with the beat of the drum. Getting closer.

Images flashed in her head. Men slipping through the dark, silent as death, pale ghosts, swooping down in the night like a hawk. They came and they went without making a sound. The only sign of their passing—homes empty of the families that once lived there. Sometimes the bodies of the missing were found. But only males. Beaten to bloody pulps.

One image after another danced before her eyes, and Lee whimpered, trying to pull back from all of it. She felt a mouth caress her temple. A soft, rough voice. "Shhhh . . . you're safe now, Lee. I promise."

Kalen—

She reached out and her hand touched his chest. She bunched her hand in the soft, stretchy fabric of his shirt, clutching it as though she could pull herself closer to him. Safe. She felt safe—Kalen made her feel safe. If she could stay just like this, wrapped in his arms, maybe this strange, scary world wouldn't seem so damned strange and scary.

* * *

She dreamed of angels, demons and dark saviors.

Demons that screamed and tore at her flesh. Fire that ate her. Weird dark eyes so black against white flesh—his mouth parted, but when he spoke, the words didn't seem to be any language she understood.

His hand on her face, forcing her mouth open. She gagged, choked and sputtered as he forced something thick and noxious down her throat. Kalen's voice: "Calm down, Lee. Just drink it. It will help." Then silence, sweet, blissful, black silence.

She floated in the darkness for a while and then it started all over again. The man with hair as pale as snow and eyes as black as midnight was back and he was trying to kill her. Had to be. Whatever he was forcing down her throat had to be poison. Nothing that tasted that toxic could be safe.

The third time he tried to get her to drink it, she spat it back out at him and punched in his direction. She caught him in the throat, and when he let go, she tried to jerk away from him. His hand came out, catching her upper arm. As it was, that hand on her arm was the only thing that kept her from hitting the floor.

He laughed and said something she didn't understand. Lee jerked on her arm and demanded, "Let me go."

Angel Boy cocked his head and studied her in a way that Lee decided she really, really didn't like. Like she was some sort of smear on a slide and he was the scientist peering through the microscope, trying to figure her out. "What? You understand me?" she demanded when he still didn't let go. Lee jerked on her arm again and very slowly said, "Let. Me. Go."

"I understand you perfectly, Lelia." He let go slowly and remained standing close enough that she could feel the warmth coming off his body.

Lee's brows dropped down low over her eyes and she snapped, "My name is Lee. Just Lee. *Capisce?*"

Now he looked a little puzzled. "Your speech is so very strange. Lelia, Lee, I shall call you whatever you wish."

What about a cab? Can you call me a cab that will take me home? she thought longingly. She took a step away and he followed her. Another step—yep, still mirroring her movements. "Can you back off?"

"Indeed. When you return to bed. If you remain upright for much longer, you will end up collapsing and then Kalen will threaten to pull out my tongue and strangle me with it." A faint smile curved his lips, and Lee got the feeling he wasn't too concerned about that happening.

She sniffed and said, "Go on. I'm fine. And if Kalen did try to strangle you, I think you can handle yourself."

A pale brow, so blond it was nearly white, lifted and he gave her a weird little smile. "Regardless, I would prefer that you return to bed. I have my hands full dealing with one patient. I would rather you not join her in the medicon."

Lee wanted to tell him to take a hike. She felt fine. Really. Well, her head was hurting something awful. Throbbing, actually. And oddly enough now, her legs were feeling really weak. But she wasn't going to let him see that. The dizzy spell had passed and that was all she cared about. Deliberately, she took a step to the side, away from the bed he was herding her toward. "I'm hungry."

She started toward the weird little refrigerator where Kalen kept food. She would have made it, too. Her legs weren't that wobbly. Really. But the door opened and she looked toward it. Saw Kalen.

Their eyes met and Lee thought, *Whaddya know . . . a man looking at me really can rock my world.* At least, it sure felt like it.

His quicksilver eyes flared and he crossed the room in three long strides. Strong arms came around her waist, and she gasped as he pulled her against him in one quick motion. He pressed his face against her neck and muttered something too quiet for her to understand.

Just that simple touch was enough to undo her. The strength drained out of her legs, and she would have fallen if he hadn't been holding her so tight. Tears stung her eyes, blurred her vision, and no matter how hard she tried to blink them away, she couldn't stop them. And once the tears started, it was like a dam broke open inside her and she began sobbing. Soft little hiccups at first, and then they turned into deep, body-wracking shudders when he lifted one hand to her head and murmured, "Go ahead and cry, sweet baby. You earned it."

Lee broke in his arms. Kalen could feel her shattering. From the corner of his eye, he saw Morne leave. As the door closed behind the deiron, Kalen lifted Lee in his arms and carried her to the narrow cot. She'd spent nearly thirty hours in that cot, unconscious yet so wracked with pain that Morne had been forced to keep her drugged just so she could rest.

The awful herbed teas the healer forced down her throat had restored her color, and Kalen could no longer sense that brittle, sharp pain radiating from her mind. No, now she was just a raw mass of confusion, fear and shock. She didn't understand what she had done. She was horrified by it. Scared.

Her hands balled up, clutching fistfuls of his shirt, and he could feel her tears soaking through the material. His heart ached, and he wished there was a way he could take this from her. Wished they didn't need her so much. Wished he could just understand why they needed her. And it all blended with guilt, because even now, in the face of her tears, he couldn't regret her being here.

Kalen closed his eyes. For the rest of his life, he was going to remember how she had looked when he got to the clearing. They still didn't know what happened—Eira wouldn't have ever let the Ikacado steal up on them like that. She would have called for help. So something had happened to Eira—all sings pointed to a stroke, but they couldn't know for sure. The medical equipment that could have definitively diagnosed such a brain injury wasn't the kind of equipment they kept on hand. Even Morne, as skilled a healer as he was, couldn't look inside the brain.

Eira had been lying near a tree, her eyes open but not really seeing anything.

A dead demon lay a few feet away, his entire body blackened as though he'd been burned. That was what cold did to the Ikacado. Cold-beam lasers were very effective against the fire creatures, but neither Eira nor Lee had a cold-beam on hand.

There was another lying at the very edge of the clearing, and he had a hole in his chest. A big hole, big enough that Kalen could have put his fist through it. No blood, though, and the edges of the wound were black and slippery, as if whatever had made it had melted the flesh. He'd seen wounds to the Ikacado like that before. Cold-beams, powerful ones, could do that, but they left a much, much smaller wound.

That wasn't the worst though. The worst had been the bits and pieces scattered all over Lee as she knelt by Eira's side. Lee had been covered with ichor, thick black blood and pieces of flesh and tissue. The small clearing looked like a body explosion, and Lee seemed to have been caught in the middle of it.

Kalen guessed that was about what had happened, too.

Lee had done that. How, he wasn't sure.

He knew she had powerful magick inside her; he'd seen

it. But the power to blow something up just by touching it—it was mind-blowing. The look of horror and fear in her eyes was going to haunt him. If she hadn't killed them, they would have killed her, and Kalen was damned glad she had been able to defend herself.

But what he wouldn't give for that to have not happened.

He'd give his very soul up if they could live in a world where none of them had to fight just to survive.

Gently, he stroked a hand down Lee's back. Her sobs had subsided to soft, broken little sighs that caught in her throat. He pressed his lips to her brow, felt the warm, damp silk of her skin.

More.

He wanted more. Lee had come too close to death—she didn't understand it yet, but that kind of magick was deadly, even to its user, until control was learned. She could have died, using a power that was too strong to be held inside a mortal body. She would be weak for a few more days, and it could be a couple of weeks before her mind healed enough to use magick again.

But his body didn't care.

All his body cared about was hers, warm and soft against his. She shifted a little, turning into him, and her hip rubbed against his cock. Already swollen, already demanding that Kalen do more than just hold Lee, the unyielding length of flesh jerked and throbbed. Lee stilled in his arms. Blood rushed to his face and he muttered, "I'm sorry."

Slowly, she lifted her head and stared up at him. Her lashes were spiky and wet from her tears, her eyes a deep, dark blue. She had tears drying on her face, and her eyelids were red and swollen. But she looked so amazingly beautiful to him.

She licked her lips and shifted. Kalen's heart thudded to a stop as she turned and straddled him, placing one knee on each side of his hips. "Don't be," she whispered. Then she lowered her head and kissed him. He tasted the salt from her tears and something so sweet, so intoxicating, he could have it every day for the rest of his life and he'd still be starving for it.

Her hands, soft and cool, cupped his face as she kissed him. He wanted to haul her against him, roll her onto the narrow cot and tear her clothes off. He wanted her naked and open for him, reaching for him. Then he wanted to mount her, push inside her and watch her face as he took her. Over and over, until she screamed his name. He wanted her addicted to him, craving his touch the way he'd craved hers for years.

Craved, but couldn't have. Not until now. She was warm and soft in his arms and he tasted the hunger in her kiss. But he also tasted the tears. She was still weak—Lee was so damned lucky she hadn't killed herself. Lucky she hadn't knocked herself out. Unconscious and vulnerable. Suffering saints, he didn't even want to think about it.

It made his hunger burn brighter. Sex reaffirmed life. Making love to her would ease—maybe ease—the knot of need inside him. But she had cried so hard. Finally broke under the pressure of all the bizarre changes life had handed her.

Easing away from her—hell, it would have been easier to stop breathing than stop kissing her. Less painful, at least. But he pulled back, bit by bit. She tried to follow him and he cupped her chin in his hand. "You don't need this right now, Lee. You need to rest. You need—"

She smiled. When God made women, He shouldn't have given them the ability to smile like that. It was like glimpsing both heaven and hell. That kind of smile held the promise of paradise and the threat of hell because when a woman smiled like that, it meant she knew. She knew she was driving a man insane, and she could either put her soft hands and mouth on him, put him out of his misery, or she could pull away and leave him suffering.

With that smile on her pretty mouth, she reached down and grasped the bottom of her shirt, pulling it off. That silvery blond hair floated free around her face in a riot of curls. Her eyes glowed like blue fire as she uncurled her body and pulled away, standing up.

At some point, one of the women had cleaned her up and dressed her in something comfortable to sleep in. That didn't include much more than that thin shirt she'd already peeled away and a plain, simple pair of panties that rode low on her hips. Plain white cotton hadn't ever looked so erotic as it did hugging her hips.

"I know what I need, Kalen. And it's not more rest." She moved toward him, and when she went to straddle his hips again, he cupped her ass in his hands and rocked up against her. Three rough, convulsive thrusts—but it wasn't enough. He surged upward and turned their bodies, putting her beneath him on the cot, just like he had fantasized. Her blond hair framed her flushed face and she gave him a feline smile, all heat and satisfaction.

"Be certain, Lee. Very certain." He held himself away from her, bracing his weight on locked arms. Hellfire, he wanted her so bad, he was shaking with it. But he had to make sure, because if this went much further—hell, any further—he wouldn't be able stop. It didn't matter if a new gate opened up at his feet and the worst Anqar had to offer came boiling up around him. Any more, even one more touch. Shit, she wouldn't even have to touch him to push him over. Just keep smiling like that—

A soft, husky laugh fell from her lips and she reached up. The soft pads of her fingers touched his lips and he caught one in his mouth, sucking it gently. "I'm certain. Actually, it's the only thing I've been sure of since . . . well, for a long time."

"Good." He covered her body with his and kissed her. He didn't rush it, though. He wanted to, suffering saints; he wanted to tear that small scrap of underwear off her, rip his clothes out of the way and shove his cock inside her. Hard, fast, until they both came, and then he'd do it again, but slower.

Instead, he traced the outline of her lips with his tongue. She opened for him and he pushed inside, slowly—so slowly that Lee reached up and fisted her hands in his hair, clutching him close as she tried to take the kiss deeper.

"No." He lifted his head just enough to break contact

with her mouth. He nipped her lower lip gently. "I have waited far too long for this—I will not rush it."

Lee lifted her legs and wrapped them around his waist. "I want to rush—I don't like waiting."

Her legs tightened, pulling him against her. Kalen let her, rocking against the soft heat between her thighs, but when he kissed her, he kept it teasingly light. He kissed his way over to her ear. She had three silver hoops piercing the lobe. He nuzzled them and then murmured, "Do you know how long I've waited, Lee?"

Lee groaned and turned her face, trying to kiss him, but Kalen was content to nuzzle her neck, or press little biting kisses to the soft, sweet-smelling flesh. "Years. I've waited years, sweet baby, and I'm not going to hurry this.

"Years," he muttered again. Her breasts were small, but firm and round, topped with pink, diamond-hard nipples. His mouth watered just looking at them. He flicked a glance up at her and smiled. "I've dreamed about this more times than I can count. I've made love to you in every way imaginable—in my dreams. But those bloody dreams can't even compare to the reality."

A weird look flitted through her eyes. "We never . . . ?"

He bent his head and licked one round little nipple. "No. Never. But we're going to remedy that, right now." He bit her gently and she gasped, arching up against his mouth. He took her deeper in his mouth with a gentle suction. With his tongue, he teased and stroked her nipple. Lee groaned. Her hands fisted in his hair, urging him on. He didn't need the encouragement, though. The woman in his arms was the only one he'd ever really wanted, in all his life.

Lee's body was an endless delight. Those small, ripe breasts; narrow torso that gave way to round hips. Long, strong legs and the most perfect ass he'd ever seen. She had a woman's body, sweet curves in all the right places, and under all those curves lay the strength of a warrior. Satin-soft and steel-strong. Her skin was pale and smooth as ivory, but so warm under his mouth. The soft, sleek muscles in her tummy rippled as he pressed a kiss to her navel.

When he pressed his lips to her sex, Lee mewled, a broken, hungry little female sound that twisted him into knots. He slid his tongue through the slick folds and she bucked against his mouth. Kalen lay his arm across her belly, holding her still as he took the intimate kiss even deeper.

Her taste was sweet and spicy, intoxicating and wild. He could do just this, forever. With slow, lazy strokes, he teased the tight bud of her clit. Under his arm, she twisted and squirmed, as though she couldn't get close enough. He pushed his finger inside her and she clenched around him with a ragged scream. She was still shuddering from the climax when he pushed up on his knees and stared down at her.

Her face was flushed. Her thick, black lashes lay on her cheeks, shielding that dark smoky blue gaze. Ragged breaths had her breasts rising and falling in an erratic rhythm. Her nipples were flushed, swollen and nearly the same shade of pink as her lips.

Kalen stroked a hand up her side and cupped her breast in his hand. With his thumb, he stroked a slow circle around her nipple. Her lashes lifted and she looked up at him. A slow, sexy smile curved her lips and she reached for him. That simple gesture was enough to shatter him. He went into her arms and took her mouth. She brought her legs up, her knees squeezing against his hips as she rocked up against him.

His patience blew apart—she was silky wet. He could feel it through his pants. With a harsh groan, Kalen lifted up just enough to free himself from the too tight confines of his clothing. He was so hard he hurt with it, his skin stretched so tight over his throbbing length, even the brush of air against his cock was torture.

He gritted his teeth and pressed against her. She was slick and warm and so sweet—she slid her arms around his neck, pulling him completely against her. Her breasts flattened against his chest. Her hips lifted to meet his and she turned her face toward his so that their mouths met.

And against his chest, he could feel the rapid, erratic beat of her heart. He dropped his shields and he could sense Lee's wonder, her staggering pleasure. The same as his own. He groaned against her lips and hooked his arms under hers, holding her so tight. He couldn't imagine ever letting go of her. Not now.

Her arms wrapped around his neck and she arched up to meet each thrust. It was sweeter than any dream. "I have dreamed of this," he whispered against her mouth. "So many times."

Lee smiled against his mouth. "Me, too. And there's no comparison."

"None." He reached down and caught her hands, linking her fingers. "Nothing can compare to heaven."

Truer words had never been said, either. She wrapped her thighs around his hips, squeezing tight. Her heels dug into his low back and she arched up, taking him deeper. A smile curled her lips and she watched him. Her sheath flexed around his cock, slow, then she did it again, and again. Kalen groaned. He reared back and slammed into her, shafting her hard and fast.

Lee's eyes widened. She whimpered, a hungry, hot little sound, and then she bucked under him. Kalen lowered his head, pressing his mouth to her neck. He raked the skin lightly with his teeth and then bit down where the neck curved into the shoulder. Lee went stiff under him, her sex clenching down around him, squeezing his cock so hard and tight.

She climaxed around him. The sound of his name on her lips, soft and ragged, as she came was the sweetest sound he'd ever heard. He rasped out her name. He kissed her, and as she continued to shudder and quake from her orgasm, Kalen gave in to his. She milked it from him with a series of slow, convulsive little pulses, dragging it out and out, until he didn't even have the strength to pull back.

His arms gave way and he collapsed against her, with their hands still entwined.

SEVEN

"Two surveillance teams, ten men each."

"Just ten?"

Kalen gave Dais a flat look. "Yes. Ten. As much as I'd like to send a full contingency, we can't spare that many men. Two teams, ten men each." Sending more than that was just asking for trouble. Somehow, the Warlords always knew when their defenses were down, and that was when the gates would open.

Kalen wasn't risking it. His gut insisted that this uneasy quiet wouldn't last much longer, and he wasn't going to send out any more men than absolutely necessary.

Dais ran a hand over his beard. He looked like he had something else to say, but instead he just nodded. His faded green eyes narrowed as he studied the huge map before them. It had been carved into a table's surface, and it was highly detailed, down to the rivers, streams, caves and abandoned villages, with the ruins of New Angeles making up most of the western edge. He tapped his index finger to the far northwestern quadrant and said, "We're running short at this checkpoint, Kalen."

Silently, Kalen thought, *Isn't that a startling piece of news?* It was always worst in the west. Out loud, he responded, "There is nowhere we aren't running short, Dais. We're doing the best we can."

"Perhaps we should send word back east. Certainly some of the camps can afford . . ."

"I've already done that," Kalen reminded him, shaking his head. He frowned a little, studying Dais's face. "We talked it over with Laisyn and we sent word. At the time, you didn't seem to think it was necessary."

With a weary sigh, Dais nodded. "Yes . . . yes. I'm sorry, Kalen. The past few days have me edgy as hell. Can't even think straight."

A wry smile appeared on Kalen's face and he replied, "Understandable. What reinforcements can be spared will be here when they can. Winter is coming as well. Sooner or later refugees in the mountains will come."

Dais's lip curled. "Refugees. And you think they will be much help? They were too cowardly to come to us and ran to hide in the mountains. We do not need refugees who would rather hide than fight. If they come to us because they must do that or freeze, we don't need them."

"That isn't fair, Dais." Kalen turned away from the former security officer and moved to the small table that he used for eating. The meal on it had long since gone cold, but he sat down and took a bite anyway. They weren't running short on food yet, but they couldn't waste it either. "Not everybody has the experience behind them that you have." He leveled a steady look at Dais and reminded him, "Not all of us were given the formal training you received."

Hell, if it wasn't for the refugees, his forces would be lesser by a third. At least. Many of them had resisted at first, thinking that the sudden influx of demons and Sirvani was something they could hide from.

There had been a time when the gates opened only sporadically. Kalen didn't remember it, but his father had. A century ago, the opening of the gate was rare, happening perhaps once or twice a year. Steadily, it became more and more commonplace, and by the time Kalen was born, Ishtan had become a world where the raids happened on a monthly basis.

In that other life, decades ago, specialized units were trained to deal with the gates. That was where Dais had been trained. Then the raids increased and the specialists were killed before new ones could be trained. They lost more and more of the people to the war. Eventually governments failed, the advancement of technology stopped and war became their way of life.

Dais made a disgusted sound. "They run into the mountains and hide, but they still cower in the night and pray for deliverance. They'd be better served to work for that deliverance than to pray for it."

"I think we'd all be better served to do both," Kalen said mildly. "And that's enough on this subject, Dais. You have teams to prep and I have work of my own."

Dais left without a word, and Kalen, appetite gone, stood up and paced away from his desk to stare outside. It was a quiet day, relatively cool and breezy. The breeze had cleared some of the smog, and Kalen could even see the faintest bit of sky far, far off to the east.

Deliverance. He had always seen himself as something of a cynic, but compared to Dais, he wasn't. Not at all. He'd spent more than half of his life praying for a way out of this. That hope had dimmed over recent years, only to burn anew when Lee came into his life.

He had to wonder, though, was it wrong to place such a burden on her shoulders? She was simply human. Just like him. Instead of the more common psy skills, she had true magick, but even true magick wasn't going to stop the raids from Anqar. Yet he couldn't shake his gut-deep belief that Lee was the key. Magick aside, there had to be something more to her than what he saw.

If magick alone could solve their problems, they wouldn't have any. Eira wasn't the only witch in Kalen's world. Her daughters had all inherited her gifts, ranging from weak to extraordinary. There were other witches out in the world. Nearly every resistance unit that fought to keep a gate secure had at least one mid-level witch. And there was nothing the witches could do to the gates themselves. They could disrupt them enough to shut a gate down, but that was only temporary.

The only way to win would be to destroy the gate.

There was a chiming sound behind him, and he glanced toward the old-fashioned clock hanging on his wall. The clock had belonged to his mother. It was old, relying on the simple mechanics of wheels instead of any sort of technology, and made of polished, smooth wood. The soft, soothing chimes at the beginning of each hour produced a sound he could remember hearing for as long as he'd been alive.

Time to go see Eira. Morne and the medics were keeping her under close watch, and visits were structured and purposefully kept short so the old woman could rest.

Leaving his half-eaten lunch behind, he headed out the door. Maybe speaking with Eira would help.

* * *

"Look at you, old woman." Kalen smiled gently as he slipped into the narrow room where Eira rested.

She tuned her head and looked at Kalen. One side of her face looked like a mask, her eye dropping down, her mouth slack. It almost looked like a wax mask with one side having been exposed to fire just long enough for the melting to start.

Neither Eira nor Lee could fill in the details of what exactly happened, so all any of them could do was guess. Eira had guided Lee into a trance, the old woman remembered that much. She'd sensed the approach of the Ikacado and hadn't been concerned—Eira's powers were formidable. After checking on Lee, she'd left the clearing to go deal with the Ikacado on her own. Dealing with a couple of firebreathers was nothing she couldn't handle.

But then something had happened; her vision had suddenly grayed out and she couldn't stand. She remembered stumbling, then falling—after that, her memories of that day were nonexistent.

It was like she'd stroked out with a couple of power-hungry monsters breathing down her neck and the only other person around had been caught in a trance, completely unaware.

When Lee came out of the trance, she'd known something was wrong, but she hadn't known what. All she'd been able to tell them was that Eira hadn't been there and Lee had known something was wrong.

It was a damn miracle *she* hadn't been found by the Ikacado. If they'd come on her while she was in a trance, Lee would have been dead in a heartbeat.

The other side of Eira's face was practically normal as she shifted a little to meet Kalen's gaze as he approached the bed. Her right eye was bright and sharp and she smiled just a little. "Old woman—aye, I truly feel like an old woman today."

Her voice was slurred, but at least he could understand her. Kalen had seen his fair share of people who'd received a serious brain injury and for whom even something as simple as talking was outside of their abilities. Being able to speak with her was nothing short of a miracle. Already, she was sitting up in the bed, aided with pillows but still, it was a sign of her strength of will that she was sitting up at all. "You look wonderful, corida."

She snorted. "Like bloody hell, that's what I look like. Don't be kind, boy. I know better." Her eyes closed and she sighed. "Your mind is troubled."

Kalen smiled reluctantly. "And I thought I was hiding it."

Eira laughed. The sound seemed to tangle inside her throat and choke her. He waited until the coughing fit passed, and then he took the water glass from the small chest serving as a table. He held it to her lips and she sipped the thickened water slowly. Some of it dribbled out and he carefully wiped it away. Eira turned her head aside but not before he caught the sadness and shame there.

"Corida, you call me. Bah. All I am is an old, helpless woman," she murmured. "We can't afford to keep somebody at my side night and day."

"We can," Kalen said in a flat voice. "And we will."

"I do not wish to argue this with you again," she said tiredly. She glanced toward the doorway, and Kalen knew she was thinking about the battle-trained medic he'd assigned to watch over her. Thinking about it, and hating it. But surprisingly, she said nothing. He was relieved, because he wouldn't argue this with her again.

He wouldn't leave her unguarded, not again. She saw herself as a weakness, a hindrance. Kalen simply saw her as a friend that he intended to protect.

She shifted a little and sighed, holding out a hand to him. "What is weighing so heavily on your mind, Kalen? Is it Lelia? Are there problems?"

He settled beside her and accepted her hand. Watching her, he caught sight of something in Eira's eyes. A flicker. A smile that was there and then gone. "Lee has always been a problem," he muttered. Then he shrugged. "All in all, I would say she is doing well. It's a drastic change she's had to deal with. It can't be easy."

"She needs some time."

Kalen swore under his breath. "That's the problem, Eira. We don't have that much time. Something is coming, I can feel it. I don't know if Lee is going to be ready. She has too much to deal with, and while she's doing her best to cope, I'm trying to figure out how to buy time and I feel like I'm running out of options. I don't know which way to go now, how to act—none of it."

"You don't act, Kalen. You react. You wait for the raids, you set traps—very successful ones, but traps nonetheless. Defensive tactics. We need offensive."

Kalen felt the dull rush of blood to his cheeks. He fought down the instinct to lash out, because even though it sounded like criticism, he knew it wasn't. "I can't think of a way to go on the offensive, Eira. The gates will not yield to us, and the few times we have gotten our hands on a Warlord, he used the gate's power to kill our men. We can't keep losing them like that."

"I know, Kalen," she said gently. Then she sighed tiredly and closed her eyes. He thought she'd drifted to sleep and he stood to leave.

"When will you send Lee to me? I have so much yet to teach her and time is no more my friend than yours."

He went stiff. Send Lee to her? Was she trying to hasten her death? She needed rest. Without turning to look at her, he said, "We have discussed this, Eira. Not until you are better."

"I'm not going to get much better, lad, and we both know it."

He didn't know that. He wouldn't believe it. "Wait a little longer, Eira." She already looked better than she had a week ago. But she wasn't ready to get back to training Lee.

"Kalen, you know as well as I that we cannot afford to wait. We cannot. There are things I must tell Lee and I will not risk my time running out." She fell silent for a moment, studying him with gentle, understanding eyes. "You call me corida and I know you mean it. You've always respected and trusted me, even when others thought I was going mad. Trust me now, Kalen. You are our leader here and none will go against you."

He shook his head. "You are too weak, Eira."

"And I will not get stronger, Kalen. This is a simple truth." He flinched at her words, and she seemed to understand exactly what was going through his mind. "I am dying, Kalen. Time and rest will not change that. What else have I to do? Lie here and just wait to die?" Eira asked quietly. "I wait already."

"You are not dying," Kalen said softly. Standing up, he shook his head and started to pace the narrow, confined space. "You're not."

But he knew he lied. There was only so much they could do for someone suffering from recurring strokes. Damage done by advancing age was something outside of a healer's ability. Morne had done what he could, but it had been precious little.

If she had another stroke, Eira would be gone.

But Kalen didn't want to think about that yet. She was a fixture in his life. Save for the war and Lee, she was the one thing that had always been there, and even more rare than that, she was a welcome constant.

The war had been raging his entire life.

Lee had been there more than half of his life, but there had been times when her presence was almost too painful, the way she came and went, appearing and then disappearing like smoke.

But Eira was constant. He could count on her honesty. He could count on her listening when he needed it. Simply put, he could count on her. He always had been able to. He wasn't ready to let that change.

"It has to change, boy."

He looked up and flushed as he realized he'd been broadcasting his emotions, his shields dropped so that he was wide open. Eira had picked up every last thought. The stroke hadn't affected that part of her brain. Slowly, he sat down beside the bed. The medic lingering at Eira's side left silently. Kalen held out his hand and Eira lifted hers. He closed his fingers around hers and squeezed.

"It is changing, boy. I'm sorry for it—you need me still. All of you. Lee is not ready. Perhaps if Elina was here, she could take my place and train your warrior woman. But she is not." Each word was slow, stilted, but her voice was determined. "Send for her. Elina will come. She can train Lee, and together, the two of you can battle back this darkness. Perhaps even defeat it. I only wish I could see it."

"You will." Kalen tightened his hand and made himself smile. But it was a lie, both his words and the smile, because he could all but see the death lurking on her.

"No." Her one good eye narrowed, and she gave him a glare he could remember from childhood. The one that meant she wasn't going to buy any innocent line he might hand her to get out of doing whatever it was he should have been doing. "You were never a liar, Kalen. Do not start now."

She tugged her hand from his and pressed the control on the bed railing. The ancient bed rose at the head, degree by degree, and she shifted around. Kalen reached over to help and she stilled. "I may be old and dying, but I am not yet dead. If I need help, I shall ask."

Finally, she settled back against the mattress with a

weary sigh. She closed her eyes and without looking, she said, "The damage inside my head cannot be undone. Some of the medics are working on an herbal concoction. Could buy a few more weeks. I'll use those weeks to do what I can with Lee. Fight me on this, Kalen, and I will spend those last weeks making your life hell." Her lids opened—well, the right one did. The left one did little more than flicker. "My brain still functions, Kalen. I am not dead yet. I am not yet useless. Let me do what I can. I have to do this."

He understood, that was the bitch of it all. He understood. If he knew his fighting days were done and death was lurking at his door, he would still want to fight in whatever way he could. But it didn't make it any easier to realize that he was going to have to let her go.

"I'm not quite ready to let you go, Eira." He tried to smile down at her, but he just couldn't.

Her fingers squeezed his, and Kalen couldn't help but notice how much weaker even that simple gesture was. Her faded eyes were compassionate and she looked at him with gentle understanding as she whispered, "Is death anything any of us can truly prepare for, Kalen? It's odd, you know—death is one of the few things guaranteed to any of us. But when it comes, it still shocks. It still startles. It still hurts. But I'm tired, Kalen. Try to understand that."

Understand it? That wasn't the problem. How could she not be tired, considering how long she'd been doing this? Kalen had been doing it twenty years and he was tired to the bone. Eira had been at it for more than sixty. So yes, he could understand it. The problem was accepting it.

* * *

Lee hadn't ever been much for meditating until Eira forced her to learn. She wouldn't admit it, but there was something very relaxing, very soothing about it. It made everything in the world fall away.

All that mattered was the beat of her heart. Each beat of her heart eased away just a little more of the tension that knotted her muscles. There was a soft, gentle breeze blowing through her hair, and she could feel each individual strand as it tickled her ears, her cheek, her neck.

She could hear leaves rustling, smell the warm scent of grass. A song. She could hear something calling to her, singing to her. Seductive and whispering of a power she couldn't even begin to understand. She could just barely glimpse the power, huge and unending.

It whispered and sang and danced. It had a tribal beat, something sensual and scary at the same time. She wanted to reach for it. Wanted to dive into that power and bathe in it. But at the same time, she wanted to run away and hide.

There was a darkness to the power. It permeated the earth, spreading through it like a disease. It rumbled and shook and shuddered deep, deep inside the land. The unrest had yet to surface. And still the drums beat. The music of it pulsed through her veins, singing to her.

Lee sighed, unaware she had done so, as she continued to peer inside the dark, shadowy storm brewing deep below and far away. Very far away. An ugly, black maelstrom and at the heart of it was the source behind the storm.

The song had gotten louder, too. Much louder—wrapping around her.

Her eyes were closed, but it was like she could still see. Her vision was weird, though. Everything felt surreal. She never moved her hands, but she could see herself reaching out. Reaching, reaching . . . until her touch sank into the earth . . . reaching . . . reaching . . . She touched her hand to that black maelstrom.

Something moved behind her. It was the quietest of sounds, faint, almost too faint to hear, so soft she never should have been able to hear it over the tribal drumbeat of the other music. The new song echoed through her head like a symphony, a wild, exotic music, so lovely to the ear—and so out of place in the storm.

It jolted her out of the trance and she froze as she realized she wasn't alone.

Even though she was still in the base camp, and thus relatively safe, terror flooded her veins. Instinctively, she tucked her body into a tight ball and rolled away. And instantly felt like a total fool.

It was Morne.

He wasn't what she'd call harmless. Not with that fallen angel face and dark, penetrating eyes. But he wasn't a threat to her, either. She didn't understand why she was so sure, but nonetheless, she was. As she stood, she brushed the grass from her pants and slid a hand through her hair. And Morne watched everything she did with a strange smile.

"Your magick grows. You must use caution when you study the Veil. There are many dangers on that path."

The guy had disturbing eyes, Lee decided as she stared at him and debated whether or not to say anything. It wasn't like he'd asked a question. He'd done what fifty other people had done since she'd arrived in this weird, terrifying world—given her advice she hadn't asked for. There was so much information flying through her head, and she couldn't make sense of it all. Sometimes she felt like if she had to take anything else in, her head would explode.

Or she would. Not physically, but emotionally. Her patience was worn so thin, it was a wonder she could have a rational conversation without ranting like a maniac. She was so tired, so scared and so freaked out, and when she wasn't trying to deal with all of the weirdness going on around her, she was trying to deal with the weirdness going on inside her.

Her feelings for Kalen. These strange new talents that seemed so out of control and so bizarre, but at the same time, still so natural. Then there was Morne, still standing there watching her with those intense black eyes.

"Are you going to tell me to—how do you phrase it . . . oh yes—shut my trap and keep my advice to myself?" Morne asked. A pale silver brow rose, and the smile on his face grew just a little.

Lee flushed. Okay, she had flown off the handle a few times lately. So what? She thought she was handling the situation pretty well. "What do you want?" Lee hadn't talked to Morne once since the last time he'd forced her to drink that disgusting tea—and she'd spat it out at him. As she sat back down on the tree stump, she grinned. It had almost been worth the taste that time, just to see it dripping off his face.

After all the times he'd shoved that crap down her throat, it seemed only fair. He still hadn't answered her. She watched from the corner of her eye as he circled around her. There was something very disconcerting about the way he watched her.

Morne crouched down in front of her. He wore his hair long, even longer than Kalen. It was even paler than her own—so pale a blond it appeared white in places. In contrast, his eyes looked black. Not dark brown, but a black so dark and deep the pupil was indiscernible from the iris. "You do not remember your magick, but your magick remembers you. It comes so easily to your call," he said. "I have to wonder how your powers would have grown if your training had started when it should have."

He reached out and touched his fingers to her face, tracing one roughened fingertip down her temple. "It glows inside of you. It surprises me that it managed to stay silent as long as it did," As he trailed his finger along her skin, he left a hot path blazing.

Something stirred inside her. It wasn't lust—not exactly, although Lee was acutely aware of the man in front of her. He was the picture of elegant masculine perfection, a contrast to Kalen's rugged, dark appeal. Elegant, even though he wore the plain basic garb all the people here wore: that matte black tunic and pants that resembled the cargos that were popular at home, but here, they served a much more basic purpose than fashion. Each and every pocket and loop was used. She could see a variety of weapons, guns, some sort of laser thing, blades. That matte black tunic was in fact armor, just as Lee had suspected. She'd been told it was strong enough to protect the wearer from laser pulses and the more commonplace blades and firepower.

Soldier gear, all of it, but Morne managed to wear it the

same way James Bond wore a tux. He moved with a sensual elegance and grace that Lee did find incredibly appealing. It was there and it was powerful.

But none of that mattered. It wasn't her body that was reaching for him. It was something else, something deep inside her—the same thing that had reached for the blackness she'd sensed inside the Earth.

Morne's hand fell and he rocked back on his heels, staring at her with appraising eyes. "Your power knows mine."

Mouth dry, Lee tried to shrug it off. "So what? According to Kalen, I've been using my power, whatever the hell it is, since I was a kid. I'm assuming you're not new to your power either and we've fought together before."

But it was more than that. A lot more. Lee knew that without him saying a word. "You and I rarely worked together. My . . . battle skills work better when I am alone. You had the luck of the saints avoiding serious injury and never needed my healing skills. Until recently. So it is not that we have meshed powers before. And I think you know that." His voice was low and hypnotic.

She could feel it again—that weird sense of something unfurling inside her, reaching out. And this time, it reached for Morne, and she could feel his power reaching out in return. His hand came up, cupping her cheek and tipping her head back. His eyes weren't black, she realized, staring into them. This close, she could see that they were blue. An impossibly dark blue, a blue darker than the midnight sky. His pupils flared, eclipsed, until even this close, his gaze appeared truly black.

She could hear the cadence of his heart beating, and it called to her like some sort of siren song. *Lub dub. Lub dub.* A heartbeat hadn't ever sounded so hypnotic. Or so loud. The beat of their hearts melded, pulsating in tandem until individual beats were impossible to distinguish. Lee wanted to pull away, but she felt frozen in place and she couldn't even blink.

"It must wake, Lelia," Morne murmured. "There is not much time."

Her tongue felt thick. She had to swallow to even speak. "Wake?"

"Not much time," Morne repeated. His gaze dropped and she could feel him staring at her mouth. "So clean," he whispered. "So untouched. Untainted. No wonder . . ."

His words ended abruptly and he pulled his hand back. When the contact broke, Lee felt like somebody had just thrown a bucket of water on her, waking her from a deep, confusing dream. When Morne spoke, his voice seemed to come from far off.

"Kalen."

Lee blinked. He didn't make any sense. None. "What?" She tried to ask, but she still couldn't speak clearly. Her throat was too dry, too tight. Morne was gone—he wasn't in front of her anymore, but he was still there. She could hear him talking.

She could still hear his heart. It no longer beat in rhythm with her own—no, his heartbeat was slow and steady while hers slammed away against her ribs in an erratic, unsteady tempo. She still couldn't move. Lee whimpered, and this time, she actually heard herself make a sound.

Lee sucked a deep breath in, and slowly, some of the fog faded from her mind. Enough that she was aware of something other than the sound of her heart beating out of rhythm with Morne's. It was Kalen's voice. Harsh and angry. Lee swallowed and looked up to find Kalen in Morne's face, his tanned face flushed even darker with fury.

He shouted something, but Morne just shook his head and smiled before he turned on his heel and walked off without looking back at Lee. Each step he took away from her seemed to clear her head, and by the time he was out of sight, Lee felt a little more like herself. She could think.

Lee could also hear, and that probably wasn't a good thing, either, because for some reason, Kalen was pissed. She wasn't quite sure why, but when she looked into his pewter gray eyes, there was no doubt about it. They glowed hot and bright, swirling from dark, thunderous gray to misty silver and back again. She hadn't heard half of what he'd said, and nothing she had heard made sense. Slowly, she stood, her tense muscles uncurling. Sitting in one place for a couple of hours sure as hell made the body stiff.

"Would you quit yelling and tell me what in the hell the problem is?" she asked when he paused long enough to take a breath.

For a second, he looked a little startled. "What the problem is? What the problem is?" One hand shot out and fisted the neck of her tunic. He jerked and she flew forward, crashing into his body. "You spent the night in my bed. You've spent the past week in my bed. And I find you letting Morne put his hands all over you?"

Fury bubbled and spilled over, side by side with shock. She shoved at his chest and snarled at him. "You bastard. He didn't have his hands all over me." Had he? Hell, Lee couldn't remember half of it. She remembered Morne slipping out of the woods. Approaching her. He had said some things, and like a forgotten song, his words lingered just beyond her grasp. But he hadn't touched her, had he?

One side of her face burned. Itched. Vaguely, she remembered his hand there. Okay, maybe he had touched her. But just her face—that was it, she thought. And she couldn't believe what Kalen was implying. He wasn't really . . . But one look up at his face and she knew he was implying just that.

Lee twisted away from him. She struggled her way free from his arms and got loose, although she knew it was only because he let her go. They might insist she was some kind of warrior here, but she sure as hell didn't feel like one. She knew the self-defense she'd learned through the Y—so what if it had seemed to come to her very easily? She'd gotten a brown belt in tae kwon do before she got bored and dropped out. But she didn't think that compared to the kind of training these people had. Not just self-defense, but weaponry, battle tactics, subterfuge. Warrior stuff. And Kalen was about as hard core as it got, when it came to that warrior stuff. It didn't make her feel any better to stand there and look at him and know that she couldn't quite hold her own with him.

Shaken and hurt, Lee faced him with her hands bunched

into fists to keep them from trembling. "You bastard," she said, forcing the words through clenched teeth. There were others things she wanted to say to him, she knew it. But for the life of her she couldn't form the words. So instead of saying anything, she just bent over and grabbed her gear from the ground. She jammed her arms into the cavinir jacket as she stomped away. The light, flexible armor molded to her skin, and instinctively, she wanted to jerk it off and toss it on the ground, stomp on it.

The armor seemed alive at times, too alien for words, yet another reminder that she wasn't in Kansas anymore. Too damned far from home, and she didn't even have a cute little dog in a basket to cuddle and take comfort from. No ruby slippers either.

Stuck here. Even though she was outside, it suddenly felt like everything was closing in on her. Lee couldn't breathe. Couldn't think. She was too hot. Hot, irritable, confused—and scared. She'd felt something rumbling in the earth, and she'd felt the echo of power whispering to her when Morne touched her. Something familiar and terrifying all at once.

She started to head toward the small unit she shared with Kalen, but instead, her feet took another path. Retreating to the space she shared with Kalen wasn't the answer. She needed someplace a little more neutral than that, although there wasn't much neutral ground to be found here. And nothing that was hers.

Lee was almost shocked to find herself standing at the medicon. Eira lay inside, and oddly enough, Lee didn't feel any of the resentment she'd felt every other time she'd been in Eira's presence.

She felt—comforted, even though the sight of the old woman was enough to make her pause. Lee had seen stroke victims before, not often, but enough to recognize that that was what had happened. Half of Eira's body seemed to work as it should. She could move her right hand and right leg, but she couldn't even hold a brush in her left hand.

As advanced as the technology seemed in this war-torn

world, they couldn't undo the damage when part of the brain died.

"Something troubles you."

Lee jerked at the harsh sound of Eira's voice. Her words were slurred and she talked a little louder than necessary. It was like each word had to be ripped from her throat, and it gave her voice a guttural tone.

Her one good eye focused on Lee's face, bright as a bird's and full of curiosity. Eira patted the bed beside her and said, "Come. Sit."

For a second or two, Lee considered leaving. But she really didn't have anywhere else to go, and for some reason, talking with Eira felt—right. More, it felt like something Lee could call her own. Nobody had forced her here. She hadn't come to train, and she hadn't even come out of duty to check on the old woman.

So instead of leaving, she edged her way around the narrow cubicle that passed as a room and settled her hip on the edge of the bed. Concern welled inside as she studied Eira's face.

A graying brow lifted. "What do you see when you look at me? A weak, sick old woman?"

With a sad smile, Lee shook her head. "A stubborn, strong one. A weak woman would have already died."

Eira closed her eyes, but the corner of her mouth tugged up, pleased. "Strength, it's something you need here."

Lee shrugged. "I don't know. I think strength would come in handy everywhere. Although it's a bit more crucial here."

They fell silent for a time. Eira spoke first. "Will you tell me what bothers you?" she asked. She spoke with odd little stops and starts, each word stilted.

Swallowing around the knot in her throat, Lee said, "Kalen. Morne. Everything." She looked down and saw Eira's hand close to hers. Cautious, she closed her hand around the other woman's. When Eira squeezed her hand lightly, Lee found it a little easier to speak, but it wasn't the issue with Kalen that came to mind.

"Can you draw power from the gates?"

Now, that seemed to surprise the old woman. Her lid flickered. Then she squinted, studying Lee's face with shrewd eyes. "You saw them?"

"Yes."

Eira's face relaxed a little and she murmured, "Good. Good . . . So you saw the gates and the power there. A great deal of power."

That was an understatement. The one brief glimpse she'd caught before Morne's intrusion had been like staring at a tidal wave. Immense and unending. "I felt it." She licked her lips and tried to puzzle her way through the thoughts jumbling in her head. There was something important about that power. She had sensed it, felt it. "The power at the gates—where does it come from?"

Eira smiled. "From life, Lee. Life is power. It sinks into the earth, all around us, and it waits."

"Why is there so much at the gates?"

"The lives of two worlds are connected there. Many lives—it creates a great deal of power."

Quietly, Lee asked, "Is the power dangerous?"

"Power is a weapon. Its danger lies in the hands of those who would wield it. But none from our world can tap into the power of the gates. It doesn't know us. It doesn't recognize us. Most of us cannot even see it, talent or no. Whatever power is needed to manipulate them, we do not possess it."

"I was told that the power there isn't stable. That you can't tap into it. Who can manipulate it?"

Eira sighed. Her chest rose and fell in a heavy sigh. There was a faint, gurgling sound to her breathing, like there was fluid building up inside her lungs. Her lids drooped low over her eyes. "Warlords."

Lee dropped her head into her hands. The Warlords. So far, she hadn't seen the men that were spoken of only in whispers, usually followed by a sign that Lee had come to correlate with a Catholic crossing himself. As though even saying the word was enough to bring down the Warlords' fury and the speaker needed divine protection. "So nobody here knows how?"

Eira's undamaged lid lifted. Her gaze met Lee's. "It is not that we do not know. We cannot. The gates recognize power, but it is selective. It does not seem to feel our power—the gate will open to a power it recognizes."

"And it recognizes the Warlords?" She started to stand up and then she stopped. Looking at Eira, she leaned over and took the old woman's hand. "Do you feel its power? I do—it's like a song in my head. It was calling me, Eira."

A small, secret smile flirted with the unaffected side of Eira's mouth. "Tell me."

So Lee did. When she got to the part about Morne, she skipped some of it. Like the way she'd felt almost hypnotized when he stared at her. The music she'd felt coming from him. And the part about Kalen. She wasn't going to share that part. But the rest . . . yes, she told Eira about the music of the storm, the drums that seemed to call her name.

"Has it happened to you?" she asked when she finally finished. "Have you felt them?"

Eira was quiet for so long that Lee thought maybe the old woman had fallen asleep. "No. Magick isn't a song to me. I haven't heard these drums. But it doesn't surprise me that you have heard them." Eira yawned. "Lee, I need to rest. But come back—tomorrow. There are things I need to tell you, while I still can."

Lee stood reluctantly. She wanted more answers. She was so confused. She murmured a good-bye, but Eira was already asleep.

* * *

"This is quite an opportunity." Char glanced at his spy and nodded approvingly. "Yes . . . yes . . . a good opportunity. Tell me, my friend, where are their other witches?"

"Gone, Warlord. The old witch's daughter left for the east. It's safer there." The spy smirked and added, "Relatively speaking."

"Hmmm. And when Eira is gone, they have no true magick left?"

The spy shrugged. "What magick remains is minimal.

A few soldiers that have small fighting magicks, but nothing impressive. There is one other powerful witch, a woman. But she's young and she doesn't know her power yet. She has mastered her minor magicks, but the true power still lurks deep inside, waiting to wake. Without Eira there to train her, she will pose very little opposition. I don't know how reliable this woman is. She's come and gone before, for years. When events take a turn for the worse, I imagine she will do as she's always done and leave. When Eira dies, she will be the only one left with any true power, Warlord. The Sirvani have captured many that have been born the past few decades. The ones with significant power that haven't been captured have either died during the battle or have left."

Char tugged on his lower lip thoughtfully. "Not many witches left in this area at all." If he didn't already have other plans for his world, the lack of witches could prove to be a serious predicament. He did have his plans, though, and the witches bred well in captivity. Already the newest generation of Warlords was in training and proving to be quite powerful.

"What about the witch's daughter? Their weapons aside, if their witches are truly gone, the Roinan Gate is all but ours. Quite a coup, yet I can't see them leaving themselves so unprotected. They would send for help."

"The only daughter she had left retreated into the east. They have sent for her, but it will take time for her to reach them. They still will not use anything but the most basic means of transport for fear of the wyrms."

Char smiled. The wyrms had been an inspired choice. The High Lord had made few very wise decisions, but the wyrms were definitely one of them. It had been a risky choice, with possibly deadly consequences, sending battalions of Sirvani to the wetlands to harvest the wyrm larvae. The wetlands were far to the south, and the entire venture had taken decades to complete. The fools across the gate had no idea how long the Sirvani had been using their world as the breeding ground for the wyrms.

Wyrms were like addil fish, growing as large as their

environment would allow. In the wetlands to the south where food was scarce and the wyrms overpopulated, the things didn't grow so well.

But across the gates, the rich, fertile soil was like manna. They grew huge, so damned big they could swallow a flank of soldiers and still have room for more. And they were drawn to the pulse and thrum within the cities and towns. The power that the people relied on was like a siren's song, calling to the ugly beasties. Or maybe a dinner gong, Char thought with a smile. The cities beckoned to the wyrms, and the wyrms learned quickly that where they sensed that pulse, they would find food.

It was the wyrms that had turned the tide. The resistance armies had held their own against the Sirvani, even against the demons that Taise had sent through the gate.

All of Taise's plans had seemed madness at the time, at least to Char, who had seen the way the High Lord deteriorated, but that madness had worked in Char's favor. Even as he shook his head in disgust at the way Taise had allowed the demons to run amok in Ishtan, Char hadn't worried.

If he had been concerned about the continued need for slaves, Char would have been more worried, and indeed, he might have been forced to take drastic measures to protect the future of Anqar. But he already knew that they didn't need Ishtan—it was like a mama weaning a babe. The babe would fight, but Char had no doubts he would prevail over it.

Once Taise was out of the way.

But the wyrms, yes, they were inspired. The resistance had proved helpless against the wyrms—they were all but defenseless. It was almost pitiful.

He heard a soft sound and glanced up to meet the gaze of his spy. A broad palm, scarred and calloused, was held out, and Char smirked. "Always the mercenary, aren't you, old friend?"

A smile came and went. Char paid him, adding a little extra because the news had put him in such a good mood. Nature had done what his men had failed to do—eliminated the old witch. She might not be dead yet, but it wouldn't be long, not if she had another attack. With the witch out of his way, the Roinan Gate would fall so much more easily. Lives would be lost, but mostly men. The resistance had finally figured out they were wise to get most of their women away from the gates. What few remained would be warriors and healers, and Char's men knew that women weren't to be harmed, if at all possible. Securing the gate and the land beyond it would take some time, but he had reliable men he would leave in charge of that.

Freeing him to seek out his child.

"Shall I go with you to tell the High Lord?"

Char glanced at the spy with a frown. "No."

The man paused, a shrewd look in his eyes. "He may have questions."

He considered lying. The spy didn't need to know his plans. However, Char had been using his services for decades, had made huge strides with his personal plans thanks to the information the spy had shared with him. Char knew the man was a canny bastard, and he also knew the man had one major personality trait that would work in Char's favor. The man had no loyalties to any save himself, and the spy also knew that Taise's grip on reality was slipping, as was his ability to rule rationally.

"If we tell Taise, the High Lord will advance his plans on the final assault." Char wasn't prepared for that yet. The final assault that Taise had in mind would have a body count unlike any they had seen before. Char wasn't fond of waste, but beyond that, he wasn't going to let the old fool's asinine ideas interfere with his own plans.

From the corner of his eye, he watched the spy. "I have certain objectives, and if he moves forward, I may never meet those objectives."

"If I may?" The spy glanced behind him as though he were worried about being overheard. "You realize that if we conceal this information, the High Lord could consider us both in direct violation of his orders."

With a cynical smile, Char said, "We're both intelligent men here. We both know that even the greatest leader will eventually make . . . less than wise decisions. Some of those decisions may not have much of an impact. Others could prove detrimental to all who would follow him."

"And not reporting back to him as ordered could prove detrimental to me."

"You don't always report directly to Taise, my friend. Often you've reported to me, and in turn, I speak with Taise. We shall just let a few details of this conversation go unsaid."

Char watched the man think it over, and when the faint smile appeared, Char knew the man would say nothing. He slid Char a squinty-eyed look and mused, "It could be worth my while to decide that I have already been gone from my post for too long." He held out a palm and gave Char a beatific smile. "It wouldn't do for my absence to be noticed."

"Not at all." More money exchanged hands and each of them smiled. They understood each other.

Char watched as the man tucked away the gold and the paper currency used in Anqar. Then he angled his chin toward the door and said, "You had best be going, before you truly are missed."

Instead of leaving, though, the spy studied Char thoughtfully. "I wonder what your agenda is. You know how unstable the gates have become—while I do not think Taise has always acted with the utmost caution, I wonder why you are not leaping into action for a full-scale assault and grabbing as many females as you can. When the gate falls, it may be permanent. Do you not fear for the future of Anqar?"

"No. I do not. Unlike Taise, I have been preparing for this. His madness has made him foolish. A full-scale assault would suit his plans." With a thin-lipped smile, Char added, "But not mine. A full-scale assault could certainly secure more slaves; however, it would end with too many lives lost."

"You do not strike me as the type to worry overmuch about the loss of life."

"Waste offends me, my good man. It always has." Part

of the reason he was so determined to reclaim his property. A man's assets should be put to work for him, not left to flounder or die.

"Hmmm."

Char wasn't fooled by the noncommittal sound. He weighed his options. He could order the spy to leave. The man wasn't a fool—he wouldn't dare to ignore an order. Ignoring orders could lead to death in this world. But the man was too valuable a tool to lose over that. A valuable tool—an asset. Assets weren't to be wasted.

With that thought in mind, he paced away from the huge war table and moved to the window. It faced east, and far off in the distance, he could see the flickering green, blue and red lights of the gate energies. If he lowered his lids and focused, he could see the rippling energy forming the actual gate, superimposed over the physical earth. He could hear it as well, that vibrant, seductive song. But over the past few years, the song of the gate energies had become tainted.

Oh, it was still lovely, but too often the sweet flow of music was interrupted by a discordant thrum. That discord was now more part of the song than not, and the gate energies were splintering even as they tried to repair the damage. "Do you know how the gates work, my friend?" Char didn't bother to wait for an answer. "It's a disruption in the energy flow of both worlds. When the powers touch, they splinter the fabric that holds our world separate and the gates form. They are sustained by the lives of the worlds. A few souls here and there passing through the gate does little to the power base, but when huge armies pass through, the gate energies are pushed to the breaking point. Left alone, the gate could repair itself. But too many pass through and there is little time for the gate energies to rebuild. Soon they will falter and collapse, and travel between the worlds will be no more."

He glanced behind him to the spy. "Does this worry you? If the gates fall, you will not be able to run back and forth between the worlds, selling information. Already it becomes more difficult to raise my personal gate to bring you to me. In time, you will not be able to cross at all."

A faint, sly smile curved the man's lips. Avarice and greed shone in his eyes. "I will manage."

Char wasn't surprised by the response. Many had reacted with outrage, but this man was too practical to waste energy on something that he couldn't control. "Yes. I imagine you will." Looking back toward the gates, he said, "Time is getting away from us. Soon, the power will be all gone and the gates will close. There is something in Ishtan that belongs to me. It was taken from me years ago and I will have it back. Once I do, the gates can collapse and never again remake themselves. I could not care less."

Ever the enterprising bastard, the spy rubbed his palms together and said with a quick smile, "If you will tell me what you seek, perhaps I could help. For a minimal fee."

Char laughed. "You're a cocky bastard. How much money do you think you can bilk out of me?"

There was a knock at the door and both men fell silent. The spy moved on silent feet to the small lounge off the side of the war room, and Char waited until the man was out of sight before he opened the door. In the great hall, he could see his servants awaiting him, but he did not call them back into the room yet. Business such as his was too delicate to risk being overheard. Instead, he stood aside and let Arnon enter the room, and once the Sirvani had passed through, Char closed the door behind him.

Arnon's eyes flicked to the lounge and he murmured, "I have spoken with the High Lord."

He said nothing else, but Char understood the unspoken words. "A moment."

It took not much longer than that to get rid of the spy. When Char returned to the main chamber, Arnon was waiting in the exact the same position, his hands linked behind him, his gaze unreadable. As tradition demanded, Arnon's head was shaved bare. His clothes, from the tunic to his boots, were spotless, and Char knew that under those clothes was a veritable arsenal. A well-maintained one, at that. Arnon was one of the most powerful Sirvani in Char's army, and the most reliable.

Char trusted no one the way he trusted the man before him. Char might not reveal his objectives to the spy, but Arnon was a different matter. Not for the first time, he considered sending Arnon across the gate to help in the quest, but decided against it.

One thing Arnon couldn't do was blend in. One look at him, and the small resistance would know exactly what he was. Warlords and their offspring weren't easy to overlook, and Arnon was no exception.

"You look very grim."

"I have heard rumors about the old witch. My own sources confirm it is indeed true. Have you told the High Lord?"

Char shook his head. "No. And I will not."

Arnon nodded as though he had expected no other response. "We are on borrowed time, Lord."

From under his lashes, Char watched Arnon and replied, "I am fully aware of that, Arnon. Have you come with useful information or will you simply parrot back what I have already heard from a number of sources?"

A cool smile formed on Arnon's face. "I simply wonder what your spy had to say about any remaining witches."

With a dismissive wave, Char responded, "Little to none. One untrained witch in the immediate area, and the others are likely weeks away."

One dark brown brow winged up, but other than that, Arnon's face remained impassive. "One untrained witch."

Char chuckled. "It would seem we have been perhaps too thorough in the raids. Most of the talented Ishtanians have already fled, or were captured during the raids. Once Eira is gone, there will be no balancing force on the other side of the gate, and it will be only a matter of time before the power fluctuations completely destroy it. We must find my daughter before that happens."

EIGHT

"Lee."

It was hours later and Lee was too damn tired to deal with Kalen or his moods, but it was pretty damn clear he didn't care. Lee could all but feel the heat of his anger beating the air around her. The afternoon she'd spent avoiding him hadn't seemed to cool his temper in the slightest.

Damn. Just ten more feet and she would have made it inside and she could have collapsed onto the bed, feigned sleep. After a minute or two, she wouldn't have had to feign anything. Lee was tired enough that she knew within a few minutes of being horizontal, she would have been dead to the world. "I'm tired, Kalen. I don't feel like talking."

"Too bad," he snarled. His hand came down on her neck and he squeezed. Lee tried to keep walking, but he'd stopped, and that unrelenting grip on her neck wasn't letting go. He wasn't hurting her, but he wasn't going to budge either.

She recognized the futility of struggling, and rather

than suffer the indignity of trying and failing, she just stood there. "What do you want?"

He glanced around and scowled. Too many people were watching them without really appearing to. Lee could feel their eyes on them, and now self-consciousness piled on top of anger. "Not here," he muttered.

Anger chased away the weight of exhaustion, and the second the door closed behind them, she said, "If you don't take your damn hand off me, I'm going to bite you."

His head lowered, and he rumbled into her ear, "Go ahead. I'll bite back . . . but first . . ."

Jealousy had a good, tight hold on Kalen, and even though common sense told him he was overreacting, he couldn't stop. He kept replaying those moments over and over in his mind: Morne bent over Lee while she stared at him with a look akin to fascination. Their focus on each other had been complete. For a few moments, nothing else had existed, not the war, not the world around them and not Kalen.

He wasn't sure what pissed him off the most, Morne touching her—or that complete and utter focus that blinded them to all else. He'd known Morne for years—the enigmatic stranger had appeared in their midst years ago. Mistrustful of the man at first, Kalen had slowly gotten to know him, grown to trust him.

Kalen also knew his people. Women went nuts over Morne. It was almost like there was something inside the man that called to women. Even in the middle of war, the man wouldn't ever have to spend a moment alone if he didn't want to.

Morne barely seemed to notice. Kalen could count on one hand how many times he'd seen the man voluntarily touch anybody unless he was doing a healing. So why in the name of the saints was the bastard touching Lee?

When Kalen had stumbled upon them, there was something weird hanging in the air. Some odd, intangible connection.

He had only touched her face. Morne's hand cupping her cheek, his fingers pushed inside her hair, their faces close but not touching. Staring at each other. Lee had looked hypnotized. It wasn't something that could be called innocent, but neither had there been anything overtly sexual about the encounter. Still, anybody touching Lee was enough to enrage him.

Kalen growled and spun away from her to prowl the tight confines of the small cabin.

He couldn't believe . . . He bounced back from the disbelief, to the irrational fury. He swung back around to her and closed the distance between them. Fisting one hand in the soft, silky shirt she wore under her cavinir, he jerked her up onto her toes. "Why did he touch you? What did he want?"

Her soft blue eyes weren't so soft as she glared at him. They blazed like blue flame, and fury flushed her face a delicate pink. She closed her hand around his wrist and tugged in an attempt to dislodge his grip. "I don't know what he wanted. And would you quit acting like you found us rolling naked on the ground?"

Oh, now, that was the completely wrong thing to say. That image exploded in Kalen's mind and he jerked Lee forward. Her soft, strong body crashed into his as he lowered his mouth to hers. "Don't let him touch you again, Lee. You hear me?"

Any answer she might have made, he smothered with his lips. She wouldn't open for him. He angled her chin and squeezed her jaw until her mouth opened. The taste of her hit his system like a lightning bolt, electrifying and breath-stealing. Lee's hands pushed at his shoulders and she twisted in his arms even though her lips clung to his. He lifted her body in his arms and turned, pressing her against the wall. "You can't understand what it does to me, thinking about somebody else touching you," he murmured against her lips. He fisted his hand in the silky strands of her hair and jerked her neck to the side.

"Let go, Kalen." Then she moaned as he raked his teeth down the arch of her neck. Her hands fisted in his shirt and she pulled him closer, arching her hips and pumping against him. She circled her pelvis against his in a mad little shimmy, and those rocking, teasing gyrations had him gritting his teeth.

"Let go?" he repeated. He slid a hand down her side, over her hip, along her thigh, until he could cup her knee and bring it up high. Then he stepped between her thighs and pressed against her. She was wet and hot, he could feel it through the layers of their clothes, and he could smell her hunger in the air, wrapping around him. He could feel her own need in the way she moved against him, the way her hands clung to him even as she tried to push him back. "You don't seem to want me to let go."

"Bastard," she muttered. He nipped her earlobe and then lifted his head, watching as she slammed her head back against the wall and glared at him. Her face was flushed, color riding high on her cheeks, and under the fringe of her lashes, her soft blue eyes glittered hot as flame.

Lee squirmed against him and then brought up her other leg, hooking her ankles together at the small of his back. Kalen snarled as need blistered and burned through him. It was a demanding scream in his brain, and he couldn't think of anything but getting her naked. Didn't she understand she was his?

"I have been waiting for you," he muttered against her mouth. "For years. For this." He tangled a hand in the silky blond tresses and pulled, arching her head back and baring her neck. He scraped his teeth down the smooth white flesh and bit down lightly where neck and shoulder joined. "Just waiting for this. Can you understand that?"

He didn't wait for an answer, just kissed her hard and rough before continuing. "Then you let another man touch you. I don't want another man touching you. Not for anything."

Her gaze was fogged and hazy when he lifted his head to look at her. The soft pink of her lips had darkened and her mouth was swollen from his. She was so perfect, soft, strong, sweet as honey and volatile as fire. Desperate to get as close as he could, he reached behind him and unhooked her ankles. He fumbled with the waistband of her trousers, and his fingers refused to cooperate. Hooking his fingers under the snug band, he jerked them down, taking the silky scrap of underwear with them. Hunkering down by her feet, he fought to get the pants off. The thick-soled boots on her feet kept Kalen from completely stripping her naked.

"Shit," he swore roughly as he managed to get one of her boots off. His patience, what little remained, evaporated, and he didn't bother with the second one. Lee leaned against the wall, her hands braced on his shoulders. She still wore the cavinir jacket, and her pants were tangled around one ankle when he leaned in and pressed his mouth to her sex.

The downy soft curls were already wet. Lee wailed out his name when he nuzzled those curls and licked her through them. The taste of her exploded on his tongue, and he reached up, seizing her hips and holding her pinned in place. He circled his tongue over her clit and then pushed inside her. She clenched down around him and moaned. He pushed her harder, alternating between caressing her clit and penetrating her with his tongue, until she exploded against him.

Lee's long body arched and trembled. Her nails pierced the skin of his shoulders. He caught her wrists in one hand as he stood up, pinning them against the wall above her head. With his other hand, he freed himself from his pants. Their gazes locked as he stepped between her thighs. With a slight dip of his knees, he pressed the rigid length of his cock against her.

She was wet and slick, hot and tight, and she squeezed tight around him as he pushed inside her. "Do you still want me to let go?" he rasped against her lips.

"Yes . . . my wrists. Let go of my wrists."

Slowly, Kalen let her go, and when he did, she caught his hands and twined their fingers together. "I don't want another man touching me," she whispered. Passion clouded and darkened her eyes to midnight. That midnight-dark gaze locked with his, and a slow smile curved her lips. "Just you. Only you."

She brought her legs up, hooking them over his hips and locking them at the base of his spine. Her back arched and Kalen dipped his head, pressing a kiss to each shoulder, the upper curve of her breasts, then to her neck. Her pulse slammed against the fragile shield of her skin, he could feel it. Her flesh was slick and gleaming with sweat.

"You're so lovely," he muttered. "So perfect."

The sexy smile on her lips widened a little. "You talk too much, Kalen." The tiny muscles of her sheath flexed around him in a teasing, rippling caress. She did it again and again, until he groaned and crushed his mouth to hers.

The miracle of touching her was that she made him forget. With their bodies joined, rubbing against the other, Kalen could forget, just for a while, that there was anything in the world beyond them. He could forget the war, he could forget the friends he'd lost, and all the years he'd spent without Lee.

The sound of her moan was like angel song to his ears, and the taste of her some rare, forbidden fruit. He wouldn't ever get enough. Greed and need had him moving on her hard and fast, determined to take as much as he could, and equally determined to give her as much pleasure as he took. Her body moved against his, so soft, so strong.

Her hands still entwined with his, he lowered them and guided hers around his shoulders. Then he skimmed his hands down her sides, cupped her hips and canted them to a higher angle. He felt Lee's reaction shudder through her body, each muscle tensing, her pupils flaring wide. She bucked against him, and a soft scream slipped free. Her hips circled against his, and Kalen groaned. The little convulsions of her pussy caressed his cock from base to tip, pushing him closer and closer to orgasm.

She wasn't quite there yet. He cupped her ass in his hands and drove into her, a series of short, hard digs that kept him in contact with the bud of her clit. Lee's breath caught—he heard the erotic, needy little gasp—and then she started to come. A series of long, hard spasms wracked her body, and a sharp scream echoed from her mouth. He caught it and swallowed it down and followed her over the edge.

When he could move again, Kalen shoved off the wall, still holding Lee's body tight against his. A few wobbly steps took them to the bed, and he tumbled them both down on it. He could smell his scent on her, and hers on him. Her lips were swollen from his, and his mouth had left little reddish marks on her neck and chest. He captured one wrist in his hand and lifted her hand up so he could kiss her palm.

"Mine."

She sighed, a sexy, content sound, vaguely feline. "Hm-mmm."

He gave his heart a few minutes to settle down, and then he lifted up onto his elbows and stared down at her. Slowly, her eyes cleared and she smiled up at him. Kalen lowered his head and covered that smiling mouth with his own.

"Again."

NINE

Kalen trailed his fingers down her arm and stared at the faint bluish marks forming on her wrists. He laid his hand over them, lining his fingers up with the bruises and brooding. "I left marks on you."

Lee popped an eye open and stared at him balefully. "Ummm. Let me rest a little and you can do it again." She pressed her face against his shoulder and snuggled in closer. "Sleep."

"Go ahead and sleep." They'd spent more than half the night making love, and Kalen was pretty sure he was drained. At least temporarily. His body was exhausted, too, but his mind wasn't shutting down. He rubbed his chin back and forth over the top of her head. The silky tresses smelled like dusk-roses. Soft and seductive. Not enough softness in his life. He didn't know how to deal with softness, and that much was pretty damned clear, as evidenced by the marks he'd left on his woman.

"You staying?"

"I'm not going anywhere," he promised. He kissed the crown of her head and whispered, "I'm sorry, Lee."

The eye opened again, and now a faint smile appeared. "What are you sorry for?"

Kalen closed his eyes and muttered, "I should have known you wouldn't make it easy." He lifted her hand from where it lay on his chest, and he kissed the bruises. "It's not this. Although I feel like I ought to be sorry for marking you, I'm not. Earlier, when you were with Morne, I was wrong. I knew even as I said anything that I was wrong." Then he opened his eyes and squinted down at her. "I still want to know what was going on."

The smile faded and she sighed. Her blue eyes were dark and troubled. Confused, even. "Yeah. Me, too. And as soon as I figure it out, I'll tell you."

She closed her eyes again, and slowly her breathing eased into a more regular pattern. "He's a weird guy, isn't he?" she murmured sleepily.

Lee never heard his response. She was sound asleep before she even finished the question.

* * *

Lee accepted the small disc from Eira. Puzzled, she stared at it before glancing up at Kalen. He took it from her and flipped it over. The minute the matte black surface faced upward, the black dissolved and colors shifted inside. He held it out to Lee and she took it back. But she almost dropped it as something seemed to leap out from inside the thing.

Not something.

Someone.

"Whoa." It was like a . . . hologram, or something. But the technology of it was far more advanced than anything Lee had seen. She'd seen some of the best technology available in her world and coveted a lot of it. Pieces of equipment that costs thousands and thousands—or tens of thousands. And all of it paled compared to the small egg-sized disc in her hand and the image it displayed. "Wow. What is this thing?" she asked, rubbing the edge of the disc with her thumb and staring at it in wonder. The image wavered and then disappeared, and Lee scowled. "What did I do?"

She caught a glimpse of Kalen's amused smile and resisted the urge to stick her tongue out at him. "If you could see some of the technology we used to have, you would truly be amazed," he said. He reached out and thumbed a tiny depression, and Lee grinned as the woman's image reappeared. "It's an emsphere. Once upon a time, we could store thousands of images on one of these but . . ." His voice trailed off and he shrugged. "We rarely have time to sleep anymore. Portraits are a hobby few of us have time for."

"Well, that sucks," Lee muttered. Then she felt stupid. When people were fighting to live, taking pictures probably seemed like a waste of time.

She looked almost real, the woman in the hologram, or whatever it was. She was smiling, almost on the verge of laughing. Her eyes were a pale, warm amber and her hair was worn in a complicated twist. It was a soft, golden brown, shot through with pale gold highlights. There was something oddly familiar about her. Those eyes—Lee closed her own and tried to concentrate, to remember where she'd seen the woman's face before.

"Who is she?"

"Her name was Aneva. Ana, my Ana. She was my granddaughter—the oldest. Ana's mother died when she was a child. Her father died in a raid. I was all she had." Eira stared at the woman with sad eyes. There was something in that look that clued Lee in. Eira didn't even have to say it and Lee knew.

Then Eira smiled. "No, that isn't fair. I wasn't all. There was Elina. Her cousin." A smile came and went. "They were inseparable, those two. Just like their mothers had been."

It took a minute for Lee to remember who Elina was. She continued to stare at the woman's image, and while she stared into very lifelike amber eyes, it finally clicked. Eira's granddaughter, the one who had headed back east with her family. "Their moms were sisters?" Lee asked as she tried to work out the family tree in her head.

"Yes. My two youngest daughters. I had five daughters.

Two sons." Eira studied the image and explained, "Only one of my children still lives. Hanel, my son, went east decades ago when his wife conceived. It was for the best—even now, it's so much safer. I wonder . . ." Her voice trailed off and she took a deep, harsh breath. When she spoke again, her voice was more garbled than before and thick with tears. "I wonder if I shouldn't have sent his sisters with them."

"I'm sorry, Eira."

A sad smile curved Eira's mouth and she murmured, "As am I, child. As am I." When she looked at Lee, tears gleamed in her eyes, but she didn't let them fall. "I never imagined this would be the life I lived, fighting a war that cannot be won. Losing my children to it. The raids were a way of life, you know. Girls went missing from time to time. On occasion, entire families. But then the raids started coming more and more often. The demons started coming, and it wasn't just a few here and there. Entire swarms of them, coming through the gate and massacring everything they crossed. They weren't content with just bloodshed, though, and they no longer sought out victims and then waited for the gate to open so they could return home. They wanted to stay."

Eira closed her eyes and fell silent for a long while. Lee wondered if she hadn't gone to sleep, but then her eyes opened and she looked at Lee. Her eyes didn't look quite so dull in that moment. They all but blazed with fury. "My girls were grown by then. Shiryn, my husband, had already died trying to fight a horde of Raviners, and two of my girls were taken by the Sirvani. That was when I realized I had to start fighting as well."

Puzzled, Lee asked, "*Start* fighting? Eira, how old were you?"

"Forty-three." Now the smile on Eira's face didn't look quite so sad and bitter. She actually looked like she was smirking a little. "Yes—forty-three, Lee. You were not the only one to come late into this life. Magick has always run strong in my family, but I hadn't ever used mine in battle until then." She gazed into Lee's eyes, and as though she heard the question circling through Lee's mind, Eira said, "That was sixty-six years ago."

Lee blinked. A little dumbfounded, she sat back and stared at Eira. She did the math and then did it again. She squinted at the old woman. Yeah, she looked old now, but ten days ago, before the stroke hit? Lee had seen men and women not even out of their fifties that looked older than Eira had. "You're telling me that you're 109 years old?"

"If I see another month, it will be 110." Eira chuckled. Her right eye gleamed with the same dry humor that had driven Lee insane just a couple of weeks ago. "Remember that next time you feel tempted to throttle me. I'm not just old, I'm practically ancient."

Practically? Hell, Eira was ancient. One hundred and ten fricking years old . . . Lee couldn't quite wrap her mind around it. Yeah, she knew people could be long-lived back home, but she hadn't ever imagined that a woman who was as active as Eira could be so old. She'd seen a century come and go. It blew Lee's mind even thinking of it. "I reckon retirement is out of the question."

Eira frowned and repeated, "Retirement."

"Never mind." She looked back at the image. The woman portrayed looked so real. Unable to stop herself any longer, she touched it and gasped, startled at the lifelike feel. If light could be touched, it would feel like this—warm, almost soft—it felt alive. "Wow."

She closed her hand into a fist, but her fingers still buzzed, kind of liked she'd gotten an electric shock. "She's beautiful." Lee wasn't sure what else to say, but she had a feeling there was something Eira hadn't told her yet.

"Hmmm. She was." Eira held out a hand and Lee placed the little disc into it. The image never wavered. Eira rubbed her thumb down the side of it and the image winked out. But instead of putting the disc aside, Eira held it back out to Lee. "I want you to have this."

Lee glanced at Kalen. He stood behind her silently and met her curious gaze with a shrug. Looking back at the old woman, Lee shook her head. "Why do you want me to have it? I don't know her."

Eira sighed. It was a sad, bereft sound. "No. You don't. She died doing her damnedest to protect you." Eira's fingers shook, but she continued to hold the disc out. "Take it, Lee. Every child should at least know what her mother looked like."

"My—my mother?"

***

"My mother."

Kalen smiled. "You've said that a good fifteen times. Does it make that knowledge easier to believe?"

Still flabbergasted, Lee shook her head and muttered, "My mother." She rubbed her forehead while she paced, but it didn't do anything to ease the ache there. "That makes Eira . . ." She heard a laugh and looked up at Kalen. "This isn't funny."

"Considering that you keep repeating yourself, yeah it is. And you still haven't been able to say it. She's your great-grandmother. What's so hard about saying that?" He came up behind her and laid his hands along her shoulders. When his thumbs dug into the tense muscles there, she moaned. Tension melted away, but her head continued to throb.

Too many thoughts whirling around in there. It was like she was standing in a crowded, smoke-filled bar, trying to listen to a conversation five feet away. Hardly anything made sense.

"She knew me."

Kalen didn't argue that. There had always been something about Lee that niggled at his brain, but it wasn't until Eira mentioned Elina and Ana that Kalen actually pieced it together. He didn't remember much about Ana. Until he'd seen her image on the emsphere, Kalen couldn't have recalled what she looked like.

He knew she'd been grabbed in a raid and that she was one of the few women to ever escape the Warlords. She'd reappeared in the camp briefly, just for a few months and then she was gone again. He didn't remember a child, but he'd been young himself. She could have either kept Lee out of sight, or perhaps she had still been carrying Lee when she disappeared.

Kalen barely remembered her. She'd been pretty, he remembered that. "She had a voice like an angel," he murmured as another memory drifted through his mind.

Slowly, Lee turned, and when she looked up at him with stark eyes, Kalen cursed himself silently. As if she didn't have enough open wounds right now, there he was rubbing salt in one of them. "You knew her?"

He almost wished he could say yes. He could see the need in her eyes, but he wouldn't lie to her about it. "No. Not really. I was just a kid when she left here. But I remember her voice."

"Do I look like her?" Lee asked hesitantly. She reached into her pocket for the emsphere, but she didn't turn it on. Her hand shook a little, and when she fisted it around the disc, it shook.

Gently, Kalen smoothed his hands up and down her arms. "I think you've got her smile," he whispered softly. Then he grinned down at her. "Eira's smile. I can see that now. Her smile, her attitude—her temper."

As he'd expected, Lee's soft blue eyes flashed. She started to snarl at him, but the look faded before it had completely formed. "Her temper," Lee said as a sad, wistful smile appeared on her face. "Why didn't she tell me before?"

"Don't you think you were dealing with enough?" He nuzzled her neck and eased her body back against his. He rubbed a hand up and down her back, and when she took a deep breath, he could feel it shuddering through her. Distantly, he was aware of the chaotic rumble of her thoughts, and once more, he found himself wishing he could do something to make all of this easier on her.

There was nothing to be done, though, beyond what he was already doing. Hold her when she needed it, listen when she talked. "You've left your world behind—your home. You come to a strange place where you don't feel you know anybody or anything, right in the middle of a war. How much more do you want to have dropped on you like that?"

"Learning I had a grandmother—or great-grandmother—might have helped. Might have made it a little easier." She sighed and snuggled closer to him. Kalen wrapped his arms around her. Lee sighed and rubbed her cheek against his chest.

"Easy isn't going to prepare you for what is coming, Lee."

Lee stiffened and pushed away from him. She shot him a narrow look from under the fringe of her bangs before moving away. Jamming her hands into the pockets of the cavinir jacket, she started to pace, long, restless strides that took her back and forth across the small room. "That's part of the problem. I don't know what's coming. I don't know what it is I'm supposed to be preparing for or why I'm supposedly so important. Nobody will give me any kind of answer."

He wasn't sure how to respond to that. His instinctive response was to tell her that he didn't know much more than she did, at least about what lay before them. But he suspected Lee didn't need his uncertainty piled on top of her own. Stalling, he moved to the small trunk that served as a table by his cot. Locked inside there was a bottle of sharn, homemade whiskey that packed one hell of a punch. He thumbed the locking mechanism. There was a faint hum as it read his DNA signature and then it unlocked.

He splashed the pale gold liquor into a glass and held it out to Lee. She took it, sniffed. "Whoa. What's this for, intoxicating the wyrms?" Lee swirled it around in the glass and stared. "I'm not much of a drinker. Hate feeling out of control . . . but right now? Right now, I think it's just what the doctor ordered." She sniffed again and then took a small sip.

She started coughing, and he watched over the rim of his own drink as she finally managed to wheeze in a breath. Lee blinked away the tears stinging her eyes and then took another sip. She managed to get it down without choking this time, and afterward she shot him a grin. "If this stuff doesn't kill me, I could get used to it."

"Good stuff. Getting harder to come by, so enjoy it." He

swirled his own glass, watched it slosh around. "Nobody here is any more prepared for what's coming than you are, Lee. You've been thrust into the middle of this mess for a reason. I don't know what that reason is, but I do know there is one."

She gave him a dour smile. "All things for a reason . . . yeah, yeah, yeah. I've pretty much always believed that, but it sure as hell doesn't seem like much of a help right now." She took another drink, a bigger one, and then grinned at him. "This helps."

"Slow down with it. It packs a punch," he advised. She started toward him and he grinned as she stumbled a little. The glass fell from her hand and Kalen cocked a brow. "I didn't realize . . ." He stared at her, concerned. This wasn't the liquor. "Lee, what is it?"

In the span of a couple of heartbeats, she had turned as pale as death and her eyes had darkened to the color of the midnight sky. She pressed her hand to her belly and looked toward him. It didn't seem like she really saw him; her eyes were tracking blindly and her voice was hollow as she murmured, "Something's wrong."

The words had no sooner left her mouth than the world exploded. Or at least that was how it felt. The ground rumbled and pitched beneath their feet, and distantly he could hear screams and crashing going on outside his unit. Lee fell to the floor, landing on her hands and knees, and continued to stare toward him out of darkened eyes.

Her body started to spasm. He tried to get to her, but the shaking and trembling of the ground made the progress slow. She started to puke, and even after she'd emptied her stomach, Lee continued to wretch and shudder. "Something's wrong . . . ," she moaned. "Everything feels—"

The spasms wrapped hold of her and choked off her words. Her face went red, darkened to an alarming shade of purple, and then she slumped. Kalen crawled his way to her, all but digging his hands into the floor as it shuddered and pitched under him. Terror wrapped him in its cold, slippery grasp, and even when he pulled Lee into his arms and felt the pulse at her neck, it wouldn't let go.

"Lee!"

She moaned but didn't open her eyes. Her lips moved, and he had to bend over to hear her. "Something's wrong . . ."

* * *

Not something. Everything.

Nearly twenty hours later, Kalen stood surveying the wreckage that had been his home for the past three years. The base camp had been one of the most secure in the Roinan territory. Probably one of the most secure camps in the west.

Now it was little more than rubble. He had no idea how many bodies were trapped under the mess of collapsed housing units and common areas. So far, the uninjured survivors numbered nineteen hundred. Nearly twenty-five hundred had been reported as injured, and the rest were either dead or unaccounted for.

Not even twenty-four hours ago there had been 6,963 refugees, soldiers, medics and scouts living in the base camp. The outlying areas had probably another four thousand in various outposts and temp shelters. Kalen had no idea how hard those areas had been hit, but if it was anything like this . . .

"Damn it all to hell," he swore. He didn't want to think in such terms, but the pragmatist in him already knew they'd lost possibly a third of their people.

"It's ready."

Kalen looked past Dais to the huge barricade that had been erected just outside the perimeter. It was actually a series of barricades, four of them, with the largest one on the inside. The barricades were crude and there was no guarantee they'd be effective, but night was coming and the camp was vulnerable.

Too vulnerable and Kalen knew it. Off in the distance, the gate was open. God and saints alone knew what was going to come pouring through it, but Kalen had a bad feeling that their time had about run out. Power had been forced into the gate, and the backlash from the power surge had caused the earthquakes. That much power was because somebody on the other side had forced the gate to open, and it was the largest damned opening he'd ever sensed. It wasn't going to be a quick in-and-out job, either. This was no simple raid. Hell, the raids alone were bad enough.

This was going to be an all-out invasion. There was also a telltale rumble in the earth that had started just a couple of hours ago. Wyrms. They hadn't arrived yet, but they would probably come when the rest of the demon bastards appeared.

Shooting a gaze skyward, he muttered, "A break would be nice."

A break. Some luck. A miracle. Kalen wasn't picky, but they were in serious trouble. Night coming, wyrms in the area—at least two—and a horde of demons just waiting for sunset. The Sirvani hadn't appeared yet, but Kalen wasn't surprised. The Sirvani would let the demons go through, and whoever lived through the demon attacks would be considered fit for capture. Strength, stamina and the ability to evade death by demon hand made for excellent slaves.

Short-term goals were to live through the night, and in the morning any and all able-bodied families were leaving. Right now, they were all preparing for the journey, packing what could be carried and leaving everything else behind. Morne was hand-selecting the warriors that would travel with the families to provide for their safety, while Dais rallied the rest of the troops and did a recon of the areas closest to the camp, searching for survivors that might have been outside the walls when the quake hit.

Kalen had activated the emergency systems and sent out a broadcast detailing the earthquake, an approximate guess at the loss of life and a request for whatever assistance could be spared. Healers had already been selected for the journey. What remained of them anyway. One of the quakes had left the medicon in ruins. Some of the healers and techs had been pulled alive from the wreckage, but none of the patients trapped inside had survived. Including Eira.

Once the families were gone, the heavy artillery would be fired up. Sooner if they had to, but Kalen didn't want to entice the wyrms until absolutely necessary. The laser cannons were only the beginning. Underneath the base, they had stores upon stores of weapons, the best technology their world could boast. They had been hoarding it like a kid hoarded sweets, and now it was party time. Most of the underground storage facilities had survived the quakes. The ones that had collapsed were in the process of being dug out.

If they lived through the night, the Sirvani were going to have their hands full.

If . . . what a frustrating word.

If they lived through the night, if reinforcements came in time—if Eira hadn't died.

That was the most enraging of all, and the most heart-breaking. Eira's broken, lifeless body had been one of the first pulled from the rubble. She was gone, and her death left them vulnerable in ways that none of them were prepared for. Elina had contacted them. She knew about her mother's death, and she'd be there as fast as she could, bringing her oldest two children with her, a witch-born daughter and a psychic. They were closer than he could have hoped for, but still, Kalen wasn't sure they'd make it.

The few witches left had minor talents, enough to start a fire or divert the natural element flow, but not one of them had the strength they would need to weaken a gate. If they combined their gifts, it just might be enough to weaken the power flow that fed the gate, but it was a chancy course of action. It was also their only course of action, because they had to close the damn gate.

The gates were a strange creation—they wouldn't open for any but the Warlords, but they did react to magick. Not directly. Magick fired directly into the gate was like feeding it, but the witches didn't focus on the gate itself. They focused their power on the energy lines running through the ground, the power that fed the gate. Hit those and it made the gate unstable, and without a Warlord there to counteract the power flow, the gates closed. It always took a few days to get the gates stabilized enough to be useful again.

A few days. Might be the time needed for reinforcements to arrive. Maybe enough for Elina to get to them. His skin prickled, and Kalen turned his head, watching as Lee picked her way through the haphazard piles of rubble, salvaging food and materials and medical supplies. The sun shining down on her head cast a silvery gold nimbus around her hair. The sight of her hit him in the heart like a fist.

He still hadn't recovered from the fear he'd felt as he watched her caught in the throes of the strange seizure that had struck when the gate opened. He hadn't ever seen anything like it, and he didn't ever want to see it again. But at the same time, he tried to work the puzzle of it out in his head. Why had it happened, what had caused it and was it going to happen again?

Holy hell, he hoped not. Fear bubbled inside his throat, digging in with sharp, angry claws. He couldn't lose her. Part of him wanted to send her away with the families and nonfighters. Not that Lee would ever go for that. If he tried to shield her like that, she was likely to bite him. Whether Lee recognized it or not, she was a fighter.

A smile curved her lips as she looked at him. Kalen started toward her. He never realized he'd moved until he had her in his arms. Burying his face in her neck, he breathed in the warm scent of her skin. *I'll do whatever I can to keep you safe,* he promised silently.

"I know."

Kalen stilled. Slowly, he lifted his head and stared at her. "I didn't say anything."

Lee cocked a brow. "Yeah, you did. You said . . ." Her words trailed off and she swallowed. "You did say something, didn't you?"

"No. I thought it."

* * *

I thought it.

It was late afternoon. It had been nearly twenty-four

hours since that bizarre moment with Kalen. It hadn't happened again, but Lee couldn't stop thinking about it. Everything and everyone had faded away for just a few minutes, and she'd felt the warmth and strength of his soul wrap around her, heard his voice murmur, *I'll do whatever I can to keep you safe*. She had heard him. But he hadn't said a word.

The brief connection had only lasted a few seconds, there and then gone again. It hadn't happened since, and that was one thing she was thankful for. Nice to have at least one thing to be thankful for, she figured.

Well, two. They'd made it through the long, terrifying night. Outside the makeshift barricades they could hear the things moving around in the forest, hear the growls, the chittering, the screams.

And the rumbles in the earth coming from the wyrms, although the wyrms hadn't advanced the way Kalen had expected. What they were waiting for, none of them knew. Most terrifying of all, though, wasn't the demons or the wyrms, although those had scared Lee plenty.

The most terrifying sound any of them had heard was music. That primitive, seductive mix of eerie chanting and the tribal beat of drums. When the music had started just a little before midnight, far, far off in the distance, it seemed every survivor had jumped.

The attack they'd been bracing for never came, and come dawn they were exhausted simply from the strain. But things weren't going to get any better now that the sun had risen.

Sweat trickled down her forehead, stinging her eyes. Her hand shook as she reached up and wiped it away. Her back ached from the strain of the pack on her back, but taking it off wasn't an option. Kalen had sent his people out loaded for bear. She knew how to use the laser in her hands, but most of the stuff in the sack was beyond her comprehension. Kalen hadn't listened to her when she tried to tell him she wasn't comfortable with the weapons, and it seemed like such a stupid thing to argue about considering what he had to deal with.

Even though she hadn't said a word, Dais seemed to read her mind as he watched her strap on her pack and rig her utility belt with the odd hodgepodge of weapons that had been given to her. "You never did care for man-made weapons," he mused, shaking his head. "Safer than magick these days. More reliable."

Lee wrinkled her nose at him. "I don't know about that. I'm less likely to accidentally burn a hole in somebody using magick. I can control that a little. These . . ." She gingerly touched a couple of the pulse charges hanging from her belt. "These, I'm not so sure about."

Dais just smiled. "If you're that nervous with them, just don't use them. But don't bother arguing with us. You'll go with the weapons or not go at all."

And that wasn't an option. Lee had to get away from the base camp for a little while, away from the stink of death, from the ever-burning fires and the morass of emotion that hung over the place like a cloud.

Part of her felt guilty, knowing that she was going out into the forest just to escape the job that lay before Kalen and the others. A grim, ugly job. Accounting for survivors. Disposing of the dead. Disposing . . . such a cold word. Like they were tossing out some Chinese food that had gone bad. These were people. Eira had been one of them.

Unwittingly, she slid a hand into her pocket and touched the disc Eira had given her. It was called an emsphere. Kalen said it could store thousands of images, but this one had held only the image of Aneva. *My mother.* Lee had few conscious memories of her mother, but looking at her face seemed to bring back memories long forgotten. Bits and pieces of songs that Lee used to hear as she drifted away to sleep. Warm arms holding her close. A soft, exotic fragrance and the most beautiful amber eyes. Just vague little things, but they were enough that Lee could understand one important thing.

She had been loved.

Ana, my Ana. She died doing her damnedest to protect you. Lee was still a little too shaky to think about the woman Eira called Aneva. Right now, although Lee hated to admit it, she wasn't ready to think about her mother yet, so she simply blocked it out. The coward's way out, maybe, but the woman was little more than a stranger to Lee, and since she had died years ago, that wasn't likely to change. Thinking about her now wasn't going to change things, so Lee decided *not* to think about her.

But even though she could push her thoughts about her mother into a neat little box and not dwell on them, she couldn't do the same thing with Eira. Eira's death hurt. Lee didn't know if it was because the old lady had been the only blood relative Lee actually knew, or if it had something to do with whatever memories she had suppressed of this place. But it hurt. The pain kept sneaking up on her, grabbing her by the throat and blinding her with the pain. Even now as she hiked through the dense undergrowth, tears stung her eyes.

She blinked them away. There wasn't any time to cry right now. No time to mourn. But if she lived through this, she was going to mourn for the odd, old woman that she really never had a chance to know.

The ground rumbled and Lee swore, bracing herself for another quake. "It's just an aftershock." She looked up and saw Morne watching her from a few feet away. He stood with his legs widespread, and the little tremors rolling through the ground didn't seem to faze him in the least.

Lee, on the other hand, felt sick, physically, mentally. Drained, exhausted, and terrified. And grieving. No, she hadn't really known Eira, and now she had the rest of her life in front of her to think about how she had treated the only family she'd ever known.

Hell couldn't be any worse than the past few days. It just wasn't possible. Nothing could be worse. The base was in shambles. The earthquake that had hit two days ago had done a great deal of damage, and what had escaped the quake hadn't necessarily escaped the subsequent raids.

Thousands were dead. Burying them all would take more time and manpower than Kalen had, so mass funeral pyres had been built. Lee had heard the words "Blessings on your path" so many times she wanted to scream.

"Blessings"—not a word to say over the dead body of a child. But it was what these people said, like "Godspeed" or something. So Lee said it as well, even though that calm, lovely phrase made her nauseous. *Blessings on your path, brother. Blessings on your path, elder. Blessings on your path, poor little baby . . .*

When she had said it the last time over the still body of a toddler, Lee had lost it. She had pulled away from the pyre and just started to walk. She probably would have walked clear out of the camp, into the mountains and on and on until she dropped from exhaustion, if Kalen hadn't stopped her.

Kalen had made a command decision and ordered the complete evacuation of all remaining families. By the time he was done, there would be only soldiers left in the camp, and Lee figured that was how it should be. Part of her wished she could join the refugees.

She wanted so bad to run. She was still trying to come to grips with the fact that what she had seen over the past few days was real.

Raviners, Ikacado, the wyrms, Sirvani—Lee felt like she had fallen into some kind of comic book but the artist had neglected to give her a decent superpower. She didn't belong here. She couldn't keep up with these people, these soldiers. They knew how to fight, and if they were scared, they didn't show it.

Lee, however, was pretty sure she had a huge, neon-lit sign over her head with flashing letters that read, *I'm scared and I can't handle this. Please send me back home.*

The ground shuddered again, and this tremor was stronger than the last. She heard some muffled voices, a couple of harsh exclamations and then a huge crack. Distantly, she heard people screaming out warnings, and she sensed Morne moving toward her with a speed that was inhuman.

She wanted to look up, but her body took over as death came hurtling down toward her from the sky. She dove to the side, rolling her body in a tight ball. Debris hit her back. Something crashed into the ground—Lee felt the rush of air on her body, and slowly she lifted her head to look.

Dust and leaves floated through the air. Lee brushed at her hair as she stared at the massive tree bough. As she gaped, one last tremor shuddered through the ground below her and then all was silent. Apparently destroying one of the forest giants was enough to appease whatever had the earth so pissed off. Lee cast a glance up into the canopy of leaves, studying the empty piece of sky. She could see the path the huge limb had taken. Smaller branches had been broken during the descent. Small by comparison at least. Some of those limbs were as big around as her waist.

The biggest limb, the one that would have crushed her if she hadn't moved, was probably as big around as a VW Bug and its branches reached upward so high, she couldn't see over it.

Morne's blond head appeared over the rubble, and he took one look at Lee before closing his eyes. Lee recognized the sentiment. As soon as she could breathe again, she was going to roll over, kiss the dirt and thank God.

Dais's voice intruded on her attempts to catch her breath. "Anybody hurt?" There was silence and she felt all eyes on her. Dais cocked a gunmetal gray brow and asked, "Are you well, Lee?"

She slowly pushed up on her elbow and looked at the older man. Under her breath, she mumbled, "Depends on how you define *well*." People started toward her and she waved them off. "I'm okay. Just give me a few minutes."

The sudden onslaught of voices was too much for her spinning head, and instead of climbing to her feet to inspect the damage like everybody else was doing, she fell back onto the forest floor. Lee squinted up at the empty patch in the canopy overhead. She could see the dismal gray clouds through the patch. It hit her like a pang, then. The sun didn't shine here. She hadn't seen blue sky in nearly a month.

God. Had it only been a month?

It seemed like a lifetime, yet oddly, it also seemed like

no time at all had passed. She could remember sitting at her workstation, the smell of the pencils she liked to use when she was sketching, the scent of paper, the weight of it in her hands, the feel of a keyboard under her fingers—the feel of the stylus. Watching the monitor as her dreams took on life before her eyes.

How many times had she sketched out memories from this world? Suppressed memories that only appeared in her dreams? It was unsettling to realize there were probably many, many memories. The piece she had been working on in the days before she fell into the bizarre place had come from a dream about the war. About Kalen.

"You aren't injured."

Lee opened her eyes and found Morne staring down at her with his unsettling blue-black eyes. "Is that a question or a statement?"

He blinked. "We need to get moving. There isn't much time before nightfall, and we must all be back at the base before then."

Lee lifted her head and stared at the limb that had damn near turned her into an ugly little smear on the ground. "I need a few minutes, pal."

He hesitated and then looked off to his left. Lee didn't bother turning her head. She just closed her eyes and concentrated on getting her breathing back to normal. If they wanted her to move before she was ready, they could damn well just carry her. But all Morne said was "You continue the search, Lothen, Dais. We'll be with you in a minute."

Dais argued with Morne. "It isn't wise to split up, not for any reason. If she isn't hurt, she needs to get up and get moving. Staying in one place is dangerous."

"I'll stay with her. She will be in no danger, Dais," Morne said, his voice dismissive.

Dais opened his mouth and Lee wanted to clap her hands over her ears, but instead, she took a deep breath and braced herself to stand up. She wasn't in the mood to listen to the two arrogant warriors argue—well, Dais would argue. Morne would simply do whatever in the hell he wished and Dais could just go screw himself for all the healer cared. But Dais closed his mouth without saying anything and turned on his heel.

He made no sound as he departed, and she closed her eyes. Leaves rustled on the ground as people headed out, and Lee heard a few twigs snap as she shifted around a little. There was a rock digging into the back of her shoulder, and the smell of fresh wood and crushed leaves filled her head. Lee cracked an eye open and looked up at Morne. "I need a minute."

"So you said," he murmured. He glanced up and looked around as though he heard something. "Take your minute. Or a few more if you need them." He turned around and walked off. As he disappeared from her field of vision, Lee shifted her gaze upward, once more staring at the sullen gray sky.

Slowly, her erratic heartbeat settled down as she reaffirmed that she wasn't trapped under the tree bough—or dead. Her hands were shaky and she had a feeling shock was moving in, so she tried to find something else to think of besides what had almost happened.

The forest here was strange. Back home when she went on a hike, she heard the call of birds and insects, but here, it was silent. She could hear the wind whispering through the branches above but little else. Just silence.

No . . . not silence. There was music. Her ears pricked and she cocked her head, trying to hear it better. It was faint, at first. So faint she almost didn't even hear it. But as Lee lay there on the damp, cool ground, she realized there was music—like the music she'd heard before, coming from the Veil.

Enticing. Enchanting. Slowly, she opened her eyes and pushed herself upright. Without even realizing that she had done so, she climbed to her feet and started to move around the fallen limb. The music grew just a little louder, beckoning to her. Her skin felt tight and hot. She pressed her back to one of the huge trees and circled around. She glanced around it and saw something glowing, just faintly, off in the distance.

What the . . .

It was a soft blue light, kind of pretty, really. Something inside her leaped at the sight of that light and she stepped forward. Her body didn't feel like her own as she placed each step with slow, precise care, never once making a sound. Her breathing was shallow and her gaze focused. *Closer—closer,* a dry, cynical bitch in her head murmured. *Somebody is up to no good and we'll find out who it is, then we'll kill him.*

All the while, there was a saner part of her mind that was screaming at her to run. Run very far, very fast. That pretty blue light spelled destruction, and no smart witch went near it.

As if all of that wasn't confusing enough, there was a third voice clamoring in the mix, the one that Lee recognized as her self, the self she knew. That voice was telling Lee she really did need to run, and she needed to keep running until she managed to wake up from this bizarre nightmare she had found herself in.

When she finally managed to do that, she was going to get herself some serious, serious therapy. No more sleep studies, either, but actual, honest-to-God, psychiatric help. The kind that came with a couch and a fifty-minute hour. Therapy was the key. Antidepressants or something would surely stop these bizarre dreams that felt so damned real.

That cynical bitch in her head seemed to laugh. *This is no dream, babe. This is real life—this is your life, and it's about time you opened your eyes and dealt with it. Deal with me. Now get your ass closer, because we have a job to do.*

Hell. She was this close to arguing with herself again, and this time, her other self wasn't going to shut up, either. This was the same cool, collected bitch that had killed the Ikacado that day when Eira stroked out. The warrior that Kalen insisted she was. She didn't feel like that woman—

Because you won't let yourself. Open your eyes. You're here. This is your reality now—accept it. Accept me. Or you will die. The last part seemed to burn through her mind, demanding that she either accept it, once and for all, or run away before she got herself, and everybody around her, killed.

Run away. Part of her longed to do just that. But Lee had already acknowledged that running away wasn't an option. She couldn't run from Kalen. Even if she wanted to, which she didn't. Leaving him was just unthinkable. She'd just met him—at least it partly seemed that way to her, but in other ways, she felt like she had known him her whole life. Had been waiting for him her whole life.

She supposed that in a way, she had. Kalen claimed that she had been slipping in and out of his life since she was a child, and heaven knew that she had dreamed about him often. All those sketchbooks back home were evidence of that.

Besides, where would she run to? Even if she tried, there was no place on this world that was truly safe. Eventually that destruction and death that lingered around the gate would find every last safe solace. If such places even existed here anymore.

Accept it. Accept me.

Silently, Lee said, *Like you're giving me any choice*—

She had no sooner thought that than that illusive curtain in her mind was destroyed. It didn't disappear. That was too silent a word to even begin to describe what happened. More, it was like an avalanche struck and that curtain was decimated under the power of it. That cool, cynical bitch wasn't just a voice murmuring inside her head. She was that cool, cynical bitch. She was the witch that stood there staring at the blue nimbus with fear in her heart, because she knew what it was.

The Veil. It wasn't just the flickering glimpse that Lee had managed on her own, either. It had been raised, completely and fully, so perfectly done that Lee could see the stark, desert landscape of Anqar and feel the whisper of hot winds that managed to blow through.

Somebody on her side of the Veil was speaking to another person through it. More—she understood them. It wasn't English they spoke, or the more lyrical version of English that seemed to be the dominant language in this world. It was alien, consisting of an odd mix of guttural phrases and musical trills that didn't seem like speech at all.

Yet, it was, and she understood it. Understood it—she who had barely managed a C in Spanish could understand these men as well as if they had been speaking English.

"This is a dangerous game, brother."

"I'm aware of that."

There was a long pause and then the first speaker, the one on Lee's side of the Veil, said, "Are you certain it's worth it? All of this for vengeance?"

A soft, sad laugh and then the man in Anqar spoke. "It isn't for vengeance. It is for her memory—and for a promise I made. I will keep that promise. The question is will you keep yours to me?"

Lee edged just a little forward and peeked around the girth of the tree, staring toward the men speaking. She couldn't see the man on her side of the Veil without exposing herself, but she could see the other man. The sight of him turned her blood to ice, and terror arced through her. Sirvani—

He wore the traditional, stark garb of the Sirvani: black pants, bare-chested, leather crisscrossing over the naked expanse of muscle there. She saw the hilts of two swords, one over each shoulder. His head was bald, but she suspected that was by design, rather than nature. His left ear was pierced with a series of multicolored gems, and her newfound knowledge whispered to her that those earrings marked him as a Sirvani of significant rank.

At the center of his chest, where the straps of leather formed an X, there was another stone, larger and glowing the same shade of blue as the Veil. It pulsed, and something about the rhythm of it made her think that it was pulsing in tandem with the Sirvani's heartbeat.

The man she couldn't see sighed, and Lee heard a world of weariness in that single sound. "I do not make a vow lightly, Arnon. I give it, I give it for always. But are you so certain that your love would want your death?"

"My love," the Sirvani muttered, his voice bitter. He

turned away from the Veil, and Lee could see him as he lowered his head. "She has been lost to me for so many years, I do not know what she would want—other than keeping the promise I made her. I cannot do that without you."

Lee heard a rush of noise, and she retreated a little more, pressing her back to the rough bark of the tree. A long string of words she didn't understand, although she did comprehend the meaning behind them. Cussing was pretty much cussing, it seemed, no matter what world you were in or what language was spoken. A brief pause followed by "Do you understand what it is you're asking of me? You ask me to stand by and watch while you all but commit suicide."

"I've been dead inside for years, brother, and we both know it. Besides, there is no way of knowing that the . . ." Lee couldn't make out those words. It sounded like "Ashni Mirn," but she had no way of knowing what that meant. ". . . will know I am the one behind the failures."

"He is no fool, brother." It was said on a snarl, and there was so much helpless fury in that voice that Lee winced. "How many are aware of his most secret plans?"

"I will do as I must. As will you." Lee felt a ripple in the air, and the blue light of the Veil slowly started to fade. "Keep her safe," the Sirvani whispered. And then he was gone.

Lee froze, uncertain if she should run or risk discovery.

A howl, almost inhuman, full of anguish and outrage, ripped through the silence of the forest, and Lee bolted. A glance over her shoulder confirmed that she wasn't being followed, and she ran as quickly, as silently, as she could, retracing her steps until she reached the spot where the tree had damned near turned her into roadkill.

She ran headlong into Dais, and his war-scarred hands caught her shoulders. He peered down into her face with concerned eyes. "Are you well? Something has frightened you."

Uncertain of what to say, she just shook her head and lied. "I got lost."

Dais watched her face with a scrutiny that was very unsettling. Lee fought the urge to squirm and pull away from him as he started to stroke his hands up and down her arms. "You are too new here, Lelia. Too new indeed. Wandering through the forest could bring you to a world of harm. Where is Morne? He was to keep you safe, not get it in his fey head to go off by himself."

Forcing herself to smile, she glanced at the tree limb just behind Dais and replied, "Even not wandering can bring me to a world of harm."

His voice—was it him she'd heard? And more . . . what exactly had she heard? She wasn't sure of anything other than that a Sirvani had been speaking across the Veil to somebody in Ishtan. It didn't bode well for them at all. Suddenly afraid, Lee looked around and realized they were alone. Completely alone. That knowledge filled her with terror. She wasn't sure why. Dais hadn't ever bothered her before, but right now he made her skin crawl.

"Morne . . . where is . . ."

"I am here." She looked over and watched as Morne separated himself from the trees. "I wished only to give you some privacy." His gaze lowered to where Dais held Lee's arms. There was an odd sense of reaction from the older man. Lee felt it in the way his hands tightened oh so slightly. His body held an odd tension, and she realized that Dais was afraid of Morne.

Terrified.

"She was running through the forest, Morne. She's pale as a ghost, you see. I was concerned." Dais looked down at her, and a reassuring smile came and went. "Looking better now though." His hands fell away.

"What were you running from?"

Lee looked at Morne and wished she could have five minutes, just five minutes, to try and clear her head. It was too busy in there, her mind working away at the puzzle of who the Sirvani had been speaking with and what they were speaking about. Dais—had it been him?

No. It couldn't be. Dais had been Kalen's right-hand man ever since Kalen had stepped up to lead this small ragtag resistance. Before Kalen, Dais had worked with Kalen's father. He was loyal to the resistance. He had to be. That certainty came swimming to the fore of the chaotic thoughts, and Lee stopped trying to imagine Dais speaking in the weird, harsh language of Anqar. It wasn't him; it just didn't make sense otherwise.

How could he have gotten here before she did if she'd left him behind her when she fled? But he looked sort of tense. Disturbed about something. Then there was the weird way he was watching her.

"Lelia?"

Lee lifted her gaze and stared at Morne. His eyes, nearly black in his face, were emotionless, and she couldn't sense anything coming off him now that Dais was no longer touching her.

Keep her safe—keep who safe? Who in the hell had the Sirvani been talking about? *Why didn't you drop that piece of information into my head with all this other crap?* she thought sourly. There wasn't a response this time, but she hadn't expected one, not now that she had stopped fighting the weird inner knowledge. It was like she had been split into a bunch of little pieces that operated independent of one another, but now she was intact and whole.

Kalen—she needed to speak with Kalen. If nothing else, she needed to tell him about the Sirvani and whoever he'd been speaking with. Maybe Kalen would know what it meant.

"I need to get back to the base camp."

Morne cocked a brow at her. "We have work yet to do out here. I cannot escort you back."

She gave him a hard smile and replied, "I didn't ask for an escort. Kalen gave you a job to do. Go do it."

As she left, she could feel both of them watching her.

Dais called out behind her, "You aren't safe to wander through the forest, Lelia. You hardly know your way around the camp."

She glanced over her shoulder. "Wanna bet?"

TEN

Kalen scrubbed his hands over his face and wished he could have just ten minutes to put his head down and rest. He didn't need to sleep, although he'd have given his eye-teeth for a decent nap. But he desperately needed a few minutes of peace and quiet.

A faint buzz lit under his skin, and he glanced toward the door just as Lee stepped through. Focusing back on the two men in front of him, he finished explaining where he wanted them to place the ion cannon. They had three of them. If they had another ten or twenty, he would be a happy man. As it was, they'd have to deal with just the three.

"Keep it under wraps until we need it. No use in letting the Sirvani know we have something a little more powerful on hand. If we keep the fires built up, it will keep all but the Raviners and the Jorniaks at bay. Perhaps even the Sirvani for a time. We've plenty of cold-beams for the fire-breathers." The Ikacado didn't really breathe fire, but they might as well have. Fire wouldn't keep them back, but the cold-beams would, and thank the Lord and saints, there was no shortage of the cold-beams.

"Kalen."

Lee's voice was soft, and he didn't turn to look at her. He held out his hand, signaling that she wait as he continued giving orders to the men. He finished, and as they headed out, he looked at Lee. Then he narrowed his eyes and studied her a little closer. Her color was up, red flags riding high on her cheeks, her eyes all but glowing. She stood in front of him with an annoyed look on her face and her hands planted on her slender hips.

"Why aren't you with Morne and Dais?" he asked shortly.

"Because I wanted to be here." Her chin went up. "You know, considering that you freaked out just a few days ago when he touched me, I'm surprised you stuck me with him on this recon deal."

Kalen shrugged. "I trust Morne to keep you safe. Although I'm not too happy to see that you are here without either of them." The last thing he needed was to worry about Lee wandering through the unsecured forest. He knew she'd needed a break away from the grisly jobs at the camp, and that was why he'd sent her with Morne and Dais. Those two would keep her safe, and far enough away from Kalen so he could concentrate.

"I can keep myself safe, buddy." She angled her chin toward the door and said, "We need to talk. Alone." Without waiting for him to respond, she turned around and headed for the door.

She strode outside. She had her curls pulled back with a thong and they bounced up and down with each step. Curious, Kalen followed her outside. There was a weird tension surrounding her. He reached out to touch her mind and ended up getting the deft touch thrown back at him by the thick, impenetrable walls. When she turned to look at him, she had a smirk on her pretty mouth.

Eira hadn't ever gotten around to teaching Lee how to bolster her psychic shields. She'd been too busy trying to get the basics of magick down to worry about Lee's rather minor psy talents. But Lee had picked up that knowledge somewhere. There was more, too.

Kalen couldn't be sure, but the vibes coming off Lee were different now—or at least different from her current norm. It was almost like he was standing with the Lee he had known most of his life—his warrior. Amazed, Kalen murmured, "I'll be damned."

"Aren't we all?" She pushed the curls back from her face and then jammed her hands in her pockets. "Somebody raised the Veil while I was in the forest."

Whatever he had been expecting Lee to say, it hadn't been that. Many of his troops were sensitives—sensing the Veil wasn't an uncommon ability. Raising it, though, was uncommon. It took more focus, more concentration and more talent than most of his men had. "Who?"

She shook her head. Some of her curls had slipped free of the restraining leather, framing her face. She looked so soft with all those blond curls, that pretty mouth and her big blue eyes. Soft and touchable—fuckable. Bleeding saints—not now, he thought as blood drained out of his head, straight down to his cock.

She said something, and it took a minute to focus on her words instead of the way her mouth looked as she shaped those words. He didn't want to think about what she was saying, not one bit. What he wanted to do was see that pretty pink mouth wrapped around his cock, and then he wanted to tumble her onto her back and press his mouth against her, taste her and lick her until she came.

But instead of that, he had to listen to whatever she was saying, and it was damned hard to think about anything with his dick hurting like a bad tooth. Finally, though, he managed to think past the desire fogging his brain. "You didn't see anybody?"

She shrugged, a graceful shift of smooth, rounded shoulders. "Not anybody on this side of the Veil. On the other side, it was a Sirvani—a high-ranking one." She slid him a look from under her lashes and said, "Whoever it was on our side, they seemed to know each other. Very well."

"How do you know he was ranked?"

Lee's only answer was a mysterious little smile, but it

was all the answer he needed. Somehow, Lee had pieced herself together: the woman she was in her world and the warrior she was in his. The knowledge was there in her eyes, in that cool, confident gaze and that arrogant little smirk.

And it all added up to trouble, because if it bothered his warrior enough that she had to come looking for him, then they had a serious problem. One he couldn't even begin to solve until he knew exactly what lay before him.

Uneasy, Kalen turned away from her and stared into the woods. "Did you hear what they wanted?"

"Hear, yeah. Understand? Not really. Something about keeping somebody safe. The man told the Sirvani he was playing a dangerous game. Asked him if it was worth it."

Puzzled, Kalen looked back at Lee. "Was what worth it?"

"A promise."

"A promise?" he repeated.

"Yeah. Should I say it again so you can repeat it again?" she asked. He glanced at her and she gave him a wide smile.

"You're awful damned cocky today," Kalen murmured. He closed the distance between them, half-expecting her to back away some, but instead, she tilted her chin up, and if anything, her grin got a little wider. "Care to tell me why that is?"

"You could say I had a near-death experience."

Kalen's heart skipped a beat. She still had that playful, amused grin on her mouth, but her eyes were dead serious. "Maybe you should explain that a little more."

She pushed a hand through her hair, tugging out the cord that held her curls off her neck, a habitual gesture that had always driven him insane. This time was no different, and Kalen watched the silken blond curls drift back down around her shoulders. She frowned down at her hand, and Kalen saw she held a leaf there. She combed her hair out a little more and dislodged more debris, more leaves, and little bits of twigs and dirt. "I just missed a close encounter when a tree came crashing down." She shrugged as though it was no big deal.

Kalen paused and then asked slowly, "Just how big a tree?"

She squinted her eyes and glanced up to the sky. Then she shrugged and said with a wry grin, "Pretty big."

"How close was the encounter?"

She glanced down at her hands and spread them out about as far as they would go. A few stan lengths. Less than the length of her body. One of the reasons he'd sent a team into the forest was to make sure there weren't any survivors—or corpses—that had been trapped by debris after the quakes. Huge trees fell; landslides from up in the mountains came crashing down and wiped out everything in their path.

Enough time had passed that it should have been relatively safe in the forest, but— Kalen cut that thought off. Letting it finish meant thinking about something he wasn't ready to think about. It would weaken him if he thought about how easily Lee could be taken from him. Slowly, he took a deep breath. "So nearly having a tree fall on you makes you cocky? It would make most people a little shaky."

"Oh, I was shaky, all right." Lee laughed. She reached behind her and gathered her hair back into a tail, wrapping it and twisting it until it was bundled into a knot on top of her head. She reached into her pocket and pulled out a couple of skinny little sticks, which she jammed through the knot of hair.

Kalen watched and wondered what she'd do if he reached over and pulled those skinny sticks out, just so he could watch the curls fall down around her face. Instead he told her, "You don't look very shaky."

She flashed him that cheeky grin. "Well, I took a few minutes. Morne sent the others on ahead, and I was sitting there on the ground when I felt it. It was kind of like when Eira was . . ." Her voice trailed off and that impertinent grin faded. "It was the Veil. I heard it, felt it, like it was singing a song that only I could hear, calling to me."

Kalen hadn't heard it explained like that before. He could sense when somebody lifted the Veil while he was close by, and when he lifted it himself, he felt the power that flowed between the two worlds. That power throbbed inside him, rippled inside his skin and warmed him from the inside out, even as it terrified him. "Let me guess—you went exploring."

She gave him a bland look. "What would you have done?" Then she rolled her shoulders, squirming around a little like she had an itch on her spine. "I heard them talking. It didn't make sense." As he watched, she flushed and looked away.

"What?"

Lee's only response was a baleful glare.

Narrowing his eyes, he reached out and cupped a hand over the back of her neck. He pulled her in close and lowered his face until they were nose to nose. "Lee . . . ," he said warningly.

"You're going to think I'm nuts."

He laughed. "Lee, if you aren't telling me whatever it is because you don't want me to think you're losing your mind, then don't bother. I'm quite convinced you lost it ages ago."

She shoved against his chest until he let go, and he grinned as she walked away in a huff. She shot him a dark look. He grinned wider. "Oh, for crying out loud," she snapped. "I could hear myself, okay?"

"Ahhh . . . hear yourself?"

"Yeah, as in there were two or three voices talking in my head, and all of them were me, but they didn't feel like me. One of them tells me I just need to accept things and stop fighting it. The other one is telling me to run away from the music I heard coming from the Veil, and me, well, I'm just standing there trying to make sense of things—which I haven't been able to do since I arrived here, by the way."

Wisely, Kalen kept his mouth shut as she continued to ramble. She started to pace, and he carefully eased his way back until she couldn't see him unless she turned her head to look at him. Lee continued to speak, her voice rising and falling, and all the confusion and fear he knew she'd been hiding finally spilled out. It was there in her pale face, in the shaking of her voice and the jerky, tense movement of her body as she paced back and forth. "She was the loudest one, though. Cynical bitch."

Now Kalen was having a hard time keeping up. She was talking about herself—right? "Lee, who are we talking about there?"

She spun around and glared at him, as though she couldn't believe he couldn't keep up with her very, very erratic train of thought. She jabbed a thumb toward her chest. "Me, Kalen. We're talking about me."

He paused for a split second and then asked, "So you're a loud cynical bitch?" He fought to keep from smiling, and other than the corners of his mouth twitching a few times, he thought he did an admirable job of it.

Her body slumped and she covered her face with her hands. "Hell. I sound crazy." For a minute, she stood there, head down. Her slender shoulders bowed, shuddered a little as she took a deep breath. "Yeah. I'm a loud cynical bitch. Look, I can't explain this without sounding crazy. But it's like I had three people talking inside my head. But they were all me. One of them kept saying, accept it, accept it, accept it . . . but it was more than just the words. It was like she was crowding into my head, pushing her way inside—told me to accept her, and I said—I think I even said it out loud—it's not like you're giving me a choice. Then all of a sudden, I could hear those two men talking again, but this time they made sense. They were speaking a language I'd never heard, but it made sense. I could feel the power of the Veil, and I could even understand why part of me wanted to run. It was a Sirvani, and the witch inside me didn't want to be anywhere near him. His kind hunt mine, and it was like instinct or something. I wanted to run from him."

She sighed and leaned back. The building at her back was one of the stone creations they'd built over the hot springs. It had come through the quakes mostly intact. Unfortunately, none of them had time to indulge in the hot springs, although Lee looked like she needed it. She was so damn tense, it was a wonder she hadn't shattered under the strain of it. "You're right to fear the Sirvani, Lee."

Her eyes moved to his face and then she looked away again. With a restless shrug, she said, "Yeah, I know. Bad news and all that. Anyway, they finished talking—I understood it all. More . . . I remember."

She lifted her eyes to his face and said it again, "I remember, Kalen. All of it. They don't really feel like my memories, but I can remember seeing you in some basement and giving you a sandwich when we were kids. Ham and cheese . . ." Her voice hitched a little and she took a deep breath. "I gave you a ham-and-cheese sandwich, and there were demons waiting to kill you."

"Lee." He closed the distance between them and cupped her face in his hands. "Yes. You gave me something to eat when I'd been starved for days. I was weak, and there were Raviners waiting for just the right moment to overtake me. You saved my life." He rubbed his thumb over her lips and murmured, "You actually remember."

She blinked, looking lost and uncertain. "Yes. I remember. And I still don't understand why in the hell I'm so important to this, Kalen. I'm just me. Maybe I'll be able to fight now and not get myself killed in the first five seconds, but I'm just me. I'm no Joan of Arc or anything."

Kalen had no idea who Joan of Arc was but he didn't need to know. He understood what was bothering her, and as much as he wished he had answers for her, he didn't. He had the same questions himself. Lowering his head, he pressed his lips to hers.

She kissed him back, sliding her arms around his neck and cuddling into him. "I'm scared, Kalen."

He lifted his head and pressed his lips to her brow. "I know. But whatever happens, I'll be with you. No matter what."

* * *

Even before the ground started with that ominous rumble, Kalen knew it had begun. He kept alternating between physical sight and the inner sight that let him look across the Veil. On the other side, the Warlords' armies were waiting patiently. Kalen could see them, and if he pushed a bit deeper, he'd be able to hear them, but he couldn't risk strengthening the contact. He had to keep his attention focused on what lay before them, not what lay on the other side of the gate.

At least not until the gate opened. Which was going to be any second judging by the tension in the air. It was hot and thick, the way it was just before a thunderstorm. The forest was crawling with demons. The telltale tremor in the earth made Kalen suspect the wyrms were going to join this little hell-party.

All around him, his soldiers waited. Lee stood at his side, finally dressed in clothes that fit. Considering that they were going to be firing up the ion cannons and all their other tech, it seemed rather pointless to not use the synthit. Her cavinir clung like a second skin, the matte black outlining each subtle curve. As though she sensed his gaze, Lee glanced at him. "You ready for this?" he asked her softly.

She smirked. "Like it's going to matter if I'm not." Then she smiled at him. "Relax. I've still got a couple of blank spots, but I think I can handle a fight. You're with me, right?"

Reaching out, he caught her hand and pressed a kiss to the back of it. "No matter what."

There was a screech somewhere out in the darkness. It was answered by a series of high-pitched hisses and low grunts. Jorniaks—cannon fodder. The Warlords always sent the Jorniaks in before a major raid, to cut down on the resistance. The ugly bastards were death on two legs. What they lacked in intelligence, the low-level bastards made up for in brute strength and sheer numbers.

"This is going to be more than a fight, Lee," Kalen said quietly. If this wasn't the final battle, then it was the one leading up to it. Their fight to survive was boiling down to all of these moments. Years of standing their ground, and if they faltered now, it was all for nothing.

"Don't think like that."

Kalen glared at Morne. The silent, spooky bastard stood just behind him, emerging from the darkness without making a sound. "Keep out of my head."

Morne shrugged. "It's not your head or your thoughts I'm reading, Kalen. That's your ability, not mine. Emotions are harder to shield—and emotions can speak very clearly." The healer moved to stand at Kalen's left, dressed in black from head to toe. His hair was pulled back and secured, covered with a hood that Morne would pull down over his face when it was time. Morne always wore a mask when he fought. When the time came, he'd melt into the shadows, silent as death, and none would know he was there until he had already killed them. "Defending your world, your way of life, how can that ever be for nothing?"

Kalen almost answered him, *If we don't win, it was for nothing.* But he kept silent. In his heart, he knew that no matter what happened, it wouldn't have been an exercise in futility. Lives had been saved, and if those lives ended here and now in battle, it was better than being dragged across the Veil and forced into slavery.

"Dark thoughts, my friend," Morne murmured for his ears alone. "They do you no good right now, and your control is so weak that I can sense every last one of them."

On his other side, Lee moved a little closer, leaning into him just a little. She was standing so close that when they saw the flicker of fire through the trees, he felt the tremor wrack her body. The Ikacado. Was she reliving those moments in the forest when the Ikacado had attacked Eira?

The ground pitched beneath their feet and Kalen moved with it, absorbing it with years of practice. "Here it comes," he said needlessly.

Off to his right, he heard Dais order, "Ready the cannons."

Seconds later, the low-level hum of the cannons powering up filled the air. There was another sound, a crackling little hiss—the cold-beams, every last one they could find. When the first Ikacado came skulking out of the forest, long, thin beams of icy cold went blasting toward them.

Smoke from their flesh filled the air, and their black blood spilled onto the ground as one after another was cut down.

Deeper in the forest, Jorniaks roared and came rushing forward. They didn't move with the grace of the Sirvani or the predatory prowl of the Ikacado. They were like lumbering bears, heavy on their feet and clumsy. An easy target for the ion cannons.

The stink of Jorniak blood was now strong in the air, growing thicker and thicker as more of the things pushed closer toward the front line. Their dying screams were joined by the cries of Kalen's people, and red mortal blood mingled with the black demon blood. Bodies fell, and soon they were so thick that Kalen couldn't tell the dead from the wounded.

Next to him, Lee's body all but vibrated with tension, and Kalen reached out, caught her hand in his. He squeezed gently and she slid him a grateful look.

It was still too surreal. Part of Lee had wanted to believe it was all a dream and that she could wake up if she tried hard enough. But the last bit of her that clung to that belief had died in the forest when she stood listening to a language she shouldn't understand but did. Accepting the reality that lay before her meant accepting the fact that she had left behind her old life, probably for good.

Instead of e-mailing with her clients, arguing back and forth over the lack of shading here or why the image couldn't be done that way, she was caught up in the middle of a flat-out battle. The things that were her former life seemed so far away now. None of the headaches she had dealt with back there could even hold a candle to this.

This wasn't a headache. It was a nightmare. Her belly pitched and rolled as she saw a couple soldiers go down on the front line. All the new memories crowding her head hadn't prepared her for seeing people cut down in front of her. She had memories of battle, memories of when she'd joined Kalen on the front line as they fought back would-be raiders, memories of late-night demon attacks on the camp, memories of seeing friends and acquaintances cut down before her eyes. They still didn't feel like *her* memories—

and some vague recollection of people dying was a far cry
from actually seeing them fall.

A soft, weird little moan filled the air, and Kalen's hand
came up to rest on her shoulder. She smothered the next
moan with her hand and had to force herself to remain silent. Silent, when all she wanted was to rush down there and
join in the fray.

The ground shuddered and shook. Instinctively, Lee flexed
her knees and managed to remain upright. But the earth
shuddered again, and again. Each progressive quake got
stronger and stronger, and then the skies started to echo
the rumble. Huge thunderheads piled up overhead, clouding the overcast sky, and as peels of thunder echoed
through the air, the rain started.

Off in the distance, just above the tree line, Lee saw the
colors flicker, so out of place in the ugly, stormy sky. Bright
ribbons of blue, jagged streaks of gold, flashes of red. The
gate stood wide open, and the entire horizon seemed to
burn with a rainbow of colors. The earth shook and rumbled, and Lee swore under her breath.

"Hang tight—it will level off in a few minutes."

Lee glanced at Kalen, envious of the way he stood so
confident and relaxed, even with the ground shaking under
his feet and rain pelting down on him. In no time flat, the
rain had soaked all of them through, and while many of them
looked like wet dogs, Kalen looked as sexy soaked through
and through as he did any other time.

It took a good twenty minutes for the rumblings from
the gate to settle down, and Lee breathed a sigh of relief
when she could finally stand on the ground without it wob-
bling under her feet like Jell-O. The Warlords and their
Sirvani were miles off, but Lee could hear them, their chanting resounding deep inside. It made her heart shudder
within her chest, that bizarre, unearthly rhythm, causing a
reaction inside her that she couldn't quite explain.

But it didn't seem to affect any of the others like it did
her. Nor could she tell if this was a new reaction for her, or
if the hypnotic pull of their chanting had always affected
her like this. She hadn't even noticed that she had started

to sway, until Kalen's hand closed over her arm and he shook her lightly. "Are you well?"

Lee blinked, feeling a little dazed. Looking up at him, she nodded. "Yeah, I just . . ."

The world seemed to explode. Lee hissed under her breath and backpedaled, crashing into Kalen. His arms came around her, bracing her weight as the ground bucked beneath them. It was different from the gatestorm. Instead of an irregular series of tremors, something seemed to vibrate and thrash in the ground under their feet.

Under—"Oh, shit," Lee whispered. She followed the impulse in her gut and turned her gaze off to the south. The wyrms were coming, fast and hard. Judging by the dust trails kicking up from the earth, there were three of them. At least three adults. There could easily be some juveniles or hatchlings, although the younger wyrms didn't pose the same kind of threat that the big bastards did.

Too much information circled through her head again, and Lee wished there was some kind of spigot she could turn that would shut the flow off, or at least slow it down a little. Her mind whirled, processing all that information.

Kalen stroked a hand down her back, and when she looked at him, he had an eerie smile on his face. "They've got some ugly beasties, Lee, but we've got something they don't."

Lee swallowed. "What would that be—a death wish?" Shit, what in the hell were they thinking? Did they actually have any prayer against something that could shoot dirt three hundred feet into the air as it traveled through the ground?

Kalen's grin widened. "No. Firepower. We've been stockpiling it all for a rainy day." He slid his glance upward at the sky, rain splattering on his face. "Looks like it's going to be raining for quite a while."

Lee had been impressed, and a little intimidated, when she saw the ion cannon in action. But that long-range weapon was nothing compared to what was hidden in the earth along the front line. The strange-looking tripod things that came out of the ground reminded Lee of the alien vessels she'd

seen in *War of the Worlds*. In more ways than one. The
things were a lot smaller than the ones in the movies, but
they packed some firepower that made the Hollywood flick
look like child's play.

The light that pulsed out of them was sliver-thin. It
didn't seem possible that it could cut through the huge trees
like flame ate through paper. Whatever that pulsing light
touched was incinerated.

"Drop!"

The order sounded from somewhere near the front, and
Lee watched as the front line fell as one. Arms came up,
protecting the head as the Jorniak demons looked around,
a little confused. There was another tripod weapon, smaller
scale. It seemed to work on auto, sighting out demons, emitting one single pulse that turned the Jorniaks into gooey
puddles of ash, one right after the other.

The rumbling in the earth was increasing, and Lee
looked away from the front line to see a wyrm as it burst
through the earth. Probably a good quarter of a mile away
but easily visible now that the tripods had cut down the trees
along that sector, it swayed in the air, dark as the earth it
emerged from, its big mouth open and gaping.

Hearing a mechanical hum, Lee turned her head, watching as the tripods turned as one, locking in on the wyrm.
Those things could cut through trees and the smaller demons, but Lee couldn't believe they'd cut through that mam-
moth monster.

Until she saw it. Its death scream echoed through the
air, and it continued to scream even as the tripods severed
the head from the body. Two of them continued to work on
the body while the other sighted on the head and pulsed
away, moving in small increments and delivering a series
of strikes along the length of it.

The wyrm continued to scream even after its body
started to melt into the earth. It shuddered and trembled,
its body jerking as though it was still trying to free itself
from the earth. A second wyrm ripped through the earth.
Two of the tripods turned on the new threat, while the
third pulsed up and down, emitting those eerie, deadly

lights that soon turned the body of the first wyrm into a decaying, stinking mess.

A little dazed, Lee looked at Kalen. "Whoa."

He grinned, but it wasn't a happy one. It was savage and just a little mean, and his quicksilver eyes gleamed with the light of victory.

"I thought the wyrms were a bigger threat than that."

Kalen shrugged. "Up until recently, you would go weeks without coming to us. We've been developing these weapons for years, but this is the first time we've really been able to use them. They power up from the so-gens."

The so-gens were the generators that converted solar energy for use in most of the weapons and transports. Some of their smaller equipment had been designed solely for use of solar power, but the larger equipment hadn't been intended for it. Modifications were made where they could be, and they had a surplus of equipment that could be fueled with the energy processed for the so-gens, but not directly. The energy was transferred to the power grid, and while Lee didn't understand the tech behind it, the basic explanation was that the power was modified, broken down into its most raw form, and from there it could be manipulated and modified to suit whatever uses they needed it for.

Of themselves, the so-gens were reliable and safe enough. They could store the energy without posing a threat, but transporting that energy was the threat. Power grids couldn't store the energy safely, so until it was needed, it was kept in the so-gen. When the energy was transferred from the so-gen to the power grids, the power grid gave off the minute vibrations that lured the wyrms.

Strange that the things that called to the wyrms were the same things that gave Kalen's army the chance to destroy them. "How strong are those tripod-looking things?" Lee asked softly.

"We call them plas-beams—same basic tech we use in the plasma rifles. Just with more kick." Then he smirked and added, "As to how strong . . . well, they cut through the wyrms."

That was answer enough. Although the knowledge still

didn't feel like her own, she knew that wyrms had skin that would make Kevlar look fragile. Under the tough skin there was a membrane of thick, nearly indestructible tissue, so the wyrms were doubly protected. A weapon that could cut through those built-in protections—damn. "Whoa."

Intrigued, Lee looked westward. The brilliant blue of the gate continued to glow against the sullen gray sky. The gates seemed to eat whatever energy was launched at them, but no matter how hungry a creation got, eventually it could eat too much. "I wonder what would happen if we turned those on the gate."

But by the look on his face, Lee guessed Kalen had already made an attempt. He shook his head. "It won't work. We don't have enough of the plas-beams, and we can only maintain the energy for the ones we have, so building more is a waste of time and materials." Aggravated, he added, "That's assuming we could scavenge up the materials we'd need. We've been working on these for years. It took ten years just to develop the idea, and another five to build them and work out all the problems."

A little discouraged, Lee looked back to the gate. Okay, so the tripod/beam things wouldn't work.

But still . . .

* * *

"How many casualties?"

Arnon murmured, "Early estimates are in the thousands."

A cut crystal goblet went flying across the room, striking the wall and shattering in thousands of tiny little pieces. Neither Char nor Arnon even flinched. As the shards fell to the floor, the High Lord turned around and looked at Arnon, his black eyes cold with fury.

"Thousands." Taise shook his head, an incredulous look on his face. "Thousands." It was as if the old Warlord couldn't wrap his mind around the number. It was as though he'd been told fleas had mounted and managed to wipe out entire contingencies of men. It had been decades since Taise had begun his slow slide into madness. At first, he hadn't seemed so irrational as he ordered more frequent raids on Ishtan. But Char had seen the damage that was being done to the Veil and had advised caution. It was as though each piece of advice pushed the High Lord that much further along on his decline into insanity. Then Taise had decided he no longer wanted to raid the offworld's female population. He wanted to own it, all of it, from the oldest crone to the newborn babe. They'd begun construction on Anqar for the massive dwellings that would be needed to contain all of the slaves.

Char, once more, had warned the High Lord against his plan. Ishtan's people might be primitive, but they were, in their own way, as arrogant and proud as the Warlords. They would not quietly go into slavery. They would fight, and they would do considerable damage. That had been nearly thirty years ago, but Taise hadn't listened then any better than he listened now. It was as though the High Lord had never entertained the possibility that the resistance wouldn't break under their full strength.

"How is this possible?" Taise snarled.

Arnon looked at Char out of the corner of his eye. Char caught the warning there, but he ignored it. "High Lord, we knew of their technology. I gave fair warning that their unusual weapons might be a bigger threat than we were prepared to handle."

"That is what the bloody wyrms were for!" Taise roared.

In a smooth voice, Char replied, "They found a way to kill the wyrms." He still couldn't quite believe what he had seen as he observed through the Veil. Yes, he'd been aware of their little weapons, but nothing could kill the wyrms. Even the Warlords hadn't had much to control them once they had sent them into Ishtan. The wyrms were indestructible. Or so Char had thought. The ugly giants were Taise's favored pet. The wyrms couldn't survive in much of Anqar—the land was too arid and hot. Wyrms required less intense heat, but more, they couldn't survive in the dry deserts that made up most of their world. The swamps where they bred were their only natural environment on Anqar, and seeing the destruction the beasties wreaked, it was a bloody good thing, Char figured.

The High Lord's voice shook as he repeated, "They found a way to kill them?" Then he threw back his head and screamed. Char fought the urge to clap his hands over his ears as the scream droned on and on. Char braced himself as the High Lord's anger spun out of control, and his magick along with it. The earth shuddered under their feet, and the glass in the windows trembled. Across the receiving chamber, an ornate mirror, dating back more than three hundred years, fell from its mounting and hit the floor. Little mirrored slivers went flying, and Char found himself staring at his splintered reflection.

"You." The High Lord stopped screaming and pointed at Char. "You will go and fix this. You cost me thousands of my men and bring me back nothing. You will fix this—or I will see your head torn from your shoulders and mounted in front of the manse."

Char cocked a brow. Finally. "Are you sending me into Ishtan, High Lord?"

Taise's mouth twisted in a mocking smile. "Yes, Char. I am. Do you disapprove?"

With a respectful bow, Char said, "Of course not, my lord." Disapprove? Hell, he had been waiting for this chance for nearly three decades. But the High Lord's most trusted hand didn't leave the homeworld unless the High Lord ordered it. As the High Lord's health and sanity declined, it was required that Char remain closer and closer to High Keep, leaving him no other choice than to try and let others do his job. Others who failed.

But it wouldn't do to appear too eager. "But are you certain that this is the wisest course of action? Your enemies are many, Devoted Uncle. I hate to leave you unprotected."

Taise's face split into an ugly smile. "Yes. I am sure you do. However, I am far from unprotected. Go, Char. And do not return until you fix the mess you made."

Oh, I won't . . . Uncle. Char forced himself to smile

politely and bow once more. "I will prepare myself for the journey then. I may be gone for some time."

Already, Taise had dismissed Char's presence and was mumbling to himself. Probably counting his new body slaves. Well, Char would make sure a few pretty ones crossed over—a sad waste, but he'd have to if he wanted the old, sick bastard occupied elsewhere while Char dealt with his daughter.

He would find her. All it would take was being in the same world and he would find her. Blood called to blood. Anticipation had his blood pumping hard and fast as he walked toward his chambers. Char was tempted to move faster, perhaps even run. But Warlords didn't show that sort of emotion. As long as he had awaited this moment, he could certainly manage to walk instead of run.

He would find her and somehow, he would learn who had helped the child's mother slip across the gate. Whoever had helped them would be better off dead. Because if Char found the man who had aided a mated Tiris in fleeing her Warlord, the man would be put to death in a manner so slow, so painful, he would plead for death long before it came. Disgusted, Char acknowledged that if the High Lord had been in his right mind, Char could have sought her out before this.

He could have gone to the High Lord and requested a raiding party with the sole intention of finding his missing daughter. Daishan were highly prized, and a sane leader would have understood Char's request. But Taise had parted ways with sanity when Char was still in formal training. Char had ascended through the ranks hearing tales of his uncle's increasing paranoia and delusions.

Taise had done the unthinkable, things no Warlord would dare, and he had done so without fear of recrimination. Not one soul dared to speak against him. He had taken body slaves that had been mated and bred, taken them away from the Warlord who'd sired the slave's children, and he claimed it was his sovereign right. Many High Lords in the past had claimed sovereign right to take what body slaves they chose immediately after a raid, but none had ever taken a slave from a Warlord who'd impregnated and claimed a slave as his own personal woman. Taise had even sunk to claiming slaves so young they were naught but children, as though he thought claiming their youth would bring back his own.

Few spoke of it, but over the past ten years, the High Lord had become impotent and many Warlords breathed a sigh of relief. The raids, for so many years, had seemed vital to their way of life, providing females for a race that was, by far, predominantly male. Raids resulted in an adequate supply of females for all the Warlords, as well as the highly ranked Sirvani.

But as the High Lord went further into madness, he'd claimed more and more females, killing them with the fervor that had once been reserved for seducing the offworld females into accepting their new fates. Killing females . . . it was something most of them found utterly repugnant, yet the High Lord killed indiscriminately in his rages.

The younger slaves were no longer brought to the manse, not even for menial labor. There was little to be done about the High Lord claiming the best body slaves presented to him, although some of the Sirvani that led the raids had turned a blind eye to the Warlords waiting at the gate for their return. Char knew it happened. While it might be his duty as his uncle's second to stop it and punish the Sirvani and Warlords responsible, Char pretended ignorance. Bad enough serving under a crazy High Lord—he wasn't going to deny the men their well-earned rewards by letting Taise claim most of the body slaves for his personal use.

Those who survived the High Lord's attentions were all but broken by the time Taise was done with them. Not because he used them too harshly, but because if they failed to arouse him, the High Lord had his personal guard beat and rape them. If they survived, no man could go near them without the woman going into hysterics.

Most of the Warlords were above using such brutality with their women. It was considered a mark of honor for a Warlord to learn to seduce a body slave so that her screams were of passion rather than rage, fear or pain. Even if she tried to run once she recovered. It was a slow, subtle possession, thoroughly binding the body slave to her Warlord, so that eventually she came to crave his touch more than she craved her freedom.

Beating them bloody was a needless cruelty that left Char with a bad taste in his mouth. It was not unheard of, but worse, too many of the younger generation saw the High Lord's brutal treatment of the body slaves and began to echo it. More and more slaves began to run away, but they were ill-equipped to function in a world as harsh as Anqar.

Which led to death or recapture. The punishment for escaping wasn't a pleasant one, and most of the escaped slaves would rather end their lives out under the harsh sun than return to a Warlord. So many wasted lives, so much wasted power and Warlords that were cutting their teeth on the ways of cruelty, undermining thousands of years of tradition. All because Taise continued to rule.

As long as that insane bastard breathed, Char wasn't going to parade his daughter in front of the High Lord. If Taise would assert his sovereign right to take whatever woman he wanted, even mated and claimed women, then what was to stop him from crossing the line and taking a Daisha? Char's gut instinct was that nothing would stop the High Lord if Char's long-lost daughter caught his interest.

So he wouldn't proceed with this under the High Lord's blessing and rule. He would find his daughter, on his own, and he would bring her back to his personal province, and there she would stay until Char knew she wasn't in danger from the High Lord. His daughter was a Daisha, the rare female offspring between a Warlord and an offworld woman with great talent. There was no telling what magicks ran in her bloodstream. She was destined for great things.

Char had always known that, and he had spent so many years searching for her, wanting to bring her back so she could claim her rightful place in their society. It was going to take time—like any other offworld woman, she was going to resent his interference in her life, but once she realized who she was, it would be better. Once she realized that she was the daughter of the man who would rule An-qar, that she would be loved, valued and worshipped, that she wasn't to be a slave, she would accept her place.

Her place as his daughter. In time, he'd present her to his most loyal men, and when she chose her mate, she'd breed. Char would get grandsons, possibly even granddaughters, off her, securing the family line. Securing his power base.

Taise was such a doddering old fool. The man actually thought that the gates were representative of his power. He was wrong, though. Char knew just how wrong the High Lord was. In all his years, Taise had failed to realize the one lesson that Char had learned early on. The gates weren't a sign of power.

Children were.

ELEVEN

Lee stood in the middle of a slaughter. At least it looked that way to her. The atmosphere was bleak, and those around her moved with a grim focus as they gathered their dead. Already the smoke from the mass funeral pyre had painted the air with its heavy, acrid taint, and the fires wouldn't stop burning anytime soon.

But from what she could tell, these people were considering the past night a cautious victory. The families and elders, along with a heavy escort, were already far away. Word had come in that reinforcements were close, closer than Kalen had anticipated.

Despite the loss of life, the general consensus was guardedly optimistic.

But Lee had lost count of the bodies she had seen. She had helped move more than fifty before she stopped counting. In a numb, trance-like state, she had moved bodies until she simply couldn't lift any more. It had been near dawn when she started, and twilight had fallen long before she stopped.

Lee had given up long before most of the others. She

had stopped frequently to empty her stomach, and though she had pretty much purged herself, she still had to fight the dry heaves. Morne had told her to leave the care of the dead to others, but Lee hadn't walked away until Kalen came and forcibly carried her away.

Guilt was eating her alive.

Kalen was so certain that she was important to this fight, and Lee had believed him. Arrogant, much? One person couldn't hope to make the kind of difference these people needed. Not unless it came with divine interven- tion. Because she couldn't figure out what it was she was supposed to do, thousands had died.

More were going to die unless she could figure out what in the hell it was. Those dark, depressing thoughts chased her through the night as she tried to make herself rest. It was an exercise in futility, she decided, after nightmares woke her for the third time. Climbing from her mat on the ground, Lee stared up at the sky. It was clouded and a dark gray that was only a few shades lighter now at dawn than it had been at midnight.

She took a deep breath and instantly regretted it. The air stank of smoke, burning flesh and putrid death. Her gut threatened to revolt, and in self-defense, she turned away from the camp and headed into the forest. Several of the men guarding the line called to her and one actually blocked her path. "We haven't completely secured the for- est, Lelia."

Lee squinted at him in the dim morning light, trying to recall his name. Reshen. Reesen. Something like that. "I can take care of myself," she said and went around him. He caught her arm as she passed by, and she stopped in her tracks and looked down at his hand. Then she lifted her eyes and stared at him.

His hand fell away and Lee turned her head to hide her smirk. She was still trying to come to grips with the mem- ories in her head. They still felt foreign, but every time somebody demonstrated that deferential courtesy, it drove them home just a little more. The cynical bitch apparently wasn't some figment of her imagination. The years she had spent sliding in and out of this world had established her reputation as one seriously *kick-ass* bitch.

Too bad she didn't feel up to the title.

As she pushed through the undergrowth, she breathed in slowly and let the scents of trees and earth fill her head. The nausea churning in her gut eased a little and some of the tension seeped out of her body. It was still riding on her, and she would have severed an arm just for an hour in her whirlpool tub back home.

The communal bathing areas had been transformed into a medical shelter for the injured, so Lee had been forced to clean up using a jury-rigged portable shower. The lukewarm water did nothing to ease the knots in her muscles even if it did clean away the grime and gore.

"You finally took that bath."

Lee looked over her shoulder, watching as Kalen separated himself from the fog. Little wisps of it wrapped around his legs as he headed toward her—the effect was both seductive and eerie. Which, she figured, described Kalen Brenner pretty damn well. He was mouthwateringly gorgeous, all that power and raw sensuality all but oozing from his pores. He was also death incarnate, and he wasn't at all satisfied to stay back from the front line when the demons and Sirvani pushed through.

He had sliced, hacked and punched his way through the demons that had tried to surround the leader. The weapons he used seemed to come to his hands of their own volition, and he used them with startling ease. Damned seductive and damned eerie.

His hair was pulled back from his face, fastened in a tail at the nape of his neck. The dirt smudges were gone from his face, and his bloodied clothes had been replaced. "You, too."

Kalen glanced down at his fresh clothes. "Morne all but threw me in the river. Then he told me to check on you." He looked around them and then looked at her. "It isn't safe out here alone, Lee. We haven't secured the forest yet. They aren't done, Lee."

Something hot and ugly moved through her. She smiled and whispered, "Good. Where can I find them?"

At that, Kalen cocked a brow at her. "Hungry for blood, are you?"

"Aren't you?"

A smile tipped up the corners of his lips. "Oh, always." The smile faded and his eyes softened as he studied her face. "You handled yourself well out there."

With a snort, Lee muttered, "I don't know about that. How much good did I do you?" The dead were going to haunt her. Lee didn't know if she'd ever close her eyes without seeing them again.

Warm hands cupped her face. Lifting her lashes, she looked up at Kalen, and the understanding she saw there undermined all her efforts not to think too much. She wanted to cry. She wanted to scream. She wanted to find someplace dark and quiet and safe so she could hide. She couldn't do any of those things, though.

So instead, she pushed up on her toes and pressed her lips to the hard, firm line of Kalen's mouth. He was unresponsive for a moment and then his hands skimmed down, closing loosely over her waist. When she licked his lips, his hands tightened convulsively.

He smelled so damned good. Clean, sexy, male, and something dark and mysterious. It was addictive. When his lips parted, she pushed her tongue into his mouth. They groaned simultaneously and, greedy, Lee pressed her body completely against his.

"This isn't a good idea," Kalen growled against her lips.

She pulled back just a little and smiled. "I think it's a wonderful idea." She tugged at his shirt. He held still. For a minute there, she thought he might pull away. But then like a spring uncoiling, he leaped into action. The world spun around as he lifted her, turning so that he could press her back up against a tree. He slid a hand down the front of the sleeveless matte black protective gear he wore, and the cavinir parted in its wake, revealing deeply tanned, hard flesh. The muscles in his belly jumped as she touched him. He caught her hands and lifted them high over her head, pressing her wrists against the rough bark for a moment, his gaze holding hers. When he slid his hands back down her arms, Lee held the position. There was a branch just above her hands and she curled her fingers around it.

Kalen unfastened her shirt and it parted. Under it, she wore a skintight tunic of midnight black. It served as both undershirt and bra, pressing her breasts flat against her chest. Kalen's dark head dipped, and Lee realized that as sturdy as the black chemise thing seemed, it was proving to be little barrier to Kalen. She could feel the heat of his mouth through the layers, and her nipples stiffened. Through the clothing, he licked, nuzzled and bit until she was moaning and rocking against him.

His hands moved to her waist and made short work of the form-fitting black pants. Her boots fell to the forest floor with a dull thud, and she opened her eyes, watching as he smoothed his palms down the outside of her legs, taking the pants with him. When they pooled around her ankles, he stripped them completely away and threw them aside.

His gaze lowered, focusing on the core of her body. He leaned forward and pressed his mouth against the blond curls covering her sex. Lee moaned and arched against his mouth. Her heart pounded, her breathing kicked up, and the roaring in her ears drowned out the memories of people screaming as they died. Under his touch, the stain of death fell away, replaced by the pleasure of life.

Hard, calloused hands cupped her hips, holding her steady as he caressed her. His tongue circled over the bud of her clit, quick and teasing. She panted and rocked against him. She lowered her hands, clutching at the black silk of his hair, trying to pull him closer. But he stopped. He lifted his head, looked up at her and then flicked a glance over her head.

Lee groaned, but reached back for the branch, locking her fingers around it. He smiled and lowered his mouth back to her sex, rewarding her by pushing his tongue inside. It was heat. It was bliss. It was heaven. He teased, taunted, pushed her ever closer to climax, and, mindless, Lee lowered her hands again, this time clenching her fingers around his shoulders. "Kalen—please . . ."

But he stopped. Again. Looked up at her. Looked up at the branch. She tried to pull him back to her, but he wouldn't budge. With a cry, she resumed her former position, arms stretched high overhead, naked from the waist down, feeling totally exposed and so damned hungry, she thought she just might die if he didn't let her come.

His mouth came back to her and he circled his tongue over her clit. One hand stroked down the outside of her thigh and caught her behind the knee. He pushed it high, leaving her exposed and open as he pushed his tongue inside her. Lee bit her lip to keep from screaming.

Closer and closer he took her, and Lee squeezed the branch so hard the bark cut into her palms. Terrified he'd stop again, she didn't dare move, but when her climax hit, her body bucked and shuddered. She let go then, reaching for his shoulders in an effort to brace herself. She sagged back against the tree and sobbed under her breath as the orgasm rippled through her body, each spasm stronger than the last.

Her breath lodged in her throat and her vision narrowed down and she could see nothing but his face. That harsh, compelling face. His eyes gleamed like molten silver as he stood up, pressing his body to hers. Layers of cloth still separated them, but she could feel him through it. His cock pressed into her belly and, hungrily, she rocked forward. Desperate to have him inside her, she reached for the waistband of his pants, and this time, he let her touch him.

She tore them open, her hands clumsy. He was naked under the pants. She made a little humming sound of approval as she closed one hand around him. His cock was hard and thick, his skin as soft as satin, his erection hard as steel. She dragged one hand up and down his length. From under her lashes, she watched as a clear bead of fluid welled from the tip. She caught it on her thumb, lifted it to her mouth and licked it away.

Kalen groaned. With one arm, he lifted her. His free hand fisted in her hair and tipped her face to his. He covered her mouth with his and muttered against her lips, "Wrap your legs around me."

Mindless, she did as he ordered, and she whimpered as

the action pressed them together, heat against heat. He shifted position, dipped his knees, and then he pushed inside her.

She arched against him, clenching around him. As one, they cried out. "I need you," he whispered. He bent his head and pressed a kiss to the curve where neck and shoulder joined. "Every day you weren't with me made me die a little inside."

Her heart melted. Winding her arms around his neck, she pulled him closer and murmured, "I'm here now."

"Just tell me you'll stay. Stay here. Stay safe."

Safe . . . Damn it, what a fairy tale. He was asking her for a promise that they both knew she couldn't possibly make, not when the road before them was still so damned uncertain. "I'm here now," she whispered. Lee brushed her lips against his. "I'm safe now . . . here with you. Make love to me."

His hands stroked down her sides, cupped her ass and pulled her tight against him. "I want you safe," he muttered, his voice harsh, guttural. "Look at me, Lee."

Her lids were so damned heavy, it was an effort just to open her eyes, but she couldn't resist that harsh, guttural command. Tipping her head back, she stared at him. "Kalen . . ."

Her lashes started to flutter back down over her eyes, and Kalen growled. "Look at me," he repeated, his voice still harsh and demanding. "Watch me . . ."

A slow, seductive smile curved her lips. "I'm looking. I am watching you, Kalen. You're all I see—even when I thought you were just a figment of my imagination."

Hunger twined with the gut-deep need for her, a need that went beyond love, beyond lust, beyond anything and everything he'd ever known. Kalen straightened away from the tree and pivoted. "I want a bed in which to lay you," he whispered. "A real bed with pillows and silk sheets."

She smiled at him. "I don't need a bed. Just make love to me."

No. She might not need one, but he wanted to give her one. Wanted something soft and beautiful for her, something like what she'd given up to come to him. Instead, he carried her to the riverfront. Huge rocks jutted out over it, and he found one that was smooth and flat. It was too early in the morning for the dim light from the sun to have warmed the rock, and when he laid her back against it, she shivered from the chill. She gasped, arching into him, and Kalen rolled so that she straddled him.

Cupping his hands over her hips, he rocked her against him. She stared down at him, her hair falling in a tangle around her shoulders. The long curls flirted with her breasts, her nipples playing peekaboo through the hair. She tipped her head back to the sky and arched as she moved against him.

Slick, silky and wet, she clenched around him. Soft and strong, she rode him until sweat broke out on their bodies and their breathing was harsh and ragged. Kalen's cock jerked inside the snug satin of her sheath, and then he swore as she smiled down at him and slowed her rhythm. He could feel the climax burning inside his balls, and from the look on her face, she knew what she was doing to him. He reached up, fisting a hand in her curls and winding the long locks around his wrist. He used his hold on her hair to pull her mouth to his, and as he kissed her, he flipped them over, putting her body under his. He came into her hard and fast, pushing deep, deeper, until she had taken all of him.

Then he pulled out, slow and easy. He thrust into her hard and fast, then followed each thrust with that slow, gentle withdrawal, and soon she was clenching and bucking and whimpering underneath him. Soft, ragged little pleas escaped her lips, and Kalen swallowed them down, crushing her mouth under his.

They climaxed together, arching into each other. Kalen tore his mouth away from hers and shouted out. Beneath him, Lee cried out his name, and when he kissed her again, he could taste tears. Shaken, he lowered his head and pressed his brow to hers. "I love you."

She pressed her lips to his. "I know. Your love is what brought me here." Lee skimmed a hand down his side. Her lashes lifted and her eyes glowed warm and blue as she stared at him.

"You're here because you belong here." He rolled off her and onto his back, bringing her with him. She automatically curled up against him, pillowing her head on his chest.

"Yes. Here with you." She glanced around them, her gaze sad. "Everything that's going on here, it's hard, it's heartbreaking. But memories of this place aren't the reason I'd wake up and want to cry, without even understanding why. When I woke up, empty and so lonely it hurt, it was because I needed to be with you. The where of it didn't matter."

* * *

She meant what she'd said. Although she was still struggling with her memories, she wasn't struggling with how she felt about Kalen. Admitting how she felt about him was actually the easiest thing in her life right now. Going back to face that battlefield was hard. Admitting to herself that she loved Kalen wasn't—she just hoped she was going to live long enough to see how this all played out.

He had left her alone after he'd checked the area and made sure it was secure. "Don't trust me to take care of myself?" she asked with half a smile.

"Don't trust anybody enough to make sure you don't get hurt." But he'd softened the words with a kiss, so she let him investigate, and when he'd left her, he had made her promise to hurry back to the base camp.

That was one thing she didn't want to do, but she couldn't hide in the forest forever. It was safe enough where she was at, for now, but that could change too easy and too fast.

Way too fast. Lee felt the ripple in the forest and her breath froze in her lungs. Everything inside her went cold as she sensed the threat whispering through the air. Instinctively, she lowered her shields and reached out, searching for the source of the threat, but the minute she did so, she yanked them back up, hard and fast.

The threat wasn't here, per se. It was on the other side of the Veil, but whoever it was, he was searching for her. That thought had barely finished forming in her mind when her skin started to crawl.

Well, damn it all to hell, Lee thought as she watched the dazzling blue of the Veil rippling into place right in front of her. She braced herself for the worst. A powerful Warlord could force up small gates, enough for one or two people to pass through, and all they needed to do it was enough energy rumbling within the earth.

There was plenty of power here.

But no gate formed. She could see through the Veil, but if she reached out and tried to touch it, all she would do was grasp at air. There was a man on the other side, and he was watching her with a wide, pleased smile.

When he spoke, it was in that same, hissing, guttural language she had overheard in the forest just a few days ago. The language she shouldn't have been able to understand.

And right now, it was a language she didn't want to understand. Right now, she would have given anything for his words to be nothing more than gibberish.

"Hello, daughter."

Lee blinked. The man on the other side of the Veil looked tall, although it was hard to tell for sure. His hair was the same unusual blond as hers, shot through with strands of every shade of blond imaginable. He had wide, wide shoulders and big hands. Long-fingered hands, and it wasn't any stretch of the imagination to picture him wrapping those hands around the hilt of the sword she could see peeking over his shoulders.

He looked like a fair-haired cross between the Sheriff of Nottingham and William Wallace. A series of intricate braids on each side kept his hair out of his face, and the rest of it fell down his back, even longer than hers. However, there was nothing at all feminine about his appearance.

He wore a thick, short chain around his neck with a big blue jewel set in filigree. The stone was about the size of a baby's fist and it pulsed. Distantly, Lee realized she'd seen a stone like that before. Just a few days ago here in the forest.

This one was bigger. Darker. And it sang—Lee could hear it. It sang to her, calling her. It was a sweet, lyrical beckoning, and if it hadn't been for the man, she just might have reached out to see what happened if she tried to touch the stone.

But the man was there and he was staring at her expectantly. Lee shook her head. The words felt weird on her tongue, and her throat wasn't used to making the words. The trills, followed by deep, almost growling syllables didn't feel natural, and her voice shook a little as she said, "Who are you?"

He smiled a little and his austere, almost cold face warmed just a bit. "I wouldn't expect you to remember. You were but a baby when she stole you away from me."

Lee said quietly, "I don't know you. I don't know who you are talking about."

"Your mother never told you?"

"She's dead." Lee clenched her hands into fists and fought not to let the old pain rear its head, but it was hard. Damn hard. She couldn't understand it. She hardly ever thought of her mom. It had been twenty years since Lee had been abandoned—or since her mother had been killed. Lee didn't remember which, and she usually didn't spend much time dwelling on it. Her childhood hadn't totally sucked, and she'd moved past the hurt feelings a long time ago.

But for some reason, staring at this man brought that forgotten pain back. Whether she had been abandoned or her mother had been killed, Lee had been left alone.

"Dead . . ." The man's gaze lowered. Something moved across his face—it almost looked like sadness. "Neve—dead all these years."

Neve. For a minute, she stared at him blankly, and then the knowledge plowed into her like a sledgehammer. *Neve*—oh, shit. *Neve*—Aneva. Lee's mother. Eira had given her the emsphere of her mother and she'd spoken of her daughter with love and pride. *Aneva—my Ana.* When Lee had looked at the emsphere's image of her mother, it had stirred memories. Vague ones. Fleeting images and little snippets of song were all Lee had been able to remember of her mother, but looking at that young, smiling face seemed to bring back memories long forgotten.

Neve—Aneva. "Aneva," Lee repeated in a hollow voice.

The man looked back at her with a sympathetic expression. "Aneva was her name from offworld. All slaves are given new names to go with their new homes. The less they have to remember their previous lives, the easier it is to accept their new ones."

Shock had her voice shaking as she whispered, "Slave?"

"Not for long, my Daisha. Neve was a powerful witch, a beautiful woman—and she bore me twin sons. I took her as my mate, and for two years, she lived with me and was afforded all the luxuries my wife deserved. She was respected, cared for. My Tiris—"

Tiris. Lee closed her eyes. That word reverberated through her, touching some odd chord for reasons she couldn't quite define. Tiris—a woman mated to a Warlord. She knew that. She didn't know how she knew, but she knew. The same way she knew that Daisha meant daughter. Daughter—

"She took you from me one night while I was with my men. You were so small, so delicate—so precious. I was so proud of my little daughter and the woman who bore her. Then she took you," the Warlord murmured. His eyes darkened with fury, and Lee flinched as sharp, discordant chords started to splinter through the air. The ethereal, haunting music turned into something ugly and violent, and the wispy edges of the Veil became darker. The lines of his face got deeper, and the rage coming off him made the air go icy. "I was fond of Neve, but in that moment, when I returned home and came to the nursery to see you . . ."

His gaze locked with hers, and the punch of his rage reached across the Veil, striking her with painful intensity and freezing the air in her lungs. She wheezed out a breath. The world swayed around her and she had to lock her knees just to stay upright. "When I found your crib empty and your nurse unconscious and bound, I could have killed Neve."

Lee believed it, too. She believed he could have killed her mother, but more, she believed every single word he said. Believed him when he said that her mother had been a slave, and that *he* was her father. A man who had kidnapped her mother. A man who came from the bastards that were trying to take over Ishtan—he was her father.

Lee didn't want to believe him. She wanted to discount all of it. She couldn't, though.

"You . . ." Her voice trailed off, a weak, breathy little sigh. Lee swallowed, cleared her throat and then tried again. "You are my father."

The fury leeched out of his face, and his glowing blue eyes no longer looked so malevolent. A smile curved his lips and Lee shivered. "Yes. I am. I've been searching for you for a long, long time, Lenena."

Lee's voice shook as she whispered, "My name is Lee. Or Lelia, if you must." A mean smile curved her lips. "Apparently when my mother took me away from you, she wanted no reminders of our past lives, either. Lelia is the name she gave me." Her heart was pounding hard and fast inside her chest, and she wanted to scream. Her mother had been a slave. This bastard had kidnapped her mother, raped her—the thoughts spinning through her head slammed to a halt and she stared at him. "You said sons. Does that mean I have brothers?"

He inclined his head. "Indeed. The twins are powerful, strong men. They will do you proud." He studied her with that eerie, possessive little smile. "You will do *us* proud. It's time to return to your home, Daisha."

He lifted a hand as though he was going to reach out for her, and Lee felt a ripple in the Veil. The power inside it strengthened as it started to shift the gate energies and re-shape the Veil into a true portal. She backpedaled away as fast as she could, drawing the blade she had tucked into her boot. It felt awkward in her hands and, at the same time, completely natural. "I *am* home, you arrogant bastard."

She tripped and ended up on her ass, and fear wrapped a chokehold around her throat as the gate energies continued to work their magick. As the Veil transitioned into a portal, she could feel the heat of the desert winds blowing, she could smell something exotic and sweet, and the intensity of the man in front of her reached out to wrap itself around her. It was an insidious magick. He hadn't said a word, but she had the oddest urge to reach out to him. To go through the Veil and let him take her away. Someplace safe. Someplace where she would be cared for, pampered and protected—

She could see herself rising, moving toward him with her hand outstretched. Her foot brushed against something, and she looked down, realized she had dropped her blade. A knife Kalen had given her, made of some dense, dark metal that glinted blue under strong light. The sight of that knife stilled something inside her.

The weird urge to join the Warlord faded, and instead of the safe, pampered existence his presence offered, she saw it for what it was. A silken prison. Yes, she'd be cared for, pampered and protected, but she would also have men paraded before her until she claimed a husband, and then she would spend months on her back as he tried to impregnate her. Any male child would be taken away and sent to warrior training. Females would be allowed to remain with her for a time, but even they would be stolen away and groomed to become mates for the Warlords.

The rush of fury cleared her head, and she took a step back just as he reached out. She watched clinically as his hand pushed through the barrier. His flesh was pale and his hand looked strong. Scarred, calloused and hard. Had he used those hands to hurt her mother?

Slowly, Lee looked up at him and shook her head. "If you want me, you'll have to do more than that." She drew her arm back like she was launching a fastball and watched as silver fire went hurtling toward his face. She heard him yell, and even as she launched out, part of her whispered, *That was a bad, bad idea . . .*

Something reached out of the gate, wispy and insubstantial as smoke. It caught her magick, sucked inside. She heard the Warlord shout out, "No!" He slashed a hand through the air, and the power fabric that held the gate together splintered as it consumed the magick. "Get back, Daisha." His shout was distant, tinny, and she must have been imagining it, but he sounded *worried*. Terror filled her as more of those smoky tendrils snaked out of the gate, reaching for her.

She jerked back, instinctively shutting down her magick.

Seconds passed as those smoky things continued to reach for her. Time slowed down, and she was excruciatingly aware of each passing second as the gate's energies tried to reach her. Tension mounted until the silence seemed to scream, and then a huge crack of thunder ripped through the air above.

The gate fractured and fell, and Lee heaved out a sigh of relief. Above, the clouds opened up, and as the torrential downfall started from above, the ground rumbled. Lee braced herself, but there was no quake. Just a series of tremors that lasted less than a few minutes. Squinting through the rain, she stared at the empty spot where the gate had stood. It was gone now, as was the Warlord—but his words continued to echo through her mind.

It's time to return to your home, Daisha.

Like hell, Lee thought. The gate might be gone, for now, but she wanted to get as far away from this place as she could. Without waiting another second, she turned and ran through the forest. Heartbreak, fear and fury pulsed inside her and she couldn't run fast enough to get away. She tried, though, running headlong through the forest, uncaring of the noise she made, uncaring of the trail she left behind her. All she cared about was getting away from the man who had stared back at her with eyes nearly identical to her own.

Hello, daughter . . .

I've been searching for you for a long, long time.

My Daisha, he'd called her, watching her with a weird mix of pride and possessiveness. Like the way Lee had looked at her first car. She didn't understand how he had found her or why he was determined to get her back, but Lee didn't have to understand it to be terrified. Even before he had said a single word, something about him made her gut clench with fear. The way he had watched her, as though he knew her, as though she should know him.

Hello, daughter . . .

Daughter. God. She could feel the scream of denial tearing at her throat, but she didn't want to scream. Not yet. She couldn't. If she started screaming now, she wouldn't stop, and she couldn't do it here. Not until she was back at the camp, with at least the illusion of safety surrounding her. Just an illusion, though. She had watched as the man forged a small gate out of thin air. She knew the Warlords had power over the gates, but facing one who had the power to create one out of thin air had shaken her to the core.

Theoretically, she knew it was possible, but she hadn't really prepared herself for seeing it.

I don't know why you weren't prepared . . . How do you think you came to be here?

That sly little voice whispered inside her head, and Lee wanted to scream as she realized the truth of those words. Lee had made her own gate. Without even knowing how or understanding what she was doing. Only Warlords have control over the gates. Kalen had told her a thousand times.

Only Warlords.

Only Warlords.

Denial burned inside her and she felt her stomach start to roil. Only Warlords. Warlords who enslaved women and turned them into little more than breeding machines. Warlords who stole away the children from their mothers, raising the boys to be good little raiders and the daughters to be obedient little whores. That scream burgeoning inside her was threatening to come loose, and Lee clamped a hand over her mouth as though that would keep it trapped inside.

Only Warlords, and you are a Warlord's daughter. More, she wasn't just a daughter. She had the power to sense the Veil, and she apparently had the power to lift a gate and shut it down; otherwise she never would have been traveling back and forth between the worlds.

Warlord—

Enemy. It throbbed deep inside and Lee slowed down, then stopped altogether. She lifted her hands and stared at them. *Enemy!*

Just ahead she caught sight of the makeshift barricades. She wanted to turn away and run. Just run and disappear. She didn't belong in there. She was a fake, a traitor. The blood of the enemy pulsed through her veins, and she had almost walked willingly to his side.

To her father's side.

No. Those voices were in her head again, but this time that cold, cynical bitch didn't sound so cold. She actually sounded compassionate. *You didn't willingly go to him. Warlords have the power of compulsion. He can make weaker people do whatever he wishes. That you resisted him is a sign of your strength.*

Lee sucked in a harsh breath and tried to still the nerves jangling in her belly, but it wasn't happening. She was shaking all over, shaking hard, and it was steadily getting worse. Lee shouldn't have stopped running. Now that she had, the tremors were getting so violent she could barely walk.

Kalen—

She just needed to get to Kalen. She pulled up the memory of his face and focused on that. Then she started to walk, focusing on nothing but that mental picture. She'd get to Kalen. Get to him and then she'd . . . then she'd what? Dear God. Lee closed her eyes and prayed desperately, searching for some kind of answer. What was she going to do? Kalen would take one look at her and know something was wrong. He'd want to know, and what was she going to tell him?

I just met my dad. He's one of the bastards that have been kidnapping your women. He kidnapped my mother, and I have two brothers, but I think they live with my daddy.

Oh, yeah. That was going to go over really well.

***

She couldn't tell him.

Lee stood off to the side and watched as Kalen spoke over the mass funeral pyre. Although his stoic face revealed little, she could feel the pain inside him, the pain and the impotent fury. He'd lost so much in his life, and all of it was because of the Warlords.

How could she possibly face him and tell him that one of those Warlords was her father? Tell him that the man was looking for her. It was even possible that her father was the reason the gate was so often raised. If he had been looking for her since she'd disappeared, then he had

probably used the gates hard and often since she had disappeared twenty some odd years ago.

A knot formed in her throat as she watched Kalen lower
his torch to the funeral pyre. She felt the heat of it as it en-
gulfed the fuel-soaked wood, the flames greedily licking
at the corpses. Still, she felt chilled.

Was all of this her fault?

He was an important man in Anqar, Lee's father. She'd
recognized the power inside him, and the size and color of
the stone around his neck meant a great deal. He was in a
high enough echelon that he could very well be behind all
of these raids.

Her gut churned and Lee swayed as a bout of nausea
struck her hard and fast. Could it be?

Please, God, no.

A sad, poignant voice rose from the people gathered around
the funeral pyre. Other voices joined in, singing a melody
that was heartachingly sad and so beautiful it barely
seemed real. Tears blurred her vision and her breathing
hitched a little in her chest as she studied the mourners.

Warriors, one and all. The families, children and elderly,
had been evacuated, and the only people who remained at
the destroyed base camp were warriors, deirons and medics. Battle-scarred and battle-hardened, they all looked as
tough as nails, but as they sang for their dead, Lee saw
their pain.

Dais stood off to Kalen's right, his head tipped up to the
sky, and she watched as the older man wiped away a tear.
Morne stood just to Lee's right, staring into the fires of the
dead, and for once, his impossibly dark eyes weren't so
unreadable.

The emotion she saw everywhere was enough to tighten
the knot in her throat until it threatened to choke her. *Dear
God—is it my fault?*

Somewhere in front of her, Lee heard a choking sob,
and unable to take it anymore, she slipped away. She waited
until the trees closed behind her before she took off running, and then she ran, ran until her muscles burned with
exhaustion and breathing was all but impossible.

Tears blinded her and she ended up tripping, landing on her hands and knees and then shoving back to her feet again and starting the process all over.

My fault—

She had no way of knowing. Not unless she asked "Daddy," but Lee wasn't certain she could handle the truth, even if she did see him. *There is no "if."* She would see him again. If he had been searching for her for twenty years, then he wasn't going to stop looking until he had her.

Power danced through the air. There was a strange, sighing little sound and then the music started. *No. Shit, I can't handle this again,* she thought, backing away. She saw the energy rising up out of the ground, coalescing in front of her. The Veil took form and Lee watched, shaking her head in denial.

"Daughter."

Lee hissed at him. Fury blistered through her and she welcomed it. It was a sweet respite over the grief and the pain, and it made her feel stronger. Perhaps it was just the illusion of strength, but as she faced the Warlord across the Veil, she imagined that the illusion of strength was better than nothing.

Warlords respected strength even if they respected little else.

"Don't call me that," she snarled.

A smile tugged at his lips. "Then what shall I call you? I called you by your name once and you told me not to call you that either."

She sneered at him. "You don't have to call me anything. Leave me the hell alone."

He sighed and shook his head. "Now, that is one thing I cannot do. You belong with your people, Daisha. People who understand your power. People who can protect you."

Icily, she said, "I'll take care of myself, thanks. Leave me alone."

The Veil's power solidified, and Lee started to tremble as the power wove itself into something more substantial. He created a gate as easily as Lee could turn on her computer back home. The power came too naturally to him. "I will not leave you alone, Lee. You will return with me."

Now his smile took on a decidedly sly bent. "You care for these people you fight with. You grieve. I feel the echo of your grief. Would you do aught to save them?"

His words froze her to the very bone. "What do you mean?"

"I think you know what I mean," he mused. "How many have already died, Lee? We will come through the gate, and I will stop at nothing until I find you. How many more must die?"

"Go away," she gritted out.

But he acted as though he didn't hear her as he murmured, "None, Daisha. No one else must die." He held out a hand. "The days of our coming to Ishtan, seeking offworld females, are coming to an end. It can end here. Now. Just return to your home, Daughter. Come home. No one else must die."

His words had the same effect on her as a sucker punch, right to the gut. She staggered back, reeling and gasping for breath. *It is my fault,* Lee realized. Sick and weak, she dropped to her knees and stared at him. Her voice was stilted as she asked, "You would call your armies off if I go to Anqar?"

He lifted one shoulder, shrugging gracefully. "This is your home, Daisha. You belong here. I understand the power that flows inside your veins. I sense it. You're strong, and you would pass that strength on to your children. Sons and daughters. You belong here."

Lee shook her head. The knot in her throat was making it hard to speak, choking her, and the need to puke was rising inside. She kept swallowing, hoping to hold the bile back, but it was getting harder and harder. "That isn't what I asked. If I do what you ask, you'll call your men off?"

He inclined his head. "That is what I said, Daisha. Warlords do not lie, not to offworlders and certainly not to our children. Come home, and your friends will be left alone. They can rebuild their world in peace." He turned his dark gaze to the gate, focusing on the perimeter. "The gates will fail—surely the offworld army you fight with has recognized how unstable the gates are. They will falter and fall." His smile turned cruel and cunning. "But do not think that to be a means to escape me, Daughter. I will not lower this gate until you are at my side where you belong, and I care not if both worlds perish from it. Or you can come to me now and save them all."

You're the key, Lee.

How many times had Kalen said that to her?

He seemed to think it was some kind of power she had inside her, and Lee had let herself believe him. Kalen was right, Lee realized, in a way. But it wasn't any kind of power she had. It was the blood in her veins. Warlord blood—and her father was willing to leave Ishtan alone if she joined him.

Her knees wobbled as she stood up. "Now?" she asked, her voice trembling.

He gazed at her with compassion, and that infuriated her until she could hardly see straight. She didn't want his compassion, and she didn't want his pity, his empathy, his love—*nothing*. She sure as hell didn't want to cross the gate into Anqar and become a good little broodmare for her Warlord daddy.

But what choice did she have?

"Now is for the best. Leaving them will not get easier for saying good-byes, Daisha. They will not understand."

No. They wouldn't. And she couldn't stand to see the hatred in Kalen's eyes if he knew. A sob threatened to choke her, and she swallowed, fighting not to let it out. Mute, she nodded. Her legs shook as she took one step. Then another.

"You are doing the honorable thing—you truly are the daughter of a Warlord," he marveled, and his eyes all but glowed with pride as he stared at her. Lee wanted to gouge them out. She wanted to hit him. She wanted to pull one of the weapons from her pack and turn it on him.

Instead she took another shaky step.

"She's not going anywhere."

Morne's voice was both a welcome intrusion and a harbinger. She saw him separate from the shadows of the forest, clad in black from head to toe, his face hidden by the black hood wrapped around him so that only his eyes showed. That dark blue snapped with a fury that surprised her.

"Lee, one more step and I will render you unconscious. You will not do this."

"I don't have a choice," she whispered. Terror and rage warred for supremacy inside her, and it made it damn hard to speak. She covered her face with her hands and struggled to breathe. She stood there, shoulders slumped and head bowed. Like nothing else, she wished she could do as Morne asked and pull away from the man who'd fathered her. She knew no loyalties to the man, and her soul rebelled at the thought of going to him, letting him place her in some silken prison and turn her into some glorified version of a broodmare.

But she did have a loyalty to Kalen. Though she had been in his world such a short time, so much of it felt familiar and she had memories of this place dating back to her childhood. If going with this strange, terrifying stranger would end the war between these worlds, what true choice did she have?

You can't trust him. That internal voice urged her to go to Morne, hide behind him and let him handle this—more, she wanted to call for Kalen. Wanted to feel his arms around her and snuggle against him. She'd feel a bit safer for it.

But there was also a part of her that did recognize some part of the Warlord. His words echoed with truth, and she knew he meant every word he said. Was it naive of her to think he would do as he said when his kind was responsible for so many deaths? Lee didn't know. She only knew that she believed him. Completely.

Slowly, Lee lowered her hands and looked at Morne. He had moved closer, aligning himself at her shoulder, and as their gazes locked, he edged in. It was a minute, instinctive moment, but she knew exactly what he was doing. Blocking her from the man who stood at the gate. "I don't have any choice, Morne."

Under that weird mask, she couldn't make out any expression on Morne's face. Nothing save his eyes. "In a way, Lelia, you are right. In this, you have no choice." He reached up, touching his fingers to her brow.

If she had known him a little better, the queer note in his voice might have warned her. But Lee was totally unprepared for the onslaught of power that struck her. It swarmed out of Morne and flooded her entire being in a matter of heartbeats. It wrapped itself around her mind, and before she could even form a single thought, her vision went dark and she slumped forward.

Morne caught her weight and lifted her in his arms before she could collapse to the ground. He slid the man standing at the gate a narrow look. He knew the man and wasn't surprised to see that the Warlord had already drawn his blade. "You do not wish to pursue this, Warlord. It will not go well for you."

"I'll gut you where you stand, you daft, offworld bastard. She isn't safe there. You have no idea how to train her, how to deal with her. She barely even understands her magick."

Behind the concealing material of his mask, Morne smiled. "She understands better than you think. And if you think safe is a fair trade in exchange for freedom, you do not know women at all."

"I could care less about *women*." He lifted his blade and made as if to cross the gate. "Just her."

Morne grinned. "Have you a Sirvani anchoring the gate for your passage, Warlord? If you think I would hand her over to you without a fight, then you're the daft fool. You want her, you will have to cut me down to get her—and all of the men who even now rush to her side. With no Sirvani anchoring the gate for you, have you the time before it falters and becomes unstable? Harder to erect the gate on this side of the Veil."

"Know so much about the gates, do you?" The Warlord paused, his eyes narrowed and thoughtful.

Morne shrugged. Obliquely, he replied, "You learn much of your enemy during war." Off in the distance, he heard the disturbance as Kalen's troops drew closer. "Time runs short for you, Warlord. What is it going to be?"

As though he, too, heard the men approaching, the Warlord eased back. He lifted the blade and held it point out, level with Morne's throat. "You will die for this, offworlder. I'll see to it."

The gate vanished abruptly. Under his breath, Morne muttered, "I have little doubt of that."

He turned his head just in time to see Kalen burst through the trees. Kalen saw Lee in Morne's arms and closed the distance between them. He grabbed Lee, and Morne let him, falling away as Kalen buried his face in Lee's disheveled hair. "What happened?" Kalen asked, his voice muffled.

Morne lied. It was easy, after all. He had been doing it for years and years. "I'm not sure. I felt the Veil, and as I came to investigate, the Warlord lifted the gate. He was trying to coerce Lee into coming with him."

"Coerce, how?"

He lifted his hands to the mask that hid his features. Instead of pushing the fabric down and away from his face, he pulled the mask away completely. As he carefully and precisely folded the material, he replied, "That is something you would have to ask your mate, Kalen. I do not know what she was thinking." That much at least was truth. No matter what the Warlord had told Lee, she shouldn't have been so willing to give up her freedom. Her life. She'd already given up much to help people she still didn't truly know. Giving up more was a price no woman should have to pay.

That she had been willing to do so only made her that much more confusing. *Fool woman,* he thought darkly. Looking up, he found Kalen staring at him with troubled, angry eyes. "Watch her well, my friend. I knew they would want her, but I did not foresee a Warlord lying in wait in the forest for her."

He hadn't, and it was nothing short of a miracle that

Morne had arrived before she had gone near enough to the gate that the Warlord could have reached out and grabbed her. Morne had been this close to failing. He didn't allow for failure. It just wasn't in his makeup. "Watch her well," he repeated and then he turned on his heel and walked away. As the forest closed up behind him, he heard Kalen barking out orders.

Lee wasn't going to be going anywhere without an escort, and Morne only hoped that would deter her long enough for him to figure out what to do now. Keeping her from the Warlord was going to be damn hard when she was so damned eager to get herself captured.

Kalen's men closed ranks around him, weapons powered up and ready. As they left the area, there was a slight rustle off to the side. For a brief moment, a face appeared in the tangled vines and greenery. Eyes narrowed and a smile came and went. Then he retreated.

* * *

"Bleeding hells."

Char stood at the outskirts, listening as his men prepared for tomorrow. There would be no more delays. No attempts to reason with his daughter and convince her there needn't be any more deaths.

He would let a thousand offworlders die, and a thousand of his own people, before he risked harm coming to her, and the longer she was outside of his protection, the bigger the risk. That ripe, wild power in her had called out to him like a beacon, and sooner or later, some of his men would sense it as well.

If it was a man who was less than loyal to Char, then the Daisha would be in danger.

He heard Arnon's footsteps and turned his head, watching as his man approached. Arnon's hairless scalp gleamed under the flickering light of the torches, and his dark eyes seemed more inscrutable than normal.

"The men await tomorrow anxiously, my lord."

Char didn't turn away from his study of the gate. It stood off in the distance, towering into the sky a few hundred lengths away from the camp. They couldn't settle too closely to it. The gate's powers were greedy, and lingering too close for long periods of time was a risk.

The gate could completely drain those around him, and the camp would be little more than a huge, walking feast. Both Sirvani and Warlord served under Char, and a good many of the Sirvani had magick talents or healing talents as well as the ability to look through the Veil. Safer all around to keep his men a good distance away.

He stood there staring at the gate and tried to battle the unease curling through him. It was more than just his fury over his interrupted attempt to bring his daughter to him, more than just his rage at the man who had dared to interrupt. Whoever the offworld bastard was, he was going to die very shortly.

It was more than that, though. Death was all around him. It hung in the air, but Char couldn't tell whose death he sensed. This close to the gate, its power seemed to cloud everything, even the ugly maw of death.

Distracted, he forgot that Arnon still awaited an answer, until the Sirvani murmured quietly, "My lord?"

Char glanced at Arnon. The Sirvani's gaze was dark and unreadable, and he looked as calm as though he were discussing the weather, instead of the most important raid of their time. "You will maintain order while I am gone, Arnon."

"Indeed." Arnon's lids flickered and a small smile danced around his lips. "You would be interested to know that I received some news while you were away."

Any man other than Arnon and Char would have dismissed him. No news save that of his daughter or his uncle interested him. However, Arnon would know this. The man seemed to know everything. "What news?"

The smile on Arnon's face broadened. "From my cousin, Weyr."

Weyr was a healer—more importantly, he was one of the few healers that Taise would allow near him. He would allow no healing magicks, but he would tolerate the occasional tonic or elixir from a select few, provided the High

Lord oversaw its preparation. Weyr was one of those select few. "And how fares Weyr this morn?"

"Busy at the High Lord's side. The most honored one has had a brain storm—minor, but there was a second one past midnight. He refused to send word, however."

Unsurprising. Stroked out and on his sickbed, the old man was likely more paranoid than ever before. "That is interesting news." Char looked back to the gate one more time.

The power was as intense as ever, but it was no longer the strong, steady pulse it had once been. Each time they raised the gate, it became more and more unstable, starting with gatestorms that lasted longer and longer.

The gates were stable now, and they'd stay that way even when the Sirvani lowered them again. But the next time they rose, Char had a feeling it would be the last. The previous gatestorm had been the strongest Char had ever witnessed, spilling back from Ishtan into Anqar with brutal intensity.

Time was running out. He glanced at Arnon and asked, "The Sirvani supporting the gate, how are they?"

Arnon bowed his head. "Steady, Warlord."

"Make sure they are spelled often. If they feel weary, get another Sirvani in place. I do not want the gate to so much as flicker." Maintaining the gates was an unimaginative but exhausting task. The Warlords themselves raised the gate, but maintaining the energy required far less skill and concentration, so that task fell to the Sirvani. While it didn't require as much strength or such a connection with the gates, it was tiring as hell. As such, it was a chore that was divided equally between teams of Sirvani.

This particular raid was turning into the longest one ever, and Char wouldn't let the Sirvani lower the gate until it was completely done. When he returned with his daughter, he'd let them lower the gate. If it was raised again, Char would make damn sure he was far away when it happened, because it wasn't going to be a pleasant event. Images of what happened at the Surachi Gate came to mind. No, Char wasn't going to be in the middle of a disaster like that, not if he could help it.

As if the gate sensed the direction of his thoughts, Char felt a nasty surge in its power. One of the Sirvani responded immediately, reaching out with a deft, unseen hand and drawing the power back inside the gate. A talented man, that one. Char made note of his face automatically.

Then he skimmed a gaze over the encampment. Thousands of Sirvani and Warlords had turned out for this one. A force to be reckoned with. "I trust you have heard no dissent regarding my orders last night?"

Arnon shrugged. "Not more than I expected. A few will always grumble when they are told no women are to be touched until they are presented to you." He paused and then slowly added, "However, have you considered explaining why?"

Char snorted. "And risk word getting back to the High Lord? Or worse, some of my rivals? There are many who would sacrifice much to take my place, including the assassination of a Daisha." Crimes against a Daisha were punished severely, as Daishan were too rare and too precious. But the protection of a Daisha fell to the father, or her mate, and if that Warlord failed to protect her, he was also punished. Char had paid dearly when his daughter had first gone missing, and over the years there had been subtle, and not so subtle, comments about his failure to protect his child. She had been long since assumed dead, and many voiced their disgruntlement that Taise had refused to replace Char as his successor.

With the High Lord's failing health, Char was in a precarious position. None must suspect that his daughter still lived. Not until Char had brought her home and taken her back into his protection. If any knew, her safety, her status, even her life were at risk.

"I chose your most loyal men, my lord." Arnon looked out over the masses gathered throughout the encampment. "Each squadron leader is a man I know and would trust implicitly. It's a hard task before you. You do not even know where to start looking." Arnon's lids flickered and he opened his mouth, but closed it without saying anything.

Char didn't bother to correct Arnon's mistaken assumption. None need know that Char has already seen his daughter. None need know that he had been just a few heartbeats from having her back under his protection.

By the Veil, she was lovely. She had the look of her mother, though her hair and eyes had clearly come from the Anqarian blood flowing through her veins. Her mother's temper as well, he mused as he recalled the way her temper flared and she sent power hurtling toward the gate.

Better off she was going to be, once Char had her safely in her homeworld. Those offworld buffoons hadn't taught her enough for her to realize just how dangerous her actions had been. Fear had frozen him for the briefest second, yet at the same time, he'd been oddly proud. His child showed no fear. She had known what he was, who he was, and what a danger he presented. He'd sensed the fear inside her, but she hadn't let it show, nor had she let it control her.

Pleased, he smiled. *We did well with her, Neve.* It saddened him, though, to realize that the fiery, brave woman he had taken as his mate had been dead all these years. He knew little of tender emotions, yet what little experience he had had come from his brief time with Neve. He knew she had felt little for him beyond reluctant desire, but it had bothered him only a bit.

More, it bothered him to think that all these years, their daughter had been alone. Completely alone, with no blood relative to look after her, no father to protect her and no mother to love and cuddle her. Children needed that, and fate had robbed Char's Daisha of that. Intolerable. Just intolerable.

"Sire?"

Char glanced up, a bit startled. For a moment, he had forgotten Arnon's presence. The Sirvani watched him with shuttered eyes, but Arnon had been with Char long enough that the Warlord knew when something was on his mind. He sighed and murmured, "Speak your mind, Arnon. I respect your insight." Char turned away from the encampment and retreated back into the lodge. The inside was lavishly draped with shisilks to protect them from the heat, sun and wind. It was marginally cooler, and he had a young body slave near the bed, fanning the air back and forth with a fan made of feathers from the flightless buisk bird. The gentle breeze blew his hair back from his face and cooled the sweat forming on his body. The body slave stared at her feet; she was clad in nothing more than thin silver bands at her neck and wrists. As if she felt his gaze, the body slave shivered slightly, and Char smiled as he scented both her hunger and her fear.

He would have liked to know her name, her birth name, not the name she had been given when brought into Anqar. But the stubborn female refused to tell him. She refused to even speak.

"Watch over this one while I am offworld, Arnon. She pleases me," Char murmured softly. "Make sure she wants for nothing—and no man touches her."

"As you wish, my lord."

Char dropped down onto the low bed and closed his eyes, relishing the cool breeze as it drifted over his body. In preparation for the raid, he had left his royal robes at the High Lord's manse and he wore battle gear. It was finely worked and every bit as elegant, in its own way, as his robes. The fine weave of the dumir tunic allowed air to circulate underneath, keeping him moderately comfortable even in the forsaken heat of the desert, yet it was solid and impenetrable to the typical weapon. Absently, he freed the toggle closures. "I am weary now, Arnon. I shall rest."

* * *

The faint light filtering in through the open tent flap struck her eyes with the same painful intensity of a thousand needles. Lee whimpered pitifully and turned her head away from the light. She tried to fling an arm across her eyes, but she couldn't even move. *What happened . . . ?*

The last clear thing she remembered was Kalen, being in the woods with him. He'd pressed her back against a tree—yeah, she could still feel the abraded flesh as she shifted on the bedding. But there was no way *that* had left her feeling like she'd been worked over with a lead pipe.

"Here. Drink this."

She lifted her lashes. Without turning her head, she could see Dais's heavily lined face and the mug he held, just out of the corner of her eye. She wrinkled her nose and shook her head. The second she did, Lee regretted it. Pain exploded through her head and she moaned. If she could have curled up in a tiny little ball and just faded away, she would have done so.

"I imagine that head hurts. Morne left you the tea—don't worry, it's not the piss you had to drink last time. This is just a soother," Dais murmured. "Come now, Lelia. Drink. The sooner you get that pain under control, the sooner you can rejoin Kalen."

"What happened?"

Slowly, she pushed up on her elbow, and when her head didn't explode, she reached for the mug. A quick sniff eased a little of the trepidation. Her head felt like it was about to throb itself right off her neck, and even if that crap tasted as bad as the garbage Morne had made her drink the last time, she didn't care. So long as it eased the pain in her head.

One sip had the headache easing back even before it hit her belly. By the time she had drunk half of it, she could open her eyes without pain shooting through her head. It didn't taste too bad either, almost like root beer, but warm and spiced. It also settled the pitching in her gut, and she relaxed back in the bedroll with a relieved sigh as she emptied the mug and let Dais take it.

"Man, that stuff is priceless," she murmured, unaware how thick and slow her voice had become.

"It does the job," Dais said. His voice had a peculiar note to it, and she turned her head, peering at him.

He had a peculiar expression on his face as well. Faces. Two faces—no, three. They wove together into one, separated into three, two . . . "Shit," she mumbled. She tried to touch her forehead and ended up poking herself in the eye.

"Best to be still. That tea was brewed from the kifer weed. It slows down reflexes, affects coordination." Dais's face continued to swim in and out of focus, but she heard the satisfaction in his voice. Loud and clear. "Within the next few minutes, you will be unconscious."

"Unconscious . . . for a headache?" She heard how slurred her words were. Something was wrong. She knew it, but it was like her brain was shutting down on her. "Why?"

Dais laughed. "It's not for the headache. It's for convenience. My convenience, naturally. You're less trouble when you aren't awake."

"Less . . . trouble . . ," Lee repeated. *Wake up . . .* She tried to throw off the sleep clouding her brain, but she just couldn't. *Wake up . . .*

Warning alarms were starting to scream inside her head, and even then she knew something was wrong. Very . . . very . . .

* * *

"The men are ready."

Char glanced at Arnon as his servant slid inside. "Doesn't it seem that sunset comes very slow before a raid?"

Arnon smiled. "I would have thought that you left that kind of nervous anticipation behind a long time ago, my lord."

The days before raids tended to be long and fraught with tension, tension that many Warlords and Sirvani burned off through sex or mock battles. Anything that might cloud the head wasn't allowed—no drugs, no ale or any other intoxicants. They needed that physical outlet, but the higher-ranking Warlords traditionally kept to themselves in the hours right before a raid.

Char's body slave lay behind him sleeping, all but dead to the world, she was so exhausted. He'd wrapped that long, fiery red hair around his hands and made her scream until she was hoarse with it before he finally brought her to completion. He'd slid his hands up and down her slender back, holding her close, but just before he would have fallen to sleep, just like that, she stiffened and shoved away from him. She'd rolled herself into a tight ball on the far edge of the low-lying bed. When he had tried to cover her with a blanket, she'd shrugged it away.

It had been years since he had taken a woman so resistant to him. In fact, Neve was the only woman that he could recall who had resisted him quite like this. Oh, most of the body slaves were resistant at first, but people usually resigned themselves to their fate after a time. Neve never did. If she had, she wouldn't have run away from him, taking their child.

This woman wasn't going to resign herself to it either. Char stared at her, feeling oddly sad. Soon he would be bringing his daughter into this harsh new life, and although she would be no slave, Char couldn't help but wonder if she would resist her new life as strongly as her mother had. As this woman now did.

"You look troubled, my lord."

Char looked over his shoulder at Arnon. "Just preoccupied. I've spent more than twenty years now moving to this point."

"Your search for your daughter," Arnon murmured.

Char sighed. He had enough to think about without Arnon's all too insightful viewpoints, but the Sirvani had served Char too long. He knew better than to discount Arnon's thoughts. Weary, he asked, "What is on your mind, Arnon?"

"You are certain your daughter still lives?"

Char lifted his lashes and stared at Arnon. "Yes, Arnon. I am." He smiled as he recalled the look on the Daisha's face when he had sensed her across the Veil and sought her out. If the shrouded outworlder hadn't appeared when he had, then Lenena would be here with him, where she belonged. Char could then have focused his time and energy on consolidating his power and protecting his child.

Yet he had to admire the strength it had taken her to resist him as long as she had. If she hadn't resisted so long, then the outworlder wouldn't have arrived in time anyway.

A strong-willed woman. It was going to be a hard task, finding a man who would match her strong will, not crush it. A thought occurred to him and he pushed up on his elbow, studying Arnon thoughtfully. "You are of high enough rank, Arnon. I sense the power inside you. Why have you never attempted to claim Warlord status?"

A pale blond brow quirked. "I know where I am of the best service, my lord. It is not as a Warlord."

The answer pleased him. Char was careful not to let Arnon see just how it pleased him. Arnon was one of the few that he had complete faith in. The Sirvani was invaluable, and for so many reasons. Loyalty like his should be rewarded. He lowered himself back into the silks and pillows at his back and murmured, "You are of an age to claim yourself a woman. Has no female ever held your attention long enough?"

Char knew the man had a body slave brought to his chambers on rare occasions. Very rare, and never the same woman twice. A good sign, in Char's opinion, because it showed the man didn't let thoughts of sex and women take over his mind. Men who had a slave in their beds every night were not always the most dependable, and not just because they were wearied from the fucking.

The Sirvani remained silent for a time, as though he had to think about his response. "Like most Sirvani, I had expectations of the time when I'd find a female that caught my eye, that intrigued me, one that I could father a child on, a child who would carry on my bloodline." Then he shrugged. "But the slaves that have been made available to me have never intrigued me. And I don't care to spend time with a woman that bores me."

"A child off you and the right woman would be a child of great worth, Arnon. Your wisdom, coupled with the power I sense within you . . ." Char nodded slowly. Yes. Yes, this could work. He would have to see how his daughter reacted to the Sirvani. And there would be talk. Especially once he took his place as High Lord. Char could handle the talk—he had dealt with it most of his life and it didn't faze him. But pairing his daughter, a Daisha, with a

Sirvani, even a high-ranking, well-respected one like Arnon, would cause upset among the ruling houses.

But if Arnon appealed to his daughter, Char would deal with the upset. The Daisha's happiness was paramount, almost as important as mating her to a man of power and wisdom. More, Arnon didn't have that streak of cruelty in him that was becoming so common among the Warlords. Arnon would treat the Daisha well. Perhaps she could even love him. Love could make it so much easier for her to accept her new life.

"When I bring my daughter back, I will present you to her, Arnon," he murmured.

With his eyes closed, Char was unaware of the look that tightened the Sirvani's face. Caught up in his own thoughts, pleased with the possibilities playing through his mind, he smiled. "Yes." *This could work.* He opened his eyes and met Arnon's steady, unwavering gaze. "It's time."

Shoving to his feet, he fastened the toggles on his tunic and donned the leather harness that held his weapons. When he turned, Arnon stood behind him, holding out Char's weapons. "You needn't play the squire for me, Arnon." He headed out of the tent, but just before he reached the thick, heavy fabric draped over the doorway, a whisper of magick slid through the air.

It blew across Char's skin like a cool wind, and he stopped in his tracks, turning to face the center of the tent. There was nothing there. His lids drooped and the power flowed through him, fluid and natural as water. The Veil shimmered into view, first a smoky, obscuring fog, deep shimmering blue, then it thinned out and the man on the other side shimmered into view.

"Dais." Char cocked a brow. "Not the best time, my friend. You should clear out. You are not in a safe place."

Dais grinned. Then he shifted to the side so Char could see behind him. It was Lenena. She lay on her back, her head turned to the side, eyes closed. Her chest rose and fell in a deep, slow rhythm, a little too slow.

"What is wrong with her?" Char demanded, his voice dropping to a rough, warning growl.

Offering a reassuring smile, Dais responded, "Nothing some rest won't cure. I just gave her some kifer root." He shifted back so that his body blocked Char's view of his daughter. "I believe this woman is of importance to you?"

Char's gaze narrowed. "If she is harmed, at all, I will gut you. Slowly."

His grin faded and Dais lowered his head respectfully. His gaze remained on the ground as he said, "My lord, I am no fool. Once I knew what she was to you, I knew she had to be protected." He paused briefly and then added, "Perhaps if I had known that you sought this particular woman, I could have brought her to you much sooner."

"You dare to question me, Dais?" Char asked, his voice soft and gentle. But the threat was clear.

"No. No, of course not," Dais responded quickly. "It is just that she has been in a very dangerous situation. I hate to think of your beloved child coming so close to death as often as she has. She has been out on the line, fighting with the resistance as though she were one of them. Any number of things could have happened to her."

Char snarled. "Do you think I am unaware of that?"

"My lord." Arnon stepped forward, discreetly calling the Warlord's attention away from the spy and to himself. "I'm certain your servant is simply voicing his concern over the Daisha."

Char gave Arnon a lethal look. "I know when I am being questioned, Arnon. Do I look a fool to you?" He dismissed Arnon and focused on the shimmery fabric of the Veil. Drawing on the power in the earth beneath him, he funneled it into the Veil, reshaping it. The gate began to take form, seamless and perfect. "Ready yourself, Dais."

Dais glanced around, a derisive smirk on his face. "Oh, I'm quite ready. I'm ready for a life that doesn't involve rising before dawn, barely scraping by . . ." His voice trailed off as he turned around to lift the drugged woman in his arms.

Dais turned just in time to see Arnon step up behind as Char continued to erect the small, temporary gate.

"My lord," the Sirvani murmured. A warning whispered through the air and Char tensed. But it was too late. The bloodied tip of a deadly torq-metal knife appeared through his chest. Stunned, Char lifted a hand to touch the blade, but his hand fell to his side, slack, before he could even lift it to his waist.

Char tried to turn, ending up stumbling and falling to his knees. He could see the Veil flickering. Energy snapped through the air. Char could no longer direct it into the forming gate, and the gate fell. Right before Dais's stunned face disappeared, Arnon said, "You'll have to live like a primitive awhile longer, Dais."

Char fell, landing flat on his back. Pain arced through him. He screamed, but it ended with a wet, garbled sound. He tried to say his servant's name. "Ar . . ."

"I imagine you want to know why," Arnon said calmly. He stood by the door with his hands linked behind his back, his face expressionless. So at odds with the fury that burned in his eyes. "Present me to your daughter, my lord?" Arnon repeated. "That was the last time you will ever see her."

Betrayal had a bitter taste, Char realized. Very bitter. He wanted to push the knife out—the icy pain seemed to burn through him. It hadn't pierced his heart, but already the deadly metal was spilling poison into his veins. Char could feel it. His limbs were already cold and his hands were clumsy as he struggled to reach behind him for the hilt. "Why you, Arnon? Why you?"

Char had battled so many assassination attempts, and yet this caught him completely unaware. Before he died, he'd know why.

A faint smile appeared on Arnon's lips. He bowed his head, that deferential nod he'd given Char so many times, but now Char saw the mocking hatred hidden behind the mask of respect. "Why, my lord? Because of Neve. You see, there was one woman that intrigued me. Your mate. We loved each other." Arnon moved closer and crouched by Char's side, a bitter smile on his face. "It was laughable, an offworld woman truly loving a man of the enemy. Me, truly understanding that love. But there you have it. We

loved each other. Then you got her with child. When the
girl child was born, we knew you would never let Neve go.
You'd force her to your bed time and again until she bore
you more and more children. You'd force her to pleasure so
that she was filled with shame and self-hatred for days."

The ice-cold of the torq-metal's poison spread more,
filling his lungs and making each ragged breath as painful
as if Char breathed out slivered glass. He choked on each
breath, struggled to get it out and take another. He had to
keep breathing until he could get help. *Help* . . . A tiny
seed of hope grew inside him. The body slave, she was still
there, watching everything with wide, dumbfounded eyes.
Char gave her a desperate look.

The little seed of hope withered and died as she met his
gaze and smiled. Hate blazed in her eyes. A ferocious,
pleased smile, the first true smile he'd ever seen from her.

"Hurts, doesn't it? Having a poison eating away at you
inside?" Arnon murmured. He crouched down by Char's
side and studied him, a nasty smile on his face the entire
time. "That is what I had to live with, every night you sent
for Neve. But you were my poison, not a piece of metal.
You're lucky, that metal will end your suffering. My suffering has been going on for more than twenty years now. I
loved Neve—would have died for her. But dying wasn't
going to save her. The only thing that would save her was
getting her away from you. After she healed from childbirth,
I knew what we had to do."

Understanding dawned slowly. Thinking was difficult,
and Char still couldn't believe that Arnon had betrayed
him. "You stole Neve away." He had spent years trying to
discover who had helped his Tiris escape, but he had never
imagined it had been Arnon. Never once had that occurred
to him.

Char had always believed that she had seduced one of
the younger Warlords. One that had managed to open the
gate long enough for them to escape. Arnon hadn't that
power then. Somebody had helped, then.

"Yes. I stole her away. But I couldn't go with her. If I did,
you'd know that it was me who had betrayed you. As your

sworn servant, you could find me easily enough through the blood bond I gave you when I entered into your service. I couldn't risk it." A smile tipped up the corners of his mouth. "However, there was another whom I had a blood bond with. One whom you had no control over."

Char closed his eyes. The sense of betrayal was painful, though not quite as painful as the poison ripping through his system. "You were the one feeding them information about pending raids." He started to cough, something thick, bitter and metallic bubbling up his throat. He choked on it and realized with horror that he was coughing up blood. "Taise was not wrong after all. We did have a traitor."

Arnon shrugged. "I had my loyalties, Char. You were not one of them. You merely thought you were." He rose and nudged Char's side with a booted foot. "You look as pathetic now as the High Lord must."

"Fuck you." Another coughing fit seized him, and by the time he was able to breathe again, he knew death wasn't far away. The lingering shadow of death he had sensed this morning had been his own. *Arrogant fool,* he thought bitterly. So certain of his men.

"All this to keep her safe—you've killed her surely enough, Arnon. She is as good as dead now. She doesn't understand her power, can't control it. She's vulnerable. Another Warlord—" Another fit of coughing overtook him and that icy darkness pushed ever closer. Desperate, Char fought it back, fought to think, to function. "Another Warlord will find her, Arnon. One that cares nothing for her."

Something flashed through Arnon's eyes. For a man who had always been so unreadable, the Sirvani was certainly showing an excess of emotion now. Char wasn't certain, but it looked like doubt, combined with anger.

He couldn't fight the poison inside him. Even now, the pervasive weakness made it all but impossible to even wipe the blood from his mouth. His voice faltering, weak, he rasped, "She's dead now, boy . . . thanks to you."

The taste of defeat was even worse than the taste of betrayal, and if Char could have hurried his death along at that point, he would have gladly done so.

Lenena wouldn't evade capture. The wild, uncontrolled power inside her would call out to the Warlords and the Sirvani like a beacon. She would be captured or killed, but it all added up to the same anyway. She was the daughter of a Warlord. Even if she didn't understand all that that entailed, Char did. She would kill herself before she'd submit to slavery.

How is it possible? After all this time, after coming so close, he'd failed her. She would never be safe, never have a chance at happiness. Her last hope for safety had been him . . . and he'd failed.

No. He couldn't accept it. Even as death drew ever closer, he wouldn't let himself admit it was over.

The answer, when it came, was faint, offering a hope so small, so slim, he never would have grasped at it—if it wasn't his last hope. Her last hope.

Her brothers . . . With the last bit of energy he had inside him, he reached for them. Even as his body shut down and death edged nearer and nearer, he reached. He'd feared there might come a time when they would need to know of Lenena. He'd feared . . . but prepared.

Those preparations just might save her.

"Daisha . . . " His words were so faint, so thick, he couldn't even understand them. "Forgive me."

Breath rattled in and out of his lungs. Trying to focus on Arnon's face, he realized he could no longer even see. The world was graying out on him, slowly deepening to black.

And the cold, bleeding hells . . . He was so cold, icy cold, all over his body and deep inside his heart. His breathing grew more and more shallow and he could even hear his heartbeat beginning to falter.

I failed . . . but perhaps they won't.

TWELVE

"I never would have guessed it was you."

Dais cut off his tirade abruptly as the low, familiar voice interrupted. Slowly, he turned and watched as Morne ducked under the low-hanging doorway. The tall man's eyes were dark against his skin and they glowed with the promise of death. "Morne, if you are here to check on your patient, she is still resting."

Morne glanced her way. "She doesn't rest. She is unconscious. I am a healer, Dais. I know the difference. I smell the roots of the kifer weed so I imagine she had a bit of help getting unconscious." A smile curled his lips, and Dais felt a ribbon of unease slide through him. "I wonder what Kalen will do to you when he learns that you have been spying for Anqar."

"Have you gone mad, Morne?" Dais asked, trying to keep his voice level. The spit in his mouth had dried up and his voice was just a bit shaky. Too shaky. The ribbon of unease grew into a bloody flood. "I've fought at Kalen's side for as long as the boy has been fighting. I fought at his father's side."

"Yes and spied on him as well. You're a clever one, Dais. I'll give you that. Whatever you received in compensation spying on these people, you kept it well hidden. You kept under the radar. I've seen you choke up at funerals and rage over the fallen body of a child. You're possibly one of the most accomplished liars I've ever met," Morne mused. He circled around the lodge, moving ever closer to Dais.

Dais turned with him, keeping Morne in his line of vision. "Have you hit your head, Morne? You're talking like a raving maniac."

A smile came and went on Morne's face. "Do not waste your time lying to me. You were seen, Dais. You aren't the only one living a double life, you know." His voice dropped to a low, almost hypnotic lull. "But *your* double life is killing people. Killing innocent people. People who share your blood. Your homeland. People who are simply struggling to live out their own lives without fearing raiders will steal away their daughters and sisters. You should have been out there shedding blood with them, and instead you have been stabbing them in the back." Morne stopped his circling and moved toward Dais, so fast his movements seemed to blur. "I wonder how they will react when they learn you've been betraying them for longer than some of them have even been alive."

Sudden, gruesome images filled Dais's head. He had a good idea of what their reaction would be. Bloody. Painful and merciless. It had always been a distant knowledge, what could happen if he was discovered, but he'd always had a quick escape plan. There would come a time when he could no longer continue his life as it had been for the past thirty-six years, and he had planned for it. But his escape route had been the Warlord. With Char dead and the High Lord on his deathbed, Dais's choices were limited.

Very limited. For the past hour, he had been working his way through those limited choices and discarding most of them. The only viable option was to get to the gate. Char was dead, and while Dais knew other Warlords, he doubted any of them knew of his connections to Anqar. His usefulness to Char had been in part because few knew anything about him. Keeping it that way had seemed wise, and lucrative on Dais's part, but now . . . now he wished he had at least a few other choices. Another Warlord he could call.

"Heavy thoughts, Dais?" Morne whispered.

Dais pulled back, getting a couple of feet between him and Morne. Angling his body so Morne couldn't see, Dais touched the pulsar at his side. If he had to, he'd cut Morne down. He had to get away—if at all possible, he needed to take Lee with him. If she was valuable to one Warlord, daughter or no, she was likely valuable to another. At the moment, she was the only bargaining piece he had.

Morne's gaze dropped, as though he could see Dais's weapon. That sly, taunting smile returned, and Morne said, "You going to use that on me, Dais? Have you got the spine for it?"

Oh, yes. Dais had the spine for it. But before he could draw the weapon, nature decided to shake things up a bit. The quakes hit hard and fast, and thunderheads stacked up in the sky high overhead. Static electricity built in the air, charging it until Dais could feel the hair rising on his arms in response.

The earth shuddered and pitched, and Dais hit the ground rolling. He kept rolling until he came up against the sturdy, ugly fabric that made up the temporary medicon. He used his pulsar to burn a hole in it and crawl out. From the corner of his eye, he saw Morne, but the healer wasn't coming after Dais. He was crouched over Lee's body, protecting her as the earth shook around them.

Dais would have a few minutes. It just might be enough. He wouldn't be able to take Lee with him, but perhaps the knowledge of her existence would be enough.

One thing was certain, his time here was done. Morne had seen to that.

From behind, Morne watched as Dais disappeared through the hole. He slithered away like the snake he was, and Morne was trapped there, protecting Lee's body with his own as supplies went flying around them. The waterproofed canvas fell down over them as the support poles shook free from the earth.

One of them struck him low on the back, and he grimaced, braced his weight on one hand and reached behind him to grab the pole and throw it aside. Then he went back to shielding Lee's body. To his left, small glass vials came raining down from the shelves. Outside he heard a tree branch break and he swore, bracing for the impact, but when it hit, it hit far off to the west. A faint smile curled his lips. Maybe they'd gotten lucky and the tree limb had fallen square on top of Dais's head.

Faintly, he heard yells. A few curses. No screams, though, and the voices outside sounded more frustrated and pissed than worried or hurt. No major injuries . . . good. Morne's priority was going to be getting Lee out of her drugged stupor so he could turn her over to Kalen's capable hands.

Then he was going after Dais, and he was going to slowly peel the man's skin from his flesh.

The trembling in the earth finally eased up. Morne remained in position over Lee's body for a few more minutes, until he was sure the quakes were over. The quakes passed, but Morne knew it wasn't over yet. He could hear thunder crack overhead, and rain started pelting down around them. As he cut himself and Lee free from the material, rain quickly soaked them through.

Behind him, he heard the sounds of people coming toward them, hard and fast. Kalen was the first to reach the tent, and Morne pulled away as Kalen reached for her. "She's fine. Just unconscious."

"Fine?" Kalen snarled. He rested his hand over her neck, and the slow, steady beat of her heart did little to ease the panic clutching at his gut. "Where are the guards I left on her tent?"

Morne gave him a grim look. "Dead, I imagine."

Kalen swore hot and furious. "Damn it, even nature won't give us a break."

"It wasn't nature that killed them," Morne murmured.

"At least, I don't think it was. There were no guards at her door when I came to check on her."

Understanding came, followed close by fury. "No Sirvani could enter my camp without us knowing. No demon." They had lost much of their firepower when Eira died, but magick wasn't completely lost to them. Aside from Lee, they still had a few witches with a weak talent—weak, but highly trained. Over the years, all of the witches had trained with Eira, and part of that training involved adding to the layers of traps and magickal alarms that lay just below the surface of the earth. Like a spider's web, they spread throughout all of the land, and a physical intrusion was sensed by the witches, and some of the more talented psychics.

They couldn't refine enough to sense any and every last ripple of the Veil. Many of the witches could train their entire lives without gaining Veil sight. But a physical intrusion Kalen's forces would have felt. Morne, damn him, stood there with those unreadable, opaque eyes, but Kalen knew there was something Morne hadn't told him yet.

Morne glanced around and then beckoned to Kalen, leading him a few feet away from the ruin of the small medic tent. They could get no true privacy without leaving, and Kalen wasn't about to carry Lee from the supposed safety of the camp. Even if she was guarded by an army of angels at this point. Bitter, he wondered if he could protect her at all. He should have known that power of hers would call out to any and every talented bastard out there. Dry leaves, broken branches and debris crunched underfoot, and Kalen shifted Lee's unconscious body in his arms. "What's going on, Morne?"

"We've long suspected that there was somebody in the army feeding information to the Warlords. We thought perhaps it was somebody under the control of a Raviner." Morne's gaze roamed restlessly along the tree line, as though he searched for somebody. "It was Dais."

"What?" Kalen sputtered.

Morne's gaze dropped to Lee's still body. "Perhaps you should lay her down."

"Like hell." If it was possible, Kalen would have held her closer. "What are you talking about with Dais? There's just no way . . ." His voice trailed off as he stared into Morne's eyes.

They glowed with a barely banked fury, and red flags of color rode high on the man's pale face. "He summoned a Warlord. A Warlord that was lifting a gate to come and take your Lee away. I stood and watched. Do not tell me there is no way."

"No." Kalen shook his head. He turned away from Morne and looked down into Lee's slack face. He pressed his lips to her cheek. She breathed out, a soft sighing sound, and Kalen caught the faint sweet scent of the kifer weed. She'd been drugged. Kifer weed was a powerful muscle relaxant—somebody had given it to her, used it to render her unconscious and helpless. Helpless.

A soft growl of rage rumbled in his throat, and he turned just a little, looked back at Morne. "You saw Dais."

Morne responded, "I saw him." He paused for a moment, his eyes closing as he blew out a controlled breath. It was as though he did that hoping to contain the rage Kalen sensed was moving through him. "I don't know . . ."

Kalen shook his head. "I don't need to know anything else." Fury and the bitterness of betrayal simmered deep inside, but Kalen wasn't going to let them take control. Not now. Dais had been one of his most trusted men, and there was very little Kalen hadn't shared with him. They were going to have to close ranks, hard and fast. They had to move to another secure area, and that was going to be risky. There were no secure areas that Dais hadn't known about.

He rubbed his cheek against Lee's soft curls. "I need her awake, Morne."

Morne nodded. He gestured back to the ruin of the medic shelter. "There is probably some moon-seal. It will make her nauseated for a time, but it will chase the drug from her system."

"Let's do it."

While Morne tended to the business of bringing Lee

out of her drugged slumber, Kalen watched from a few feet away. Gathering his men around him, he sent a party of ten into the woods to search for the missing guards. Another small troop was assigned to go through and give the orders to break camp. People were already searching for injured and collecting everything that could be salvaged from the quakes.

He heard a soft moan and looked over at Lee. Morne stood over her, and when Kalen approached, the other man backed away. Kalen glanced out toward the camp. "Make sure nobody needs serious healing. We leave here within two hours."

It took less than an hour and a half. The missing guards were found in a fraction of that time. One had been attacked straight-on, his skull caved in. No defensive wounds on him, and Kalen knew why. He'd known his attacker and hadn't been on his guard. Probably left his position to take a piss, and Dais had been waiting for just such an opportunity.

The second guard was on the eastern side of camp, his throat a gaping, bloody wound, slit from ear to ear. "Dais probably sent him out to find his partner and followed him," Morne murmured as he rose from his study of the body.

Kalen blew out a harsh breath. It was still so hard to grasp, the knowledge that Dais had been betraying him for years. But the old warrior was nowhere to be found, and a check of his tent revealed that most of his clothing and all of his weapons were gone. Three scouts reported having seen him running through the woods heading westward, as the quakes rumbled the earth.

Two troops had also seen him, leaving camp. But nobody had thought anything of it. Why should they? Dais was one of their leaders, exceeded in command only by Morne and Kalen. Kalen wanted to hit something. No. Not something. Someone. Dais. He wanted to pound the man bloody and then have Morne heal him so he could do it all over again.

Unfortunately, there was no time for it.

People rushed all around. It was organized pandemonium. They had spent enough time on training and drills that it was all second nature. He crossed over to Lee's side, distantly aware of somebody throwing water on the campfire Kalen had just left. Wood sizzled and smoke wrapped around his ankles, its acrid scent filling his nostrils. He crouched by Lee's side and reached out, running his fingers through her tangled hair. "We have to leave. How do you feel?"

She didn't move at all. Yet Kalen could feel her withdrawal all the same. She wouldn't look at him as she responded, "Fine."

"You're angry with me," he whispered softly. "I know you are and I can't blame you. I—"

Lee's blue eyes briefly met his and then she looked away. "I'm not angry with you."

"Then what is wrong?" Kalen asked, keeping his voice low. He glanced around and cursed their total lack of privacy. Nothing to be done for it. He eased a little closer and cupped her face in his hand. "You haven't said more than three words to me. You won't look at me. I don't blame you for being angry—I promised I'd keep you safe and then one of my own men tried to hurt you."

"What Dais did isn't your fault," Lee said. She shifted on the bedding, wincing a little. She started to push up, and Kalen slid an arm under her, easing her the rest of the way up. For one brief second, she leaned against him, but then she moved away until there was a good six inches between them. "Dais is responsible for his actions, Kalen. Not you."

"He was under my command. He was a traitor and I never knew." Then he shook his head. "I am responsible and it's something I'll deal with. But if you aren't angry . . ." He covered her hand with his, lifted it and pressed a kiss to the inside of her palm. "Why do I feel like you're not really here with me?"

Lee quirked a brow at him and smiled. It was a forced smile, though. It never reached her eyes, and her voice was flat as she murmured, "I am right here."

Frustrated, Kalen blew out a breath. There was a wall between them now and he wanted nothing more than to tear it down. But first he was going to get her to someplace safe. His people to somewhere safe. Once he did that, he would focus his attention on finding Dais and gutting him, on securing the line and waiting for reinforcements—bloody hell, the way things looked now, it could be another couple of months, if ever, before they were safe and he could devote some time to finding out why Lee was pulling away.

"Son of a bitch," he swore. Somebody called his name, and he looked up to see Roshan, one of his men, standing by the funeral pyre that had been built for the guards Dais had murdered. Eve, one of his witches, stood waiting to burn the pyre in a quick, controlled burn. Once she had put the flames out, they would leave.

Kalen didn't even have two minutes to spend with his woman and try to undo the damage Dais's betrayal had caused. The spiraling sense of helplessness and futility grew large enough that it felt like he was choking on it. But instead of trying to get through that distant wall, he leaned forward, hooked a hand over the back of Lee's neck. Kalen pulled her against him and kissed her, fast, hard and deep, taking in as much of her taste as he could, as quick as he could. "I love you," he muttered, pulling away just enough that he could say the words against her lips. "I love you and I haven't waited this long for you only to lose you now."

Then he stood and stalked off, leaving Lee behind him.

Miserable, Lee closed her eyes. She lifted a hand and touched her lips. They seemed to burn from the brief contact with his. Sobs built inside her chest, and Lee could barely breathe around them. She wasn't going to cry, though. Not yet. There was no time for it.

The army moved in a quick, controlled fashion, speaking very little, never once pausing. Even the dead were dealt with economically. Lee lost track of all the people who paused very briefly by the funeral pyre, and once it was set to flames, only Kalen and some witch Lee didn't know remained by the burning bodies.

They were leaving—because of Dais. Lee had pieced together what had happened through little bits and pieces of her memories and snippets of overheard conversation. Dais was a traitor. She vaguely remembered him coming into the tent, but not much after that. He'd drugged her and was getting ready to take her to her father. Everything felt foggy and her gut churned. Her head pounded from the drugs in her system. Morne had given her something that was basically a chaser, flushing the debilitating drug Dais had given her out of her system. She felt mostly better physically and she could move, but she wasn't so sure that was a good thing.

Morne's treatment had also left her head painfully clear.

Clear enough that she realized how much pain could have been avoided if Dais had succeeded. If he had gotten her into Anqar, her father would have left Kalen's world alone.

Maybe he still would. Lee was going to have to bide her time, but if she was careful, she could slip away from her guards. All she would need was a few minutes. She could raise the Veil. Maybe she could even force a gate up. She was, after all, a Warlord's daughter, and when she had watched her father construct that gate, something inside her had recognized and understood what he was doing.

Get to him before he unleashed his armies on Kalen's world. Get to him before he could kill anybody else. A cold fist of pain wrapped itself around her heart as Lee watched Kalen. His long hair was pulled back from his face, exposing the clean, almost harsh lines. His eyes were focused, intent. Occasionally, he'd glance her way and she'd see either guilt, rage or a yearning that shook her to the core.

She wasn't going to see that look again. Tears blurred her vision as she let herself acknowledge that. She'd spent years waiting to find him, and now after just a few brief weeks, her time with him was over. Lee wouldn't ever lie under him again and feel that strong, sleek body moving over her, moving within her. She wouldn't stare into that quicksilver gaze and see her own need reflecting back at her.

This isn't fair, she thought bitterly. Everything that had happened, everything she had learned and everything they had gone through, and the only way she could save them was to turn herself over to a man who was going to lock her in a silk cage and throw away the key.

One life—she closed her eyes and tried to make herself focus on something other than what lay before her. If her life was what it took to save Kalen's world, then that wasn't such a big price to pay, right?

"What is going on in that head of yours?"

Lee looked up into Morne's eyes. She didn't bother responding. She focused on bolstering her mental shields, keeping him from sensing her emotions. It was easier now than it had been before, even with the pain and nausea dancing throughout her system. Figures. Just when she finally started to get a handle on all the weird abilities, it was all going to hell.

Or she was. After all, what else could Anqar be? A hot, dusty place filled with demons, wyrms and men who had complete and utter control over her life. Yeah, that sounded like hell, all right.

"You think those damn shields will keep me from knowing what's going on inside your head?" Morne murmured. He crouched down in front of her and waited until she looked at him. "Do I have to tell Kalen what really happened when I found you speaking with the Warlord? Do you want him to know how close you came to getting captured?"

She glared at him. "Don't you dare."

Morne coolly replied, "Then do not give me reason."

She looked away. "I'm going to do whatever I have to, Morne. That's what we do, right?"

Long, narrow fingers closed around her wrist and she looked down, staring at the way his big hand manacled her there. Then she looked up at him. "Yes, Lelia," Morne said in a voice devoid of emotion. "That is what we do. And I'll do what I have to—even if that means finding some hole in the ground and throwing you in there until I know it's safe to let you out."

Lee leaned forward and whispered, "Morne, try it and I'll shave you bald while you sleep." Then she jerked and twisted her wrist. He let go, but she had the bad feeling he did it only because he felt like it.

He glanced down at the long, pale hair spilling over his shoulders. "I've had that experience before. A bit cold in the winter, perhaps, but nothing I can't deal with." He stood and tapped a finger against her nose. "Remember what I said, Lee. I *will* tell Kalen. If he doesn't wring your neck, it will be nothing short of a miracle."

* * *

"A Daisha."

Dais fought the urge to roll his eyes as the Warlord continued to murmur to himself. From what Dais could tell, everything in Anqar was in upheaval. Wisely, Dais hadn't mentioned a word of what he had seen the last time he had peered through the Veil. He didn't know if they had Char's killer and he didn't care. All he cared about was securing the trust of a Warlord strong enough to bring him over.

The backfire from the previous gate's rise and fall had finally settled, and it would be safe to lift the large, central gate. Dais planned on being front and center when it opened. He was leaving this harsh, godforsaken land and going to a place where a man of his talents was appreciated. Appreciated with lots of liquor, lots of gold, warm soft beds and warm soft women.

The waste of the last thirty-plus years was finally coming to an end. All of his sacrifices would soon pay off. That is if this bastard ever stopped pacing, thinking and muttering to himself. "Char's only child," Dais offered helpfully.

"Yes." The Warlord grinned, a wicked grin that looked a little too gleeful, a little too mean. "A Daisha at my side could help me secure my place as High Lord. It's just a matter of hours, really, before the current High Lord goes to greet the earth."

"A Daisha is indeed a fine prize."

"Hmmm." The Warlord—his name was Yashin—tugged thoughtfully on his lower lip. He was a bit young for his rank—his hair had barely grown out past his collar, and he had yet to begin showing any sign of aging. But the stone at his neck didn't lie. It was a deep, rich shade of blue, just a few shades lighter than Char's had been. Young and powerful—both qualities would work in Dais's favor. Youth often went hand in hand with recklessness. Dais didn't need a Warlord that was going to think through every single move he made, although Yashin wasn't proving to be as impulsive as Dais had hoped. And the power—that power was going to lift and hold the gate so that Dais could leave behind his destroyed homeworld.

"You can lead me to this Daisha?" Yashin asked. "You know where to find her? If somebody has already tried to grab her once, she will be watched closely."

Satisfied, Dais grinned. "Yes. I can find her." He had no doubt that Kalen would be moving the camp, and if Dais knew his so-called leader, then he knew Kalen was going to lead the army. There was one place where Kalen's men wouldn't be able to travel in the secure formation that Kalen preferred. They would have to travel in a long, narrow line, traversing through a dangerous, rocky gulch. On the other side there lay safety. The narrow gulch could be guarded by a relatively small force, and there were plenty of niches on the mountain face where troops could lie in wait for an attacker, picking them off by twos and threes.

But to get there, they had to get through that narrow, treacherous passage. All Dais had to do was wait there with enough men. A few minutes' time was all he needed, and the Warlord could gate in, get Lelia, and they would be gone before the gate weakened and fell.

It would be so very simple.

* * *

Lee paused and stared up at the towering rock face off to her right. It stretched up and up into the sky, blotting out the sun. Time was running short. She knew where she was, thanks to these bizarre memories. Her memories, yet not hers. There was a veritable rock fortress on the other side of this passage, and once Kalen and his forces were in there, nothing less than a nuclear blast could get them out of there.

Which meant Lee had to make her move before then.

"Lee."

She turned her head to find Kalen standing just a breath away. He stared at her, and she saw the echo of some suppressed emotion in his eyes. Pain, almost. She'd been acting like a cold bitch to him ever since they had pulled out of the camp hours ago—barely looking at him, shying away every time he reached for her. She could see why he thought she was mad, and she hated knowing she was adding to his problems.

Like he didn't have enough to deal with.

It's going to hurt leaving him, no matter what. Pulling back now isn't going to help. Might even hurt him more—don't disappear from his life and leave him thinking that you blame him for anything.

Some of the best advice she'd ever given herself, Lee supposed. She was debating how to close the distance she'd forced between them when Kalen sighed. His shoulders slumped just a little and he turned away. Lee reached out, caught his arm. When Kalen paused and looked back over his shoulder at her, Lee closed that distance between them, pressing her body to his. She slid her arms around his waist and snuggled close. Lee felt the slow, steady beat of his heart against her cheek and the brush of his breath against her hair as he wrapped his arms around her and held her tight.

"I love you," she whispered quietly. "I didn't realize love could come like this, so hard, so fast. So completely. But it did. I love you and nothing will ever change that."

Hearing his sharp intake of breath, she lifted her head and stared up at him. "I'm not mad at you, Kalen. Not about anything."

Rough, calloused fingers touched her face, tracing over the arch of her brow, along her nose, lingering on her lips. "Not mad? You don't blame me for this? I forced you here,

Lee. If I hadn't kept pressing, you might have remained in that safe world your mother sent you to, ignorant of all of this. Safe from it."

"And I wouldn't have ever known you were anything more than a dream." Turning her head, she pressed her mouth to the back of his hand, kissing him gently. Then she forced herself to smile at him. "I don't blame you—not for anything."

Kalen's eyes closed and he pulled her back up against him, tucking her close and tight against his body as he bent over hers. Not even a breath of air existed between them, and for a few brief seconds, Lee let the warmth and strength of his body surround her. She felt so safe there. So loved. And accepted—completely and totally. Without her saying a word, Kalen seemed to understand the chaotic mess that had been inside her since she'd first come to him. He seemed to understand her frustration, her confusion, and the way she missed some of the things from the world she'd left behind.

She wasn't going to find that in Anqar. The way her father had told her about slaves being given new names as a way to eliminate any and all connections with their past lives, no, she wasn't going to end up with some guy that loved her and respected her and understood that she missed coffee, computers and chocolate.

It was a bitch to know that this was probably one of the last times she'd be able to really feel like she was her own person. But Lee wasn't going to wail and moan about what she had to do. She was losing enough—she'd be damned if she'd lose her dignity and pride as well.

"What's wrong, Lee?" Kalen said softly against her ear. "You're so quiet. If you're not angry with me, then it has to be something else bothering you."

Mute, she shook her head. She could lie. Tell him she was just shaken by what had happened, the close calls of the past day, but if she talked, Lee had a bad feeling she might start crying. If he saw her crying, he wouldn't leave her alone. He might even try to look inside her thoughts and see if he couldn't find out the problems himself.

That wasn't about to happen. So instead of replying, she just stood there and let him hold her.

***

"The gate!"

"Shit."

"Through the ravine, hurry!" Kalen called out, yelling so that he was heard over the worried voices of his men and women.

The earth rumbled below, and Kalen felt like his stomach dropped to his knees. Tension hung in the air, and the overcast sky suddenly went black as thunderheads piled up overhead. They could only move through the ravine in groups of people seven or eight across. Considering he had thousands of troops to get through, that wasn't fast enough.

"Archers and snipers to the ridge," he said, his voice grim as he started moving to higher ground. Less than half of his force was through the ravine, and the gate was being forced open with a speed that was going to unleash a hellacious storm right on top of them.

The ground rumbled again, and somebody off to his left cursed long and hard. "Wyrms, last bleeding thing we need . . ."

Kalen shook his head, smiling a little. "This close to Sojourn Gap, the ground is rockier than hell. There are sheets of pure rock all around us." He kicked at the thin soil under his boots and grinned. "The wyrms try to come after us here, they'll end up with one hell of a headache."

Even those colossal bastards couldn't move bedrock.

Morne appeared at his side, and Kalen jerked his chin back toward the steadily moving line. "Go with them—get them to the Gap and make sure all is secure."

In a mild voice, Morne replied, "You are the commander, Kalen. Would make more sense for you to get your ass to safety and leave somebody else to bring up the rear."

"Morne—"

The earth pitched under their feet, a violent upheaval

that sent Kalen to one knee. Down below, his people staggered, and Kalen shouted, "Keep moving, damn it!" In a lower voice, he said to Morne, "What in the hell are those crazy fools up to, forcing a gate that fast? They want to kill themselves along with us?"

Grim, Morne muttered, "We need Eira right now."

"Maybe I can help." The voice came from overhead. Both men looked up, and then immediately jumped back to avoid being landed on by a tall, tanned blur that came hurtling down from above. Elina smiled at them, a mischievous, amused grin as she jerked on her climbing rope. The retractable claws on the grappling hook came free, and the thin rope came slithering down the mountain like a snake. She wound it around her arm and hooked it to the utility belt around her waist.

Stunned by her sudden appearance, Kalen glanced up the sheer face of the mountain and then back at her. "You got here fast" was about the only thing he could think of.

Elina's sunny smile never faded. "I had a feeling I wouldn't be gone long."

"Your children?" Morne asked, his voice just a little too censuring.

Elina gave him a cool look. "My kids are at Elswic. About as safe as I can hope for. I'm raising my kids the way Granna Eira raised me, to understand their responsibilities and to have honor. How responsible would it be if I stayed safe in the east while all hell is breaking loose here?"

"The kind who is also a mother and has to put the needs of her children first?" Morne suggested.

Kalen started to object, but Elina glanced at him and shook her head. Then she faced Morne, a disdainful look darkening her pretty, vivacious features. "I am, you overgrown idiot. If the resistance of Angeles does fall, the rest of Aishen will follow close on its heels. Saving this territory means saving the rest of our sorry asses." Then she sniffed and gave him a derisive look from head to toe. "Although some of the sorry asses are less deserving than others."

With that, she shifted the pack on her back and headed down the steep path, moving west toward the gate at a fast pace. Over her shoulder, she called out, "Keep the line moving, Kalen. I'll do what I can about the gate."

Kalen looked at Morne and found him staring after Elina with narrow eyes. "I forgot how much she likes you," he said.

Morne shot him a malevolent look.

With a laugh, Kalen said, "Come on. Get to the Gap, old man. This isn't over yet."

Morne's dark eyes followed the slim, long form of Elina for a moment longer, and then he looked back at Kalen. "You should go, Kalen. Stay by your woman. Keep her safe."

"Responsibilities," Kalen murmured. He shook his head. "You keep her safe until I can get to her."

That said, he dismissed Morne and moved down the incline to organize some of the troops that had started milling around when the quake hit.

One of the archers whistled out a warning, and the out-riders moved to form a shield along the tail end of the line. The stink of sulfur filled the air only moments before the pale, bone white flesh of the demons became visible through the trees. The forest gave way to rocky soil and boulders along this stretch of land, giving the demons little cover to hide behind. The sun was still tracking slowly through the sky, moving toward the west, but sunset was still a few hours away.

If the Warlords had sent the demons out before sunset, things were not looking good. "Ready the cold-beams," he called, and the order echoed up and down the line. Bron, the lieutenant who had served under Dais, stood at Kalen's side, and Kalen jerked his head toward the line. "You stay with them. Keep the line moving. If I fall, you make damn sure they get to the Gap."

Bron lingered, apparently under the same delusion that Kalen should find someplace safe. Safety was becoming more and more of an illusion at this point. If they wanted safety, they were going to have to make their world safe. "Get to the line, Bron. That's an order."

Bron beat a quick retreat, and Kalen muttered under his breath, "Don't worry, kid. I'm not going down here."

Not yet. Not now. Lee was waiting for him.

*　*　*

The discordant music of the gate jangled in her head like a kid banging on piano keys. Lee wanted to hide under a pillow, plug her ears—anything to drown out that harsh, dissonant melody.

It sounded ill. Weak. Almost like a death scream. Part of her understood why—the gate was being pushed too hard, too fast, and it was resisting. It was like somebody had taken a piece of clay, and instead of gently molding it into shape, they had grabbed at both ends and jerked.

The resulting work was a mess—ugly, brittle and weak.

But she sensed the power of the Sirvani working underneath that mess, strengthening the gate, shoring up the weak points. The gate wasn't going to fall. Not yet, at least. Not without help. Part of her wanted to reach out, find the weakness and the frailties, the evil strains and the darkness hidden within the gate power, find them and fix them. She could even feel that weird yet familiar gift unfurling and reaching out.

Something within the gate recognized and reached out in return. The magick in Lee recoiled, and something immense seemed to open up around her, recognizing the dual magicks within her and wanting them. Lee tore herself away.

She shivered. Morne had paused by her shelter briefly and tucked a blanket around her. That had been hours ago, and although he hadn't approached her since, she knew he was watching her. Watching over her, while Kalen was still overseeing the battle waging outside the Gap.

Sunset had come and gone, and with the sun's disappearance, demons came boiling up out of the forest like ants, striking in organized little hordes and trying to break the line of troops. So far, they hadn't succeeded. People milled around Lee, their voices a raucous cacophony in her ears. So many people, so close—realistically, she had known Kalen was in charge of this many people.

But knowing it and actually seeing it were two different things.

She hadn't ever seen so many people in one place, not at a rock concert, not at a ball game. It was maddening.

It was also the chance she'd been waiting for. From the corner of her eye, she watched Morne, and finally, he edged just out of sight. He'd left two men watching her, and one of them was busy trying to fix a jammed pulsar. The other kept one eye on her and the other on the aperture in the mountains. Sojourn Gap, the last stronghold Kalen's men had.

Getting out and into the gulch was going to be a challenge, but with all the fighting she could hear going on, she could manage. Her chance to slip away had come too quickly and she wasn't ready. *You won't ever be ready,* Lee told herself. *Might as well get it done now.*

She slid away, melting into the crowd of people and keeping her ears pricked for any sign that somebody had noticed her absence. She'd almost made it through the crowd when a hard, strong hand closed around her arm. Morne jerked her to a stop, and she looked up into his furious face. "I told you not to try," he warned her in a pitiless voice.

He started to drag her away from the aperture, and Lee jerked furiously against his hold. "Damn it, Morne. Don't you get—"

Thunder boomed overhead. Over the past few hours, the quakes had settled to tremors, but now the earth started to shudder again. It felt like one of those moving floors in a funhouse, though, not a real earthquake. From the corner of her eye, she saw Morne turn his gaze to the west. Lee imagined he couldn't see much over the foothills and the trees, but she saw what held his attention.

Since the sun had set, the brilliant blue of the gate had cast neon shadows against the sky, illuminating the clouds. But now the brilliant blue was fading, and fading fast. A slight smile curled Morne's lips and he muttered, "That's a good little witch."

"What witch?" Lee demanded as he once more began dragging her through the crowd.

But he didn't answer. He kept pulling on her arm, taking her farther and farther away from the narrow crevice that was the only exit. Sheer rock cliffs surrounded them on all sides. Sojourn Gap had one way in. One way out. Water was supplied through an underground source, and Kalen had long since had the foresight to prepare all the strongholds for a day such as this.

Damn near impenetrable, Sojourn Gap could be protected simply by placing troops along the steep slopes of the gulch and picking off invaders as they came through. But the very things that made it such a safe haven were the very things that were going to keep Lee trapped here.

The cave in front of her yawned like a big, black mouth and Lee struggled in earnest, but Morne ignored her. "I'm not going in the fucking cave," she snarled. *Have to get out . . . have to have to have to . . .*

Voice cold and uncaring, Morne responded, "Oh, yes. You are."

When she stopped walking, he picked her up and threw her over his shoulder. Lee continued to struggle and buck and squirm, and he let her, doing nothing to stop her until she managed to land a kick in his midsection. Then he clamped an arm around her thighs. "Any more and I'll spank your pretty butt, Lelia. Kalen might kill me later, but it will be worth it."

She just fought harder. For all the good it did her. The man had a grip like iron. And apparently, absolutely no tolerance for disobedience, Lee realized. He dropped her down on the cave floor and backed up. Lee surged to her feet and started forward, only to realize they weren't alone. At Morne's back stood twelve of Kalen's troops. She recognized each and every one of them.

They stared at her with a dead-serious cast to their features, and she sank back down to the floor.

She wasn't going to be able to slip away again.

***

Sleep came on her like a summer thunderstorm, totally unexpected and turbulent. Vivid, brilliant dreams, like the ones that had plagued her for so long, followed her once more.

In her dreams, she stood at the narrow entrance to Sojourn Gap, staring out at the rocky, uneven path that led out of the Gap and straight into hell. The gate seemed larger than life, and on the other side, she saw her father. He stared at her, and for some reason, there was sadness in his eyes. Regret, even. *Too late, Daisha. I was too late to save you. You must run.*

Run where? she asked him, bitter and angry.

Away. Away. Away. He kept saying it over and over, until a red flower blossomed on his chest. A closer look revealed it wasn't a flower, but blood. She could just barely make out the knifepoint protruding through the front wall of his chest. Another Warlord appeared beyond his shoulder, and as her father fell down, the new Warlord took his place. He looked at Lee with cold, clinical eyes that made her feel like she was some specimen on a lab slide. *You'll do,* he told her, his tone bored, almost indifferent. Then he looked away, staring at somebody she couldn't see. *Finish it, man. I'm ready to leave this forsaken rock and plant a child in her.*

Finish what? Lee asked. But she already knew.

They came storming through the gate. Hundreds. Thousands. *Millions . . .* Warlords and Sirvani, the Sirvani with the smooth, naked scalps and the Warlords, their pale hair bound away from their faces. Each of them had a blue stone that glowed either on a harness crossed over the chest or set in an elaborate collar around the neck.

Leave none of them alive. We're done here. The Warlord looked at Lee and smiled. *Come, offworlder.*

Lee shook her head. *No. I won't come if you plan to invade.*

He laughed. *Like you have a choice. You didn't truly think you were meant to save an entire world, did you? One lone woman? Pretty you might be, but you aren't worth that much.*

She turned away from him, wanted to run. Her legs felt weighted down and she couldn't even move. She wasn't supposed to, Lee decided. What she was meant to do was find her father and stop this damn invasion. End it. All of it.

Lelia—this isn't the way.

It was a woman's voice that spoke, coming from nowhere and everywhere. She looked around, searching for the speaker, and there was a soft, husky laugh. *You won't find me out there—I am within you. Just as the power to end this lies within you—you, not in your womb or between your legs. But inside you, where two powers meet. The gates shun power. They gobble it down like children with sweets, but then they jerk away, hiding before they can eat their fill.*

The balance is within you—use it, push it through the Veil, push your power into the gate.

Lee nodded. Little of that made sense, but she understood the gate. She had to find a gate and get to her father.

Perhaps . . . perhaps—she couldn't leave here and make her way to the permanent gate. But she just might be able to make one.

After all, her father had.

No, Lelia. That isn't the way—

The woman's voice was still echoing in Lee's ears as she forced herself to wake up.

THIRTEEN

It wasn't over. Not by a long shot, Kalen knew. But as he stood at the entrance to Sojourn Gap and mopped the sweat off his face, he breathed out a sigh of relief. The relative quiet would be short-lived, he knew. Elina had only bought them some time, but that time had allowed him to get most of his troops into the Gap, with minimal casualties.

Now he just needed to find Lee, bury his face in her hair and sleep. Just an hour. If he could get an hour's sleep, he'd be ready to go again. He paused by Sanchez, one of his lieutenants, and left orders for the cleanup. He passed by the huge shelter that would serve as a communal dining area and had the galley workers start preparing some field meals for those who would keep watch for what remained of the night.

There was precious little of it. His bones ached with every step he took, and there was a burn low on his right hip that was going to need treatment before too long. The Ikacado had gotten close enough, just barely, to leave a mark on Kalen before Kalen turned the cold-beam on the thing and blasted it into the next life. Sweat, grime and blood covered him, and he paused just long enough by one of the many streams to splash water on his face.

There was a waterfall at the far end of the Gap, and as soon as he could find the time, he was going to take Lee there. Scrub every last inch of his body and then make love to her under that waterfall.

But right now—sleep. That was all that mattered.

The ripple of power that rolled through the air filled him with dread. No. Kalen stopped dead in his tracks and shot an angry look up into the heavens. "Can't You give us a little time to catch our breath?" he asked. "Just a little?"

He turned to go back to the front line, but something caught his sight. Just out of the corner of his eye. Something flickering a pretty, bright blue—a blue that was damn near the same shade as Lee's eyes, he realized. Why hadn't he noticed that before . . .

"No."

It was a gate. Not the powerful, permanent bitch that was the source of so much grief for his world, but a small one. Temporary, only big enough for a few people to pass through at a time.

Or in this case—one person. Lee. They'd found her.

Kalen started running, shouting for Morne, then calling his other troops to his side. The thunder of hundreds of feet surrounded him as they all converged on the source of the light. It was coming from one of the hundreds of shallow caves that dotted the rock face.

And right in front stood Lee.

A startled breath escaped Kalen, and he froze in his tracks. It wasn't a Warlord lifting the gate. It was Lee. Horror flooded him as he realized what was happening. The gate was being forced open—from this side. Power swelled in the air, making it feel heavy and thick. It spun in the air, unseen by the naked eye, but he could feel it. Sense it. The hair on the back of his neck stood up, and goose bumps broke out all over his flesh. His gut knotted, his muscles were tense and ready, all over something he couldn't even see. It was like a monstrous cyclone was forming all around them and they were caught in the maelstrom.

And in the center of all that horrible, fascinating power was Lee—her head tipped back, gazing up at the sky as though she followed the direction of some unseen guide, spinning a gate out of nothingness. Kalen stared at her, trapped in place and mesmerized as the power formed in front of her. Lee stood right at the mouth of the cave, and as Kalen watched, the shimmery gray of the Veil appeared between them, obscuring her features.

With every breath, the Veil solidified. She stood with her arms spread in front of her, palms facing out, and an unseen wind tore at her clothes. Kalen could smell the hot desert air, and he knew Anqar was just a breath away.

He came to a halt at the mouth of the cave, just an arm's length from Lee, but he didn't touch her. Kalen wanted to grab her and haul her away from the forming gate, but that power was too unpredictable. He was forced to watch and wait—although if she tried to go through that gate, he was grabbing her and consequences be damned.

***

This isn't the way.

Lee would have plugged up her ears if she could. That annoying, intrusive voice just wouldn't shut up. "Yeah, it is. It's the only way."

Giving yourself over to them? You think that is a solution? It's not—the solution lies within you. It's your magick. Flood the gate with it. It knows you, accepts you. Use it!

Lee snarled, "Would you just leave me the hell alone?" She wasn't sure if she spoke out loud, and she was even less sure who that voice belonged to. It could have belonged to herself—it wouldn't have been the first time she'd argued with herself. Sadly, it wouldn't be the last either. Lee imagined there was going to be plenty of time for her to look back and question the wisdom of this decision.

And yet she couldn't stop those words from circling through her head. *It knows you, accepts you. Knows you . . .*

Like an echo, they kept repeating through her head. She shuddered, and as the answer finally made itself clear, her knees buckled with relief.

She didn't have to give her body over to the Warlords. But her magick—to the gate. It was just days ago, two . . . maybe three . . . when Lee had watched those rather innocuous tripods as they decimated the wyrms. She remembered wondering what might happen if those things were directed at the gate.

It would take a huge burst of power, massive; one strike was all they'd get before the gate shut down. It would shut down at any sign of foreign power, and Kalen's men simply didn't have the amount of firepower it would take to hit it hard and fast.

Lee's power, though—the gate accepted Lee's power. Accepted, hell, it seemed to crave it. Lee could feel it pulling at her, and it wasn't the first time she'd felt like this either. Unlike the other times, though, she was right up close and personal with the gate, and pulling away wasn't an option.

The thing felt almost sentient. She sensed its hunger as she funneled more and more power into it. *This is the answer.* Satisfaction blazed through her. Yeah, she was probably going to go down with the gate, because she could feel the thing wrapping its power around her, pulling her inside.

But if she went down in a blaze of glory, it was a damn sight better than spending the rest of her life in some silken cage.

* * *

Kalen came pounding into the Gap like the hounds of hell were at his heels, but it was all for nothing, Morne thought bitterly. Lee hadn't tried to escape again, but it would be so much easier if she had. Had she run away, even if she'd been caught, Morne could have pursued her, straight into Anqar if necessary. But she was now caught up in a game of chance with the gate. Gate energies were turbulent, and if she faltered, Lee was dead. Possibly along with every last soul in the Gap.

"This isn't happening," Morne muttered. He pressed his fingers to his eyes and swore long and hard. Focus and concentration danced out of his reach, but he had to get control. With sweat dripping from his brow, he closed his eyes and opened that part of his mind that let him pierce the Veil. He didn't lift it—the last thing he needed was the reaction the troops would have if they became aware of one of his many secrets. Instead, he just reached through, connecting with Arnon.

His twin waited on the other side, and Morne sensed Arnon's uneasiness. *What is going on, brother?* Arnon demanded, his mental voice quivering with rage.

Aneva's precious little girl is opening the gate, brother.

Arnon's thoughts stumbled to a halt and then, for a brief moment, all Morne could sense from him was a casual dismissal. *She can't. She's no Warlord. She's a woman.*

She's also Eira's granddaughter. You've sensed the woman's power before, Arnon. Lee's father would have been the next High Lord—he was the most powerful Warlord in Anqar. No, she shouldn't be able to open the gate, but that is exactly what she is doing. And Morne should have been prepared for this—he'd seen how she reacted when the gate's power acted up around her. She recognized it—and likewise, the gate seemed to recognize her. Gate energy was something the Warlords had long accepted as a sentient being. Not one they could fully comprehend, but it didn't act or react like conventional magickal energy.

When gate magick existed within a person, using that magick was practically instinctive. Mastering it took time, but once gate magick revealed itself, using it was just a matter of time. Lee was damn young, too young for the gate magick to have already revealed itself. Yet it had. Morne should have been prepared for this, the moment he realized she could hear the musical call of the gate. Recognizing it and using it weren't that far apart, not when the talent ran strong.

Seven hells, this is bad, Arnon whispered. As one, the twins shifted their focus. Although they saw none of it with their physical sight, they knew what would happen once Lee managed to fully raise that gate. If she didn't get sucked into the maelstrom of power, then the Warlords would come hunting her, and they wouldn't give up until they had her. Nothing in hell would stop them.

We have to stop her. Stop her now, Arnon demanded.

Morne snarled. *And pray tell me how I'm to do that without killing her?* Along with every one around them, if the power backlashed.

Arnon's voice, by contrast, was gentle. *We have no other choice, Morne. If they realize she can do this, and they find her, she will wish for death. Long before it comes. Both of us know it. It must stop now, regardless of how it ends.*

A woman with gate magick. She would be hated, coveted, and as long as the Warlords had a chance of finding her, her life and her freedom would be in danger. Morne looked at the air, watching as it fully manifested. The gate was open—just a small sliver of it. Like a rent in the air, he could see the dry, arid lands of Anqar just through the gap. Just a little. Hot desert winds, smelling of the sands and spice, wafted through. On the other side of the ever-widening gate, he saw two faces.

His twin. And a Warlord. He was staring at Lee with disbelief. It faded, though, quickly replaced by an avaristic greed that made every protective instinct Morne had go on red alert. He opened his senses—it felt like something tore inside his mind as he tried to reach out with too much of himself, spread too thin.

Distantly, he sensed what Lee was thinking.

He knew what she had planned, knew it could quite possibly kill her—and at the same time save her mother's homeworld. The idea itself was simple, so simple. So beautiful. Something that was born of the twin magicks she had inside her, magicks that should never have been forced together inside one person. He felt Arnon's touch on his mind, felt him recoil in horror as Arnon realized what Lee was going to do. *It won't work,* they thought as one.

But then Morne shook his head. *It will—if her magick can sustain her.* Lee's connection to the earth was tenable, at best. Already she was faltering. She might not realize it, but the twins did. Distantly, Morne was aware of Kalen and all the men watching and staring in horror. They couldn't rush in and grab Lee away—the magick she was pouring into the gate would suck them inside, and death would be the easiest fate, but not the likely one. The men would die, and Lee would never again breathe free air.

She needs more power, Arnon murmured. He said nothing else, but Morne knew what he wanted.

Pain spasmed through him as he stared at his twin's face. *If this works, it will level everything on the other side of that gate.* It had happened once before, and the crater of Yorkton was the result of the power surge. This time the power surge would happen on the other side of the gate— right where Arnon now stood.

Do it, Morne.

If I do, she'll likely die, Morne said. So will you. He didn't tell Arnon his final words, but his twin knew none-theless. Those unspoken words hung between them as they stared at each other through the unstable gate.

Arnon smiled gently. *I have been dead inside for years, my brother. You know this. It will come as a blessing, if I but know she is beyond the reach of our kind. And if you don't, she'll die anyway. They'll find her, for certain. How well will she tolerate the silken slavery of being some War-lord's Tiris? She will be fought over, claimed by the stron-gest Warlord. With strength too often comes brutality—at least among our kind. I do not want that for her. Nor do you.*

Still . . . *Brother, I can't.*

You have to, brother, Arnon murmured. *Do it now be-fore her power wanes.* Their silent communing had yet to catch the attention of others, but it was just a matter of time.

Morne stared at his brother and searched for some other way. But there wasn't one. He knew it. His brother knew it. Arnon's face was calm, accepting, even as he said aloud, "You made an oath to me, brother. You will keep it."

The Warlord standing at Arnon's side glanced at him,

puzzled by those sudden words. Eyes narrowed, he followed Arnon's gaze, tracking it across the gate and landing on Morne. Eyes went wide and Morne saw the recognition. *Arnon, you bloody fool . . .* His twin had given them away, and on purpose if Morne knew him at all well.

"Do it, Morne. *Now.*"

Morne closed his eyes. Whispered softly the proverb he'd heard often since coming to this world so many years ago, "Blessings on thy path, brother." And then he reached down deep, reaching into the earth for the power that lay dormant. Just waiting for the right hand to touch it, use it. He gathered it inside and then turned his focus on Lee, funneling it through her, solidifying her connection to the earth. It struck her with a force that was nearly palpable, and Morne saw her body react, spine arching, mouth falling open. Her blue eyes gleamed, and some ethereal light seemed to emanate through her pale skin.

"Don't falter now, Lee," he whispered. Her body jerked hard. He could feel her pulling away from the sudden onslaught of energy, but just when it all threatened to overwhelm her, she steadied.

He watched as she anchored herself in the vast energies of the earth—connected to them through him. Morne's abilities as a healer gave him a deep, unending link to the earth, and Lee's natural witch talent did the rest, converting that earth energy into pure, sheer power. The gate sucked it up like a thirsting man drank water, quick and greedy.

When Arnon added power from across the Veil, light flared and shone so brightly that Morne could barely see anything else. But still, he continued to look into the gate, staring at his brother. He stared, even when the light blinded him and he could no longer see anything at all. Even when he could no longer feel Arnon, he continued to stare.

* * *

Some distant part of him wanted to screech in denial as Kalen watched Lee. The power flowed out of her, straight and true, flowing into the gate. Too much power—Kalen could see little wisps of energy trying to escape; he could sense the gate trying to shut down, but Lee wouldn't let it.

She controlled the gate as though she had been doing so all her life. Perhaps, in essence, she had. She'd been born with the ability inside her, and the evidence of it had been in front of him all this time, yet he hadn't ever seen it. All these years, Lee had been gating back and forth between their worlds in her dreams. The question *how* . . . only made a passing appearance in his mind. How was it possible—there was only one way.

Aneva hadn't been alone when she escaped the Warlord who had claimed her. She'd had a child with her—a Warlord's child—Lee. Or rather, Lelia. She was born of a powerful bloodline on both sides, and those powers joining together had resulted in something Kalen had never even thought of. A witch who could control gates—more, a *female*. Witches, by nature, had a stronger connection to the earth than any other known talent. Only healers came close to equaling that power. With that ability to tap into the vast resources of a world's energies, and the ability to manipulate gate energy . . . As if pieces of a puzzle were abruptly falling into order, Kalen realized just why it was Lee was so damn important.

He'd always known she was. He'd anticipated some great magickal power, or some sudden insight that would end the war. But he hadn't expected this. Lee was going to end Anqar's hold over Kalen's realm.

By destroying the gates. While they all watched, Lee continued to pour more and more magick into the gate realms, that ephemeral plane between the worlds. She was going to flood it with more energy than the gate could hold, but the gates were greedy. They would take more and more, until they self-destructed.

Sudden blinding clarity hit Kalen. Yorkton. Somehow, something similar had happened in Yorkton. The crater that remained was the result. "Dear God," Kalen prayed.

He'd been willing, in theory, to sacrifice his army if that secured their world's safety. His men felt the same in gen-

eral. It was something they had talked about time and
again, but looking at it theoretically and watching as it
unfolded were so vastly different.

Kalen felt sick. Sick and frustrated because there were
only two possible outcomes. Both resulted in the destruction of the last large gate that remained in their world, so in
the end, his world would finally be safe. Either way, however, his life was over.

Either they'd all die when Lee's control slipped and the
gate's backlash killed them all, or as the gate shut down
one final time, it would suck Lee inside. She'd be dead—and
so would he. Even if his heart continued to beat for another
fifty years, when he lost Lee, it was going to kill him.

Then I go with her, he thought. Caring very little, Kalen
glanced around at his men. His gaze lingered briefly on
Morne, and he knew that the task of leading his men would
fall to the healer. With Dais being a traitor, no other had
the experience.

It would be well, in time, Kalen decided. He spared one
glance at Morne and saw the intense focus on his face, and
then Kalen looked back at Lee. As he stepped toward her,
he heard someone speak. The Sirvani, speaking in the
harsh guttural language of Anqar. Like most of his men,
Kalen had a fair grasp on the alien language, but the Sirvani's words meant nothing to him. The man might as well
have been speaking gibberish.

Then Morne spoke. Although Kalen understood the
words themselves, the context made little sense. The look
on the man's face when Kalen glanced at him made even
less sense. Morne was gazing through the ever growing
gate, at the Sirvani. Ignoring the Warlord completely—the
man who was the biggest threat, yet Morne didn't spare
him even a glance.

Instead he gazed at the Sirvani with a look of sadness as
he murmured, "Blessings on your path, brother."

Kalen felt the power shift then as Morne threw his
strength in with Lee's, aligning their powers. Lee began to
glow with the enormous power channeling through her
body. The gate shuddered—Kalen could feel it. It shook

the earth down to the bedrock. Not the violent rattle and roll of a quake, but trembling, almost like the tremble of leaves on a branch in the wind. But this trembling seemed to go to the very core of the Earth.

"Lee," Kalen whispered. He went to her, but power came up, punching him back, knocking him away, as though the gate feared Kalen might do something to stop the deadly infusion of energy. "Lee!"

He shouted out her name and she turned her head, looked at him. He saw it in her eyes, the acceptance of what was coming. "If you're going to throw yourself into death, then I'll damn well follow you," he swore, surging to his feet.

"You can't," Lee whispered. Her knees gave out, as though the power flowing through her had sapped her strength. She went to her knees and still the magick funneled through her. Light flashed, so incredibly brilliant it left them all standing there blinded.

The trembling in the earth grew and grew, and the tension in the air seemed to stretch itself out into infinity, and still the gate guzzled up the power. Kalen felt another ripple in the magickal energy and realized somebody else had added to the power flow. A foreign presence, one he didn't recognize—he snarled, realizing that even now, while death hovered all around them, one of the bloody Anqarians were trying to steal from them, trying to drive through that power.

But he didn't pierce it. Didn't try to wrest control from Lee or Morne. Instead, the power was added to the flow. This third, final power punched through like a laser turned onto ice. The world exploded.

Or at least it seemed that way. Lee screamed. Behind Kalen somebody cried out. He wanted to scream himself as he saw Lee's body catch the impact of the backlash. She went flying through the air and Kalen ran toward her. He couldn't move fast enough. He'd never get to her in time. It wouldn't matter though, the sane, functioning part of his mind whispered. The power surge was going to strike back out at them and they'd all be gone.

This surge was going to level them all. That gate would shatter—

Then shatter, damn it, Kalen thought bleakly. *Be done with it. Just let me go with her.*

The few seconds seemed to stretch out forever as her body hurtled through the air. Something moved between Kalen and Lee—someone. A tall, blond blur that moved with a speed that was inhuman. Kalen recognized Morne as strong arms came up, grabbing Lee out of the air just before she would have crashed into rock walls with deadly force. Slowly, Morne turned, holding Lee cradled against him.

The ground rumbled; rocks and boulders came crashing down the mountain as the power surge came. Yet the final end that Kalen expected never hit. The power surge struck and the world continued to spin. There was indeed the gatestorm that Kalen had been prepared for, but it was . . . muffled. Almost as though it had hit elsewhere and all they felt was the echo.

The rumbling of the earth continued as the gate closed in. There was an echoing boom that resounded through the foothills. Then it was done.

The land was still intact.

And the gate was gone.

Relief never had time to move through him. He went from the taciturn acceptance that Lee would die but at least he would follow her, to stark and bitter denial. Lee wasn't breathing. He closed the distance between them, hoping that it was a trick of the light, or just the space between them that made her seem so still.

Morne tried to turn aside, still cradling Lee to his chest. "Kalen—"

"Give her to me!" Kalen demanded, grabbing her away from Morne. His heart seemed to have taken up residence in his stomach, and he couldn't breathe as he searched for some sign of life. Lee wasn't breathing. Her face was so pale it seemed translucent, and huge, dark circles ringed her eyes.

Hands came up to pull her away from him. Kalen turned

to the side, cradling her lifeless body protectively against his own. "Kalen, there's no time," Morne snarled. He ripped Lee from Kalen's arms with an unnatural strength.

"How can I trust you?" Kalen asked, forcing the question out through his gritted teeth. Pieces of the puzzle fell into place as he looked into Morne's face with its exotic, foreign features. The man's speed as he moved to catch Lee's body as it flew through the air like a living, breathing missile. The tempered strength that had caught her body like she weighed little more than air. "You're a fucking Warlord."

"Yes. I'm also the only healer strong enough to bring her back—but only if I do it now." Without waiting for any kind of response, Morne sank to the ground, cradling Lee in his arms. One hand came up, resting in the shallow valley between her breasts.

Kalen went to knock Morne's hand aside. "Don't touch her," he growled. Arms came up from behind, catching him before he could reach out for Morne or Lee.

He struggled against their hold, tried to tear away from them, and just when he managed to jerk his arms away, more hands came up to hold him. Arms wrapped around his waist; bodies came up between himself and Morne, forcing him back. As the distance between Lee and Kalen grew, he struggled harder and harder. "Damn it, Kalen—he's trying to save her," somebody said. Kalen had no idea who spoke or who held him. He didn't care. He just wanted to get to Lee. To hold her in his arms, to lie down beside her and simply . . .

Her chest moved.

The strength drained out of his body and he sagged. If all those restraining hands hadn't been holding on to him, he would have collapsed to the ground. "Lee . . ."

Her head turned to the side, and a harsh, high-pitched noise left her lips. Followed by a spasm that seized her body. Kalen started to struggle again. "Let me *go*," Kalen roared. He jerked away, freed so suddenly he hit the ground, landing on his knees. He scrabbled over the distance that separated them. A weak, pitiful moan escaped

Lee. Kalen grabbed her away from Morne, and this time Morne let her go.

Kalen pressed his cheek to hers and whispered her name. Her body remained limp in his arms, although he could hear the soft, shallow sound of her breathing. Slowly, he looked up at Morne.

Voice weary, Morne murmured, "She will live. Overextended herself—again. It will take her some time to recover, but she will recover."

Hoarse, Kalen whispered, "Why help her? Us? Why save us?"

A bitter smile curved Morne's mouth. "It wasn't about you or your world, Kalen. Not at first. I blame you little for not trusting me." He reached down and touched Lee's hair gently. "I was here only to fulfill a promise and had no use for you, your world or the futile way you continued to resist the inevitable. It was that futile, senseless determination that brought me around, though. Hard not to admire that kind of stubborn pride."

None of that made sense. Kalen whispered, "I don't get it, Morne. Why? Did you start out to be a spy or what?"

"Spy?" Morne repeated. Then he shrugged. "I never set out to be a spy, although I did become one . . . of sorts. Just not the way you mean. I came here to keep a promise, Kalen. To protect her." He reached out and touched Lee's face once more, and then he turned away, disappearing from sight.

FOURTEEN

Seven days.

Kalen hadn't slept in seven days, and he sat by Lee's bed, gritty-eyed with exhaustion, almost dumb with it. Lee lay just as still as she had for the last week. She slept on the jela pad that had been brought to the Gap four days ago. It cradled her thin, pale body, but Lee could have been lying on a bed of rocks and it wouldn't have mattered, not to Lee.

She hadn't moved on her own since Kalen had taken her away from Morne, and after that one pitiful moan, the only sound she'd made was soft sighing breaths.

He sensed the presence behind him, but he couldn't even find the energy to care. The tent flap lifted, letting light briefly spill inside, and it was dark once more as the flap fell down behind Morne. "What do you want, Warlord?"

"Technically, the term would be Sirvani," Morne said, his tone reserved. "I never completed the training required to be called Warlord."

A thread of disgust curled through Kalen. "How upsetting for you." He glanced over his shoulder at Morne, and then he stilled.

Morne had come to the Roinan Mountains more than twenty years ago. In all that time, the man hadn't seemed to grow any older at all. Yet in the week since Morne had saved Lee, it seemed as though the man had aged a good ten years. Lines fanned out from his eyes and deep grooves bracketed his mouth. His hair was all but gone, Kalen realized abruptly. The waist-long blond strands had been cut almost brutally short. His dark eyes were sunken and his features had thinned out, giving him a hawkish appearance.

Morne had always seemed almost too pretty to be a man, almost angelic in his features. He met Kalen's gaze levelly. "If being a Warlord meant so much to me, I never would have left Anqar." He looked at Lee and then back at Kalen. He cocked a brow and murmured, "If I take a look at her, are you going to cut my balls off for touching her?"

Kalen curled his lip in a sneer. He'd rather the bastard be nowhere near her.

Yet . . . Begrudgingly, he rose from the stool. His stiff body protested, muscles screaming out at him after so much time of inactivity. "You look like hell," Kalen noted.

"You, too," Morne murmured, smiling a little. He cupped a long-fingered hand over Lee's neck, his thumb resting in the delicate hollow. "Her mind is healing. Her body . . ." His voice trailed off and he finally shrugged. "The strength of her body will return if she has the will for it. It seems as though the truths she faced and the actions she was forced to take have drained her will."

"She'll waken," Kalen said softly. He closed his eyes. It was more of a prayer than anything else when he repeated it, his voice stronger, "She'll waken."

With a slow, thoughtful nod, Morne said, "If your will alone will do it, then indeed she will wake." He stood, but instead of moving aside, he rubbed his hands over his face. "The gate is destroyed."

Morne really did look like hell, Kalen thought. He looked like he barely had the strength to remain upright.

Kalen didn't want to care. Not one bit. He reached for some kind of fury, a passionate need to rip Morne apart with his bare hands. Might have to take a metal pipe to his head and knock him unconscious first, he figured. But if he did that, he could pull out a blade and happily go to work.

And if it was any other Warlord in front of him, he would have had no problem finding the anger he reached for. But he couldn't. He'd have liked to tell himself it was only because Morne's intervention had saved Lee's life, but it would have been a lie. It was going to be hard to totally put Morne's true identity aside, though. In a mocking tone, he said, "Going to make going home hard on you, isn't it?"

Morne glanced at him, his eyes empty. It wasn't the careful mask that Kalen had seen so many times before on Morne, something designed to keep people from reading any emotion. No, this was more a lack of emotion. As though some part of him had died.

"The Roinan Gate is gone," Morne murmured. "What little energy remains in the gate will not sustain anything more than a small gate for a few moments. And that only for a finite amount of time. Now that I know Lee is healing, I'll take my sorry ass off. There may still be a few small gates that haven't totally shut down yet."

"Why?" Kalen demanded. "You homesick?"

"Homesick?" Finally some show of emotion. Morne's eyes flashed with fury and the air around them crackled with hostility. Instinctively, Kalen braced himself. His hand went to the pulsar at his waist, but no attack ever came.

Morne looked away. "No. I am not homesick. Anqar hasn't been my home for years. In truth, I doubt it ever was."

Kalen couldn't stop the sneer. "You're a Warlord."

Morne looked down at his hands and spread them wide, flexing them and then closing them into empty fists. "I said once already—if being a Warlord meant so very much to me, I wouldn't have spent the past twenty years on your primitive world, Kalen."

"*Primitive?*" Kalen demanded. "That coming from a man whose race enslaves women just to use them as incubators?"

A faint smile came and went. "A race that has fewer and fewer children born to it with each passing generation. They seek only to survive, Kalen. And yes—a primitive world. My kind sees the refinement of magick as the ultimate mortal achievement. Using technology or manual labor when magick could be used instead—primitive."

"Must have been damn hard to live in such a primitive world all this time," Kalen muttered. A muscle twitched in his jaw. Some of that anger he had expected finally worked through his exhaustion.

"Oh, for the love of the saints," Morne snapped. "Come down off your pedestal, you blind bastard. I was born and raised to be a Warlord, Kalen. Born and raised to believe it was my right, my duty to seek a bride from offworld. Just like you were raised to believe that anything that comes out of Anqar is something evil and to be hated. I learned long ago how skewed my beliefs were. " He nodded toward Lee. "You've only got a finite amount of time to figure out the same thing for yourself. You know now whose blood flows in her veins."

Furious, Kalen growled, "This isn't about her. It's about you and how long you've lied to all of us."

"And had I come to you and told you that I came out of Anqar, that I came here years ago to watch over a child, protect her, what would you have done?"

"Protect her—she wasn't here for you to protect."

"And how do you think she came to be here, Kalen? On her own? By some random twist of fate?" Morne asked with a small smile. "I assure you, it was not." He turned back to Lee and reached down, brushing her hair from her still face. "Love her well, Kalen." He sidestepped around Kalen and moved to leave the tent.

"Morne." Without looking back at the man he'd thought of as a friend, Kalen said, "Was the gate truly destroyed?"

"Yes."

"How did she do it? How did we live through it?"

There was a moment of silence and then Morne responded, "Everything, every person, has a breaking point. Even the gate. Lee simply fed it more than it could handle, and the power of the gate splintered from the burden. As to how we survived—power flows forward unless it's made to flow elsewhere. She shunted it through the gate and it kept flowing. When the power surge broke, it flowed forward through the gate."

"What about those on the other side of the gate? The Warlords."

He glanced back as he spoke, just in time to see the flash of grief before Morne blanked his features. "Only one was a Warlord. The other was a Sirvani."

"Was?"

Morne looked up. His eyes were haunted. "Yes. Was. He was my twin. My brother." Morne was quiet for a moment, and then he reached up and pinched the bridge of his nose. "Arnon, my brother, was serving as a Warlord's personal Sirvani when Aneva, Lee's mother, was brought through the gate. The Warlord chose her as his body slave and she conceived, almost immediately. He declared her as his mate—she bore him two sons. And then Lee. But Neve loved my brother. The boys were taken from her—it's customary that boy children be removed from their mother on their fourth birthday and placed into training. When Lee was born, Neve knew that she had to run, or else the girl would suffer the same fate she had, a broodmare. She was a prisoner. Her cage was gilded and soft, but it was still a cage. Neve didn't want that for her daughter—neither did my brother. They were in love. Arnon would do anything to help her. When he came to me for help, I couldn't tell him no. He'd find a way, no matter what, and if I helped him, I could do my best to keep him from getting caught—and killed."

A bitter smile curved his lips. "And I did. Arnon knew if he disappeared at the same time Neve went missing, his Warlord would suspect him. Arnon had a blood oath to the Warlord, and that bond could be used against him. So I brought Aneva and Lee back into Ishtan, and Arnon stayed behind. I remained to watch over them. But I couldn't keep her safe here, not after the Warlord started searching Ishtan for them. The answer lay even beyond the Veil, farther than my kind had ever looked. Lee's adopted world. She'd be safe there. Neve was meant to go with her—but we were caught unaware. She shoved Lee through the gate into that strange, unknown world. I told her to follow. But she stayed by me to fight the Raviners. They're magick bloodhounds, you know. Give them a whiff of your magick and they can find you even if you hide in hell. We killed them, but Neve was fatally wounded." He fell silent for a moment. "I meant to go after the girl. But people in that world had already taken her. She was being cared for. She was safe. And I knew the Warlords would never look for her there. So I left her there."

"Alone," Kalen said, his voice flat.

"Yes. Alone—and she was safer there than she would have ever been here. After a time, it was assumed that the Warlord's missing daughter and wife were dead. They stopped looking. But as long as they searched for her, she was in danger. What else should I have done, Kalen? I had my hands full just keeping demons off my ass. There was no way I could have kept a child safe, not while I was busy killing every last Sirvani, demon and Warlord that came searching for her."

That was how Morne had come to the attention of the resistance. There had been rumors of a man in the mountains who fought like he was possessed, killing any and every alien creature that crossed his path. Nothing out of Anqar had been safe when Morne crossed its path. But now Kalen saw it all differently. Yes, Morne was a fighting machine, but he'd been fighting to keep his secret—and his brother—safe.

"We all make choices, Kalen. Not all of them are easy," Morne said quietly. "Not all of them are right. But I stand by the choices I've made. I did it to protect my brother, to protect Lee." Then he ducked outside the tent, the flap falling closed behind him.

Indecision froze Kalen. He felt as though that self-righteous anger should burn through him, color every choice he made. But there were too many years of friendship—he couldn't overlook them any more than he could ignore what he knew inside. Morne was no enemy—and this was the man's home. Kalen ducked out of the tent and called out Morne's name.

Morne paused, but he didn't look back.

"There's no reason for you to leave here. Not unless that is what you want."

He was quiet, quiet for so long, Kalen suspected he'd get no response. But then Morne turned and stared at him, and in those dark eyes, Kalen saw a deep, overwhelming grief. "What I want . . ." He laughed, but there was no humor in the sound. "In the past twenty years, I've only allowed myself to want a very few things: my brother's safety, and to protect the child of the woman he loved. I've never let myself think beyond that."

Glancing over his shoulder toward Lee, Kalen thought back to those moments when he'd been sure Lee would be lost to him and she would have been . . . if not for Morne. He could have lost her before he even had her, if not for Morne. Looking back at the other man, Kalen said softly, "She's safe now. Maybe it's time you let yourself think about wanting something more."

Morne smiled, and all the sadness Kalen had glimpsed in his eyes showed in that smile. It was as though the weight Morne had carried for so long had finally crushed him. "Kalen, I honestly wouldn't know how." He looked past Kalen's shoulder into the tent, and the smile on his face changed just a little. "But she's safe. That's something."

With that, he turned and left in silence.

* * *

It was faint at first, a soft, whimpering little moan. Sprawled facedown on a thin mat, Kalen slept, dead to the world. Another little moan came from the bed, and Kalen lifted his head, glanced around. Head muddled with sleep, he couldn't figure out what had woken him up, and he dropped his head back onto the pillow with a grunt.

Tired. So damned tired.

He was almost back to sleep when he heard it again. For a second, he couldn't even move. His heart pounded in his throat as he scrambled on his hands and knees over to Lee's bedside. For the past eight days, she had been still and motionless, barely making a sound even when she breathed. Now she lay on her side, curled into a tight ball. Her teeth were chattering.

Kalen grabbed one of the blankets and flipped it up over her body, tucking it tight around her. He lay a hand on her cheek and murmured her name. Lee didn't open her eyes, but she turned her face into his touch, trying to burrow closer. Lying beside her, he whispered, "Lee."

Since the backlash from the gate had knocked her into this catatonic state, Kalen hadn't been able to pick up anything from Lee. Until now. He dropped his shields and nearly laughed as the flood of half-conscious thoughts assaulted him. She didn't like the lights, she was cold, she wanted coffee . . .

And the last barely formed thought was enough to make him groan.

Kalen . . . mmmmm . . . She turned her nose into his chest and sniffed at him. She draped an arm around his waist and muttered in her sleep. He thought she might wake up, but the senseless jumble of thoughts faded away and she dozed back into deep sleep. He retreated from her, comforted by those brief, erratic thoughts.

With her warm, soft body cuddled up against his, Kalen closed his eyes.

***

Kalen woke to heat.

Warm, soft, wet heat, gliding down his chest while busy fingers worked to push his trousers down. He reached up and fisted a hand in Lee's silky curls. He pushed up on his elbow and looked down at her, watching as she circled her tongue around his belly button. "You're awake," he said inanely.

Lee lifted her head long enough to grin at him. "So are you," she replied. She wrapped her hand around his cock, stroked him from tip to base and back. "Wide awake." Then she lowered her head and continued her downward path. She tugged at his pants, and he obligingly lifted his hips so she could push them down. Lee licked the head of his cock. Kalen was certain his eyes crossed. She scraped her nails over the sac of his balls. His spine bowed up. She looked up at him, a smile flirting with the corners of her lips. She held his eyes and then lowered her head and took him in her mouth. Air left his lungs in a rush.

She continued with her teasing, sucking on him, lifting her head to give him a coy smile, then dipping her head so she could lick his rigid flesh like a kid with a stick of candy. Sweat gleamed on his skin; his heart pounded so damn hard it stole his breath, and the urge to come was so strong, he hurt with it.

"You're cruel," he muttered.

Lee smiled up at him. Then she threw a leg over his hips and straddled him. She was naked. Somehow, she'd managed to shimmy out of her panties, and now she was pressed naked up against him. Kalen stared at the wispy blond curls that covered her sex. She rocked back and forth against him. Kalen gritted his teeth and looked up to her face. She smiled down at him, held his gaze and took him inside. They groaned in unison. Lee leaned forward and linked their fingers together. Kalen lifted his head and captured one nipple in his mouth, sucking deep.

He circled the pebbled flesh with his tongue and then bit down gently. Lee's fingers tightened around his. She arched, trying to get a little closer. Kalen shifted his attention to the other nipple, working it until it was swollen and pink. Then he lowered his head back to the thin excuse for a pillow. Eyes hooded, he stared at her. She rode him slow and easy. Her spine arched and her pretty breasts lifted up, her pink nipples still wet from his mouth and gleaming.

He freed one hand and slid it up her thigh. He sought out the hard, peaked flesh of her clit and stroked it. Lee's steady rhythm faltered. His heart skipped a beat as she clenched around him, her long, slender body shuddering. Tight as a fist. He pivoted his hips, rising to meet her downward strokes. But it wasn't enough.

The fear, the emptiness of the past week caught up with him and his patience snapped. He tensed and then flipped their bodies. He took their linked hands and pressed them down beside her head. Their lips met and Kalen kissed her deep, hard and quick. Then he muttered, "I ought to spank your pretty little ass for scaring me like that."

Then he kissed her again and started to move on her, taking her with hard, deep thrusts. Flesh slapped against flesh. The harsh, ragged sounds of their breathing filled the air. He could smell her, the hot, sexy scent of a hungry female. Her body arched under his, those sleek, perfectly made curves.

"I love you," Kalen rasped against her lips. "You crazy female, what in the hell were you thinking?"

He didn't wait for an answer, didn't really want one. He just had a week's worth of fears, nerves and needs that he had to burn off, and he figured that doing this to her, pumping in and out of her sex, listening to her moan, feeling her body shudder under his—after a week or two of this, he just might feel a little more normal. Maybe. Releasing her hands, he skimmed one palm down her torso, over the subtle flare of her hip, and lifted her. He moved higher on her body, and shifted so he could rub against her clit with each stroke. Lee cried out his name.

He cupped her chin in his hand, tilted it up. He bit her lower lip gently, sucked it in his mouth. Lee's nails bit into his shoulders. She bucked against him, moving her hips in a mad little shimmy as though she was trying to take him deeper. He leaned into her, using his weight to still her movements. Lee groaned. "Now who's being mean?"

"You deserve it—you put me through hell." Kalen would like to draw it out, make it last and last. But it wasn't going to happen. Already he could feel his balls drawing tight against his body, the warning tingle dancing down his spine. "I need you too much or I'd really make you suffer."

He slanted his mouth over hers. Their tongues met. He could have died happy in that moment, her body under his, her taste filling him. The silken tissues of her sheath tightened around his cock, and Kalen pounded into her harder, faster. She screamed into his mouth and came, her sex vising down around his cock like a fist. He erupted, coming so hard it felt like the top of his head came off.

The strength drained out of his body and he slumped down, resting his head between her breasts. "I'm still thinking about spanking you," he mumbled.

Lee made a little humming sound under her breath. "'Kay. Gimme a few minutes because I wanna enjoy it."

"You're not supposed to enjoy it. I am. It's for my enjoyment, for you scaring me to death." He took a deep breath and flipped over, bringing her with him so that she lay sprawled over his body. "I thought I was going to lose you, Lee. You could have died."

She lifted her head and met his gaze. "Yeah. I kind of thought I would." She pressed against his chest and Kalen let go. He pushed up on his elbow, watching as she settled at his side and folded her legs. His mouth went dry and his cock twitched. The way she was sitting exposed the pink, wet folds of her sex. He'd thought he'd have to wait a few minutes, but now . . .

Lee's husky chuckle caught his attention and he looked up at her face. She grabbed something and flipped it over her hips, hiding her lower body. He recognized it as his shirt. "You really ought to ask before you borrow my stuff," he murmured, reaching out. He caught the edge of the shirt and tugged. "Maybe I want to wear that."

She slapped at his hands. "You can wear it after we're done talking." Her eyes sobered and she caught his hand, held it in hers. "I know I scared you. I can't tell you I'm sorry. I did what I had to do. You kept telling me that I could stop this, and you were right. I figured out how, but there's no way I could have done it and guaranteed you that I'd stay safe."

Kalen narrowed his eyes. "If you're trying to use reason and convince me that I shouldn't spank you, don't bother. Reason has absolutely no effect when a man has to watch while his woman practically commits suicide in front of him."

"Heaven forbid I be reasonable," she said drolly.

"You can be reasonable all you want." Kalen lay back on the thick cushion of the gel pad, pillowed his head on his free hand. "Maybe in a few years, I can look back and all your logical reasoning will make me feel better. Right now . . ." His voice trailed off. Kalen closed his eyes and sighed. "Right now, I don't want to think about it."

Without opening his eyes, he closed his fingers around her wrist and jerked her closer. She landed on top of him and Kalen grunted with satisfaction. Wrapping his arms around her waist, he looked up at her. "Right now, all I want to do is hold you close to me and convince myself that you are safe."

She kissed him, a chaste, gentle kiss. "You're holding me now. I am safe." Then she closed her eyes and pressed her brow to his. "*We're* safe . . . right? The Veil, the gate—I can't feel them anymore."

Kalen looked up at her. "We are safe. All of us. The Roinan Gate is destroyed. There is remnant energy left in the Veil, but it could only support a small gate. When that energy is gone, so are the gates."

Her eyes closed. "We're safe." She started to relax against him, but then she tensed and tried to pull away. Kalen tightened his hold. "Remember what I said? Me, holding you? I'm not done holding you."

Lee's eyes darkened and she struggled. "Let go of me."

Kalen's shields were still down, and he caught one of the random thoughts circling through her mind. Not a thought—a memory. A Warlord. Tall and intimidating. *Hello, daughter.* He sensed her shock, her denial—and her self-disgust. Like a puzzle piece had settled into place, Kalen understood her sudden attempt to withdraw. "I'm not letting go. I don't care what kind of blood is in your veins. I only care about you, Lee. I had a week to think about what my life might be like if you died. I've lived a life without you and it was empty. I don't want that life again, Lee. I want a life with you. I love you."

He threaded his hand through her hair and pulled her face closer to his. He kissed her, soft and slow. "I love you, Lee."

Eyes closed, she licked her lips and made one of the sighing little hums under her breath. "How can you be so easy about this? How can you be so perfect?"

Kalen laughed. "Darling, I'm not perfect. I'm just a man who spent a long, long time waiting for you. Nothing is going to come between us. Nothing." Then he squinted up at her. "You do want to stay with me . . . right? You're not going to try to find some way back to your world?"

Now it was Lee's turn to laugh. She wrapped her arms around his neck. "Kalen, this is my world. You're my world."

If she didn't have sex with something soon, she would burst out of her skin.

She plunged through the blue-shot water, driven by a whisper on the wind, a pulse in her blood that carried her along like a warm current. The lavender sky was brindled pink and daubed with indigo clouds. On the beach, fire leaped from the rocks, glowing with the heat of the dying sun.

Her mate was dead. Dead so long ago that the tearing pain, the fresh, bright welling of fury and grief, had ebbed and healed, leaving only a scar on her heart. She barely missed him anymore. She did not allow herself to miss him.

But she missed sex.

Her craving flayed her, hollowed her from the inside out. Lately she'd felt as if she were being slowly scraped to a pelt, a shell, lifeless and empty. She wanted to be touched. She yearned to be filled again, to feel someone move inside her, deep inside her, hard and urgent inside her.

The memory quickened her blood.

She rode the waves to shore, drawn by the warmth of the flames and the heat of the young bodies clustered there. Healthy human bodies, male and female.

Mostly male.

***

Some damn fool had built a fire on the point. Police Chief Caleb Hunter spotted the glow from the road.

Mainers welcomed most visitors to their shore. But Bruce Whittaker had made it clear when he called that the islanders' tolerance didn't extend to bonfires on the beach.

Caleb had no particular objection to beach fires, as long as whoever set the fire used the designated picnic areas or obtained a permit. At the point, the wind was likely to carry sparks to the trees. The volunteers at the fire department, fishermen mostly, didn't like to be pulled out of bed to deal with somebody else's carelessness.

Caleb pulled his marked Jeep behind the litter of vehicles parked on the shoulder of the road: a tricked-out Wrangler, a ticket-me red Firebird, and a late-model Lexus with New York plates. Two weeks shy of Memorial Day, and already the island population was swelling with folks from Away. Caleb didn't mind. The annual influx of summer people paid his salary. Besides, compared to Mosul or Sadr City or even Portland down the coast, World's End was a walk on the beach. Even at the height of the season.

Caleb could have gone back to the Portland PD. Hell, after his medical discharge from the National Guard, he could have gone anywhere. Since 9/11, with the call-up of the reserves and the demands of homeland security, most big city police departments were understaffed and overwhelmed. A decorated combat veteran—even one with his left leg cobbled together with enough screws, plates, and assorted hardware to set off the metal detector every time he walked through the police station doors—was a sure hire.

The minute Caleb heard old Roy Miller was retiring, he

had put in for the chief's job on World's End, struggling upright in his hospital bed to update his résumé. He didn't want to make busts or headlines anymore. He just wanted to keep the peace, to find some peace, to walk patrol without getting shot at. To feel the wind on his face again and smell the salt in the air.

To drive along a road without the world blowing up around him.

He eased from the vehicle, maneuvering his stiff knee around the steering wheel. He left his lights on. Going without backup into an isolated area after dark, he felt a familiar prickle between his shoulder blades. Sweat slid down his spine.

Get over it. You're in World's End. Nothing ever happens here.

Which was about all he could handle now.

Nothing.

He crossed the strip of trees, thankful this particular stretch of beach wasn't all slippery rock, and stepped silently onto sand.

* * *

She came ashore downwind behind an outcrop of rock that reared from the surrounding beach like the standing stones of Orkney.

Water lapped on sand and shale. An evening breeze caressed her damp skin, teasing every nerve to quivering life. Her senses strained for the whiff of smoke, the rumble of male laughter, drifting on the wind. Her nipples hardened.

She shivered.

Not with cold. With anticipation.

She combed her wet hair with her fingers and arranged it over her bare shoulders. First things first. She needed clothes.

Even in this body, her blood kept her warm. But she knew from past encounters that her nakedness would be . . . unexpected. She did not want to raise questions or waste time and energy in explanations.

She had not come ashore to talk.

Desire swelled inside her like a child, weighting her breasts and her loins.

She picked her way around the base of the rock on tender, unprotected feet. There, clumped like seaweed above the tide line, was that a . . . *blanket*? She shook it from the sand—*a towel*—and tucked it around her waist, delighting in the bright orange color. A few feet farther on, in the shadows outside the bonfire, she discovered a gray fleece garment with long sleeves and some kind of hood. Drab. Very drab. But it would serve to disguise her. She pulled the garment over her head, fumbling her arms through the sleeves, and smiled ruefully when the cuffs flopped over her hands.

The unfamiliar friction of the clothing chafed and excited her. She slid through twilight, her pulse quick and hot. Still in the shadows, she paused, her widened gaze sweeping the group of six—*seven, eight*—figures sprawled or standing in the circle of the firelight. Two females. Six males. She eyed them avidly.

They were very young.

Sexually mature, perhaps, but their faces were soft and unformed and their eyes shallow. The girls were shrill. The boys were loud. Raw and unconfident, they jostled and nudged, laying claim to the air around them with large, uncoordinated gestures.

Disappointment seeped through her.

"Hey! Watch it!"

Something spilled on the sand. Her sensitive nostrils caught the reek of alcohol.

Not only young, but drunk. Perhaps that explained the clumsiness.

She sighed. She did not prey on drunks. Or children.

Light stabbed at her pupils, twin white beams and flashing blue lights from the ridge above the beach. She blinked, momentarily disoriented.

A girl yelped.

A boy groaned.

"Run," someone shouted.

Sand spurted as the humans darted and shifted like fish

in the path of a shark. They were caught between the rock and the strand, with the light in their eyes and the sea at their backs. She followed their panicked glances, squinting toward the tree line.

Silhouetted against the high white beams and dark, narrow tree trunks stood a tall, broad figure.

Her blood rushed like the ocean in her ears. Her heart pounded. Even allowing for the distortion of the light, he looked big. Strong. Male. His silly, constraining clothes only emphasized the breadth and power of his chest and shoulders, the thick muscles of his legs and arms.

He moved stiffly down the beach, his face in shadow. As he neared the fire, red light slid greedily over his wide, clear forehead and narrow nose. His mouth was firm and unsmiling.

Her gaze expanded to take him in. Her pulse kicked up again. She felt the vibration to the soles of her feet and the tips of her fingers.

This was a man.

* * *

Kids.

Caleb shook his head and pulled out his ticket book.

Back when he was in high school, you got busted drinking on the beach, you poured your cans on the sand and maybe endured a lecture from your parents. Not that his old man had cared what Caleb did. After Caleb's mom decamped with his older brother, Bart Hunter hadn't cared about much of anything except his boat, his bottle, and the tides.

But times—and statutes—had changed.

Caleb confiscated the cooler full of beer.

"You can't take that," one punk objected. "I'm twenty-one. It's mine."

Caleb arched an eyebrow. "You found it?"

"I bought it."

Which meant he could be charged with furnishing liquor to minors.

Caleb nodded. "And you are . . . ?"

The kid's jaw stuck out. "Robert Stowe."

"Can I see your license, Mr. Stowe?"

He made them put out the fire while he wrote them up: seven citations for possession and—in the case of twenty-one-year-old Robert Stowe—a summons to district court.

He handed back their driver's licenses along with the citations. "You boys walk the girls home now. Your cars will still be here in the morning."

"It's too far to walk," a pretty, sulky brunette complained. "And it's dark."

Caleb glanced from the last tinge of pink in the sky to the girl. Jessica Dalton, her driver's license read. Eighteen years old. Her daddy was a colorectal surgeon from Boston with a house right on the water, about a mile down the road.

"I'd be happy to call your parents to pick you up," he offered, straight-faced.

"Screw that," announced the nineteen-year-old owner of the Jeep. "I'm driving."

"If I start giving Breathalyzer tests for OUIs, it's going to be a long night," Caleb said evenly. "Especially when I impound your vehicle."

"You can't do that," Stowe said.

Caleb leveled a look at him.

"Come on, Robbie." The other girl tugged his arm. "We can go to my place."

Caleb watched them gather their gear and stumble across the sand.

"I can't find my sweatshirt."

"Who cares? It's ugly."

"You're ugly."

"Come on."

Their voices drifted through the dusk. Caleb waited for them to make a move toward their cars, but something—his threat to tell their parents, maybe, or his shiny new shield or his checkpoint glare—had convinced them to abandon their vehicles for the night.

He dragged his hand over his forehead, dismayed to notice both were sweating.

That was okay.

He was okay.

He was fine, damn it.

He stood with the sound of the surf in his ears, breathing in the fresh salt air, until his skin cooled and his heartbeat slowed. When he couldn't feel the twitch between his shoulder blades anymore, he hefted the cooler and lumbered to the Jeep. His knee shifted and adjusted to take his weight on the soft sand. He'd passed the 1.5 mile run required by the state of Maine to prove his fitness for duty. But that had been on a level track, not struggling to stabilize on uneven ground in the dark.

He stowed the evidence in back, slammed the hatch, and glanced toward the beach.

A woman shone at the water's edge, wrapped in twilight and a towel. The sea foamed around her bare, pale feet. Her long, dark hair lifted in the breeze. Her face was pale and perfect as the moon.

For one second, the sight caught him like a wave smack in the chest, robbing him of speech. Of breath. Yearning rushed through his soul like the wind over the water, stirring him to the depths. His hands curled into fists at his sides.

Not okay. He throttled back his roaring imagination. She was just a kid. A girl. An underage girl in an oversize sweatshirt with—his gaze dipped again, briefly—a really nice rack.

And he was a cop. Time to think like a cop. Mystery Girl hadn't been with the group around the fire. So where had she been hiding?

Caleb stomped back through the trees. The girl stood with her bare feet planted in the sand, watching him approach. At least he didn't have to chase her.

He stopped a few yards away. "Your friends are gone. You missed them."

She tilted her head, regarding him with large, dark, wide-set eyes. "They are not my friends."

"Guess not," he agreed. "Since they left without you."

She smiled. Her lips were soft and full, her teeth white

and slightly pointed. "I meant I do not know them. They are very . . . young, are they not?"

He narrowed his gaze on her face, mentally reassessing her age. Her skin was baby fine, smooth and well cared for. No makeup. No visible piercings or tattoos. Not even a tan.

"How old are you?"

Her smile broadened. "Older than I look."

He resisted the urge to smile back. She could be over the legal drinking age—not jailbait, after all. Those eyes held a purely adult awareness, and her smile was knowing. But he'd pounded Portland's pavements long enough to know the kind of trouble a cop invited giving a pretty woman a break. "Can I see your license, please?"

She blinked slowly. "My . . ."

"ID," he snapped. "Do you have it?"

"Ah. No. I did not realize I would need any."

He took in her damp hair, the towel tucked around her waist. If she'd come down to the beach to swim . . . Okay, nobody swam in May but fools or tourists. But even if she was simply taking a walk, her story made sense. "You staying near here?"

Her dark gaze traveled over him. She nodded. "Yes, I believe I will. Am," she corrected.

He was sweating again, and not from nerves. His emotions had been on ice a long time, but he still recognized the slow burn of desire.

"Address?" he asked harshly.

"I don't remember." She smiled again, charmingly, looking him full in the eyes. "I only recently arrived."

He refused to be charmed. But he couldn't deny the tug of attraction, deep in his belly. "Name?"

"Margred."

Margred. Sounded foreign. He kind of liked it.

He raised his brows. "Just Margred?"

"Margaret, I think you would say."

"Last name?"

She took a step closer, making everything under the sweatshirt sway. *Hell-o, breasts.* "Do you need one?"

He couldn't think. He couldn't remember being this distracted and turned on since he'd sat behind Susanna Colburn in seventh grade English and spent most of second period with a hard-on. Something about her voice . . . her eyes . . . It was weird.

"In case I need to get in touch with you," he explained.

"That would be nice."

He was staring at her mouth. Her wide, wet, full-lipped mouth. "What?"

"If you got in touch with me. I want you to touch me."

He jerked himself back. "What?"

She looked surprised. "Isn't that what you want?"

Yes.

"No."

Fuck.

Caleb was frustrated, savagely disappointed with himself and with her. He knew plenty of women—badge bunnies—went for cops. Some figured sex would get them out of trouble or a ticket. Some were simply into uniforms or guns or handcuffs.

He hadn't taken her for one of them.

"Oh." She regarded him thoughtfully.

His stomach muscles tightened.

And then she smiled. "You are lying," she said.

Yeah, he was.

He shrugged. "Just because I'm—" *horny, hot, hard* "—attracted doesn't mean I have to act on it."

She tilted her head. "Why not?"

He exhaled, a gust between a laugh and a groan. "For starters, I'm a cop."

"Cops don't have sex?"

He couldn't believe they were having this discussion. "Not on duty."

Which was mostly true. True for him, anyway. He hadn't seen any horizontal action since . . . God, since the last time he was home on leave, over eighteen months ago. His brief marriage hadn't survived his first deployment, and nobody since had cared enough to be waiting when he got out.

"When are you not on duty?" she asked.

He shook his head. "What, you want a date?"

Even sarcasm didn't throw this chick. "I would meet you again, yes. I am . . . attracted, too."

She wanted him.

Not that it mattered.

He cleared his throat. "I'm never off duty. Until Memorial Day, I'm the only cop on the island."

"I don't live on your island. I am only . . ." Again with the pause, like English was her second language or something. ". . . visiting," she concluded with a smile.

Like fucking a tourist would be perfectly okay.

Well, wouldn't it?

The thought popped unbidden into his head. It wasn't like he was arresting her. He didn't even suspect her of anything except wanting to have sex with him, and he wasn't a big enough hypocrite to hold that against her.

But he didn't understand this alleged attraction she felt. He felt.

And Caleb did not trust what he did not understand.

"Where are you staying?" he asked. "I'll walk you home."

"Are you trying to get rid of me?"

"I'm trying to keep you safe."

"That's very kind of you. And quite unnecessary."

He stuck his hands in his pockets, rocking back on his heels. "You getting rid of me now?"

She smiled, her teeth white in the moonlight. "No."

"So?"

She turned away, her footprints creating small, reflective pools in the sand. "So I will see you."

He was oddly reluctant to let her go. "Where?"

"Around. On the beach. I walk on the beach in the evening." She looked at him over her shoulder. "Come find me sometime . . . when you're not on duty."